CW01072456

ISRAFEL

By Anthea McLean

 FriesenPress

One Printers Way
Altona, MB R0G 0B0
Canada

www.friesenpress.com

Copyright © 2024 by Anthea McLean
First Edition — 2024

All rights reserved.

No part of this publication may be reproduced in any form, or by any means, electronic or mechanical, including photocopying, recording, or any information browsing, storage, or retrieval system, without permission in writing from FriesenPress.

ISBN
978-1-03-919650-6 (Hardcover)
978-1-03-919649-0 (Paperback)
978-1-03-919651-3 (eBook)

1. Fiction, Romance, Science Fiction

Distributed to the trade by The Ingram Book Company

None sing so wildly well
As the angel Israfel

—Edgar Allan Poe

And the angel Israfel, whose heartstrings are a lute, and who has the sweetest
voice of all God's creatures.

—Edgar Allan Poe, Attributed to the Koran

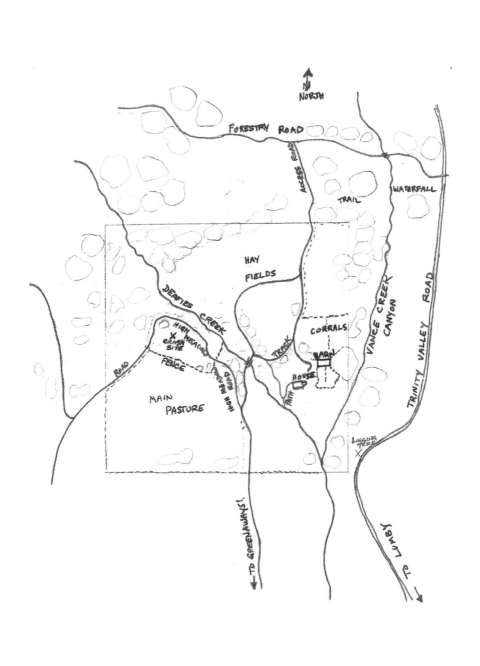

PROLOGUE

THE MOMENT THAT IMPERSONAL RENTAL car came bumping over the frozen ruts of our yard, I retreated into the hostile silence that had become instinctive. I didn't want to talk to him.

He was just one more predatory reporter, here to assault me with the same old questions, the same indignation when I refused to answer, the same disruption to the thin, frail order of my day. That car was one of hundreds that have been here before. Those fine leather shoes were just as out of place in our British Columbia wilderness as all the others that had tramped through our springtime mud and churned up the summer dust. I'd seen too many of those Madison Avenue suits, in our barn, on our doorstep, soaking in our mountain rain or stifling their owners in the heat of our summer sun. In the cold of this November, he was covered by an expensive camelhair coat, but I saw at once the bulge in the pocket where the everready notebook lay. I turned back to the barn, to the horses I was giving their afternoon feed.

"Mrs. Tremayne, I've come a long way—"

"That's not my fault," I said rudely and clumped away from him in my heavy boots. They'd all come a long way, some from the other side of the world – as if that made any difference. Everything I was trying to protect was precariously balanced on a narrow ledge between the push of guilt and the knife blade of suspicion. I dared not talk to any of them.

"But it is."

His voice followed me, chiding, faintly accusing, but also holding a surprising note of kindness. I hesitated at the doorway of the barn, half turned, caught by that touch of sympathy and reminded again of the guilt.

"My name's Frank McKinnon," he went on. "I'm with Time Magazine."

When I made a dismissive motion with my hand, he said, "I know we've been here before. But I haven't. And I just don't understand why you're still refusing to talk after all this time. It's been six months. Can't you let go now?"

Six months! I thought, staring at him, my eyes beginning to burn. *Do you think I don't know? Six months since that last desperate day. Six months of loneliness and regret, of accusation, and this burden of guilt growing heavier and heavier. Six months, every minute counted, since Israfel's mind reached mine for the very last time. For six months my husband and I have been trying to restore our lives to the semblance of a former stability. For six months I've been hiding my feelings, keeping silent, while jealousy and suspicion have been used as weapons against me.*

"I know," he said, watching my face. "You're sick of the lot of us, and I can't say I blame you. We've probably hounded you to death, and I realize what you've gone through. The whole affair must have been a trial, and the coverup . . . it was a coverup, wasn't it? You've been asked, or told, to keep quiet? Maybe even threatened?"

My eyes still burned, and I felt my lips trembling, the fiber I had so long braced myself with beginning to bend and shake. Coverup? Oh, yes, but in many more ways than one.

"I know you've turned down millions for exclusives," he went on. "I'm not going to pressure you. But I can never stop wondering why you've stayed silent so long, unless you have been threatened . . . or it isn't true."

Threatened, I thought. *But not in the way you're thinking.*

"Is your husband home?" he asked, his eyes flicking to our old log house, massive and heavy among the firs and pines beyond the lawn. The windows were all in darkness.

"No," I said. Jesse was back in Los Angeles, working on another score. I was here, alone but for the horses and one dog. There wasn't that immediate hawklike rapacity in his eyes that I'd seen in most who tried to question me when Jesse was away. "Aha! She's all alone, vulnerable, and we know how emotional she gets, don't we? Now's the time to crack her. Hit her hard, fellas! Maybe this time she'll break."

"Lots of work for you," he said, looking over the enormous barn, the crowd of mares standing at the fence, then back to my slight stature and thin tired face.

"I'm used to it," I said and moved on through the doorway.

"Mrs. Tremayne . . . Laura . . . " He tried to stop me. "Please, talk to me for a minute."

"I'm not telling you anything," I said out of habit, not thinking, and heard the rough hissing sound of satisfaction deep in his throat.

I had walked into a trap of my own making, I realized too late. Of course, there were a thousand things to tell. The coverup had been thorough and efficient, but the news and publicity make its own stories. If he'd had any doubts, I'd just dispelled them.

"So, it is true!" Now his eyes were as piercing as those of the hunting hawk. "I'd always thought so. But why, why then, won't you talk about it?"

I stood there, caught, too tired by disappointment and regret to erect any defense, worn out by a battle I could never win.

"Because I don't wish to," I said feebly.

"I know, but why, still now?" He was pressing, yet his tone was softened by that appealing note of kindness. "It's been six months. People forget, Laura. Maybe now it wouldn't be such a big deal."

"So why is it for you?" I asked, trying to stall him. "I mean, coming all this way when you know how we've refused to talk . . . "

"Curiosity, hope, a persistence or stubbornness I seem to have been born with. A story too good to let go. I've always believed it, Laura. And I don't like coverups."

"Neither do I," I said. But I had gone on, struggling to guard the walls of a fortress when the invader was already within.

Frank McKinnon was watching me, reading my uncertainty and distress, my tremulous lips and sleep deprived eyes. If he'd tried for further advantage then, I'd have turned my back and left him. But he said nothing, waited, looking at me with the sympathy and understanding I'd found so rarely. My guilt burgeoned, swelled, overshadowed everything I have tried for so long to protect.

"I have to think," I whispered. My throat tightened. I could feel my heart thudding against my ribs. If I told him . . .

I held out my hand. "Give me your card. Maybe . . . Someday . . . Perhaps . . . "

He delved into a pocket of his coat and then pressed that significant card, the first I'd accepted, into my cold palm. "I'll wait," he said.

I pushed that meaningful scrap into my jeans, my eyes blurring and mouth going dry. I heard another voice, deep inside my head, say the same words. The unforgettable voice that was music, haunting and lingering like the ghost of a troubled spirit, tormenting me with regret. Israfel's voice.

CHAPTER ONE

THE FIRST TO BEHAVE STRANGELY was the dog.

We were high on the northern shoulder of Copper Mountain, deep in the forest of pine, fir and birch, following the old logging road that skirts the summit. Gray clouds descended all around us, and a spattering of rain had made me turn the horse I was riding homeward. The afternoon was cold, the air raw, and I had no wish for a soaking.

This year, the glories of fall were lingering, mellow and nostalgic. There were still russet leaves on the birches, red berries, and white on wild roses and twinflower bushes that edge the roads. The stubble of the hay fields glowed gold and green in the rich light of the low-lying sun. The cold stillness of the air, the untroubled sky and motionless trees lent a sense of permanence, as though this frozen earth and crystal sky would remain inviolate to heavy snow and massing clouds, the fierce onslaught of winter.

Last year, in the misty gray of that November, restless, impatient northerlies had torn away the colored leaves, brought storms and heavy skies that intruded rudely after the golden days of October. But there had still been beauty in the smoky mists and cloud wreathed mountains, a lingering of colors in rifts and sheltered valleys, pleasure in the golden leafy carpet underfoot, and I had ridden whenever I could. Now, I was happy because Jesse was home. Our year had been a good one, and we found so much pleasure in our North Okanagan home, we could forgive the weather's occasional inclemency.

I was riding a young bay stallion named Gallant who was four years old and had just started under saddle in the spring. I was always prepared for an occasional bout of temperament but not for the sudden strange behavior of the dog, Sally. Her merry trot far ahead of us, plumed tail waving, and eager questing nose all altered to a frantic terrified dash to a precarious position just behind Gallant's heels.

"Sally! Get away!"

She ignored me, made nervous darts from one side of the hard and dangerous hooves to the other with her tongue lolling and eyes glazed with fear. There was no thunder to frighten her, no roaring chainsaws felling trees in the woods. So, what on earth?

Gallant jerked to an abrupt halt. I jolted against the saddle horn. He threw up his head and snorted, and I felt all his muscles bunch and tense, his neck hardening against my hand. Sally disappeared beneath him.

"Easy," I said, "Sallee . . . "

Neither animal paid me any heed. The horse's ears switched nervously, and I felt the increasing beat of his heart thudding against my leg.

On the slope below us, tall cedars and firs fell away. As far as I could see, there was nothing between their boles but for trees and meadows. Our 160 acres undulated to forest and the hills across the road on our eastern boundary. A murky cloud was descending there, hiding the hills, obliterating the peaks of the distant Monashees. Nothing else to see.

I strained my ears, could hear only the creak of the saddle as Gallant shifted, the crunch of stones beneath his feet, Sally panting and the horse's anxious breathing, the drip of raindrops onto wet leaves.

Then, what was it? A hunter? A wounded bear or deer? That wouldn't explain Sally's behavior.

"Sally!"

A nervous head came into view from below my heel. She whined, looked up at me, her eyes frightened and bewildered. The horse moved again, an uneasy sidestepping.

I urged him on, thinking motion would ease his fear. A bare hundred yards further he stopped again, snorting and tossing his head. Sally cringed at his heels.

Then a faint sound came to my ears. A fluttering, accompanied by a thin hissing, came from behind the trees to my left. It was moving down the mountain, but its source remained invisible as I peered between the branches.

Gallant began to plunge, trying to get his head down and fighting the bit. His neck was damp with a darkening sweat, and every muscle in his body bunched and writhed. I held him, somehow, while still trying to see what was frightening them so.

It had to be flying, for the fluttering sound was now coming from far below us, and it was heading toward a long upper pasture we call the High Meadow. I urged Gallant on again, and as the road turned across the southern slope of the mountain, taking him away from the sound, he did go more readily. But his ears were stiff and his gait a very cautious, hesitant trot. Sally clung to his heels.

Then, through a gap in the trees, I glimpsed a blazing orange light. There was no time to identify its source as it immediately hid behind the trees again, but I heard with horrifying clarity the shrieking and rending of metal, trees cracking and branches snapping, the hissing sound sputter and stop.

Gallant tried to spin around, almost unseating me, but all I could think of was the plane that had crashed on the High Meadow. The fluttering sound was that of a useless engine; the orange blaze must have been a fire. I slammed my heels into the horse's sides, forced him on down the hill. He fought me, shaking his head, stiff legs jolting me as he resisted the gallop I held him to. Foam flew from his mouth, splashed my coat, and flecked his already lathered neck, and I could hear resentment and fear in the sharp snorts that fluttered his nostrils. I kept my legs close against him, urging him on while I clung to his wild and uncomfortably choppy ride. I had forgotten Sally.

A sharp turn brought us onto the old trail that paralleled the top fence of the pasture. The horse, coming closer to home, began to move more freely. But the muscles of his neck remained tense and hard, and his ears jutted forward in a constant listening. I leaned into the streaming hair of his mane and thought frantically of Jesse, ambulances, getting help quickly, and what I should do if the craft was already blazing.

We raced along the hillside to my right. Beyond was the strip of woodland that separated it from the High Meadow. I couldn't see any fire, heard only the pound of the hooves on the wet and stony ground, the horse's moaning breath.

We galloped through the gateway that we left open now that the horses were no longer out to grass. Here the road, matted with russet fallen leaves, ran between tall trees – cedar, larch, fir, and birch – then made a sharp turn into the meadow. We swerved around the last of the trees and came onto the grass at the same wild gallop. An extraordinary sight met my eyes.

Gallant skidded to a stop. I was glad he did, for it was no plane that had crashed into a grove of cedars and birch on the high side of the meadow. It was, or had been, round, and it shone with a light that seemed to come from within the material of the hull. A thin yellowish vapor rose from it, but I could see no flame. There were two silverclad figures beside this strange craft, helmeted, staring toward me through tinted visors. They were carrying another, either dead or unconscious, but they froze into stillness the moment they saw me.

What was this? Some NASA space vehicle that had malfunctioned and gone terribly off course? But there hadn't been any recent shots. Then they must be Russian. Oh, Lord! My heart sank in dismay. Now what? What would this mean? All kinds of bureaucratic red tape? Our property placed out of bounds? Would the army come rushing in? The press in droves? What should I do first? Who should we call?

Still, they stood motionless, staring at me.

Gray clouds were lowering on the mountains, and a few drops of icy rain fell onto my face. A permeating dampness would come into being as soon as the sun was gone on that November day. Already the early darkness of short winter days was closing in, and smoky mist was flowing between the trees. I urged Gallant toward them, but he refused, standing as motionless as them with every muscle prepared for flight. I slid to the ground and led him.

In an instant, the two figures laid their burden down. One hurried to the strange craft caught among the trees and went in through a hole gaping in its side. The other remained, watching my approach. Gallant hung back at the end of the rein, dragging his feet on stiff and unwilling legs. The pull of the rein was stretching his head to the limit of his neck, and the whites of his eyes shone in constant alarm. Sally, now catching up with us, no longer followed, staying where she was with fear glazed eyes and her tail tucked miserably between her legs.

The figure emerged from the craft with several pieces of strange looking equipment in his arms. He carried them back to the others and set them on the ground. I stopped and waited, bewildered and anxious.

They did something with a small boxlike object, and a soft humming sound rose from it. Gallant snorted and reared, flinging up his head, wrenching at the rein, my arm. Sally barked once. I hesitated, uncertain. Were they Russian? They must be. And why didn't they remove their helmets? Should I be rushing home for aid, Jesse, to call an ambulance, the police? Or should I wait to find out where they were from, whether that other one was badly hurt? Then the one who had been to the craft did remove his helmet, and the other immediately followed suit.

"Are you all right?" I called and dragged Gallant forward again. "Are you hurt?"

They did not answer. Oh, Lord! They must be Russian. Now what?

I now saw that the one who had first removed his helmet was the taller of the two. He had thick black hair that fell below his ears in soft loose waves. The hair framed a face that was lean and strong and classically elegant. But his eyes riveted me. They were dark, brilliant with intelligence, and verging on the enormous. I was vaguely conscious of the other figure kneeling beside the one on the grass and removing his helmet, but my eyes couldn't leave those huge and dazzling dark eyes as he began to come towards me, carrying something that looked alarmingly like a weapon.

"This is Canada," I said for want of something to say. "Where are you from? Are you American? What happened? Do you understand me?"

He made a sudden movement with a gauntleted hand. The thing on his hand pointed right at me. I stood still, trying not to show the alarm beginning to rise within me. Gallant reared again, and I clung to his reins and struggled with him and the fear beginning to impart itself to me.

These men were strange, very strange, and so disturbingly silent. The round craft with its luminous shine and curious yellow vapor wasn't like anything I'd ever seen before in my life. The terror of the animals was inexplicable. The face before me was different in a way I couldn't at once define. The glossy suit he wore looked unearthly in the pallid gray light, totally out of place in this rough upland meadow beneath a foggy sky. This was the backwoods, and he didn't belong here, here in this untamed wilderness where only a week ago we had seen a cougar in our yard.

That different craft . . . this different face . . . the weird thing he was aiming at me . . . the most uncontrollable of all fears, that of the unknown, tried to pierce through all my common sense, numb my mind, and let the fierce hand of panic seize me by the throat.

Desperately, I sought reason. If only he would speak . . . If the sun were out and bright, none of this would seem so ominous. It was the grayness, the mist, the fading light, the frightened horse and cringing dog . . . I forced myself to think about the one lying so still there on the grass, about getting him help, about Jesse – who wasn't so far away – about the police, the army, NASA control. They must know where this thing is. Surely, they must!

"You speak this language" The voice came suddenly, startling me. It was deep and melodious but enunciated the words awkwardly, as though speaking in an unfamiliar tongue.

I tried to pull myself together. "Yes, English. This is Canada. Can I help you? Your companion . . . " I looked toward the figure lying on the grass. "Is he hurt?"

The hand fell. He came a few steps closer, and Gallant snorted with alarm and threw himself back on his haunches, dragging at the reins. I tried to calm him while keeping an eye on that approaching figure.

"That is an animal?" he asked.

What an extraordinary question! My fear had abated at the sound of his voice, but now I wished I hadn't dismounted, had waited where I had first stopped, that I still had Gallant's speed and strength beneath me.

"Yes," I heard myself say. "A horse." I took a surreptitious backward step, gathered the reins, stroked the damp hair on Gallant's neck.

He stopped as though aware of the horse's distress, but his huge eyes began to examine me with a blatantly open and thorough scrutiny, as though I were something he had long waited to see, a curiosity he had heard strange tales of but had never met. Gallant wasn't responding to my soothing hand, and I knew as he kept pulling away with muscles bunched and eyes rolling that I didn't stand a hair of a chance of regaining that saddle that was so inviting on his back without a fight that would reveal my fear.

"Your companion . . . " I said again, trying to ignore his eyes, their unrestrained probing, wondering if Jesse would hear me if I screamed.

The air grew colder as gray cloud crept closer, hiding the mountain, shrouding the trees, isolating the meadow, me and these men – these strange men who weren't behaving at all as one would expect under the circumstances.

And this one still stared at me. Then he spoke again. "We are in danger," he began slowly. "Your . . . army . . . must not find us." The dark eyes bore into mine, intense with meaning. "We must return."

Such strange eyes . . . but they must be Russian – had to be. Yet why that question about the horse? And what danger? What had they done? Or did that craft hold something highly important to the USSR, and a volatile situation would arise if it fell into western hands? Or the craft itself? Round, domed, with that strange silvery translucence. I had seen enough photographs and television pictures to know this was totally unlike the space capsules of our own technology.

But these men did not look in the least like Russians. This one so dark and refined, and the other, now coming toward us, had a face as delicately structured as an angel in a Botticelli painting. He had the same lifted poise and perfectly cut mouth, hair that shone like gold and eyes as blue as a summer sky.

It was then that I began to suspect the seemingly impossible. Could it be? Could it possibly be? That these beings – that the strange craft was from another world? A terrifying weakness drained my limbs. I tried to tell myself the notion was impossible, a fantasy to explain the yet unexplained. This being was a man, speaking to me in my own language, with a craft that must only be secret and new. But the seed, once sown, wasn't so easily uprooted. Their clothes, their faces, that craft . . .

The dark eyes were watching me, compelling me. "Will you help us?" I dragged myself together, forced my whirling head to steady. I looked at the heavy sky, the damp gray mist, the sodden earth and stubble of grass. What an unwelcoming landscape to crash into! Dark and ragged trees floated in the mist and fading light. Even the sky, gray and leaning close, seemed ominous.

I looked at the other, at the golden hair and wide blue eyes, and saw a sensitive face white with shock. The eyes stared back at me and were vivid with horror and dismay.

From the south came the whining roar of a jet engine. It thundered toward us and passed overhead, the plane invisible through the cloud. Its furious noise echoed dully from the mountains, muffled by the mist.

I looked at the wreckage of trees and craft, the figure lying so still on the soaking ground, at the shocked blue eyes and the appealing dark ones. And then I felt nothing but sympathy.

"Will you?" There was no demand or even pleading in the voice. Only a natural appeal.

"Of course," I said. "Of course, we will." They were human, in trouble, asking me for help in my own language. And in this rural community, help was always forthcoming.

But maybe I spoke too readily, too soon, for I saw a caution narrow his eyes, a wariness that disturbed me. Again, he studied me, and I became uncomfortably aware of a cuff hanging down on my faded jeans, that the seam's edges were white with wear and the knees becoming threadbare. That suit of his was a soft and lustrous silver, sleek despite a bulkiness. My sheepskin coat was old, stained, the sleeves creased and elbows rubbed. My boots' only value was their comfort – his looked like gold lame. While their hair was immaculate, my ordinary brown was in its usual curling mess and blown into tatters and tangles by the wind during the passage down the mountain. Maybe he was wondering if my words were as disreputable as my appearance.

I summoned a smile and felt how it was more of a nervous grimace than a reassuring expression. The impetuosity that Jesse was always accusing me of – that had followed me from my youth into my mid-twenties – had made me speak too soon.

"Believe me. We'll help you. I promise."

Skepticism. Doubt. Caution.

"Don't worry," I said. "Please. You can trust me. Really, you can." I looked from one to the other, my face stiff with that awkward smile, my lips stretched and dried.

Eyes with the endless depths of cave water, the other's as infinite and blue as a sunlit sea, penetrated mine with a searching, probing stare. The dark head titled slightly, as though he were listening to something only he could hear, but this steady gaze didn't waver once.

I tried to meet them with conviction, to assure them that I meant what I said and could be trusted. All the traces of my fear were miraculously replaced by the need to have them believe me. I no longer saw that strange craft in the broken trees, the inert form lying on the grass. I was unaware of the pull at the reins in my hand by my frightened horse. There was only the doubt to be dispelled from the faces before me.

At last he began to relax, and then he released me from his gaze. "Thank you," he said with an unexpected formal courtesy, and his lips softened into what I interpreted as a smile.

They must be Russian, I thought again. They were anxious about being found because that craft was highly secret, and for them to lose it to a western power would be highly embarrassing. In which case, had I been too hasty? Maybe this was something our forces should know about. If I had only reacted out of fear of the unknown – and what kind of help was I even supposed to supply? But . . . Lord alive! There was also that question about the horse!

I stared at the arresting elegance of that face, the lightly gold skin without a flaw, and those enormous, luminous eyes. No. That was not a Russian, nor an American, nor any breed of human on this earth. And neither was the second one, even though he was different than the first.

He forbore my scrutiny, as I might a child's. A kind of smile lingered at the corners of his mouth, making him look tolerant, kind, and sensitive. I drew a deep breath, shuffling my feet on the soggy ground. I had promised him.

"I'll go," I said. "I'll get my husband and a truck."

"Husband?" The wary look was back in an instant. "Truck?"

"The man I'm married to. A truck to carry you and your companions. We'll take you to our house."

There was a quick assessment of my words. "I understand," he said.

I glanced again at the third figure who was lying so still. I moistened my dry lips. "Um . . . what about this? Should I call someone?"

"Please call no one else. We will be able to . . . " He broke off, searched for words, then gave up as though there were none. "We will do what is necessary," he said.

I turned away and gathered the reins with fingers that felt as though they weren't properly attached to me. Gallant's neck was wet against my hand, and he swung away from me when I prepared to mount. Again, I tried to soothe him. I looked back at those watchful eyes. "And you? Are you all right?"

"Yes, thank you."

I shortened the near rein until I'd pulled Gallant's head right around and held it bent to his shoulder. He lay his ears back and shivered when I touched him, but I was able to jam my foot into the stirrup and swing myself up. He wheeled in a tight circle, pivoting on his forehand, and foam flew from his mouth as he fought the bit. I steadied him with my legs and hands, and brought him around to face those alien beings. Now the eyes were intensely curious, watching me find the other stirrup and adjust the reins while the horse danced and sidestepped as though this were some strange performance with an extraordinary climax yet to be revealed.

"I'll be back in a few minutes." Gallant tossed his head and tried to spin around. I forced him forward again and smiled more easily down at them. There was security in being lifted above those strange men, in having Gallant's strength and speed beneath me. "And don't worry. We'll help you."

For some reason it never occurred to me that I was speaking for Jesse without his consent.

CHAPTER TWO

THE HORSE WAS WHITE WITH lather by the time we reached the roadway leading to the house. But the furious pace of his racing gallop never ceased. I crouched over his neck, his mane whipping my windbitten face. Where had they come from?

"Jesse!" I screamed when I saw the mares and yearlings streaming along the fences and heard their excited whinnies as they were caught up in this wild race. "Jesse!"

Gallant hurtled around the final bend, and I hauled him to a skidding stop before the barn.

"Jesse!"

He appeared in the doorway, a pitchfork in his hand, hazel eyes widening beneath his battered hat as he saw the lathered, sliding horse, I was on the ground and running, leaving Gallant. Sally dashed past me and flung herself at Jesse, uttering piteous, whimpering cries.

"Laura! What in the hell are you doing?"

I tried to speak, but my throat refused to function, and my jaw locked tight.

"What's happening? What's the matter?" He flung the pitchfork down and came striding towards me. Jesse was solid and self assured in his competence. He wore denim pants and tooled leather boots, long hair framing his ordinary, comfortably familiar face.

My voice broke free. "Hurry! Jesse, quick, get the truck. Put some hay in the back." I snatched at the swinging reins as Gallant tried to dash past me into the barn. "A . . ." But couldn't tell him, not yet. "There's been a crash . . . up on the High Meadow."

He had to jump aside as Gallant swung, brought up short by my jerk on the rein. Then I was rushing through the door, dragging Gallant with me. "Jesse, hurry. Get the truck." I flung open the door of the nearest stall, forced the horse inside, tore at the cinch with trembling fingers.

"But Laura! Just a minute now. You mean a plane? Shouldn't we call an ambulance, the police, someone?"

"No! Jesse, please!" I pulled the saddle from Gallant's steaming back, trying not think about him getting chilled. "Just the truck. I'll explain as we go."

"But . . . Laura . . . " He was standing in the stall doorway, thick brows gathered in a frown.

"Please!"

"Okay. Okay."

He was gone, and I fumbled with fingers that felt like sticks at the tiny buckle of the throat latch. What if the one lying so still was badly hurt? How would we get medical treatment? Suppose he was dead or dying. Then what? What should we do? And the craft . . . So alien, so strange, crushed among the trees on our meadow. Cold out there, and damn miserable . . . Oh, Gallant! Stand still! Hurry! Hurry!

I heard the rumble of the Chevy pickup engine, saw the flow of its lights pass across the barn doorway. I slid the bridle from Gallant's head and ran from the stall.

Darkness was thickening among the trees, grayed by dampness, and I anxiously thought again of the one lying on the cold wet ground as I clambered into the truck and slammed the door.

Jesse drove fast and the truck bounced on the bumpy road. "How many? Any injured?"

"Three. One may be hurt."

"I didn't hear anything, but the horses sure seemed scared of something for a while there."

"Yes." I remembered Gallant's fear, the cringing Sally. I had to tell him. "Jesse, it isn't a plane."

"It isn't? But you said . . . "

"It's some kind of spacecraft."

"Good God!"

"But . . . Jesse . . . I don't think it's of this world."

He drove on in silence for several seconds, his face intense and hands gripping the wheel. Then the enormity of what I had said hit him as though I'd stuck him with a rock. Astonishment was followed by a look of utter disbelief that turned to anger. His foot jammed on the brake and the truck skidded on the wet road, slewed sideways, and jolted to a stop.

"What the hell kind of joke is this? Laura! For chrissakes!"

"It isn't a joke."

"Aw, c'mon! What's gotten into you?"

"Look, how often do I bring a horse home in a lather?"

He sat there, stiff with anger. "So, what in the hell are you playing at?"

My voice shook. "There's a crashed spacecraft up on the High Meadow, and it isn't American or Russian."

"Then we should be calling the police! The army! Dammit, someone!"

"No, Jesse, we can't."

"We sure as hell can!" He thrust the transmission lever into reverse gear. The engine roared as we hurtled backward onto the stubble of the hay field.

"Jesse, please! I promised them!"

"You what?" He hit the brake hard and jerked the wheel over.

"Promised we'd help them. Jesse," I implored. "Please! Think!"

He rammed the lever in the forward gear. "About what"

"What'll happen if we give them up."

"So? Yes?"

I yelled, furious now. "Will you just stop for a minute and listen to me?"

The truck swayed to a halt. He glowered at me; brows drawn into a fierce frown. "Laura, be sensible. We must call someone – if they are as you say."

"And then? They'd be taken away, and in all probability, nothing would ever be heard of them again. The whole thing would be hushed up. We'd be discredited if we ever said anything."

"C'mon, Laura!"

"It's possible, though. Isn't it? Think of how people – responsible people – who've reported strange sightings have been ridiculed. Airline pilots and police officers told they were chasing Venus, made to look like idiots."

He listened, but the frown didn't leave his face. He ran a distracted hand into his hair, dislodging the old, weathered Stetson, leaving a tangle over his ear.

"Nobody would believe us if we told them afterward, would they? And if they did, the same kind of denouncement would soon shut them up."

He said nothing.

"But Jesse, the thing is, I promised them we'd help them. Come and talk to them at least before deciding anything further."

Drops of rain began to gleam on the windshield. The mountains were gone into the mist, and darkness lay across the fields. I thought of them out there, waiting and worrying, alone and perhaps hurt, in an alien world, a cold and wet depressing world fraught with danger.

"Look," I said. "It's raining. Let's not leave them out there in this, anyway."

He sighed with resignation and began to turn the truck around again. "Okay, Laura. But only for now."

This is really happening, I thought as Jesse drove on. There were three beings and a spacecraft up there on our meadow, and they just had to be from another world. I did understand Jesse's prudence. We were taking three totally unknown strangers into our home, and alien beings at that, perhaps harboring dangers of which we were entirely unaware. But there was also a deep, heart pumping excitement. History was standing on our doorstep – and who could be impervious to that?

We had both always loved the unique and rare, finding as much adventure in our lives as we could. That's why Jesse wrote his music and rode in horse races. That was why I wanted to live here instead of California, where our friends all thought it wiser for us to be. But there was adventure in these mountains and forests, in seeing bears and cougars, deer and coyotes from our windows or on wilderness trails. And the old log house, built by my grandfather fifty years ago, was beautiful and unique. When he had left the place to me, I had been overwhelmed.

Jesse worked well here and loved the land; I had my pottery studio and kiln in the cellar. And we had the horses, the Arabians, most stemming from the mares my mother had given me when I had been fourteen years old and horse crazy. They had been the concert of our lives, a unison in which we had danced at the high notes, been in tune at the low, and always with the excitement of what was yet to be. What ribbons and trophies would be won? What foals would be born? Where would our young stock go? But all these adventures paled into nothing beside what happened on this cold gray November afternoon.

We drove through the gateway into the meadow, and the truck began to bump and lurch over the rough terrain. Its beams of light were dusty in the drizzling rain, the distant trees ghostly through the grayness.

"Over there." I pointed, peering through the mist.

The truck began to climb the slope, and then I saw them. The smooth surface of the craft gleamed amid broken scrubby trees, and the two figures stood beside the third lying on the grass.

"They look like us," Jesse said, and there was relief in his voice, an easing of the frown. "Are you sure they're not American? Or Russian?"

"Positive. Why? What did you expect? Star Wars Wookiees?"

"I thought you were kidding."

He drove straight towards them, and they began to look defensive. Both held something in their hands and aimed it at us. I felt my stomach tighten.

"Jesse, maybe you should stop here."

He did so, sitting and staring at the silvery figures with the frown back on his brow.

In the darkening mist, with the headlights shining on falling rain, they were indistinct, veiled by a shimmering curtain of bright water. But their faces and eyes had a luminous quality we could see, and the sheen of the suits they wore reflected the light with a strange clarity. A pile of equipment heaped beside the body on the ground was as equally unfamiliar, and I heard Jesse's sharp intake of breath, as he too realized how out of place they were in this wild mountain meadow, that these beings did not belong here.

I got out as they began to come toward us, and Jesse turned off the engine, switched off the lights, and also got out. We stood together before the truck, unable to go any further. The only sounds were the pattering of raindrops and the ticking of the truck's engine as it cooled. Neither of us could find a single word to say as we stared at our unlikely visitors in a breathless, frozen waiting.

They stopped a short distance from us, and again it was the dark one who spoke. "We will not harm you," he said carefully. "All we require is your help . . . until we can obtain assistance."

His huge eyes were even more compelling in this near darkness, and I found my voice. "Of course," I said, trying to sound reassuring while the misty cold was creeping through my clothes and down my back. The fear of the unknown lurked within its chill. "Our house isn't very far away. We'll take you there now. But . . . your companion . . . is he badly hurt?"

"Not severely. He is our commander." He hesitated, apparently struggling to explain things in our language's limited words. "He will recover in . . . " Again, he paused, and I saw the distinct expression of worry on his face. Then he smiled. "I am trying to calculate your time," he said.

The smile bridged the gap of strangeness; the look of worry made him human. I wonder now what we would have done if they had been seven feet tall and covered with long brown hair, if we could have related to them at all. Cultural shock and fear of the unknown were already enough to struggle with. But his smile erased our fears, and we even forgot they were alien beings from another mysterious world.

"We'd better get him to the house," I said.

The smile became warm. "I must apologize," he said, "for inconveniencing you in this manner." He pulled off a gauntlet, revealing a long, very fine boned hand. "I believe it is your custom to hold the hand upon meeting. My name is Farrand, and this" – he turned briefly to the other one standing near him – "is Celene."

I took the hand. How cold it was! I tried to convey warmth and sincerity in my touch. "I'm Laura, Laura Tremayne. And this is Jesse, my husband."

Jesse accepted the hand, and with it, apparently, the situation. "I'm sorry," he said in a rush, "but you must see this has been kind of a shock to us."

The eyes studied him, faintly puzzled. But then Celene stood before me, holding out his hand. It was even colder than Farrand's, and shock and dismay were still vivid on his face. He didn't speak, and I couldn't think of anything to say. His clasp was very brief, and after quickly touching Jesse's hand as well, he immediately drew away.

But Jesse didn't seem to notice. He hurried to help them load their commander and equipment into the back of the truck, gave them a hand up (although they didn't seem to need it), and drove away with a considerate amount of caution, as though he realized how rough this vehicle must seem to them, how comparatively violent its ride could be.

As we rolled down the High Meadow Road, he began to shake his head. "I don't believe it," he said. "But where else could they have come from?"

"We'll have to ask them." My voice was pinched by a constriction in my throat, and I was numb with strain and excitement.

"Funny that we didn't."

"Too many other things to think about."

The lane was a softly lit tunnel in the lights of the truck, paved with leaves, walled and roofed with branches, needles, and twigs. Some brushed the side of the pickup as it passed between them. Familiar sound, familiar road, well-known vehicle . . . and in the back . . . my God!

Jesse slowed to turn the sharp corner at the bottom. "If I'd ever thought about it at all, I'd have said that something like this would be an earthshaking event – not a crashed ship in a small backwoods pasture."

I huddled on the seat, my hands clasped between my knees. "It may yet be."

"Be what?"

"An earthshaking event."

"I don't know. I get the impression they want to leave as soon as possible."

"Yes," I admitted, "and Farrand did say earlier that they were in danger and the army mustn't find them."

The bridge's timbers rumbled beneath the wheels.

"That craft," he said. "What a weird thing."

"Mmm . . . And if that's what we've always called a UFO, or flying saucer, wouldn't the US Air Force, or the armed forces here, just love to get their hands on it?"

"That's what I'm beginning to think. And if they did, I guess they'd want to keep it secret. And that would mean the disappearance of those on board."

"I think that's what they're afraid of."

An instinct to protect began to overcome my other emotions: the excitement and the alarm. They were people with names, alone with a wrecked craft in the cold wild mountains of our planet and had turned to us for help. They were trusting us, were putting themselves into hands that must be as alien to them as theirs were to us.

Jesse was silent, negotiating the curves on the hill where the road ran up from the creek to the hay fields. They opened before us, wide and rolling in the beams of the headlights. In the valley below, the lights of the village shone hazily through the mist.

"So, what do we do?" Jesse asked suddenly. "Be loyal to our nation or to them?" He jerked his head, indicating the occupants in the bed of the truck.

"To them," I said without hesitation. "Because I promised."

"But if there's so much more at stake . . . that craft . . . "

"I promised," I said obstinately. "Jessee!"

"In the heat of emotion. I've always said you're too emotional. A promise like that was damned stupid."

"Maybe it was, but when I saw them there, on such a miserable day, helpless, one hurt or even dead—"

"He isn't dead," he interjected.

"Well, anyhow, I thought you felt it too. Farrand apologized for being an inconvenience."

Again, he was silent, He turned onto the road that led to the house. I hadn't noticed the rain cease, but it was starting again. He switched the wipers on, still in silence.

"We haven't had time to think properly," he said at last. "But we're sure going to have to . . . and very carefully," he added, throwing me a look dark with warning.

But when we reached the house, he again hurried to help them, expressed concern for the inert form as they carried their commander into our spare downstairs bedroom, and seemed to have forgotten his doubts.

I was the one who became uncertain when I saw how out of place Farrand was here. In the soft light of the rustic lamp, with the heavy log walls and dusky ceiling's wooden glow, he was as unbelonging as he had been up on the High Meadow. The silverclad body of his commander lay at his feet on the shaggy Scandinavian rug and was just as alien. Jesse had gone to help Celene bring their equipment in, and I was alone with them.

"What can we do for him?" I asked, trying to force away that persistent fear of the unknown, to dispel a debilitating sense of inadequacy. I gestured to the figure lying on the rug.

"I have all that is needed," Farrand said.

"Oh."

I turned away from those alien eyes, their compelling water covered depths. I took pillows from the top of the closet, brought linens and an extra blanket, and began to make the bed. He watched my every move, intense, curious.

"I'm sorry," I said, "but I don't know what you're used to – whether you even sleep in beds."

"Beds? What are beds?"

"This is a bed," I explained. "We sleep in one at night and stay in one if we are ill or hurt."

For a moment he stared at me, and then that warm smile touched his face. "We came to see," he said. "So now we are seeing."

I've heard that the course of history can be changed by a smile. Maybe I'm exaggerating if I say Farrand's changed ours. But without it I think the train of events wouldn't have followed the road it did, that I might have broken my promise and let Jesse have his way. Without it I think it could have been me who betrayed them. For my first look at Israfel was shattering.

CHAPTER THREE

FARRAND KNELT ON THE FLOOR and began to remove his commander's outer suit. I finished making up the bed, eased again by his smile, until I was done and went to where Farrand still knelt. He was touching his commander's head and neck with gently exploring hands.

Without the bulky suit, the figure on the floor was incredibly slender, dressed in ivory colored velvety garments with a wide band of gold across the chest. The same golden metal boots were on his feet, and his hands were long and white. Then I saw his face, and a painful tearing rent my chest, and the floor rocked beneath my stumbling feet.

In all the excitement, the hurry and the faded light, I had not paid close attention to this one. Now I was looking at a truly unearthly face.

Motionless, as pale as alabaster and with eyes firmly closed, the face still revealed an intensity of life force that took my breath away. Power, strength, and discipline were carved into the fine honed molding. Maturity shaped his mouth, and intelligence was written in every line, a wisdom far beyond the human pale. Silver hair winged away from the high forehead, and there was youth in the smooth translucent skin, blue veins at the temples as fine as thread, an overall sensitivity. But that was an illusion, dispelled by the imprint of age and vast knowledge, the engraving of purpose and authority, and by an aloof aura that set him in a realm apart. He looked as pale and brilliant, as distant and cold, as the star from whence he must have come. He was ethereal in a godlike magnificence that was impossible to regard as human.

My mouth dried to dust as I looked at that face, so beautiful but so foreign in its expressive composition. Life that shone in that face, even when it was so pale and still, the eyes invisible. Unconscious, he was electrifying and frightening. Too much so, I found as I stared. He was terrifying!

An inner trembling began somewhere deep in the center of my being, vibrating with the beating of my heart, and my throat tightened so I could scarcely breathe. I stood there, shaking and dreading his return to consciousness. I desperately wished we had called the authorities, anyone, and let others far more capable take charge. I couldn't handle this.

Farrand was lifting him, rising to gaze at me with his perceiving eyes. He read my face across the body he held in his arms seemingly without effort.

I stumbled at the threshold of betrayal, barely resisting the urge to turn and run, when I found myself remembering the promise I had made to this manlike being with the gentle face and warm, winning smile, the reliance he was placing on me.

I forced myself to meet his eyes, my face to compose. But my voice seemed to echo in the empty drum that was my head. "What . . . is his name?"

"Israfel."

Coincidence, I thought, as in the muffled rooms at the back of my memory, a door opened for one brief moment. The name merely sounded like something else, was familiar only in my imagination. I couldn't have heard it before. That instant of recollection was another figment of confusion, created by the turmoil of my brain and shaken wits. No doubt the same disturbance was allowing the primitive fear to surface, the terror of the unknown that is atavistic and inherent, powerful enough to smother logic and common sense when the mind is dislodged from the familiar and secure.

I looked around me, drew strength and stability from the stout log walls, the solidity of my house, the sanctuary of my home. And Farrand was as human as Jesse, I told myself. His commander hurt and unconscious, just as we could easily be.

Farrand relaxed visibly when I summoned a reasonably confidant smile, and I tried to ignore another disconcerting thought, one that seemed to come of its own volition: what might he have done had I fled the room and run to the phone to summon authorities? Surely, they weren't entirely defenseless.

I turned to the bed and drew the covers back. Israfel's hand

The uneasiness persisted, and when I went out into the hall to turn up the thermostat (Israfel's hand had felt like ice when mine had inadvertently touched it as I had covered him), the feeling deepened. Alien equipment was scattered across the floor – strange boxlike objects of a bluish black substance, some covered with tiny buttons, others obviously broken. Jesse came through the door carrying another one of those objects, almost staggering beneath its weight while Celene carried an identical one with the greatest of ease. The darkness beyond the open door resounded with the distant thunder of a jet engine far away, and a wash of cold night air swept around us, chilling me.

Impressions, short and swift, making marks of anxiety. That plane out there, was it the same one I had heard earlier? Why was it flying here in the dark and the low and heavy clouds? Celene's angelic face was cold, and he obviously avoided sharing any of his distress. Jesse had put the box thing down and was talking with Farrand at the bedroom door. Something about the ship. Another problem.

Farrand's voice was warm and quiet, speaking our language easily now. I tried to pull myself together, to pay sensible attention. "Could we bury it?" he was asking.

"Bury it?" Jesse frowned.

"That would be the most satisfactory."

"I guess it would, but how?"

"Have you a . . . a machine?"

"I've a tractor with a frontend loader, but that would take all night." Jesse ran a hand through his hair, knocking his hat to the floor. He didn't notice. "We'd have to dig a damned big hole, then drag it there somehow, and cover it all up again."

"I will help."

Jesse frowned again, obviously thinking Farrand didn't realize the extent of the work involved in such an undertaking. Celene had gone out. I remembered my mission, turned up the thermostat, then went to our room at the front of the house and took an electric blanket from the closet.

When I returned to the hall, Jesse and Farrand were still discussing the difficulty of hiding the ship.

"I've been doing some clearing near there," Jesse was saying. "But it's the digging—"

"I will help," Farrand repeated. He went back into the spare bedroom and scooped up Israfel's suit and gauntlets. "These should be hidden also."

"I'll get some plastic bags to put them in," I said, following him. I spread the electric blanket quickly over their commander and plugged it in, then headed for the kitchen. Activity, I found, took my mind off the problems, and familiar things made the word *alien* seem less ominous.

But when I returned with the bags and Celene and Farrand had divested themselves of their outer suits, the word sprang before me in capital letters.

The sleeves of the tunics they wore were closefitting, revealing how remarkably slender their arms were. Their shoulders had the fragility of children, and their bodies were slim and willowy. Yet I had seen both lift seemingly heavy weights with ease. But the greatest strangeness was the fabric of their clothes. With a sheen of velvet, the material was so soft, like the fur of a chinchilla, that I could scarcely feel it when I had the opportunity to touch it. Smooth and fine, it yielded to every movement, flowed and fitted as only a perfect cut can. But I could find no seams. The metallic bands of gold around their chests were strangely distinctive. Celene's was narrower than Farrand's, and neither was as wide as Israfel's. And again, there was that odd stirring of my memory, the uneasy movement of some distant recollection, that I again dismissed as only fancy or some unconnected similarity. I opened a bag and folded one of the suits into it, trying to ignore the alien texture between my hands. Cold, slippery like plastic, but not . . .

Jesse was at the door. "We're going up with the tractor to see what we can do."

"Okay. But you'd better find a coat of some kind for Farrand."

Ten minutes later they were gone, carrying three green plastic garbage bags, Farrand in boots and an old coat of Jesse's. And yet he was taller than Jesse, and the thick Melton wool coat concealed his slenderness.

The tractor rattled away into the darkness, and I went back to the spare room to arrange the electric blanket.

Celene was there, standing unhappily by the bed. And he looked at me with an expression of extreme distaste. In his spotless ivory tunic, with his shining golden hair and pure waxen skin, he looked as though no speck of dust had ever touched him, and he was obviously disgusted by my soiled clothes and the aroma of horse that was emanating from me.

In defense, I tried to smile, to make a joke. "Life on the farm isn't all roses," I lightly spoke.

His only response was to step away from me, but when I went to the bed and began to slide the blanket's cord under it, his brilliant eyes flashed with warning.

"What are you doing?" he demanded. His voice was clear and sharp, and I realized it was the first time I had heard him speak.

"Making sure he's warm," I said.

He looked down at the bed, frowning recognizably.

"Feel it," I said.

He did so, signals of danger in the quick glances he kept hurling at me.

These too I tried to ignore. "Now," I said, forcing a lightness to my tone, "I must go and attend to our horses. Then I'll be able to get out of these grubby clothes."

I left him there, standing on guard beside the bed, a glorious vision of peerless ivory and gold, entirely out of place and already nurturing the resentment that would grow into hatred.

CHAPTER FOUR

GALLANT GREETED ME WITH AN indignant whinny and impatient tossing of his head. Sally came slinking from behind some bales, eyes reproachful, tail unhappy. Lather had dried the horse's coat to a sticky stubble that was impossible to brush out, and there were still damp patches on his neck and flanks. I rubbed him down and blanketed him, but none of my words of assurance would soothe the horse.

I let the foals and yearlings into their sheds, mixed their grain ration, hauled hay out to the mares, and fed the stallions. Old and beautiful gray Shadrach, dry boned, dark eyes, was the only one who was quiet. Young and high mettled Alla Bay, with his bright chestnut coat, paced his stall with his nostrils flaring and ears taut, tearing hay in spasmodic snatches. The mares were nervous too, flinging their heads up to gaze wide-eyed into the black forest at unseen dangers, their hay forgotten, trailing from their mouths.

I too stood staring across the yard, at windows flooding with light that were normally in darkness at this hour. Beyond those walls were two beings not of this earth, one with a face I tried not to think about. Far away was the distinctive rattle of the tractor engine. Jesse, in fine rain and falling night, was trying to bury an alien spacecraft beneath the stones and sod of a meadow on our property, and with him was another being from a different world.

How could we be doing this? What were we taking on? How could we possibly assume such a dreadful responsibility? Again, the debilitating malaise of inadequacy leeched my strength and weakened my resolve. Who were we? A young couple, relatively unworldly, living on a lonely farm in the wilds of the country to which we owed our allegiance, hiding not only something of inestimable value from government but also from the world, concealing the answer to question millions have asked: are we alone in the universe?

But the alternative . . . I remembered Farrand's words. There were dangers to consider. The capabilities of that small and simple ship would be priceless. The knowledge stored in the heads of those on board would ensure victory in the space race. And what rights would they have on this earth, where sacrifices were readily made for power and political advantage?

Farrand's smile. Celene's unhappy eyes, his stricken face there in the cold gray damp of the High Meadow. And their commander . . . helpless, not knowing even where he was . . . that pale and beautiful face so definitely alien and so definitely promising of superior ability and extreme wisdom. What secrets to the universe might he own? What means could be used to extract them in the endless quest for power? What defense would these three have against all the resources, equipment, and methods available and resorted to in our corrupt and greedy world?

I hugged my arms to my chest in a new and different fear. I stared into the darkness as I pondered these alarming thoughts, my eyes trying to pierce the black depths of the trees, the dark hollow of the roadway, the shadows around the barn and house. The desire to protect brought new strength.

Rain still fell softly, but I saw nothing else, and Sally, following me as I walked across the yard, gave no warning. I let myself back into the house.

What do they eat? I suddenly wondered as I stoked the woodburning furnace. There was the larger portion of a roasted hen in the fridge and the remains of a rhubarb pie, but would that do for them? And I simply had to change my clothes.

Celene turned from the window as I hovered at the door of the spare room. He looked at me with despairing eyes.

"Celene," I said gently, sympathetically, "are you hungry? What do you eat?"

"We have food in the ship."

"Did you bring any in? Is it in the hall?"

"Farrand said to leave it."

"Do you know what chicken is?"

"Chicken?"

"Look, I'll just go and change my clothes and get cleaned up, then I'll show you."

The hostility and scorn in his eyes weren't quite as pronounced as before, but he obviously still regarded me as very inferior.

"I'll show you," I muttered, digging to the back of my closet and pulling out a long formal gown that I had only worn once before. I showered, dried my hair into waves as elegant as hard brushing and a blower could produce, and even indulged in a dab of perfume Jesse's mother had sent as a heavy hint last Christmas. Then I casually invited him to the kitchen.

If he was impressed by my pashmina and daisy perfume, he didn't show it. But astonishment must have been a billboard on my face when he said, "Fowl," as I took the chicken from the fridge.

"Where did you see all this before?" I asked, amazed.

"They are universal," he said. For the first time he smiled. There was one second of dazzling beauty before the cold disdain was back. "A very long time since we had seen one."

"Then today you shall. But" – I remembered the still figure in the spare room – "your commander, is there anything we can do for him?"

"My commander," he said softly. "Israfel . . . " His voice strengthened. "This is a terrible thing to have happen!" Anguish filled his eyes, and his face became even paler. I moved to touch his arm in a conciliatory gesture, but he jerked himself away.

"Celene, it'll be all right. Please, try not to worry."

Anguish became despair; disdain turned to anger. "You cannot know," he began, then broke off. The blue eyes froze. "How can I not worry?"

"Okay. Okay," I said, the chill of his eyes seeming to penetrate the soft warmth of my silk. "I know you are. But it won't help right now. And we're doing all we can."

The most precise discipline I had ever seen began to stiffen his lips, his whole body, and brought a total dispassion to his eyes. My skin prickled with icy goose flesh as I saw all traces of emotion vanish from his face. The speed of the transformation was equally unnerving. I stood as though cemented to the floor and stared at him. This being wasn't only alien but dangerous. The lack of emotion in his face was chilling as the unrelenting cold of winter. And he was here, inside my house. My house . . . my home, I reminded myself.

And he was within at my invitation. Their presence brought enough fear without him intimidating me in my very own kitchen!

I raised a defiant chin in a discipline of my own. "We're trying to help you," I said. "We don't have to, you know."

The cold eyes focused on my face as if from a vast distance. I met them with my ordinary brown eyes, curbing my temper, resisting the insidious tickle of fear crawling on my back. Open enmity would be intolerable. The whole affair was hard enough to deal with as it was. But I couldn't just stand here, in my own house and home, letting him cow me with his arrogant disdain and supercilious eyes.

For a long time, I held his gaze, and then he blinked, as though surprised by my display of defiance. He blinded me with a smile as dazzling as the sun.

"We are in your debt," he said. "But I am most concerned about what has happened. I have never experienced anything like this before."

"Neither have we," I said. "Believe me!" Relief made me generous; the fears of antagonism forcing me into the acceptance of a truce. And his smile was enough to make me forget anything.

"And if I may help prepare the food—" he began.

"No, No!" I gathered my wits at this unexpected offer, and I was just as disturbed by this new Celene. "There isn't much to do. Just tell me how you like things. Do you like peas? It'll be a bit of a hodge podge, but tomorrow I'll be better prepared."

Mundane tasks lent stability and took my mind off the being from another planet with his lightning changes of personality. His clear unhappiness did draw sympathy, and his frequent journeys across the hall to check on Israfel were a reminder of concern, even though the elegant grace with which he moved made me feel like an ox. I made a salad, prepared vegetables, sliced a loaf of French bread, and managed not to cut myself once even though my hands hadn't ceased to shake since I had raced away from the High Meadow on Gallant.

Our dining room was warm, cozy, and inviting. My grandfather had built the fireplace from stone they'd collected on the property and had made the pegged plank floor of birch. I kept it polished to a satin shine. My best Swedish flatware and Venetian crystal shone on a blue linen tablecloth, and I put out the dinner service I had made myself: heavy pottery glazed with tones of sage and lavender swirled onto an ivory background. I could tell that, to Celene, it was all as primitive as a cave. But as I closed the handwoven drapes that match the shade, and the rich greens, blues, and hints of orange enclosed the room with mellow warmth. I didn't care. This was my home, and we liked it.

He was no more impressed by the room I showed him upstairs.

"There's another," I told him. "But it isn't any better than this."

Then there was that sudden switch. He smiled. "May both Farrand and I stay there?" Here he looked at the single beds, the brown and cream Scandinavian rug on the polished floor, at the angled ceiling beneath the roof. "This will be fine for us. Thank you."

I made up the beds, again declining his help, and wished had been the one to go and help Jesse instead of Farrand. Then we heard the tractor as it came back into the yard and practically ran down the stairs in relief.

"Were you able to do anything?" I asked as they pulled boots off in the utility room. "You haven't been gone very long."

Farrand smiled. He looked tired but pleased. Jesse sat on the bench by the door and stared at me, one boot still on, his hat forgotten, tilted precariously on his head. I took the hat and hung it up. "Well?"

"Incredible!" he said. He pushed a hand into his hair. "Just incredible."

Farrand padded out of the room in Jesse's socks and went to look at Israfel. I hovered in the doorway. "Yes?"

Jesse began abstractedly to remove the other boot. "All I had to do with the tractor was loosen the soil and help drag that thing with a chain."

I took the boot from his hand and set his slippers before him. "What happened?"

"Farrand . . . He . . . " He shook his head, stared at me without seeing me. "I don't know . . . "

"Yes? What?" My voice was beginning to rasp.

"Well . . . he just kind of did something . . . and the earth flew up out of the hole. And when we moved that thing . . . the tractor couldn't pull it . . . he got behind it, lifted it with his hand. It came quite easily." Again, he shook his head. "Incredible!"

"Telekinesis," I said.

"What?"

"You know, the ability to move objects by using the power of the mind."

"Oh . . . yes, I remember. But something like that!"

"You know what else?" I spoke. "They eat the same food we do. Celene said that what I showed him is universal."

"Laura . . . I . . . "

"Yes?"

"I don't know about all this."

"It's been too much, too sudden," I said, trying to sound sensible. "We'll feel better tomorrow."

But he looked doubtful, and I told myself it was only natural that I should feel the same. For who could know what tomorrow would bring?

That night we went to bed in a state of total exhaustion, but I found it impossible to sleep. The incredible events of the day rampaged through my mind like a movie that couldn't be turned off. Several times I heard soft sounds in the room next door and knew that either Celene or Farrand was there – alien, alien, alien – tending Israfel, their commander – more than alien. And the faint memory of the name annoyed me with its elusiveness. Where had I heard it before? The very certainty that I had was as disturbing as my inability to remember. Israfel. Israfel. Where? Where? Where?

Had he recovered consciousness yet? I strained to hear. But there was never the sound of a voice, nothing to indicate what was happening in the room next door. If he had . . . my skin prickled and my heart fluttered. Celene was intimidating enough, but Israfel . . .

I tossed and turned, plumped up my beaten down pillow. What were those things they had aimed at us up there on the High Meadow? Weapons? They must have been. But then weren't they in danger? Jesse and I merely had to telephone for help. They couldn't. So, what would happen about their rescue? Was there another craft like theirs close by that could even come tomorrow? Oh, God! I hoped so.

At least they'd come down in a relatively safe place and could speak our language . . . How? How! For pity's sake! Why hadn't I wondered about that before? And why did they look so much like us? And it wasn't coincidence that Israfel's name should strike like something else. I had heard it before, or seen it . . . somehow, somewhere . . . where were they from? Why hadn't we asked them? Was that craft a UFO? On and on, the questions teemed and seethed, until I got up in desperation, crept to the bathroom, and sneaked a sleeping pill.

〰

I woke to pouring sunshine and struggled back to what I knew was a shocking present before I could even remember why. The curtains had been opened. Jesse was gone, his pajamas lying in a discarded heap on the far side of the bed. And I could hear voices – his and someone else's coming from the room next door.

Recollection hit me, making my stomach lurch, and an ache pierced through the fuzziness in my head. My God! What had happened yesterday?

I went to the window, looked out across the lawn to the roadway and corrals beyond. A skiff of snow had fallen in the night and was already melting. Powdery avalanches fell from the trees, and the eave of the house dripped steadily beneath a golden rising sun and delphinium sky.

The mares stood at the fence, watching the house for the first sign of movement that would herald their morning feed. Already late, I saw, putting on my watch. Nearly eight thirty and nothing done yet.

The fuzziness was clearing from my head, movement bringing back some power of thought. And trepidation returned, taking hold of me as I left the room. We had three aliens in the house, and what was going to happen today?

CHAPTER FIVE

"FIRST," JESSE WAS SAYING, "I'LL cut down some more trees, and the damaged ones, pile all the branches where we buried it, maybe even get a fire going. I've been doing a lot of clearing up there," he added. "It won't look strange."

They stood around Israfel's bed, their faces intent and serious.

"And we must listen to the news," he went on, "see if anything's been reported."

"It's almost time for the eight thirty," I said.

Celene looked at me with the usual coldness, but Farrand smiled. He didn't notice the hair I'd forgotten to comb, the loose strands unraveling from yet another fraying sweater.

"I'll go and turn it on," I said, then, caught by the stillness of the figure on the bed, I added, "Israfel?"

"Not yet," Farrand said, and his smile was gone. "I hope later today."

I found myself wishing he had woken because a familiar sound was coming to my ears. The drone and beat of the helicopter, coming up the valley, and toward us.

This wasn't totally unusual. Forest companies and government helicopters often took this route, going north in the early morning and coming back in the late afternoon. But on this particular morning it was alarming, too . . .

" . . . near Kelowna. No names have yet been released," the voice on the radio droned. "In hockey last night . . . "

They had said a small plane had come down somewhere between Dawson Creek and Kelowna. Did that explain the helicopter? Or . . . I no longer heard the voice on the radio. Was that why they'd sent that aircraft to search our area? Were there parties hunting through our woods? What happened when a plane went missing?

Farrand and Celene stood near me.

"Small plane?" Farrand asked.

"That's what they said."

"You look worried."

"It could mean search parties all through here."

"What are Kelowna and Dawson Creek?"

"Towns, due north and south of here."

It was hard to explain mileages in a way they could understand. I found a map of British Columbia and showed them the places concerned and where they were in relationship to us. But it was still hard to convey scale, that our place was only a pinprick.

"What facilities does this country have for such a search?" Farrand asked at last.

"Planes and helicopters, mostly," I said. "And most planes do carry a transmitting device that emits a signal by which they can be found."

They considered this in silence, their faces expressionless.

"Did anyone see you yesterday, do you think?" I asked, wondering why I hadn't thought to ask that before, then realizing it was only one question in probably a hundred or more. And how much time, or thought, had there been on the preceding day for such questions?

"We were shot at," Farrand said, "by a fighter plane. It disabled us."

"Shot at?" My voice sounded strange.

"That's what damaged our ship."

How stupid I'd been! Of course. How, otherwise, would that gaping hole have been torn in its side? But this realization was no less disturbing. Someone else had seen the craft, shot at it, and brought it down. They would be searching – the army, the police, Defence Department people – questioning, invading. Oh, hell!

"I am sorry," Farrand went on, "that we should inflict this trouble on you."

It was trouble, I knew. He obviously wasn't expecting any rescue in the immediate future. And their commander still lay in another room, unconscious and helpless, a further liability. Again, I wavered between the burden of helping them and the sincerity in Farrand's voice, the awesome responsibility and their difficult predicament.

"I wish it had never happened," Farrand said quietly.

I sank into a chair at the table and looked up at him. What should we do? How could we possibly cope with this? How large his eyes were, how clear, despite their darkness. And they were deep and intent and compelling, fixed on mine. His face . . . so strong, so well-formed. He was slender and slight, vulnerable, dislocated into a dangerous alien world.

"Don't worry," I heard myself saying. "If they don't know where you are, we'll manage somehow."

Jesse came back, dusting hay from his sweater and snow off his slippers.

"The more normal things look around here, the better," he said.

I broke away from Farrand's gaze, struggled to my feet, and began to gather cutlery and plates from the dishwasher and carry them to the table. "There was a report of a small plane being overdue," I told Jesse, setting out the plates.

"Oh?" He was still picking at bits of hay caught in the wool of his sleeve. "Where?"

"It said on a flight between Dawson Creek and Kelowna."

"A big area."

"There's something else," I said. Farrand was still watching me. "The reason they crashed is because they were shot at."

Farrand spoke, his attention turning to Jesse. "I must repair our communicator, reach a base ship. It will come for us then."

"How long will that take?" Jesse put his slippers by the stove to dry.

"I should be better able to tell you when I have examined it."

A slight uneasiness appeared on Jesse's face. "Is it with those things in the hall?"

"Yes."

"We're going to have to find somewhere to hide all that stuff."

"I was thinking that also."

They went out into the hall, and with Farrand's departure, a pressing sense of urgency began to inflict itself on me. There was so much to do: hiding places to be found, plans made for handling questions, stories to prepare as forearming. And what about when friends dropped in? What would we do if the police came with a search warrant? Would the damaged trees and scarred earth have been noticeable from that helicopter? What if it came back to investigate? They must be searching. Something strange had been shot at, brought down. Could they already have some idea of where it might be?

I spilled cream on the floor, scrambled eggs on the stove, and went to the pantry to find – I had forgotten what for. That missing plane – was that true? It was more likely, I told myself, throwing bacon into a pan that was too hot, that the report was a ruse, an explanation for planes and helicopters and search parties – that they were in fact looking for something else. And if such a precaution was being taken, secrecy observed, then our alien visitors could well be in the danger I had imagined.

I was going to help them. I knew it. Was Jesse? He had talked about a hiding place and making things appear normal, had worked to bury the craft the night before. But this morning he looked uneasy, and even more so when they had come back. Farrand was obviously upset.

"It's most badly damaged," he said unhappily. "It will take much time to repair."

Celene turned from the window with cold dismay reflecting from the icy glacier of his face. I stood by the stove, urgency becoming panic as I saw their new distress. Worry piled on difficulty until it towered above me like the mountains that surrounded us.

"Don't worry," Jesse said, rescuing the toast that was burning on the stove. "As long as it's reparable, don't worry about it."

I stared at him, uncertain that I was hearing him correctly. Only a moment before he'd been worried. Now he was doing the same kind of lightning change as Celene. He passed around reassuring smiles and put more toast on the rack, exuding confidence with every movement of his strong musician's hands. His hazel eyes were clear and steady as he smiled at Farrand, and his mouth was sure. Every trace of worry had vanished from his face.

Calm spread its soothing influence, and my anxiety stilled. Even Celene looked less troubled, and Farrand produced a smile. Jesse turned the toast, put more wood on the fire, pulled another flake of hay from the cuff of his sweater. Farrand sat down and Celene's cold face thawed a couple of degrees. I measured coffee beans into the grinder and found I could keep count. I sliced more bread, put out preserves, and let the comfort of peace and the warm ambience of the kitchen allay those other apprehensions. All around me were earthy tiles and oak counters, glass jars of herbs and cereals, hanging ivies and copper pots glinting in the sun. African violets crammed on the windowsills wore familiar faces, and heat came from my grandfather's antique cookstove as it cooked our breakfast and took away the morning's chill. Daylight brought its own security, and even the fact that our guests were extraterrestrials no longer seemed to matter. They were human and needed us. Even Celene, standing by the window and looking sadly out at the sun gilded trees and snow mottled hills, provoked only sympathy. For some reason all was well.

But later, when I felt it was my duty to go and look at Israfel, a different sense of disquiet erased what after all had only been a false sense of security. Here we had a very real problem, and one that none of us could eliminate.

Israfel had slipped into a deeper unconsciousness, a disturbing one. The vitality of his face was fading, the life force checked. Instead, there was a look of secretiveness, as though he had consciously drawn away from any contact, away from us and a danger he could possibly sense, gone into a place inside himself where none could reach.

Farrand's eyes, dark and troubled, met mine above the still form. But he said nothing, went with Jesse up to the High Meadow to cut down the damaged trees, pile their branches, and burn them. And I, worried now about Israfel, went to town for extra supplies and met a police car in the forest.

All my insides lurched horribly when the chrome grille and dark blue came suddenly before me, the distinctive and unmistakable rack of red, blue, and white lights standing across the roof. The road was too narrow for our vehicles to pass, and I was glad of that much, at least. I hoped I could parry his questions and turn him back, but my heart was thumping at the shock of suddenly seeing this unwelcome visitor. We both stopped, and he got out while I sat winding my window down and dragging in deep breaths of calming air.

I had seen him before, down in the village, recognized his serious face, which a scattering of freckles didn't make youthful. A young police officer but typically old before his time. He came alongside my door.

"Mrs. Tremayne?"

"Yes." I tried to smile, to appear politely curious, while my heart turned somersaults and my lungs seemed paralyzed.

"I was just heading for your place."

"Oh?" Surely that wasn't my voice. "My husband's out doing some clearing he's been working on. Can I help?"

"Well, I just wanted to know if you might have seen or heard anything unusual yesterday?"

Oh, God! What a question. If he only knew! I frowned, blinking as I felt my eyes begin to freeze. "Unusual?" Would he realize that wasn't my normal voice? Could he see how my hands were clenching on the wheel? I tried to relax them and hung an elbow on the top of the door as Jesse would do.

"Yes."

"Like what?"

"Well, like a plane in trouble."

"Oh!" A plane? Was there really? "I heard on the news this morning that a plane was missing on its way to Kelowna. Is that it?"

He made a noncommittal sound. What did that mean? That there wasn't a plane?

"I was riding yesterday afternoon," I continued, "but the only plane I heard was a jet. Could that be it?"

"No. A light plane."

"You think it could've come down around here?"

"Possibly."

"Oh, dear. And it was miserably cold and damp last night."

His eyes were watching my face, observing it far too closely for my liking. A hot sweat was damp beneath my arms, irritating against my clothes. I tried to imagine a plane, with wings and a tail, a propeller and wheels, down in the mountains, these tangled forests.

"How many people?"

"We aren't sure. Possibly two."

I frowned again, wondering if I had answered his questions by suggestion. But his eyes were still fixed on my face.

"Jesse and I could go out on horses after lunch, search the forest and mountainside up there." I waved a vague hand to the west. "We're very familiar with all the trails and old logging roads. As far as the power line, anyway. Would that help?"

"It sure would, if you don't mind."

Had that satisfied him? It almost seemed so. So maybe there was a plane. Surely, he would have tried to discourage us from searching if he knew it wasn't. My hopes rose, if somewhat thinly.

"We'll call you as soon as we get back, even if we don't find anything."

He nodded, a trace of gratitude in a faint smile. I swallowed the guilt of my deception. After all, I had told no lies, said nothing blatantly untrue.

He gave me his name, some parting words, and headed back to his car. I sat and watched him, my heart still jumping, dampness spreading to my hands and neck. That little bit of hope was already drifting away. This could only be the beginning.

He backed up and pulled the car off the road into the small layby. I was longing to see him turn around, go back the way he had come, but there wasn't enough room on the narrow road between the dense trees of the forest reserve. He waved me on, and I had no alternative but to comply.

I watched for as long as I could in my rearview mirror. I saw him pull back onto the road and continue toward the house. Then a curve in the road hid him from my sight.

There was nothing I could do to warn them. I had left Sally in the yard, but she, hearing the sounds of the chainsaw and tractor, might have gone up to the High Meadow to join Jesse. I rushed the truck along the narrow bumpy road, roared and slithered down the hill, and raced along the highway and the village streets. Now I was in a desperate hurry to get back, and then I ran into a friend in the grocery store.

Concealing my haste and anxiety was as much a trial as not telling her what had happened to us. She was buying cabbage and wanted to know my method of making borsch, and I had to stand there, trying to be natural, to remember the recipe, while my whole inner self was shaking from reaction and the desire to share my extraordinary news. She was a friend, close, and we had few secrets.

Oranges, apples, broccoli, tomatoes, people pushing carts, the smell of the cabbages and green onions, the jangle of the cash register, a little girl in a pink coat proudly bearing a Cabbage Patch doll, two men leaning on their buggies and talking about a dance at the Legion Hall – such familiar sights and sounds and scents, life going on around me, and I was not a part of it, detached by my extraordinary secret. *I must get away*, I kept thinking, *I must get back. What had happened? Where is that police car now? Where are Farrand and Jesse?* And Maureen went on talking about the borsch and cabbage rolls and the latest prank of their spoiled little daughter.

"Hey, Laura," she said suddenly. "Are you okay?"

"What? Oh, sure." I tried to pull myself back to cabbages and beets, oranges and apples, and that I mustn't forget a sack of potatoes.

"You look a bit strange."

"I do?" I shrugged, smiled. "I was just thinking . . . " Oh, Lord! If that didn't sound as phony as hell. "Jesse and I must ride out this afternoon. There's a plane missing. I said we'd go and look for it."

"Oh, wow," she said. "I didn't know."

"There was something about it on the news this morning." I began to put radishes and green onions into a bag. What else did I need? I tried to think.

"Did it crash?"

"What?" I only just caught myself from saying yes.

"The plane – has it crashed?"

"They seem to think so."

"Oh, wow," she said again. "I'd hate to walk into something like that, though. Wouldn't you?"

The temptation to tell her what I had walked into was again unendurably strong. I moved away. "I'd better get going, Maureen. I still have a few things to do."

"Sure." Her large brown eyes were still watching me, her vivid face filled with concern. "I'll call you later, see how you made out, tell you how the borsch is."

Borsch! I thought as I waved goodbye to her. I wished that was all I had to think about.

((()))

By the time I turned onto the access road, I was a nervous wreck. I had seen nothing of the police car. I had driven like a maniac all the way back; stress had filled my mind with nightmarish images that I was certain had become reality.

Tire tracks on the forestry road told me nothing. My own had crossed those made by the tractor, and so had another's, I saw, on the road to the house. I slewed the truck into the yard and scrambled out.

Sally bounded to meet me, tail whirling and ears strained back against her head. She was making small whimpering sounds, a sure indication that someone had been here during our absence. I could see where the car had turned.

Celene met me in the kitchen. His eyes were blazing with a blue and furious glitter, his face as white as chalk. He faced me like a tiger confronted by fire.

"Celene! Is everything all right? What happened? Did he see you?" Words tumbled from me in my desperation to know, but he didn't answer. "I met him in the forest. I thought I'd managed to put him off. Did he come to the door? What did you do?"

What had happened? Celene was furious. I shivered in the icy glare of those freezing eyes.

"The dog spoke," he said at last. "And a machine came near."

"It was a police car. But did he see you?"

"No."

"Did he come to the door?"

"No. He turned slowly, looking out. Then he went."

My sigh of relief was more of a moan. "Thank God for that!" I said.

The cold eyes blinked. " 'Thank God'?"

"It's as much a figure of speech as anything." Relief and the breaking of stress made me gabble. "If something turns out right that could just as easily not have . . . " My voice trailed away as his face became a mask of disbelief. "Anyway, everything's all right."

"No," he said. His eyes clouded with unhappiness and his mouth softened into a shape of pain. "I am not accustomed to having to hide from one such as—" He broke off abruptly, and I wondered what it was he had been about to say. Then my thought was forgotten as the beautiful smile suddenly dazzled me once more. "Forgive me. I overlook that I am a guest in your house, what it is you are doing for us. I am worried about my commander, what could happen to us here, about the danger."

"Celene . . . I . . . " I moved toward him, longing to assure him, to let him know I was sympathetic to his fears. But he drew away with that quick lifting of his head, a discernible distaste. I pressed on. "I understand how you feel, really I do." What incredible eyes, what a strange mixture of sensitivity and anger, of unhappiness and vulnerability and guarded threats and warnings. I wish he could have been happier here, but his high idealism never allowed it.

There was scorn in his voice. "I don't think you can even begin to know."

"But I do!" I protested. "I fully understand why you should be absolutely appalled at suddenly crashing down into this cold damp wilderness, to find yourself with people of another world in what must seem to you a very primitive house. And your commander lying there so helpless and hurt. Celene, I quite understand why you're upset."

For a long time, he stood and considered me, his face now totally enigmatic. I waited, trying to retain a sympathetic and encouraging smile, to assure him by my demeanor that I was steadfast and sincere.

"Thank you," he said at last, "for trying."

It was something, I supposed, and he would have regarded me pressing any further pressing as presumptuous. I let the matter rest.

"What about Israfel?" I asked. "How is he?"

"The same," he said, immediately unhappy again. He left me and walked away with his easy grace, back to the room in which Israfel lay.

⬖

True to my word, Jesse and I rode out in the afternoon and traversed the mountain to the west. We followed every passable trail and logging road, leaving our tracks for anyone to follow. Privately, I hoped they would. One small plane flew over while we were out, but we saw no other signs of a search.

Darkness had fallen by the time we got home, and we were cold, our hands and feet uncomfortably so. I dismounted and looked toward the house, anxiety constantly preying on me. The snow had melted from the road, and nothing had crossed the tracks left by our horses when we had ridden away, but that was only one of the worries that had beset me.

The house was in darkness. I pictured them there, listening always for Sally's bark of alarm, waiting for us to return – three beings from a world of which we knew nothing.

"Jesse," I said, "we still haven't asked them where they're from or anything like that."

He began to lead his horse into the barn. "I know. Several times this morning I meant to ask Farrand but always seemed to get sidetracked or something."

"What did you talk about?" I followed him into the familiar, sweet, warm interior, Andante clopping behind me.

Light flooded as he flicked the switch. *Farrand and Celene must know we are back*, I thought, *and perhaps Israfel has recovered consciousness in our absence.* This last thought also had its element of alarm. That perfect face with its stern lines and discipline, its authority and supreme intelligence, alive, comprehending and aware, could be far harder to deal with than Celene's aloof disdain.

"The best ways we can hide them," Jesse said.

I unbuckled the cinch and pulled the heavy saddle from Andante's dappled gray back. There was also all the equipment now in the room upstairs. And a search did seem to be in progress.

Jesse led Astra into a stall. "I told him I could close off one side of their room where the ceiling slopes down. It would be a small place, only large enough to take their stuff and with just enough space for them, if needs should be."

Celene didn't like hiding. I took Andante to her stall and began to unbuckle the bridle. "I wish we knew for sure just what is going on, why that cop was here today."

"I guess we'll find out soon enough."

We fed the horses in a thoughtful silence. I was cold, tired after the exertions and strains of the day, and filled with fresh doubts and anxieties. Jesse too looked pale, troubled, and as tired as I was. *What have we taken on?* I asked myself silently, measuring oats into a pail, stirring in syrupy molasses. *Are we doing the right thing? Could we be making a terrible mistake?*

But then, when I saw Farrand a short while later, his warm smile at seeing us, his gratitude for the meal I served, my doubts all evaporated as the daylight. They returned tenfold, though, droving me to the edge of panic, because that night Israfel began to die.

CHAPTER SIX

JESSE PHONED CONSTABLE PAUL, TELLING him we had seen nothing and where we had searched. He asked the constable, with justifiable inquisition, if he couldn't be more specific. Were they certain the plane had come down in our area? What color was it? Did it not have a signaling device on board?

"He's being purposely vague," Jesse said when he had hung up, his brow furrowing, his eyes thoughtful.

"But there's one thing I'm just about certain of," he went on. "There isn't any plane."

"It's much easier for us to cope with questions if we assume there is," I said. We drew the drapes over all the windows, turned the yard light on, left Sally out on guard, and stoked the fires against the night's cold. Warmth and light filled the rooms. The log walls glowed, the copper and colored tiles in the kitchen shone and gleamed, and fires crackled in stove and hearth. Rich smells came from the roast I had left in the oven, soft music from the radio Jesse had switched on to hear if there were any further reports on a missing plane. The house was an illuminated and living world of its own in the empty darkness.

This was my home, cozy and serene, alone in the isolation of our hilly piece of wilderness with the only visible lights coming from the village far below on the valley floor. They could be seen through the trees from our living room windows but were too far away to pose any threat of watching eyes or questioning minds. Those below were quite disconnected from the strong and heavy walls that enclosed us in our secluded sanctuary. It was so tempting, when I was tired and strained, to put away the memories of the policeman's face and eyes, the vehicle on our road, the morning's helicopter, to return to the house's warmth after the cold of the mountain in the afternoon, to forget what had happened here yesterday. Israfel was still a concern, but his face was less disturbing, his stern discipline frozen into a waxen immobility, as though he had made some decision and was less troubled. His pallor had increased, and blue smudges were forming below his eyes, but they made him, for the first time, appear vulnerable and defenseless. My urge to protect was even stronger, for Celene too had lost his arrogant air, was immersed once more in deep unhappiness, and would scarcely leave Israfel's side.

"I think your idea is good," I said to Jesse, "to build a hiding place in the room upstairs."

We were sitting by the living room fire with Farrand. Celene was with Israfel. Neither would drink tea or coffee, so Jesse and I sipped at steaming mugs of the coffee we loved while Farrand was quite content with a glass of icy water fresh from the creek.

Wearing one of Jesse's sweaters and a pair of his socks, Farrand looked very human. Only his exceptionally large eyes and the creamy color and texture of the slacks he wore indicated he was anything else. And he integrated himself with us and our lifestyle so rapidly that it soon became hard to remember he was a stranger, not just to this continent but to this very planet.

I must buy some clothes for them, I remember thinking, letting warmth and tiredness daze my senses, relaxing in the stillness of the house and the silence of the dog. *Even Celene would look far less sublime if he were dressed in jeans and a shirt. His eyes looked something like ice on the day they came . . . when was that? Was it only yesterday?* My eyes closed, and my head fell back against the curtains behind my chair.

Farrand and Jesse went on, talking about how to structure a hiding place, build a partition with a concealed door, make it look like an established wall.

We must ask Farrand where they're from, I thought dreamily. *We must ask them what they were doing here . . .*

Their voices were only a blur of sound, indistinct beyond a blanket of sleep that was muffling my brain. It had been so cold out on the mountain that afternoon with no way to get warm on a horse. How beautiful the fire was, how warm the house, the mug held between my hands. How lovely to relax, to sink into soft cushions, to forget a policeman's questioning, his observant eyes, the car heading toward the house . . . so quiet here, so peaceful, now . . .

"Laura!" Jesse's voice suddenly thundered in my ears.

I leaped into wakefulness with a painful jerk. "Oh! What?"

He was standing between me and the doorway, alarm written all over his face.

"Farrand. He suddenly rushed out of the room. He was in the middle of saying something, then he stopped, just like that, got up and ran."

I struggled to my feet, following Farrand. I hurried after him, my head whirling with all sorts of too vivid imaginings, none of which made any sense. For the dog hadn't barked; nobody was banging on the door; there were no strange lights in the yard. I caught a glimpse of Celene racing up the stairs as though his life depended on his speed and saw Jesse ahead of me in the doorway of the spare room and Farrand bending over Israfel, one hand moving through his hair and the other pressed to his chest. His intense silence spoke more loudly than any words of desperation, and his face and whole body were rigid with concentration. We were forgotten as we stood there in horror, for Israfel wasn't breathing and Farrand wasn't following any of the standard life reviving procedures we were familiar with. Yet we dared not interfere.

Celene rushed by me, only having eyes for the figure lying so still in the pool of soft light on the bed. He flung a curved piece of bluish metal down on Israfel's chest, a series of wires trailing from the device's row of buttons. He grasped one of the wires in one hand and passed Farrand another. The wires glittered a sapphire blue, and a soft humming sound began to rise from the object, gradually filling the room.

Jesse and I watched in frozen fascination as Israfel began to breathe, slowly and spasmodically, but apparently on his own. I moved closer and looked at him. His face was deathly white and devoid of life. The blue smudges below his eyes were even darker now, and the same blue tint had spread to his delicate nostrils, the fine skin surrounding them, and his lips. I turned to Farrand and saw deep anxiety in his eyes.

"Farrand," I said, "what is wrong with him? How is he hurt?"

He frowned, searching for words. "He was hurt to crash . . . it is an unconsciousness . . . his mind . . . is hurt . . . he is our commander, responsible for the craft . . . for us."

"Yes, I know. But you said he would soon recover. Now he is close to death."

His face paled and his eyes darkened. "Such a thing has not happened before. He blames himself. He was responsible."

"What? For causing the crash?"

"Yes."

Jesse spoke. "But that wasn't his fault. You said you were shot down."

"Yes. He should have avoided that."

I struggled to understand. "How badly was he hurt?"

"Not too severely. I repaired that."

"How?"

Again he frowned, regarding me unhappily. "There are not words in your language to explain."

"Then . . . " Could this be? "This unconsciousness is . . . is a way of escaping . . . the knowledge that he is responsible?"

"Part of."

"But . . . Farrand . . . " This couldn't be right! "He's your commander! He should be able to bear the responsibility for being responsible . . . if you see what I mean."

Farrand considered this, his eyes on the figure linked to him by the gleaming wire held so tightly in his hand. "He is of the highest hierarchy," he said. "He has a mind that can embrace all the laws of the universe, transcend time, make instant equations of distance and space. He is trusted, revered, most highly respected. He cannot fail."

"But anyone can make a mistake," Jesse said when Farrand's voice trailed away unhappily.

"Indeed. But Israfel would never permit it in himself."

"But what about you?" Jesse continued. "You said he was responsible for you."

Farrand stared at him, apparently perplexed.

"He should be thinking of that responsibility – of helping you now."

"His mind is hurt," Farrand said again, as though that explained it all.

I didn't understand, and I could see that Jesse didn't either. But we moved on from the subject to the more pressing concern of Israfel's current condition.

"Farrand," I began cautiously, voicing a worry I had been harboring for quite some time, "just how similar are you to us? I mean, you look like us – well, more or less. You eat the same food . . . "

"We have a common root," Farrand said.

"Then we should try putting him on an intravenous food supply."

"A what?"

I could see by his face that he had no idea what I was talking about, so I explained it to him as best I could. He began to look interested and faintly surprised. So did Celene.

"We don't have one," I finished up. "But I can go out and get one in the morning."

⊗

Morning came at last. Farrand and Celene were pale with exhaustion, their eyes glazed with tiredness and anxiety. A bleak depression reflected in the slowness of their movement. Farrand admitted to me that they were giving their own lives to Israfel through the device placed on his chest. They were transmitting their heartbeats to his, the reflexive action of breathing, the pulses and impulses – the whole life process passing from them to him. His life was hanging on by the threads tied to theirs, the fragile lines that were, after many hours, wearing thin. Once more, I thought longingly of doctors, of a hospital with professional care, and had to put such thoughts far from me.

Precaution had prevailed. We had decided that I would leave as soon as reasonable and go to Vernon to purchase what we needed. Buying these supplies locally could provoke questions. Even though I would hint that a horse required them, smalltown concern could quickly bring well meant but unwelcome attention, and this must be avoided at all costs.

Once again, I had to leave, drive the twenty odd miles to Vernon, buy what I required, and obtain instructions for its usage. "We breed horses," I explained to what I was sure was an overly curious druggist. "We lost one foal last year that I'm sure we could've saved if we'd had one of these." *How devious I am becoming*, I thought. *It's amazing how you can give indirect explanations and convey intent without telling a direct lie.* And I managed to conceal my dismay at the size of the needle and assure the man I knew how to find the jugular vein – the jugular vein! My blood ran cold at the thought.

"Dextrose," I said shakily. I suppressed an imaginary sneeze to cover the tremor in my voice as I answered his question about my plans for the horse's feed.

I hurried from the store, ran to the truck, and raced along the highway once more. Relief at obtaining the dispenser was replaced by doubts about whether it was going to work. We had fine needles at home, and the veins on Israfel's hands were thin but stood out clearly, dark and very visible under the translucent skin. But this outfit was intended for an animal – Israfel was an entirely different entity. God! How different!

What might the dextrose do to him? Could the substance be poisonous to him? What if he did die? The worries multiplied, and by the time I climbed the last hill on Trinity Valley Road, I was again close to a state of panic.

Spotting a strange pickup in the forest treated me to another dose of alarm. We squeezed by one another. I tried to find a casual neighborly smile. He passed by, wearing a typically local peaked cap that looked too new, a nylon coat that shone a shade too bright. Lots of people used the road in the fall and went up into the mountains to gather firewood, but the back of this truck was empty.

Had he been to the house? It was impossible to tell from the tracks at our turnoff. The snow had practically disappeared. Only a few patches of tampeddown ice remained, which gave little indication of the ways vehicles had passed.

I raced along our road, the truck bucking and twisting over the bumps and potholes, springs groaning and tailgate rattling, the steering wheel straining my hands and wrists. Who was that man? What had been happening at the house during my absence? A nervous headache was forming behind my eyes with an accompanying queasiness in my stomach that the lurching and jolting of the truck wasn't making any easier.

Jesse must have heard my wild approach and was at the opened door before I had reached the house. I slewed the truck to a rocking, skidding halt and scrambled out. "Jesse! What happened? That man – did he come here? Who was he?" I dragged my precious package across the seat. "Israfel – is he still alive? What's happened? Jesse!"

"Hey," he said. "Take it easy. No one's been here. But I sure hope this is going to work. He doesn't look good at all."

The man's absence was a small comfort in the face of Israfel's condition, the despairing hopelessness in Farrand's eyes, Celene's pinched pallor as he regarded me and my purchase with the greatest mistrust. My hands trembled as I changed the needle, filled the bag, and found Dettol, gauze, and tape. I was dealing with a completely unknown entity, and if this didn't work . . .

I could see Farrand's doubt, but he said nothing as I carried all the paraphernalia into the spare room. Celene's eyes blazed with their customary cold glitter, but he too remained silent. Jesse's face was as filled with anxiety as mine must have been.

Israfel's breathing was shallow and uneven, his face waxen and blue and completely withdrawn. Dark shadows lay beneath his eyes, and his lips were almost gray. There was little doubt that he was dying, and my own uncertainties fled as I found a vein in the long fine hand and slid the needle into it. The skin had little more substance than tissue paper, offered no resistance, and was deathly cold. We had nothing to lose by trying this.

I taped the needle into position while Jesse brought a chair to hang the bag from, and then all we could do was wait. And wait we did while my mother's grandfather clock out in the hall loudly ticked away the seconds, and each beat echoed an empty measure as the pale face before us did not change. Farrand still clung to the wire in his hand, and I could see the hopelessness in his eyes increasing.

The house was still, Sally blessedly silent, and even the telephone did not ring as we waited and waited for the slow seconds to tick by, for time to prove whatever it would.

The clock chimed softly at the hour and ticked steadily on again to the quarter, the half, then another quarter. My legs were stiff, and my feet were growing numb, but I couldn't bring myself to move – not while Celene and Farrand stood there, so still in their sorrowful vigil. Jesse, too, was as motionless as they.

The liquid in the plastic tube dripped steadily into the dark blue vein. Alien, I reminded myself unhappily, and I thought again of the differences in properties, of substances that could be poisonous or toxic to that being from an entirely different race. *No*, I prayed. *Please, no.*

The relentless metallic hammer of the clock went on and on, interminably, and sunlight reached the window, marking the passage of this awful waiting time. Another hour, the distant whinny of a horse, an answering neigh. Gallant. I recognized his voice. Tick tock, tick tock. Farrand's hand was white above the glittering wire that ran from it, and I could see a slight vibration, as though his hand was trembling. He showed no acknowledgment when I reached out and touched his arm in a consoling gesture. Celene's face was becoming even colder, even more merciless, and his body was poised in a threatening stance as he took in the ugly needle, the syringe taped to his commander's hand, and the human being standing by who had done this thing. My headache was becoming intense.

Jesse turned and gave me a meaningful look.

What? my raised brow silently asked him.

His head turned back again, his eyes to this still form on the bed. I stared.

Was it a trick of the light? Was the yellow sunlight making the blue color appear less distinct? For, although thin, the light was brighter, more illuminating. I moved, let my shadow fall over the face, and felt my heart lurch. He was lying there so pale and still, but the blue had faded. Couldn't Celene see that?

"Laura!" Farrand's harsh whisper shattered the silence. He held out his hand, and the wire lying across it was no longer shining. "Laura! He has stopped taking life from me."

Celene stepped forward and lifted the device from Israfel's chest. He stood, staring down at his commander.

What was this? Stopped taking life? My vision was hazy and blurred, the pain in my head preventing me from understanding.

Celene's voice was indistinct at first, an additional rasp on the raw nerves of my ears. But then I realized what he had said: "He breathes! Laura, Jesse. He breathes, and on his own."

Relief drained the last of my strength. I scarcely heard Celene's voice, his grudging words of thanks, and felt only distantly the grip of Farrand's hand on my arm. Israfel was alive, living, because of what we had done. I stood beside them unable to move at all.

I have often wondered what Celene would have done if Israfel had died during my ministrations. The unknown, unfamiliar crudity of what I had done would certainly have prompted him to lay some blame at my feet. But he looked at me and smiled, and I know that, although I hadn't made a friend, he was less of an enemy than he could have been.

CHAPTER SEVEN

THAT NIGHT, FARRAND GAVE US a container made of gold.

"It held a fuel cell," he explained. "And I understand this is a valuable metal."

"It is," Jesse said, looking at the thick sided box of around sixteen square inches. "But why are you giving it to us?"

"In repayment for all you are doing for us."

"We aren't doing much at all—"

"But you are, and we may ask you to for a long while yet. To repair our communicator is going to take much longer than I had thought, and then we'll still have to wait."

Jesse lifted the box. "This is worth a fortune."

"We want you to have it. We wish to not be indebted to you."

Farrand's face still wore the strained pallor from the morning. All afternoon he had worked on the damaged communicator, taking it apart, examining a myriad of broken pieces, sorting them into a multitude of little heaps. Celene, equally pale and worn, had refused to leave Israfel's side even for a meal, convinced that the improvement in his commander's status heralded an imminent return to consciousness.

"He must not be alone when he wakes, here," he said, casting a disapproving glance at the roughhewn walls that surrounded him, the beamed ceiling overhead.

Several planes passed over during the day, and the familiar helicopter returned, flying on a course slightly more eastward. The only visitor was a neighbor, Mark Raven, wishing to borrow a jack. Celene and Farrand remained out of sight while he had an after lunch cup of coffee with us in the kitchen, talking desultorily about the trouble he was having with his car. And we, so relieved by Israfel's improvement, were able to sit and listen to him without giving in to any of our earlier urges to tell someone about our unlikely visitors. Overcoming that desperate emergency had stilled our first excitement.

But Celene and Farrand looked exhausted; Israfel showed no sign of awakening. My anxieties were again beginning to show their worrisome heads. The missing plane had been mentioned again on the news that evening, and I couldn't forget about the man in the unfamiliar pickup on the forestry road that morning. Jesse had spent the afternoon taking measurements in the room upstairs, figuring how to build a dummy wall under the sloping ceiling, estimating the materials required. But how safe would such a hiding place be? How secure? And for how long? Farrand was obviously very concerned about the extent of the damage to their essential communicator. What if he wouldn't be able to repair it at all?

"Farrand, your own people – won't they come looking for you? Surely they'll realize you're missing . . . " My voice trailed away as he regarded me strangely.

"They will look for us, but not for a very long time."

I wanted to ask him why it would be a long time, but something in his eyes prevented me. Reticence, regret – I don't know what it was. I heard my voice trying to assure him that everything would be all right.

"Our craft would be most valuable to your armed forces," he said.

"I realize that. But as long as no one knows you're here, we'll manage."

I wondered where else we could hide them if the house became untenable, if we could make a place deep in the woods. But winter was already reaching across the hills; the first snows were lying beneath our trees. No. We'd have to keep them in the house, and there was still Israfel to consider.

My own anxieties seemed trivial when I thought of Farrand's, and I pushed them away. "Get some sleep, Farrand. If Celene trusts us, Jesse and I can sit with Israfel tonight."

Jesse nodded in agreement, but a wry smile touched Farrand's face.

"Celene is very young, very distressed. You do understand? He never expected anything like this to happen."

"Neither did we," Jesse said.

"No. I see that." He smiled again and rose to his feet. "But he needs sleep more than I do. I will stay with Israfel."

"Wouldn't he let us?" I got up from my chair, glancing from one to the other. "Jesse and I are night people. We could take it in turns. Couldn't we?"

"Sure."

Farrand was obviously doubtful.

"You both need sleep," I said, turning away. "I'll ask Celene."

Farrand followed me from the room and across the shadowed hall. Celene rose the moment he saw us and regarded me with scarcely a trace of animosity. But his face changed abruptly when I told him what we'd been discussing.

"I do not wish to leave my commander," he said.

"I know. But you can't go on like this, not after giving so much of yourself."

"Trust us, Celene," Jesse said. "We'll take care of him."

I watched him struggle with distrust and exhaustion, resentment and uncertainty, determination not to yield and eyelids he could scarcely lift. He turned to Farrand and seemed to have some kind of short exchange with him. Maybe Farrand convinced him – I don't know. But at last, Celene agreed, although with a reluctance so obvious I almost told him to forget about it, to sit there until he atrophied.

"Call me at once, please, if he should wake."

I held my tongue.

"If you'll stay until midnight," Jesse said to me, "I'll come after that."

"Okay."

"Then I'll stay until you wake up," he told Celene.

"I would prefer that you wake me before dawn."

"Fine."

Resigned, he turned away. Farrand gave us a grateful smile before following Celene from the room. And Jesse and I were left alone with their unconscious commander. This moment marked an enormous amount of trust, and we were committed now. We had accepted their gold and given them our assurances. There could be no turning back.

Jesse took a sharp, deep breath. "I'd better go and do something with that gold." His voice was very subdued. "We're not going to be able to use it until after they're gone, you know. It'll have to be hidden until then."

I nodded, lost in thought.

"And I'll stoke up the fires," he continued, "then get some sleep before it's my turn."

"Okay," I whispered, my eyes on that alien being now in my care. Oh, God! What had we taken on?

Jesse brought a small lamp from the music room and some magazines for me to read, but I couldn't concentrate on them at all. We were totally committed, rightly or wrongly, and surely I was far too young and incapable to bear such a responsibility. Had Jesse really realized the enormity of what we were doing? Jesse took most things in stride, but wasn't this far more than we should even be considering?

I sat there, miserable and afraid, while the long hours of darkness hung interminably in the house. I wished Israfel would awaken, even if it happened while I was there. At least it would ease my worry. Celene would be happier, and someone far more intelligent than me could deal with the problems. Perhaps he'd find a faster way to get them away from here and back where they belonged.

Although I watched until my eyes ached and eventually blurred, my mother's antique clock ticked steadily on in empty measure as Israfel lay there, pale and still, showing not the slightest trace of awakening.

The soft burr of the alarm clock in our room next door made me jump. I seemed to have lost all sense of time, despite the ticking clock. Jesse came in, and we spoke in whispers.

"Anything happen?" he asked.

"Nothing." I rubbed a cold, numb foot. "Did you sleep?"

"You know me, anytime, anywhere. Your turn now."

I slept that night and the next, but not a few nights later.

The following day passed more or less without incident. Israfel was just the same – no better and no worse. Jesse began to build the partition in the room upstairs, using the lumber he had on hand from his store in the back of the barn.

Jesse's love of woodworking had come as a complete surprise to me. He had not only built all the loafing sheds and the box stalls in the barn, but he had also done all the refinishing work in the house and had made the round birch table for the kitchen. Mark Raven had helped him with the table, and in return, Jesse had given Mark a hand with the sauna he had built down by the creek behind his own beautifully crafted house. But I had suffered many a qualm when I had seen hammers and chisels and buzzing saws and other tools coming dangerously close to Jesse's precious musician's hands. For his music was his livelihood, particularly the scores he wrote for motion pictures. Many of his songs and themes have remained popular for years. Woodworking was one of the last things I'd thought he'd turn to, and he hadn't really been able to explain it himself.

"Maybe it's because I can feel it in my hands instead of in my head," he had said. "Maybe it's because I can see it and touch it, know it will last. Music only exists when it's played."

Jesse was a maze of conundrums and contradictions. We had met at a horse show where he had been riding a friend's horse in the races.

I thought of the rather plain young man with the unformed face and toolong hair, his hands carefully encased in heavy leather gauntlets, only reckless and odd. His name had meant nothing to me, as we generally only heard the performers. There was no associating the composer of *One Sunshiny Day* and *Love Never Mattered Before* with the sport of horse racing. Then, when he'd had the nerve to laugh at me, I'd became thoroughly indignant.

"Why do you do it?" he had asked as I'd slipped down from my mother's prided gift after the English pleasure class. "When it's so boring."

"Boring?"

"Utterly." He grinned.

"Boring!"

"Totally. And I didn't see you smile once."

"Does one have to smile?" I hadn't known how to deal with such brashness, such rudeness, and had tried to brush past him.

But he had caught Calliope's rein. "When it's like yours, yes."

My flushing cheeks had only made a farce of the icy dignity I'd tried to assume. "It would appear," I'd spluttered, "that horse racing causes a permanent state of recklessness."

He'd laughed. He'd shoved an ornate leather hat to the back of his longhaired head and laughed. I'd jerked the rein from his hand, turned my back, and left him, hoping I'd never see him again.

He had sent me a record. It had been a privately cut single, his own voice, his own music, his own accompaniment on the guitar to "When Laura

Smiles." I had been stunned. Never, in my then twenty years of life, had I dreamed of anyone doing something so beautiful just for me. And I'd felt guilty for misjudging him. I'd needed to write to him and thank him and apologize. I'd married him six months later.

Jesse, deeply entrenched in the Hollywood scene and Californian lifestyle, true to his strange diversities, had been just as ready to move up here, to this old and lonely house a mile from the nearest road, to the forest and mountains I had come to love with a strong and tenacious passion. And he'd found a swift affinity for woodworking when we'd fixed up parts of the house, expanded the kitchen and enlarged the living room windows.

So, while Farrand worked with remarkable skill on his mysterious fragments of strange little keys and thin broken plates – and I went to set the kitchen table and Celene resumed his watchful guard – Jesse began to construct the dummy wall that would provide a place of concealment for months to come.

The planes and helicopter still passed overhead, and it was Farrand, dressed in Jesse's clothes, who slipped out before breakfast and fed hay to the horses while we slept on after our vigil of the night. Nobody came, and the radio and television newscasts mentioned nothing, but a few new days later my anxieties were promptly reinstated.

On a trip to the village to pick up nails and a few groceries, I met a convoy of army vehicles on Mabel Lake Road. There were six of them: four Jeeps and two trucks. In the summer, cadets used the army camp at Vernon to train. At no other time had we seen such vehicles. But here they were, heading purposefully north.

The moment I reached the village, I phoned Jesse and told him what I had seen. I rushed around the stores, grabbing what I needed, dreading the sound of any familiar voices that must stop and talk. Luck was with me, and within minutes I was racing home.

Where the small convoy went remained a mystery. At least it hadn't arrived at our door. But worry persisted. Why were those vehicles here at this particular time? Where had they gone? Up on the High Meadow, the earth and trees still bore signs of the recent activity that Jesse's burning hadn't eliminated entirely. I quickly imparted my anxieties to Farrand and Celene, and we discussed the advisability of moving Israfel upstairs.

"I don't know," Jesse said. "Until I get the wall finished, you'd be trapped there. Let's suppose we do get visitors – police, the army, whatever. While we're talking to them at the front, you could slip away out the back, go down into the ravine below."

So, we left Israfel where he was, and I joined Celene in his watch at the window.

Then, in the afternoon, it began to snow. The soft white flakes came down and down, concealing everything with a smothering blanket. Never have I been so glad to see snow. I prayed for several more feet, for then our road would be practically impassable and only four-wheel drive vehicles or snowmobiles could venture in. But the snow stopped when barely two inches lay on the ground, frustrating my hope.

However, the work done up on the High Meadow was well concealed. Jesse rode up on a horse just before dark, went all the way around through Silver Farm, and came back via our neighbor's land to the south. He reported that the meadow was smooth and white, that one of the burn piles was still smoldering, and that the police had called our neighbors too and advised them of the missing plane. Jesse had said nothing to the neighbors about the convoy I had seen earlier, feeling that the less curiosity we aroused, the better.

But memories of those vehicles plagued me. I could see their dark green color and blocky shapes so clearly, their glassy headlights coming toward me as they headed in our direction. And we had no way of learning where they had gone, if they were still here, and why they had come.

Jesse had erected the wall's framework and was trying to decide where he should saw the panels for it. Doing the work out in the barn would require explaining what we were doing to any neighbors who might come by. Doing the work upstairs would save trips in and out, but it would also make a mess of dust.

We all looked worried. Israfel showed no sign at all of waking. He lay still and motionless as always in his deep and unchanging coma. A dark, violet colored bruise was beginning to spread across the back of his hand where the lifegiving needle had to remain, and we only had enough dextrose on hand to supply him for a few more days. The thought of buying more from a curious druggist was an additional anxiety.

But the evening passed with no disturbance, and the others went off to bed early, leaving me to take the first watch of the night.

I tried to read, but it was hopeless. The waiting silence of the house hung like a motionless pendulum, as though time were standing still, as if dawn would never come. I no longer heard the ticking of the clock in the hall. I listened only for sounds outside the house: Sally's bark, engines, a heavy boot crunching snow, or thudding on the entry steps. My skin itched and felt hot, my throat sore with dryness. I paced about the room restlessly, imprisoned by anxiety, all my nerves strung taut with tension. From the door to the bedside to the window, I paced and peered out at the black and gray world surrounding the house. The lights of the village glowed in a frosty aura far away. Clouds banded the sky, edged with silver by the light of the moon. Back at the bed, I looked at my alien charge. He reminded me, very slightly, of Mel Ferrer in the old movie *War and Peace*, lying on a sick bed, wounded, young, pale, and ethereal, with a pure and princely quality. Although the face was so very different, there was a similarity in the pose, the pallor, the still quiet discipline. I stood there and wished desperately that he would awaken, or that there was something else we could do.

The dryness of my throat drove me to the kitchen. I filled a glass with water and drank it quickly.

On my return, something was different. At first, I could not determine what, and I looked around with puzzled eyes. Then I realized. The shadow on his face had changed. Before I left the room, the small lamp's light illuminated only one side of his face. Now his head was slightly turned toward it, allowing the light to touch the wider expanse of his forehead, the lid of his other eye, a tiny portion of his cheek. I stared, uncertain. Was it really so? His soft and shallow breathing was the same, the bruised hand in exactly the same position. But I became increasingly certain that he had moved – only a fraction, but he had. I hadn't touched the lamp. I was sure. It was near the window and the chair that stood there. But I had been beyond the chair. He had moved.

Oh, Israfel, I implored him silently. *Wake up. Wake up. Please wake up.*

I stood and watched, my eyes itching with strain, trying to see the slightest trace of movement. But there was nothing. He lay as still and immobile as before. *At least I'd have something to tell Jesse and Celene in the morning,* I thought.

I sat in the chair once more and tried to relax. Far away a coyote howled, the wild voice echoing across the wintry night. I went to the window again and looked out.

The sky was clearing, a bright halfmoon floating free of the dwindling dusky clouds, its light scattering sparkling diamonds on the snow. *It must be cold,* I thought. *Cold and frosty.* A shiver passed over me. Strange, when only minutes before my skin had felt so hot. It must be the cold, with the sudden drop in temperature that was not uncommon at this time of year and at this altitude. There was a chill coming off the windowpane. And then, without any warning, that sense of cold turned into an extraordinary sensation of alarm, then to despair and a terrible anger.

I gasped, stricken with inexplicable fear. Something was threatening me. There was an awful danger aimed right at me. It paralyzed me, gripped me with terror, turned my bones to milk. My head reeled, but I forced myself to spin around, confront it, try to ward it off.

Israfel was looking at me with incredible, unearthly, glittering silver eyes.

CHAPTER EIGHT

THIS WAS MY NIGHTMARE, A terrifying dream that would sometimes come in the night for no detectable reason. I would try to escape from some awful but invisible danger and would be unable to move a single limb. My whimpers of distress would wake Jesse, but even after he had pulled me out of it, I would lie awake for a long time, flexing my ankles, wrists, fingers, toes, keeping my eyes wide open, afraid to go back to sleep again.

This, however, was no nightmare. This paralysis was as real as the brown and orange wooliness of the rug on the gleaming floor, the familiar log walls reflecting yellow lamplight – as real as those inhuman eyes and the mask of dreadful anger covering that perfect face.

My hands remained half lifted; my feet were cemented to the floor. My swift turn had unbalanced me, so I leaned at a slight angle, and my mouth was partially open, molded by my gasp of fear. And there I was caught, held in midmotion, as though a film had suddenly stopped and I was only an image frozen on a screen, but one that would continue its movement when the projector rolled again. I couldn't even move my eyes, and they stared in horror at those that looked like living metal. Now I could see the danger, and I was shackled to the reality of my nightmare.

Jesse's name formed in my mind, tried to escape my throat, but was choked by a constriction that felt like a hand. And another fear joined the one that already gripped me, one I had almost forgotten but came flooding back as my struggles to move proved futile: the chilling, insurmountable fear of the unknown. I was bound by a power entirely alien.

Terror beat at me, the pounding of panic. Jesse wouldn't be waking me from this nightmare, for this was no dream. And he couldn't even hear me, for still no sound would come when I tried to scream.

The eyes flashed like spears as they stabbed into mine.

Who are you? Where am I? Where are my companions?

Questions forced through a muffling darkness, through the hood of fear cloaking my head, and streamed into my mind – questions that weren't mine.

My ship? Where is it? Destroyed? Farrand and Celene? The danger . . . the failure . . .

Words, ideas, and fears – other fears – began to fly through my head with the velocity of a jet stream, gaining even greater speed until they were only a blur of silent sound and streaking movement. I gasped inwardly as my brain was drawn into the vortex of their passage, to tumble helplessly, buffeted and bruised.

The silver eyes widened and fixed on mine with a piercing intensity, and suddenly darkness lay behind my sight and the streaming thoughts were torn away.

He raised himself up, still staring at me, now with a strange conjecture in his eyes. The look of fury slipped away, and the face was beautiful again. But I was still held prisoner by that unearthly power.

Then he saw the needle in his hand. I could almost feel the leap of his own shock, and he tore the hypodermic away in a single wild movement, plaster ripping, tearing the fragile skin, with his face white and the silver eyes blazing fiery stars of new anger.

No! I tried to cry. *That needle . . . it's keeping you alive.*

No sound issued from my nerveless lips, but the eyes sprang back to my face in some kind of answer.

Who are you?

The question came in silence, but I heard it clearly in this frightened turmoil in my brain.

Laura, I tried to say. But still no sound would come. *Laura Tremayne. This is my home.*

What continent?

Canada . . . North America.

Am I captive?

No.

Slowly, the paralyzing grasp relinquished its hold. The raging glare began to fade in the unearthly eyes. A deep trembling started within me, spread to my hands and knees. His face wore no expression.

Farrand and Celene?

Safe. I can get them for you?

My ship?

Hidden.

His head lifted and he studied me openly, considering, the eyes probing, and then I was allowed no thought of my own as his mind went searching into mine. I could feel its force, its strength as a ruthless invader, impervious to any barrier of resistance I tried to throw in its path as it traveled all the corridors of my intellect, explored each room of knowledge, examined every cabinet of memory. Any rights to privacy were ignored, and I jerked my hands up to my head in pained protest and an instinctive indignation, anger making me forget my fear.

A door seemed to close, and the intruding mind was gone. But I felt like a shell, drained of strength as even my anger vanished. The silver eyes swam before mine, rocked in the darkness of an emptiness in my head. I felt as a victim of the inquisition must have – brainwashed, bereft of all identity, with little memory and any knowledge uncertain.

I recognize your truth. The silent words came again, and the tones were surprisingly soft. *And I understand now what has happened. I must offer you gratitude, appreciation for what you have done. But I wish you had let me be.*

His words echoed in my head. Their meaning took shape. My wits began to gather, hazy and unclear, confused at first. But then they sharpened as recollection resumed.

And why? the voice in my mind said, so soft it was as a whisper. *Why can you read my mind?*

I shook my head, pressed a hand to my aching forehead, drew in some deep breaths. How could I possibly answer that?

The eyes were pewter, the face made even more beautiful by the sadness now etched upon it.

You should have let me be. I have failed, failed my trust, my command, Farrand, and Celene. They are stranded on this dreadful planet because of me.

My craft may be hidden now, but for how long? They should have destroyed it and let me die.

No! The word formed in the hollow of my head, drew walls of thought and windows of focus around it, opened doors to the scattered parts of my identity. *They need you,* I tried to say, seeing their faces once more, their anguish and despair as they had stood here in this very room.

The mind closed off from me. The silver eyes were shadowed, secretive, the face wholly unrevealing. Purplish blood was running over his hand from where the needle had been, and I turned my attention to that.

"Let me get them for you. And then I'll fix your hand."

The sound of my voice, freed from my preoccupation with something else, rang loudly in the room. His head lifted again, and his eyes flashed briefly.

"You speak this language?" he asked, so quietly the words were scarcely audible.

And I realized that all our communication had only seemed to be in English, that the words were only my translation of thoughts transmitted, things perceived, as had been his.

I nodded.

"My hand will recover." The voice was stronger but cool, dispassionate, and his expression evened as I watched him take the stance of an aloof and disciplined commander once more. "And I would like to see Farrand and Celene."

I found myself on the way to the door, obeying his wish as though it were an order. The withdrawal of his mind made me feel disconnected, dismissed, small, and even abashed, subjected to another lesson in inferiority. I was wary of the cold hard scrutiny of his eyes as they followed me with their disturbing silver gaze.

Somehow, I stumbled up the darkened stairs, not finding sufficient wit to turn on the light until I reached the top. Celene leaped up as soon as I touched his shoulder and knew immediately why I had come. No words were required to send him flying down the stairs as though on wings, and Farrand went racing by me in pursuit before I even realized he was awake.

I hurried after them but stopped in the doorway, feeling not only like an intruder at Farrand's and Celene's so visible joy but like I was once again wholly disconnected. The privacy of their silence, the fervent grip of Farrand's hand on the bleeding one of that alien being, and the cold hardness of those arrogant silver eyes I had no wish to face again, the invading of the mind, the frightening paralysis, that awful sense of danger. No!

I turned away, began to go toward the closed door of our own room, to Jesse. But then I remembered the dislodged hypodermic, the torn skin and flow of that strange dark blood, and once again concerns of a practical nature brought stability and pushed aside the fears and those improbable figments that must have originated in the too fertile imagination of midnight. Food, he must need food. Something light and plain, easily digested. Toast, milk, honey. And a bandage for his hand. Sound log walls surrounded me, the warmth of my house, curtains drawn against the night. Silence, security. Why had I been afraid?

Turning on the lights, I made my way to the kitchen, drenched my eyes with the blues and greens and earthy tones of the tiles, the gloss of ivy leaves and African violets and familiar copper pans. Shining glass and polished furniture, heavy iron and gleaming blue enamel of the stove, still warm. It seemed impossible that in another room of this strong old house, my home, was an alien being with silver eyes who could read my mind.

I took eggs from the fridge as well as butter and milk, set out a bowl and two small saucepans, found bread for toast, put a plate to warm, brought myself up short. Then what was I doing here, breaking eggs into a bowl in the kitchen in the middle of the night?

The strangely fluctuating uncertainties that had plagued me in the beginning returned. For days and nights, I had longed for Israfel's awakening, and now it had come but bore little joy. I had done all I could to save his life, only to find that he had no wish for it. Adjusting to Farrand and Celene, accepting them, had been difficult enough. But how was I ever going to tolerate this other being, so alien and cold, with his unearthly eyes and ruthlessly penetrating mind? I put butter in a pan, set it on the range, began to beat the eggs. There was the awful sense of danger that had assailed me as I stood by the window, the nightmarish paralysis of my limbs. He was as terrifying as my first impression of him had been.

I stood still, the beater forgotten in my hand, the task I had undertaken gone from my mind.

The aura of power was no illusion. The bonds that bound me had been inescapable, breakable only by him and had come from him – not from my own fears, I was certain. And the dangers . . . those had existed, were real, no illusion either.

The phone stood on a desk in a corner of the kitchen, and I turned and eyed it, considering.

A small movement behind me made me jump. Celene stood there, looking at me most strangely. I know I paled, caught on the brink of treachery, experienced a new fear, as surely he must have realized what I had been about to do.

But Celene had other concerns. "Laura . . . I . . . " He stumbled over the words he was trying to say, apparently suffering from his own bout of confusion. "Laura . . . I must thank you . . .We both do . . . but he is most distressed." Never had I thought to see Celene look so bewildered. "He wishes we had let him die. Laura, I had no idea he would want that. You providing us with safety made the situation seem less desperate. I thought we would repair the ship and carry on, that he would want the same."

"I don't understand," I said. "But surely, once he realizes how important he is to you, he'll come around."

"That is not enough for him. All he sees is his failure."

"Failure?"

"He is revered and admired. I was honored to be with him, to be chosen for his crew. He cannot tolerate this fall."

This seemed the height of egoism and vanity to me, and incongruous in someone of such obvious intelligence. But I knew to say so would only offend Celene. I mumbled platitudes, suggesting that once Israfel was over the shock and had recovered his strength, he'd feel better. "I'm making some food for him," I added, gesturing toward the bowl on the counter.

"Thank you. He must be in need of some."

"Only scrambled eggs on toast."

"Let me help you."

For the first time since he had arrived, I felt a little closer to him. I was happy that he'd shared some of his concerns with me, appreciated his apparent resolve, his assistance there in the kitchen in these silent midnight hours. Only fleetingly did I entertain the thought that he'd been aware of my intentions and was making sure to keep me and the telephone under close surveillance.

Jesse turned sleepily toward me when I climbed in beside him. "What's up?"

"He's awake."

"Thank God for that!"

I snuggled against him, wishing the occasion were a happier one, trying to forget the disquieting thoughts. But Jesse spoke again.

"You know, I've been thinking. The best way to hide them would be to have them right out in the open, dressed like us, building a new shed or something."

"That wouldn't work with Israfel."

"Why not?"

"He has silver eyes."

There was s silence. No sounds even came from the adjoining room. But Jesse was fully awake.

"Silver? How silver?"

"Like the metal."

"Oh."

Another silence, then, "Tinted glasses."

"Maybe." I wished he'd go back to sleep, that I could and forget those eyes, the power, that strange communication.

"It sure is quiet," Jesse said. "Have you noticed that they never speak to each other out loud?"

"Mmm."

"Must be telepathy or something."

"Guess so."

Why didn't I tell him that the same thing existed between Israfel and me? Perhaps because I didn't really want to believe it myself, or because Israfel was disturbed about it, even angry – but why didn't I tell Jesse? He was silent, and soon his deepened breathing told me he was asleep once more. But sleep would not come to me. My mind seethed in restless turmoil, keeping me distracted and awake. Why could I read Israfel's mind but not Farrand's or Celene's? How long would we have to hide them? How long would we be able to hide them? And why hadn't I told Jesse of my moments of panic at Israfel's awakening?

At last, in what must have been the very early hours of the morning, an awareness came from beyond the wall, followed by a sudden sense of quieting. The troubled thoughts immediately ceased, and darkness stole into my mind, a warm and soothing relaxation. I must have been asleep within seconds.

CHAPTER NINE

WINTER CAME DOWN FROM THE north the next day, riding on determined winds that bent the treetops in surging waves, whirled dried leaves and the husks of flowers from the last remaining crannies that were sheltered and dry, flung twigs at the windows where they pattered like rain, and brought the taste of snow and the cold of the Arctic wastes. An iron gray sky blew with the winds, carried heavy snow laden clouds that passed threateningly overhead and massed against the surrounding mountains. No snow fell in our valley, but ice formed everywhere. Smoky breath surrounded the horses, and the ground became hard and unyielding beneath their feet. Hoof prints were frozen into place, edged with delicate rims of crusty frost, and icicles hung from all the eaves. Winter had come.

Farrand was waiting for me in the hall when I ventured from our room upon waking. Jesse, rising earlier, had already gone outside to feed the horses and check the water systems. There was no sign of Celene and Israfel, and I was relieved to see the latter's door firmly closed.

"Laura." Farrand came toward me, stretched out a hand in a beseeching gesture. "Please – don't be disturbed by my commander."

I waited for him to go on. How was I not to be disturbed by such an alien and alarming being? One who carried such a threat of danger, could freeze my limbs and penetrate my mind and regard me so disdainfully? I hoped Farrand could put my mind at rest, but he appeared to be equally perturbed. His face wore an expression of deep unhappiness, troubled and dark, and his eyes were somber with distress.

"Laura, I wish I could have woken him, that it had not been you – and that you had not undergone such stress. But it was as severe a shock to him as it was to you. Please understand. And Laura – I'm so grateful to you."

Why was he expressing so much gratitude to me now?

"But I wish he would stop blaming himself," Farrand went on. "And nothing I can say will alter his decision."

A new uneasiness crept into my heart. "Farrand . . . you don't mean . . . that he might try to take his own life?"

"No, not that. He knows now that we are safe, that I am repairing the communicator. He will do what he can to ensure our safety, but he does regard our crash as his failure, and as I said before, he will permit no failure in himself."

My sympathy was aroused. *Surely*, I thought, *it is a rare being who regards personal failure as such an ultimate dishonor.* And I reminded myself what a shock awakening in such a strange environment must have been for him, considered how I might have reacted under similar conditions.

"Farrand don't worry. I think I'm beginning to understand. And surely in time he'll feel better. When he realizes you don't blame him, don't you think he'll feel differently?"

He smiled, the warm human smile that was so endearing, that smoothed away the rough edges of uncertainty and fear, made him so hard to resist.

"I hope so. And if you can bear with him, overlook the differences you find in him, then our worries will be far less."

I tried to smile back, glanced cautiously at that firmly closed door. "What's he doing now?"

"Sleeping, very deeply. We conversed until late in the night." He turned, drew me towards the kitchen, where, to my surprise, Celene was setting the table. "And thank you again, Laura," Farrand said, before going to the stove and stretching his hands above it to warm them.

Celene gave me a trace of his beautiful smile. "This morning is so cold," he said. "Is it often so cold here?"

"Nearly all winter," I said absentmindedly. I had an uncomfortable feeling, as though I had forgotten something or missed something, and was disconcerted by Celene's smile. His sudden helpfulness made me uneasy, and Farrand was no longer looking at me.

Jesse came in, stamping his feet and swinging his arms, shouting, "Brrr!" as another gust of icy wind swept around the house.

"Guess I'll go to Vernon and get paneling for the wall," he announced, joining Farrand by the stove. "And I'll buy you guys some warm clothes."

I almost said I'd go with him. I didn't want him to go and leave me here.

"Thank you," Celene said. "I have never been so cold."

I turned from the fridge, cream jug in hand. Celene was standing by the table, putting out knives, and I saw how pale and pinched his face was. I looked at Farrand and saw his was the same. He smiled at me with reassurance, and my anxiety about Jesse going away was forgotten.

Several times at the breakfast table, I caught Celene and Farrand studying me with curious eyes. But each then smiled disarmingly, talking politely about the weather or offering to make more toast.

Jesse's mind was taken up with paneling and estimating our guests' clothing sizes. He was presumably relieved that Israfel had recovered and noticed nothing out of the ordinary. And why should he have? There was nothing tangible, nothing noticeably different. And I, reconciled to Jesse's going, making up a shopping list and planning the day's menus, had forgotten my misgivings. Farrand and Celene volunteered nothing further about Israfel, his state of health, or his mind. I was just as prepared to ignore the subject, and as long as that far door remained firmly closed, he could stay behind it with his strange thoughts and disturbing power for as long as he liked. I wouldn't complain.

Nobody came, the cold deterring would-be visitors, smothered the trees, isolated us in our small world and the closed warm oasis of the house. Jesse set out for Vernon, and Farrand went back to work on the communicator, but after lunch, Celene picked up the magazine I had left in Israfel's room the night before and asked me if I would show him how to read it.

I stared at him blankly. How in the world was I supposed to do that?

His eyes met mine with some defiance. "Just show me," he said.

I was filled with doubts but lit the living room fire and made a pot of the mint tea I had discovered he would drink. We settled down on the hearthrug with cups and cookies and the magazine, and I was subjected to an overwhelming lesson in inferiority. Celene's brain had the capacity of a boxcar in comparison to the nut sized faculty of mine, and his ability to learn reduced mine to that of a mouse. I had only to show him each letter, explain their sounds, the consonants and vowels, the rules of pronunciation and the exceptions I could think of at the time.

"Thank you," he said and appeared to begin to read the magazine.

Nonplussed, I sat and stared at him. Once or twice, I saw him hesitate over a word, but then apparently reach an understanding and go on. Then, within minutes, he was turning the pages after only a cursory glance at each.

"Celene," I said tentatively.

"Yes?" The brilliant eyes raised to mine.

"Would you rather have something more interesting? You seem to be skipping through that."

"Skipping?"

"Only reading a bit here and there."

"No. I am reading it all. But it is only about horses."

"Reading it all?" I said, dumbfounded. "That quickly?"

"Most certainly. I understand it, from your explanation. Thank you."

At a loss for words, feeling very small and squashed, I sat still and struggled to come to terms with this. What an incredible brain! What astounding ability! No wonder he regarded me as most inferior. How could he possibly do otherwise? And that other one, their commander – Celene was watching me with his eyes still politely raised.

"What would you like to read?" I said, my tongue stumbling over the words.

The blue hardened into an icy coldness as the gaze intensified. "Anything about what is happening in your world."

I tried to think. We were subscribed to *National Geographic*, *Time*, and *The Vancouver Sun* as well as our personal magazines. In a daze, I found a pile of back copies in the music room, took them to him, and left him by the fire.

Jesse was bringing fish home for our evening meal, but as I had nothing prepared for dessert, I went to the kitchen and began making two pies with apples I'd stored in the freezer back in early fall. Work was still the best remedy to quell disquieting thoughts.

The kitchen was warm from the stove, beautifully illuminated by Jesse's cleverly placed fixtures, glowing with color in the early darkness of that winter afternoon. I rolled pastry, drained apples, wondered how Jesse was faring, if snow might be falling in Vernon or on the highway, how soon he might be home. As I concentrated on the near and familiar, the pastry forming beneath my hands, with the house silent, it was easy to imagine myself being there alone, waiting only for Jesse to come home.

I put one pie in the oven and began rolling out the pastry for the other. There were crumbs caked on my hands, and a smudge of flour was dusty on my cheek where I had pushed at a straying wisp of hair. The fire crackled and snapped in the stove, and the aroma of apples was fragrant and made me nostalgic for the sunny day in fall when I had gathered them from the ancient tree my grandfather had planted many years ago. I was reminding myself that in the heritage of my home, I was free to be as I wished – to do as I pleased, have flour on my face, and forget the extraordinary brain of that being in the living room – when I realized someone was behind me. He had come as silently as Celene, but it was not Celene standing just inside the room. There were no words, no communication – only a still and disciplined waiting.

Dread suffocated me. A painful tightness wrapped around my chest, locking my throat. I didn't want to turn around, but I had to.

Israfel was a vision of silver eyes and shining silver hair, as ethereal as a figure in a stained-glass window, emanating a strength and power that filled the room like smoke in darkness, invisible but warning every sense of danger.

This was what I had expected of him the first time I had seen him. That cold authority and the inhuman aura of supremacy, a vast alien intelligence. To him, Jesse and I would be nothing, not worth considering, meaningless—

Laura.

There was no sound. My eyes were drawn, I swear by him, to meet that metallic gaze. I tried to swallow, but my throat was locked by fear. *Jesse is going to loathe him*, I remember thinking as I saw the molded discipline of his face, the stern mouth, the imperious carriage of the deceptively slender body. This was the embodiment of my freewheeling Jesse's detestation.

Laura.

So much command in that silent voice, accustomed to being obeyed. And he was tall, much taller than I had realized. His feet were bare on the darkly stained floor, pale, looking cold.

How is it that you speak to me? he silently asked.

I . . . I . . .

As I stumbled in the darkness of fear, I saw something different. A trace of concern softened the autocratic mouth, and the strange eyes blinked. He took a step toward me, and I froze.

Laura, what is this? You are behaving strangely. I see in your mind – what is it? Fear? Why?

"Don't . . . Don't come near me!"

He stopped, stood there in the soft light of the lamp, an alien, the luminous ivory and gold of his clothes totally out of place amid the wood and tiles, the plants and flour and pastry of my kitchen.

I mean you no harm. Laura, please. Don't be afraid of me.

Just like Celene, he began to change as I watched. The silver of his eyes muted to pewter; the discipline yielded to some kind of vulnerability. Suddenly the mouth was sensitive and pained, and the straight shoulders lost their militant bearing. He became the being I had spent long hours beside, wishing he would waken. The strength and power must only be an illusion, or even a pose, he had adopted for so long that it seemed natural. This was the one I had been trying to protect while he had lain unconscious and helpless in our spare room. I found I could breathe again, manage a smile.

"You took me by surprise," I said.

I apologize. There is much I don't yet understand. And first I must ask why you brought me back.

"Brought you back?"

Yes. Farrand and Celene don't need me. I'm a liability to you, to them. They knew that.

I spoke out loud as it seemed to maintain a degree of distance between us. "They thought they could repair your ship—"

Only because they were in a situation they hadn't been in before. They should not have made such a judgment.

"How could they? How could anyone?"

They should have. They were most lax in their duty not to.

"You aren't showing much gratitude," I muttered, remembering Celene's long vigils and ceaseless concern, Farrand's constant purpose, my own hours of anguish.

Gratitude? The face was cold again. *Why should I show gratitude? I failed my command, lost a valuable craft, put them into jeopardy—*

"You obviously don't realize all that's been done for you," I began. My face was beginning to burn, my neck to dampen beneath my hair. "If you'd seen them—"

There was a strange flash from the silver eyes, their blade-bright glare restored. *That was not their purpose*, he told me.

"Good God! Doesn't it matter to you that they cared?" I was forgetting to be intimidated.

They were mistaken.

"What does it matter? If they were mistaken or not? You could at least show some appreciation for their care!"

All right. I will. But that doesn't alter the facts.

"Facts? Facts?" My voice cracked with anger. "Well let me tell you! For days we've been caring for you, done everything we could to save your life. They've worried about you, given you some of their own lives. And not just because they need you but because they care. Dammit all! They're your crew! Don't you even know that much about them?"

They've never been in this kind of situation before.

"So have a little charity, for pity's sake!"

Charity? They're my crew, trained for a purpose. They don't need charity.

Strain and temper got the better of me. I glared at him in fury. I no longer saw the alien eyes and autocratic face, the lips again stiff with discipline. This being was only cold and inhuman and undeserving of the care and attention we'd given him. I let my disappointment and frustration speak.

"Yes," I rapped. "We were all mistaken. We shouldn't have bothered with you, should have let you die. Then you wouldn't have had to face up to your responsibilities, would you? You could've taken the coward's way out—"

My voice was slammed back into my throat by an invisible fist. The cold rage of his eyes froze me once again, and my heart shook as I realized what I'd said to this terrifying being from another world.

What do you know of me? You miserable little creature! My command was a trust, never to be broken. Without that I am nothing. My life is done, gone, finished, over. Do you understand that? Can you?

I struggled to free myself, had to speak in silence, tried to defend my words.

Then make something else of it. Don't just give up. A hot tear suddenly ran down my face, but when I tried to dash it away, I found I still couldn't move. *And release me*, I demanded. *How dare you do this to me?*

He changed again. Even his strength was gone as I found myself freed. He looked bewildered and bemused, and that concern appeared once more on his lips as I stood there trembling while my chest still heaved with rage.

You are strangely emotional— he began, but I cut him off.

If I weren't, you wouldn't be here.

And I see little reason or logic in your mind.

Then don't look at it! I lashed out blindly while furious tears spilled from my eyes.

But I have to. Yours is the first mind on this earth that I can read.

I dabbed at my face with my sleeve, spreading more flour. The pastry was hardening on my heated hands, forming an uncomfortable crust.

And please, Laura, don't be upset.

At first, I couldn't believe his last words, the soft sincerity of their tone. I stared at him with open doubt, then wondered how I could ever have thought him dangerous. So slight, his eyes a muted pewter and mouth forming what I took to be a small smile of regret. He was the one in danger, not I. Dislocated into an alien world – one in which he would have no rights, one in which his knowledge and abilities would be priceless – and a new thought took shape. Wouldn't he be safe if he willingly shared his secrets with our western powers?

No, Laura. I will not. And that's why the time may come when I, or all three of us, may have to die.

I began to protest, but he stilled me.

Nor must my craft ever fall into human hands. We may have to destroy it yet. Farrand and Celene would have already done so if your military had found it before your husband so kindly concealed it. Farrand allowed himself to hope. But not I, Laura. I'm a law to myself, responsible only to a universal council. One moment of inattention has ended that, but until I can officially resign, I shall do what I can to help Farrand and Celene. But remember, although our minds are strong and we aren't completely helpless, we do have our limitations, and we are only three.

All my instincts suddenly shifted to protect. "Israfel, don't think about it anymore." I drew a chair near the stove, seeing again the tint of cold on his bare feet. "Come and sit there and I'll make you some of the tea Celene seems to like."

Thank you, but no. He turned from me, looking defenseless, frail, and vulnerable.

"Don't go," I said.

I'll sleep just for a little while. He began to walk away. *You can wake me easily enough, it seems.*

For the first time, I really heard his voice, noticed its timbre and extraordinary lilt. And again, I could scarcely believe the sound of it. It was what I'd imagined a Celtic bard would sound like, musical and melodious, a voice with which to sing madrigals and cantatas and minstrels' songs of long ago, a voice that would echo from old stone walls or ring clearly from the tops of hills, rise like a lark's in the morning sun. Then I scoffed at the absurdity of the notion. How ludicrous! From where did I get such a silly idea? This was an incredibly advanced being from beyond our own space age, one from an entirely different world. He might not even know what a song was. And a Celtic bard?

There was a turmoil of total confusion in my mind as I watched him go.

CHAPTER TEN

JESSE'S ARRIVAL HOME WHILE I was setting the table made me look at the extra place setting with new trepidation. I was going to have to invite Israfel to our table, and how was Jesse going to react to this authoritarian being with his cold, hard eyes and commanding face? I could imagine it all too well. Jesse wasn't going to like him one bit.

I became more and more nervous as Jesse unloaded the bags and packages, the coats and sweaters and warm slacks he had bought, the boots and slippers and extra socks. Their impending meeting was as inevitable as the onset of winter, as unavoidable as the falling snow. It could prove just as incisive. Jesse was as slow to change his mind as the winter ice to thaw, and we didn't need any more problems. Israfel's door remained closed, and I sensed he was waiting for me. Waiting for me to ask him to join us, to make the necessary introduction, for me to take the next step on this risky road.

The sauce was made, fish cooked, potatoes mashed, and vegetables ready, and at last I couldn't put it off any longer, forced myself to his door. He opened it at my timid knock, and a vise of anxiety closed around my heart.

Oh, God! He was so daunting! Those inhuman eyes and that aloof and alien face, the militant, disciplined poise. Jesse stiffened at his first glance, and I saw that aversion to uniformed authority curl his lips and tilt his heavy brows as his eyes narrowed. His chin began to jut, and the muscles along his jaw flexed and tightened.

Israfel was polite. "I do thank you for all you have done for us, for concealing our craft, giving us shelter. I realize how difficult it has been for you."

Jesse said nothing, but he did take the long thin hand held out to him, held it for but a moment.

I opened the safety valve of words. "Jesse brought clothes for you all. You'll need them. It's cold here in the winter. And slippers, for your feet."

His were still bare and looked just as cold. But his stern dignity was unaffected, his aloof and constant authority. He would look just as commanding if he were dressed in rags, I was certain.

My torrent of words kept rushing. "Dinner's all ready. You must be hungry. I hope you like fish. Do you drink coffee? Farrand and Celene don't, but I can make a mint tea, too . . . "

I sent Israfel a silent message. *If only you'd smile, try to look the least bit human, then maybe Jesse would warm to you, find you more acceptable.*

I only smile when it's sincere.

I swallowed, stared beyond him longingly at the doorway to the kitchen. But I couldn't leave them now, not while Jesse stood there bristling with spiky antagonism and Israfel gazed at him with polite but cold formality.

Then I saw Israfel's lean chest heave, a softening change the firm line of the mouth, the color of his eyes become pewter. "We are most grateful to you," he said, and his voice was music in what was becoming an awkward silence. "We are deeply indebted to you, and I wish we were able to fully repay you. What Farrand gave you is not enough."

Jesse blinked in surprise, and I saw his lips move. But there was no declining the offered courtesy, the apparent sincerity in that beautiful voice. A slightly crooked grin lifted a corner of his mouth. "That's . . . that's okay," he said. "It's been a bit of an adventure for us."

"As long as it doesn't become more than that."

"Time will tell, I guess."

"And we may be here for much of your time."

Jesse's shoulders lifted in his eloquent, expressive shrug. "We'll manage. Now, would you like a glass of wine?"

Too relieved to wonder about the double transformation I had just witnessed, I hurried to the kitchen and began piling vegetables into serving bowls. I could hear their voices and Farrand's coming from the dining room, and I heard Jesse laugh once. Celene came and helped me, for which I was grateful, as my hands seemed clumsy, the fingers stiff and disconnected.

The meal passed, somehow. I know I talked too much, and Jesse was slightly challenging Israfel from behind a veil of studied charm. Israfel gave a flawless performance of an honored yet grateful guest, and a stranger sitting at our table wouldn't have noticed anything particularly amiss in our behavior. Only Celene, silent, abstracted, apart, indicated that not all was as it should be.

In the days that followed, I could see how Israfel was attempting to adjust. They wore the clothes Jesse had bought for them, Celene with an unhappy tolerance, Farrand too busy with what he was doing to be concerned, and Israfel as though what covered him was of no importance. Behind the reflective dark glasses Jesse had found for him, his eyes were only gray, enigmatic. In a thick sweater and woolen slacks, his body was still powerful but not so alien. He kept his mind closed to me and spoke when necessary but was always formal and polite. Jesse seemed to accept this, and as they fit their lives into ours with careful studied deliberation, neither of us could complain.

Curiously, Israfel was the first to befriend Sally. She had barked wildly at Farrand and Celene, the hair on her back raised and her white teeth bared. They had needed many days of careful contact to gain her confidence and acceptance. But it was not so with Israfel. She sniffed at his hands and feet while I watched with heart-thumping apprehension. Her eyes were wide and dark with instinctive fear, her shoulders hunched, and legs poised ready to either leap or run, and I knew she could tear that paper-thin skin with one slash of her teeth before I could even shout. Then she raised her head and looked at him with calm brown eyes, her ears falling back in soft acceptance. She even offered him a hesitant paw. Israfel, to my astonishment, appeared to be charmed. He bent down and touched her silken hair, a faint smile smoothing the stern lines of his face.

The horses had seen Farrand, but only from a distance as he had thrown hay over the fences to them, and it seemed only sensible that they get used to one another. But the animals' reaction was most odd. Gallant reared and plunged in his stall, his eyes rolling wildly, and a dark sweat broke on his neck. The moment Jesse went in and stood beside him, he calmed.

Alla Bay bolted. He dashed out into the corral, raced to the far end, and stood there, his tail curled over his back and head held high, rigid, staring back at the barn with huge black eyes. Only Shadrach remained. And again, it was Israfel who made the first contact. The lean dry head of our aged Egyptian stallion stretched out to the alien from another world.

I loved Shadrach, and a strange lump rose in my throat as I watched. His mane hung in a silver curtain on his neck, and the long forelock swept in soft curves behind the prominence of his eyes, framing the sculpture of his face and fine ears, the chiseled bones and velvet muzzle. Israfel touched the flared nostrils, the smooth white hair, and the arching crest of the reaching neck, and I wished I were a painter, not a potter, so that I could capture the sheen of the wintry sunlight washing through the dusty window behind him, the iridescence of silver hair, and the shimmering mane, a moment of great rarity.

The other horses' acceptance came slowly, and then only a veneer on the surface of the instinctive fear that always lies beneath the training and discipline, the domesticating by humans. But it seemed necessary to do this. Our animals' fear had been striking and would certainly have caused any visiting friends or neighbors to comment. Such a meeting was bound to take place before long.

But I was puzzled about Israfel. How had he been able to quickly build rapport with some of our animals when he always seemed so cold and withdrawn, so aloof and remote and lacking any visible emotion? He appeared neither happy nor unhappy, and seemed no more concerned about his current life than the death he had narrowly escaped. He didn't seem worried about the communicator's damage or confident that Farrand would be able to repair it. The prospect of being rescued or permanently stranded here – neither seemed to trouble him at all. But there was no apathy. Life burned in those distant eyes, and discipline always composed his mouth. I found him impossible to understand, and he never gave me any indication that he was aware of my thoughts.

The trio's attitudes toward each other were equally difficult to determine, for they only spoke out loud to us. Farrand was the one who acted as the spokesperson. Israfel was always withdrawn and silent, and Celene only stayed in our company out of necessity. I had no idea whether Israfel still felt blameworthy, responsible for their crash. Since our altercation in the kitchen that afternoon, he had said little more to me other than *thank you* and *please*, and he had given cursory answers to all my questions with his usual polite formality.

However, they were obviously taking pains to avoid unduly disrupting our routines. How they were trying to fit in. They observed everything we did, from the way we held our knives and forks to our method for lighting fires, and they helped whenever they could. Celene, though, was visibly appalled by the labor involved in caring for the horses, the rudimentary equipment of my kitchen, and the horror stories of murder, warfare, assassinations, rape, starvation, and corruption that he listened to aghast on our radio and television newscasts.

We had to listen, even though I suffered a certain sense of shame, wishing my world appeared in a more favorable light to this critical being from another planet. But the search for the missing plane had become intensive, and we needed to keep ourselves as informed as possible.

The details were still vague. The number and identities of the passengers were never revealed, nor was the color or make of the aircraft. Then we heard that the search was focused on an area bounded by Tappen, Salmon Arm, Falkland, and Sicamous. This conclusion was based on reports that a rancher, bringing cattle in off the range, and two hunters had filed. Low cloud and poor visibility were hampering searchers in the area, and an airsea rescue helicopter had been called in to lend assistance as soon as the weather improved.

Jesse and I sat and digested this news with mixed emotions.

"That's great," he said, "if they're looking up there."

"But are they?"

"That's what it said." He frowned, switched the set off. "Maybe there is a plane after all."

But I shook my head. "Why are they so vague about it, then? They still haven't even said how many people were supposed to be on board." And the thought passed through my mind that Israfel must have taken some evasive action to bring his craft down in an unexpected location far from the area their pursuers suspected.

" . . . no plane." Jesse's voice intruded on my thoughts. "And they do know what they shot down. The search will just keep on expanding in ever broadening circles, and it won't be long before that area stretches to us."

"And in the meantime, the snow's getting deeper."

"Snow," he said. "That could be our greatest asset."

"I hope we get six feet."

He smiled faintly. "Why are we doing this, hon? Don't you think sometimes that maybe we're being foolish?"

"No. Yes." I forced a laugh. "Sometimes the thought does cross my mind. But then I always think of Farrand and Celene – the way they looked that first day. And that I promised to help them."

"And there's that gold," Jesse murmured. "They're paying us a fortune."

※

It snowed that night and the next. The sun came out again during the day and melted much of it away from the roofs and roads, but in the woods, it lay thick and white. Then the police called us. This time it was the officer in charge calling from Kelowna, asking whether we could supply horses for a mounted search party.

Jesse, his face tight, tried to explain casually that our mares were all in foal, our stallions too valuable to take out in such conditions, and our other stock all young and unbroken. "The only ones we have," he said as helpfully as he could, "are my events horse and my wife's personal saddle mount."

There was a short silence, during which he looked at me with worried eyes. It was late afternoon. Israfel and Farrand were upstairs, Celene in the living room with his head buried in a book. Jesse and I had just been getting ready to go out and do the chores.

"We've already been out once," he went on, hitching a hip on the kitchen counter, trying to appear relaxed. "We rode all over between here and the power line. . . . Well, sure, we can go again. . . . Okay, further north. We're not as familiar with the territory up there, but sure, we'll go."

He listened for a moment longer, then obviously steeled himself. "But do you think there's any chance of survivors? I mean, well, hell! It's been damned cold. . . . I know. . . . We must keep looking. But I heard last night that it was thought to be up around Tappen or Salmon Arm . . . Oh, I see. . . . How many did you say? . . . What? . . . And we still don't know what color . . . Oh, okay. . . . Sure. . . . Yeah. I'll call you tomorrow."

He took down the number, replaced the receiver, and turned to me with a worried frown.

"It was seen passing over Tappen. They say it must have been off course and was trying to get back onto it, heading in this direction."

"Oh, Lord!"

"They've got the army out all over Silver Star. The army! Imagine!"

"And around here somewhere," I reminded him.

"It kind of looks like they know what they're looking for, doesn't it? To have the army out—"

"So why call us, then? You'd think they'd want to keep Joe Public out of it."

"Yeah, unless they want to make it look as though there really is a plane."

"Hmm."

"I said we'd go out again tomorrow, search to the north."

"I wonder why they asked us," I began slowly.

"If you want to be scary about it, we're alone here – or so they think. We're a mile off the road, at least that from the nearest neighbor. We know this country. And that cop who was here . . . they do know it came down around here somewhere. They must do."

"Jesse! What are you saying?"

"Quite frankly, that we'd be easy to shut up if we happened to be the ones to find it. And in the meantime, we're very conveniently looking for a downed plane, helping keep that story alive."

I wrapped my arms around my chest as a chill suddenly came between me and the heat of the stove. My warm and cozy kitchen filled with the cold gray shadowy specter of fear; the strong log walls seemed as frail as glass.

"You really think . . . " I said, my heart pounding, but then I could not bring myself to speak the ugly, intolerable words. Danger stared me in the face. We had already found what they were searching for, had concealed the enormous prize of an alien space craft on our property, and were hiding the three on board. We could well be in as great a danger as they were.

Jesse only looked at me with his answer in his eyes.

⬳⬳⬳

He spent the evening finishing the wall in the room upstairs. He did most of the work right there, figuring he could do it more quickly if he didn't have to keep trekking to and from the barn and the house with all the necessary changes of clothes and footwear in between.

Farrand worked doggedly on, undeterred by the racket and dust that assailed him constantly, and Israfel was there most of the time, lending a hand to either when he could. He held boards and passed nails with swift and willing cooperation, but even when working together, the distance between him and Jesse remained, totally unbridged, a vast gulf of difference.

Once we had swept up all the sawdust and small ends, burned the rubble in the furnace, and cleared away the tools, the wall became an integral part of the room. A cunningly concealed door at one end could be firmly locked from the inside, and fitted molding rendered all the joints invisible.

The space behind was small, but we were able to stack all their equipment in the far corner, and I found an old tray that would just pass through the doorway. Farrand moved his communicator work onto this tray so he could pick the whole thing up and slip it away if need be.

Jesse insulated both the wall and door so tapping on them would produce no hollow sound, and the door, when locked, became as solid as the wall.

The rooms they occupied bore few traces of their inhabitants. We had hung some of their new clothes with ours and hidden the rest behind the wall. They also stored their few toilet articles there when not in use, along with the blankets, sheets, and pillows that they'd strip from their beds every morning. Nothing makes a room look more unused than a bare bed.

I remember all these details so clearly because, again and again, I was impressed by the simple necessities entailed in the enormous undertaking we had embarked on. Seemingly insignificant or trivial details could become critical vulnerabilities if left unattended. We could not afford to lose anything for want of a nail.

CHAPTER ELEVEN

WE RODE OUT AGAIN THE following day, wrapped in our warmest clothing, leaving the house locked and Sally on guard.

There was little warmth in the low lying yellow sun, and the woods were thick and soft and white with snow, shaded and cold. Laden branches hung low over the trails, smothering us with powder and crystals when we brushed against them, spilling their icy burdens onto our woolen toques, over our faces and shoulders, and across the horses' backs. We were constantly trying to dust ourselves off, but the snow clung in small hard cakes to every fiber and hair, to the wool of our coats and the fabric of our jeans and crusted like jewels in the horses' manes.

My gloves became knots of snow, frozen stiff, with sharp little beads that scratched my face when I tried to dust snow from it, and our noses ran perpetually in the thin cold air. Soon the cuffs of our sleeves were in a similar state as our gloves.

"I can't take too much of this," Jesse said, scattering icy lumps that had found their way inside his collar.

"We must," I said. "The more time we spend, the more distance we travel, the less likely it is that others will come and search through these woods."

"Don't try too hard to convince yourself of that," he said. "Remember what we said yesterday."

I tried to repress a shiver, but it was hard with my fingers beginning to burn with cold and my feet growing numb.

"And we have ourselves to consider," Jesse went on. "What would happen if we came down with pneumonia or something?"

I hadn't thought of that, tried to stop the notions that began to crowd at his words. If we became sick . . .

"We'll have hot baths when we get home," I called to him as Astra began to bound up a steep hillside. "Hot lemon with rum and honey. Go to bed early."

I leaned low over Andante's neck as she followed Astra, slowed her when she was at his heels again, the trail leveling. "We must go on, must allay any possible suspicions by appearing willing to hunt for this supposed plane."

Jesse rode on in silence for a while. The snow squeaked beneath the horses' hooves and slid from branches with swift, smooth rustlings. Andante's feet occasionally flicked up packed and frozen lumps of ice to thump hollowly against my boot.

The trees rose high above us: evergreen cedar, fir, hemlock, and pine, their needles and branches choked with snow, and the seedlings and saplings at their feet bent beneath the thick white weight. The trails were smooth, bright ribbons, tracked only by hares and the tiny prints of squirrels, slots of deer, and the occasional doglike pads of coyotes.

We saw no animals other than a squirrel that chattered with shrill indignation at our intrusion, and once we heard a raven cry, saw the black winged shape cross our narrow sky. But raising our faces invited the unwelcome slap of another mass of icy snow. We were forced to keep our heads bent low, eyes on the trail before us or searching the deep forest, just in case there really was a plane.

"This is so futile!" Jesse said in exasperated tones, flinging the words suddenly back at me over a snow-covered shoulder.

"Not really," I protested. "We're diverting suspicion from ourselves."

"But what a way to do it!" He threw up an arm to ward off a heavily laden branch. Snow cascaded all over him. "If it weren't for Farrand, I'd call this whole thing off."

I felt a sharp stab of dismay. "You mean today? This searching?"

"No. The whole affair. I'm tempted to call the police, the army, before we get in any deeper. And the press. Laura, if enough people know about it, we should be safe. Public knowledge would be good protection."

My heels drummed against Andante's sides as I urged her on, hastily, pushing up beside him in spite of the branches and snow that smothered me.

"Jesse, no! How could you even think such a thing?" My heart was thumping with painful alarm.

He turned an unhappy face toward me. Snow was encrusted to his thick eyebrows and all around his toque, plastered to his coat and gloves, and melting into his jeans. I, riding behind him in the passage he'd cleared, had fared considerably better.

"Well, not only should we be thinking more about ourselves, but . . . well, don't you get the impression, kind of . . . that Celene despises us? And Israfel is so blasted superior—"

"Yes! Yes! But it's inevitable." An icy branch swept across my face, filling my eyes and mouth with frozen crystals. I gasped, jerked involuntarily at the reins.

"And then we wouldn't be out here, going through this," Jesse said, leaving me behind as Andante stopped at my sudden rough treatment, tossing her head with resentment.

I dashed snow from my eyes and collar, pulled icy lumps haphazardly from my hair, then pushed an irritable Andante on again. I came alongside Jesse once more.

"Stop a minute. Jesse, please!"

He reined to a halt and faced me, his hazel eyes red rimmed and troubled. He looked utterly cold and miserable.

"They're bound to feel superior," I said. "Their minds are way above ours, their intelligence, their culture – everything."

"I know. I know." He made a dismissing gesture with his hand. "But Farrand is entirely different."

"So, think about Farrand. Forget the others."

"Easier said than done when I have to sit and look at their cold and arrogant faces every day."

"Try putting yourself in their place," I said, dabbing my dripping nose against the icy crust of my sleeve.

He regarded me thoughtfully, then turned his horse and moved on.

"And there's that gold," I reminded his retreating back.

But another cascade of snow fell over him, and he hunched his shoulders up around his ears and appeared not to hear. And I hadn't the heart to repeat my words as he dug lumps from inside his collar and flung them aside angrily, swearing beneath his breath.

We rode on again in silence, struggling with the snow, the cold, our thoughts.

At midday we stopped and dismounted, ate the sandwiches we had brought, drank hot coffee from a thermos, and warmed our hands gratefully around the cups.

"Do you know where we are?" I asked.

"Haven't a clue," Jesse said, stamping his feet to get the circulation going again.

I looked behind us, at the trampled snow that marked our trail. A wall of snow-thick forest enclosed us, and laden branches hung low, barring our path as usual.

"Maybe we should go back," I said.

"You mean the way we came?"

"Yes."

"That would narrow our search area. Halve it, in fact."

"I guess you're right," I said grudgingly.

"Now that we've come this far, we might as well do a proper job of it." He swung himself back into the saddle and gave me a sudden smile. "We'll find the power line, then go back."

"Okay."

"When I think about Farrand, forget the other two, I do feel more like going on with it."

"Great!" I smiled at him, climbed into my own saddle with a lightening heart, and fell in behind him once more.

The power line cut across a wide swath of land between the mountains and hills to the west and north of us. The great woven metal pylons spaced along it were incongruous after many hours of riding through dense and wild forest, on steep and narrow trails that were so heavily overgrown and indistinct, it was hard to believe they had once been logging roads. Where the only life was wild, the tangled trees and rotting windfalls appear untouched by human hands. Several wooded canyons and gorges were impossible to enter or cross, and it was shocking to emerge from the forest into the sudden clearing and see the pylons there, huge, intricate, marching one behind the other along the broad expanse of stripped land on which they stood.

We came out of the forest on a northern slope and could see the undulating line of monstrous structures stretching away for miles, rising and falling until the swath became only a ribbon, disappearing into the far mountains.

To the south, the last visible structure reared against the yellow winter sky from the crest of a hill, its stark and rigid lines an incredible contrast to our eyes after hours of being filled with tangled forests of nature's rampant hand, the soft and random shapes of snow.

A narrow roadway twisted and turned around the humps and dips of the rough terrain, cutting from one side of the swath to the other as it traced the easiest route from pylon to pylon. And we followed it, heading home.

Snowmobile tracks were plentiful – but they usually were. There were, however, the marks of heavy tires. Free at last of the snow laden branches and the steep and narrow trails, we had eyes only for the wide-open spaces, even found some warmth in the last of the yellow sunshine. We urged our horses to a gallop.

They snorted and tossed their heads, shaking their bridles and jingling their bits. Snow flew up in spuming sprays from their flying feet, and the cold wind of our sudden passage bit sharply into my face, across my still running nose, and through the dampness of my toque to my ears. I squinted my eyes against it, tried to huddle deeper inside my coat, thought about the fire waiting for us, hot drinks, warmth for my frozen fingers and toes. Soon! Soon we would be home.

We crested the hill of the ridge before us and began to plunge down the other side. Then we both reined to an abrupt and startled halt.

There were no fewer than a dozen army vehicles standing along the trail, some trucks but mostly Jeeps, with white vapor curling from their exhausts. Groups of men on snowshoes were gathered beside them, and there were two others on snowmobiles, the engines idling.

We moved on, rode slowly down towards them.

The men turned and watched us come. They were dressed in warm parkas, caps with earmuffs, and heavy boots and gloves, all unmistakably army issue. Some carried guns, and I saw more weapons in the back of the first Jeep we passed. We stopped before the first group.

"Hi," Jesse said, wiping his forearm across his nose in a most undignified but essential move. "What's up?"

The men, their faces roughened by the cold, eyed us with caution. Then one detached himself from another group and came toward us purposefully.

His marching walk and the rigid carriage of his head and wide strong shoulders all spoke of command. His parka was unfastened, and I caught a glimpse of a pistol holstered in smooth brown leather on his belt, the miliary uniform beneath. Apprehension soared within me as he reached us.

His whole demeanor revealed businesslike intent, indicating how important he considered his mission here in this wild and mountainous terrain to be. The face was young and smooth, and appeared unaffected by the cold. Pale blue eyes regarded us – our snow-encrusted clothes, our windbitten faces – with a dispassionate nonchalance, his wide, thin lips firm beneath a neat dark mustache. There was no smile of greeting, no recognizable sympathy for our obvious cold discomfort. I began to feel colder still.

"Would you be the Tremaynes?" he asked crisply, the tone of loud authority in his voice.

Jesse has a swift aversion to officialdom, born, I believe, of many customs inspections. His long hair and the hippy style of dress he wore when traveling had many times provoked immediate suspicion and a thorough search of his belongings. The flippant manner he seemed to adopt at the mere sight of a uniform didn't help, either.

"That's right," he drawled, again wiping his nose on his sleeve, the gesture followed by a loud and determined sniff.

"Captain Forrest. Where have you searched?" The pale eyes registered nothing, not even disapproval.

"I guess you'd call it nowhere, for there wasn't a single placename. Didn't see any signs, roads had no names, and didn't see a soul we could ask."

I repressed a giggle, then grew fearful as the cold face before us showed not the slightest trace of humor. This man could be a bad enemy – and enemies were the last things we needed.

"Between our place and here, all over the eastern slope," I said, "to a northerly point about half a mile from here. Wherever there were passable trails."

"And?"

"All we got," Jesse said, "was bloody cold."

"You saw nothing?"

"Trees and snow, that's all," Jesse continued. "Not a crashed plane in sight."

"Is there anywhere down there where you haven't been?"

"Christ!" Jesse said irritably. "There's miles and miles of woods all over. We've been everywhere we can. If a plane came down anywhere near where we were, we would've seen it, or some trace of it. But it's impossible to cover every blasted acre! There're fallen trees everywhere, deep ravines where one wrong step would break your neck, trees too dense to even walk through. And it's bloody miserable riding through there, I can tell you, in all this snow." He made a gesture that displayed his encrusted jacket and gloves, the frozen knobs clinging tenaciously to himself and the mane of his horse. "If it's around here somewhere, I'd say the best way to find it is by air."

"We're using every means at our disposal," the captain said brusquely.

"Yeah, but I'm kind of surprised to see the army out in such full force," Jesse said, somewhat daringly, I thought. But then such a statement was probably quite logical in the face of what we were supposed to be confronting, and I was probably just looking for trouble.

The pale eyes didn't even blink. "Why not? We have the men and machines, the training."

"But turned up nothing either, eh?"

The straight back became even more erect. "We've searched from Vernon to Silver Star to Lavington and were just discussing whether we should move on to the east when you came along."

They stared at each other in restrained hostility.

"Have you no maps? Nothing systematic to show me exactly where you've been?"

"All I can tell you," Jesse said, "is that we've been everywhere possible for a horse to go. And I'd just promised my wife here that once we reached the power line, we'd go home."

"I see. So how much terrain would you say you have missed?"

Jesse slouched in the saddle and wiped his nose again. Captain Forrest's officious tone was beginning to make him angry. I could see it. But his anger must have also reminded him of the folly of provoking enmity, of the necessity to retain self-control.

"If you'd care to follow our tracks along the line here, you'll see where we came out of the bush. That marks the northern boundary of our search area. Last time we were out, we came up as far as here and covered every trail between the south side of Copper Mountain. Then I reported back to Constable Paul."

"So, you went no further south than that?"

"No. If it had come down on the eastern slopes beyond, it would be visible from the road or the village."

"And above those slopes?"

Jesse shook his head.

"Very well. Then we'll go on and search there."

Jesse pulled off his gauntlets and blew on his hands to warm them. "Would you like me to come with you? Show you where we left off?"

"That won't be necessary." Forrest pulled a neatly folded map from his pocket. "You can simply show me here."

Jesse slid to the ground and held one side of the map with a hand stiff from cold.

I gazed at it anxiously. Jesse's precious hands! What if he got rheumatism in them? Then my eyes saw only the map. It was one of those highly detailed forestry maps, and great areas had been crossed off with neat red lines, section by section. The only parts left unmarked were obviously the mountainsides to the east, Trinity Valley, and our place.

Jesse became slightly apologetic. "I never thought to take a map. But look, I can show you roughly where we've been." A finger of his other hand moved across the light-colored paper. "These trails aren't all exact, of course. And there are others that aren't on the map. But we've been all over here – nothing, and we'd have seen it for sure if it were there . . . or here . . . or anywhere around in here. This trail doesn't end here but goes on, joins another that isn't marked . . . oh, I guess up around here. We went all through there, and here, and along every deadender that we came to. Nothing."

"So, the only places you haven't really been at all are here and here." A hand in a leather glove pointed while I craned to see. East, near the road, an area slightly off-centre, and north, further up the valley.

Jesse nodded. "I guess that's it."

"Which way were you planning on going back?"

"Down here." Jesse's hand looked so cold, bluish. "We refer to this as the main road. But we came that far the other day, to the south side of it, that is."

"Are there many side roads off it?"

"No, not many."

"Would you check out any you do see on your way back?"

I knew by the slight lift of Jesse's shoulders that he sighed. He turned the motion into a shrug. "Okay."

"And would you report to me tomorrow?"

"I have a number to call in Kelowna – the officer in charge. Maybe you could check with him."

Jesse's aversion to officialdom was asserting itself once more, ensuring he tried to get the last word.

"Very well." Nothing, it seemed, could ruffle that icy reserve, bring any expression to that disciplined face. I thought of Israfel, whose power and authority were inherent in his whole structure – not a facade as this man is so apparently learned. And yet Israfel, to my never-ending incomprehension, had acted in a totally unbelievable manner, entirely out of context, when he had regarded himself as having failed.

Jesse was climbing back into his saddle, gathering up the reins. I studied Captain Forrest curiously, wondering how he would behave should he fail in his mission, almost forgetting for a brief moment what his mission actually was. Then I found myself staring at him even harder. Did he know what he was really looking for?

"Mr. Tremayne." The voice was still crisp. "If you should happen to see anything on your way down, would you come back and tell us? I shall be here for at least another hour."

Though it was spoken as a request, the note of authority still made it a command.

Jesse shrugged, began to turn his horse. "If we see anything," he said lightly.

There was an automatic straightening, a reflexive movement of the hand that raised in the beginning of a salute by Jesse as we rode away.

I glanced back once, saw Captain Forrest examining his map once more, and thought about what finding our three visitors might mean to a coldly ambitious young armed forces officer deeply instilled with a sense of duty. And the vision of Farrand, Israfel, and Celene being taken prisoner by one such as him filled me with sudden revulsion and a cold, uncomfortable sense of dread.

CHAPTER TWELVE

COLD AND ANXIETY RODE WITH me all the way down the steep and winding logging road that brought us to our turnoff in the Ecological Reserve.

Captain Forrest's systematically ruled-off map haunted me, the unmarked areas to the east. Would he regard our search as thorough enough to draw those neat red lines all over the sections that would encompass our immediate environs? I doubted it. Would he not rest until he and his men had crisscrossed the mountain slopes and forests, our fields and woods, the High Meadow? I feared it might be so.

What if he found the craft? Then what? Should we lie, deny all knowledge of it for the sake of protecting our three guests? Would we still be able to hide them? And what could happen to them if they were caught, taken away? I trembled at the thought.

With horses eager to be home, the wider road giving us freedom from snow laden branches, we were back at the house in good time but chilled to the very marrow of our bones.

Hot baths, hot drinks, and a blazing fire soon thawed my body. But that icy anxiety still froze my mind and clung as tenaciously as the snow that had fallen from the trees, gripping me in its cold hard hand. And Israfel saw, suddenly spoke into my mind.

Laura, why are you so troubled? What is this darkness I see, the fear I can feel?

I was surprised, for this was the first silent communication between us in many days. I raised my head and looked at him.

We were in the living room, curtains drawn against the early dark, Jesse and I still toasting our toes before the fire. He had told them quickly and succinctly of our day's experiences, the army vehicles and personnel we had encountered, their uncomfortably close proximity, and Captain Forrest's map. Celene had been the only one who showed any apprehension, his lips tightening as Jesse spoke, the blue blaze flaring in his eyes. But he hadn't said anything, and we had all retreated into silent thoughts. Until Israfel had come reaching into my mind.

Laura, what is the cause of your distress?

Unavoidably, the images formed – of men and vehicles, guns and maps, pale eyes in a dispassionate face, the military marching step.

Today I met someone who's actively looking for you, someone who would be ruthless if he found you, a man who has been trained well in the course of duty – like you, but not like you.

Do you think he knows what he's really looking for?

I don't know. I wouldn't be surprised if he does.

And it bothers you to visualize us falling into his hands?

Of course.

Why?

I told him the first thing that came to mind. *I haven't gone to all this trouble for you . . . just to let it go.*

A strange, indecipherable thought – a form of emotion – came to me briefly. Then it was gone. The mind withdrew, locked itself away behind the barrier again. But then he spoke to Jesse.

"We are sorry you had to endure such an unpleasant day on our account. And please believe that we do appreciate your efforts on our behalf. We realize how difficult our situation could have been for us without your help."

He spoke stiffly with his customary formality, but the underlying note of sincerity was unmistakable. And for the first time I saw Jesse let a smile go in his direction.

⦀

"We'd better decide what we're going to do about Christmas," Jesse said.

"Christmas?" I asked.

"It's only three weeks away, and we're going to have to let Mom and Dad know."

We were in the barn on a cold and snowy morning, mixing the grain for the weanlings' feed.

"We did say we could only go if we had someone to look after things here."

"I know."

Jesse was chopping carrots with a lethal looking machete he used for the purpose, which I always wished he wouldn't. But I no longer even saw it.

"We can't go away and leave them," I said.

"You don't think so?"

"I'd worry the whole time."

"Nobody's been asking questions for at least two weeks now."

"They're still looking for the plane, though."

"Not so intensively."

"Only because they think there's no chance now of survivors."

He swept the carrot pieces into a pail and gathered another handful from the sack. I measured oats into another pail, poured diluted molasses over them, breathed in the oatmeal's syrupy scent.

"Mom and Dad have been looking forward to us going."

"I know. But—"

"And we can't very well ask them to come here."

I grinned. "Hardly."

He chopped at the carrots. "So, what do we do?"

The question was a difficult one. We had spent the preceding Christmas here; his parents having gone to Hawaii where one of Jesse's older brothers managed one of the big hotels. Their invitation to us for this Christmas was one of long standing, which we had accepted on the condition that we found someone to look after the horses. Needless to say, that was something we hadn't even tried to do.

"We have no one to take care of the horses," I said.

"Farrand would."

"I know. But what would happen if someone came?"

"Farrand could carry it off, explain he was here only as a caretaker."

"I'd still worry," I said unhappily.

"If we stay here, then we'll probably get invited down to the Greenaways' for dinner on Christmas Day. What do we say? That we have three house guests? You know they'd be invited, too."

"Mmm."

He chuckled. "Can you imagine it? Farrand would be okay. But Celene and Israfel? In the middle of the Ransoms' horde of children, Helen's brother-in-law telling his terrible jokes, and if Dan and Roger got into another of their arguments about Fords versus GMCs—"

"You really think it would be that impossible to have your parents here?"

"You know Mom. Curiosity's her middle name. 'Where were you born? Mars? Oh!'"

"Yes, I was forgetting."

Jesse's parents were warm, friendly, smalltown people from Oregon whose only complaint was that their children were all so far away. But I was forgetting his mother's bright-eyed curiosity. "Where did you meet Laura and Jesse? Why do you wear dark glasses in the house? Who are your parents? Where do you live?" Lord, no!

"Maybe we could take them to the Greenaways' with us," Jesse said thoughtfully.

"But five of us?"

"If they do invite us, that is. But sooner or later, someone's going to know they're here. And I still think the more open we are about it, the better."

I was doubtful, worrying again. "Maybe."

"And in ordinary clothes, they do look more like us."

This was true, and the tinted lenses did conceal the true color of Israfel's eyes. But that was only part of the problem.

"We'd have to give them whole new identities," I said, sitting down in the sawdust, my task mixing grain forgotten.

"That isn't impossible. But in the middle of a crowd, with everyone a bit smashed . . . " Jesse began on another batch of carrots. "That could be the easiest way to let the neighbors meet them," he said.

"But who would we say they are?"

"I don't know. But we can think of something," said Jesse.

"Some of your freaky friends from California? Musicians you used to play with? That'd explain the oddities. Guys out of your lurid past."

"Mmm. Wish they were," he said.

"Heavenly bodies – ha, ha!"

"I know! Darth Vader and ET, and . . . " Jesse replied.

He snorted. "That'd explain Celene and Israfel, but what about Farrand?"

"Celene and Israfel? Darth Vader and ET?" I giggled. "Oh, brother!"

"Far out?" His eyes glinted.

"I don't see how you could be farther out, unless you're getting really spaced!"

"Christ!" He threw up his hands, and a shower of carrots flew high into the air. "Spare me!"

⬡

I called in at the Greenaways' the next day. Sitting at the table in Patty's bright white kitchen, I mentioned that we had three house guests, friends of Jesse's who would be staying with us over Christmas. Patty, with her quick smile and clear English voice, immediately invited us all for dinner on Christmas Day.

I hesitated as all my doubts and fears promptly surfaced.

"Well, thanks an awful lot, Patty. But that would be five of us. And I don't want to bring total strangers into the middle of your family festivities."

"No trouble," she said breezily. "The more the merrier. And as long as Jesse brings his guitar, we don't mind at all if your friends come."

"But five!" I protested.

"Don't worry. The Campbells are going away this year, so they won't be here. Your friends will make up the number."

"They're . . . " For a moment I wished I could tell her.

"Yes?" She put cups on the table regarded me with her honest blue eyes.

"Like most of Jesse's friends. A bit odd."

She laughed and went to the refrigerator for cream. "But are they nice?"

"Oh, yes." Surely Jesse was right. This would be the best way to introduce our guests to the neighborhood. My fears were only borne of my constant tendency to worry. Farrand at least was charming and delightful, and would easily fit in. The others were polite, considerate, and well-mannered. "Yes," I said again. "Very."

She was coming back to the table, and I tried to change the subject.

"Well, look, if we're all coming, then let me help at least."

"No, really, Kevin will help me. There's no problem."

"I insist on bringing some mince pies or a pudding, then."

She smiled again. "Okay. Some pies would be lovely."

I left soon after, feeling fraudulently committed and worrying about both my friends and our guests.

※

By the time Christmas came, the search for the missing plane had supposedly been called off. Or so the local radio station reported. But there were still trucks and snowmobiles going up and down the forestry road in a far greater number than was customary at this time of year. The extra snow that had fallen did little to deter them, it seemed.

We weren't asked to participate in any further searches, and this brought a mixture of worry and relief: relief that we didn't have to go out and struggle through the cold snow filled woods, that the search wasn't that much in evidence; and a niggling anxiety that we were being kept in the dark about what was really going on.

Casual mention to neighbors of the traffic on the forestry road brought little enlightenment. One, who had a team of sled dogs that he exercised regularly on the road, was as mystified as us. Yes, he had seen the tracks going up but never a vehicle, and he only rarely encountered a snowmobile. "Then it's either kids or Mac Anderson going up to fish through the ice on Bardolph Lake. So, they must go up first thing in the morning," he said, his eyes on the tire ridged spot in the snow, "and come back late at night."

We listened occasionally but never heard anything, and we were left to only wonder.

Celene, Farrand, and Israfel accepted the Christmas invitation with reluctance and doubt.

"It's bound to come sooner or later," Jesse said, "that you meet some of the neighbors. And it's better this way rather than someone seeing you accidentally and wondering why we haven't said anything about you."

Farrand, naturally, was the first to become amenable to the idea.

"You'll have to tell us what to do, what to say, how to answer questions," he said.

"And," I said, "we'll have to change your names."

So, to friends and neighbors they were to become Randy, Len, and Rafe.

"Len?" Celene said in pained tones.

"The closer it is to your real name, the less likely Jesse and I will make a slip," I explained.

"But what does it mean?"

"Actually, it's short for Leonard."

"And that?"

"Something to do with a lion, I guess."

"A lion? You mean an animal?"

I smiled at his disdainful face. "Celene, the name change is only for your protection."

Farrand laughed. "I won't ask what mine means."

"No, you'd better not. But it's short for Randall or Randolph, and don't ask me what they mean, for I've no idea."

Israfel was silent, but suddenly his mind asked me about his new name.

I spoke out loud. "You'll have to tell anyone who asks that it's the way some people pronounce Ralph."

Why don't they use the names they were given?

"Some do. We do. But so many are customarily changed or shortened to something else."

For a moment he laughed. It was the first time I'd heard it, and we all stared at him in surprise. Then the icy curtain of reserve fell over the beautiful face; the eyes retreated into distance, and the lips thinned. That moment of laughter might never have been.

I was disappointed, angry, and I attacked him in the most stupid way imaginable.

What's the matter with you? How can we ever integrate you into the community when you can't even laugh without regretting it? You stand up there on your lofty pinnacle, nothing but arrogant and aloof, with never a smile for anyone. No wonder Jesse doesn't like you! I can't understand why Celene and Farrand do. What are you? A machine? A brainwashed automaton? A robot without any feelings or sensitivities? Why do you always have to be so distant and cold—

My impetuous attack was brought to an abrupt halt as the silver eyes clashed with mine, brilliant as polished metal, honed to the sharpness of a sword. And they were filled with a raw fury that left me cringing in all my nerves and senses. But their stab was nothing compared to the slash that came from his mind. I reeled as it struck me.

Who do you think you are? You minuscule creature of no rank or position! You presumptuous barbarian, feeble little victim of uncontrollable emotions, you—

Suddenly the mind sealed as though an iron door had slammed over it. The thoughts vanished, and the blazing anger in his eyes was extinguished as a flame by a deluge of cold water. I shook my head, still reeling at his onslaught, and waited for it to come again.

Nothing happened. I looked at him and saw a trace of puzzlement in his eyes, then curiosity as they again met mine.

Shaken, I was angry once again. I glared at him, and then I understood his hesitation.

So, you can lose your cool, can you? You're not as unemotional as you'd have me believe, are you? In fact, you might even be downright human!

At this, he stiffened, and the coldness returned to his eyes. But I pressed on, dashing willy-nilly along my foolhardy course. I was only dimly aware that Farrand and Jesse had left the room, and that Celene was standing watching me with blazing eyes in a face white with fury.

I blundered on. *Smile, Israfel! It won't kill you. It won't even hurt you! Try it. Just for once, go on. Smile!*

A faint flush stole into the pale, translucent skin. From the corner of my eye, I saw Celene take a menacing step towards me. The hair moved on my scalp, and all my nerve ends prickled. The room was filling with danger, palpable, threatening, strong, and deadly. I knew I had gone too far.

Paralyzed, my breath freezing in my throat, I stared at Israfel, at the remote distance of those alien eyes. How could I have been such a fool to attack him in that fashion? Surely an iota of common sense would have told me I was playing with fire.

I'm sorry, I tried to tell him. *It was unforgivable of me to say those things to you. I don't blame you for being angry.*

A strange intensity came into his face, and the eyes lost their distance, pierced mine once more like blades.

Laura . . . My name came hesitantly. *Laura . . .*

He made an abrupt motion with his hand, and Celene turned from me to face him. The danger drifted away like smoke.

A torrent of thoughts came racing through my mind. They came from Israfel's stream of consciousness but were snarled with elements of confusion. Hesitant knots were all I could separate from that rushing flow.

Slower! I pleaded. *I can't keep up.*

Again, the door slammed shut; the thoughts were gone. He stood there in a flood of yellow sunlight, slight and all at once seeming vulnerable, his eyes shading as he looked at me. After that single motion of his hand, he had become still, appeared to be deep in thought. The trace of a frown lowered the smooth brows, drew a fine line between them, and his mouth lost its look of strict discipline. I waited, unable to move, scarcely breathing.

I don't know how long we stood there, me clinging to the back of a chair with stiff fingers and damp palms, knuckles white; he so still and silent, withdrawn but no longer aloof. It could have been only minutes, even seconds, but it felt like hours. My heart was an anxious pulse in my breast, beating so loudly I could hear it. My mouth was dry, throat tight and sore. Celene stood near the fire, vigilant and waiting, watching us both. I could do nothing.

A glitter sparkled in the unearthly eyes, and I saw his lips move into what I interpreted as a wry twist.

I've told you. The words came to me softly, quietly. *I only smile when there's a reason.*

For a long time, we stared at each other. The expression on his face precluded any argument; I was weak with strange relief. Then again, there was that slight movement of his lips, followed by a brief bend of his head – as though he were dismissing me and anything else I would say. He turned without haste and left the room, moving with his easy grace and effortless step but with none of the usual militant bearing. I fell into the chair I was leaning on and closed my eyes. I didn't hear Celene go, but he had gone when I finally pulled myself together.

For a while, I thought Israfel had forgotten the incident, for he behaved as though nothing untoward had happened when next we met. He was, as usual, polite and considerate, distant and quiet. But when I began to instruct them on what to say upon arrival at the Greenaways' – on introductions, describing the people we knew would be there and warning them what to expect – I noticed that Israfel was unusually cooperative. He asked the kinds of questions that meant he was paying serious attention to the problems they could encounter, and he showed a remarkable willingness to remember names and descriptions, conversation topics and subjects to avoid. He appeared to have taken my words to heart about integrating him into the community.

They absorbed everything so easily. I knew none of them would forget what I had told them, but there was one thing that never occurred to me.

CHAPTER THIRTEEN

"WHAT ARE YOU DOING?" FARRAND asked, staring in astonishment at the green fir tree we were dragging into the house.

"It's traditional," I said and went on to explain the customs we observed, year after year, and the festivities, special music, and gift giving of Christmas.

"But where is your history of those times?" Celene asked me in amazement. "That was such a short time ago. Where are the facts? Surely records were kept!"

"I think they were burned," Jesse said slowly, "in the library at Alexandria."

"So! You live with these . . . these myths?"

"I don't think they're myths."

"But they have been made into mysteries, and those are myths."

I felt Israfel's mind move. It brushed against mine with the swift lightness of a bird's wing, but no thoughts came to me. He was looking at Celene, and I saw the latter hesitate, his eyes flicker in some acknowledgment, then turn away.

There was a strange silence in the room that Farrand suddenly broke. "What are you going to use this tree for?" he asked.

"Decoration," I said, wishing I knew the story of the Christmas tree, intending to look it up, so conscious of Farrand's eyes I forgot Celene's last words and what appeared to be Israfel's intervention.

⚛

"I wish we'd never agreed to go," I said to Jesse on Christmas Eve. The worries I had been steadfastly gathering had accumulated into an oppressive harvest of anxieties, and with dinner at the Greenaways' now imminent and impossible to avoid, I was miserable with fear.

"You worry too much," he said, his head bent over his guitar as he replaced a worn string. "They'll be able to handle it."

"How can we possibly be sure?" I pulled with nervous fingers at a button dangling by a single thread on my cardigan, one that had seen better days. But I liked its warm comfort and wore it in the face of Celene's censorious disapproval. "We can't know at all."

"Hmm. I don't think they're nearly as helpless as you like to think."

"What? But they're stranded here, with a wrecked ship and no communication! Goodness only knows how far from home they are, totally dependent on us to protect them—"

"Okay. Okay. But don't forget their intelligence. And that brings me to another thing. I think they're keeping all kinds of things secret from us. Which is probably okay – unless it's for the wrong reasons."

At this I was silent. Again, here was the opportunity to tell him Israfel and I could read each other's minds. But still I said nothing, keeping this knowledge to myself and not knowing why.

⚉

With the truck wheels chained, we went down to the Greenaways' on the back road. Jesse drove Farrand and me down first, with the mince pies in boxes balanced on our knees and the slippers for all of us in a tote bag.

"Just you and Farrand arriving first will make their differences less noticeable than if we all arrive at once," he had said as we'd dressed in preparation. "And it's too cold out for anyone to ride in the back."

As we crossed our boundary and began the last steep descent, the road narrowed and became untracked in a treelined, snow filled gully. I looked at Farrand's long fine hand on the box he held, felt my arm brush his as the truck jolted on the bumps and ruts, and wished with helpless desperation we were not taking him away from the relative safety of our home. And then Celene and Israfel. Surely, we should never have even considered this.

My hands were damp, my throat dry, and as we rounded that last bend and an aura of house lights spread over the snow, I began to feel miserably unsure. What might this lead to? If only we could tell them all, take them into our confidence, enlist their support!

But no. Out of fairness to everyone, we had to keep our secret, let the subterfuge continue for as long as we could.

Familiar vehicles were parked before the barn. I eyed them uneasily.

A dark brown Ford Bronco stood defiantly beside a blue and white GMC Blazer; the Ransoms' huge station wagon crouched beyond. Mac and Helen's red Toyota shone bright and new behind Maureen and Ted's compact Dodge. A new sticker adorned the bumper of the blue Chevrolet that belonged to Sarah and Todd, Helen's sister and brother-in-law. "Carpenters make better studs," I read as Jesse turned. Typical!

He stopped at the footpath leading to the house, and we climbed out. I took a deep breath, keeping a firm grip on the pie as the truck began to move away, and we headed for the wreath-decorated door.

I could hear Jesse beginning to grind up the hill, the rattle of the chains and the rumble of the engine, the laughter and the steady roar of voices coming from inside the house, the crunch of our feet in the snow. Then all these sounds were drowned by the wild roar of the Greenways' two dogs as they flung themselves from the steps in a frenzy.

Part husky, part Doberman, part something else, the friendly floppy pair transformed before my eyes. Hackles raised and teeth bared, they barked furiously at Farrand while their bodies cringed, tails tucking down and eyes glaring white with fear. I froze, stood staring at them in horror and dismay.

The door was flung open. "Chummy! Chip!"

The dogs ignored Kevin's cheerful voice, drowned it with the roar of theirs, whirled in circles in the snow.

I turned to Farrand and saw him watching them, an intensity growing in his eyes. Kevin yelled at them again.

The dogs fled abruptly, disappearing under the balcony at the front of the house. The sudden silence that fell was numbing.

Kevin came down the steps. "Sorry about that, Laura. Don't know what got into them. Come on in, and Merry Christmas."

Somehow, I set my feet once more into motion, and then we were in the bright kitchen with voices and faces and shouts of "Merry Christmas" all around us. Children chased by us, trailing paper chains, and Patty was taking the pie from my hand. "How lovely!" Farrand stood beside me on the mat, smiling his warm and gentle smile, still holding a pie and the tote bag.

"This," I managed to say, "is . . . " For one awful moment, I couldn't think of the name we had given him. "Randy," I gasped at last.

Kevin relieved him of the other pie and shook his hand. "Get your coats off and come and have a drink. Everybody's getting ahead of you."

Warmth and people and delicious aromas enveloped us. Glasses of mulled wine were pressed into our hands. Laughter and conversation and the excited cries of children surrounded us. Ted was hugging me and giving me a hearty kiss, Mac demanding to know what I'd done with Jesse.

"He's gone back to fetch the others," I explained and began to edge Farrand towards a vacant chair in the living room next to Helen. Helen, with her shy grace, would not bombard him with questions. Helen, in a long black skirt with a white lace blouse, her beautifully groomed and pure white hair, her calm gray eyes, and her gentle smile stood in marked contrast to the weathered, windburned face of Mac, with his fun-filled eyes of sun-bleached blue and noisy laughter, the massive shoulders that could lift a horse – and sometimes had – broad beneath a bright plaid western shirt, was the ideal one to leave Farrand with. She smiled when I introduced him to her, and I sighed inwardly with relief as she appeared to accept him without question.

But Maureen was curious. She collared me as I went back to the kitchen. "I didn't know you had visitors," she said in a faintly accusing tone. "And where have you been hiding yourself lately? Haven't had a peep from you."

"Sorry," I said, trying to sound natural. "They've kept me kind of busy. And they haven't been with us very long," I added, hoping she'd accept that and believe me, that she wasn't really hurt by my recent lack of contact. I gave her a quick hug, then began to admire her dress. "Haven't seen that before. New?" And when she nodded, I added, "Was Santa good to you? And how did Deenie like her presents?"

Maureen dived into her extensive discourse on her little girl's reactions to the opening of parcels, and the wild barking of the dogs intruded loudly. Patty, a mixing spoon in hand, went to the window and peered out.

"Those dogs! What on earth's the matter with them?"

My stomach did an uncomfortable somersault. I joined her at the window. "It's Jesse and the others," I said. "Here comes the guitar and the wine." I tried to keep my voice steady as the dogs' barking reached a crescendo.

"Oh," she said, her concentration on the dogs. "Did you bring wine, too?"

"Of course."

Three figures came into the light pouring from the window. The dogs whirled around them.

"You didn't need to, and the pies look lovely." She frowned, went to the door, and opened it. "Chummy! Chippy! Will you shut up! Sorry, Jesse. I don't know what's got into them."

"Too many strangers," Jesse said.

I stood by the window, found myself trembling. Kevin was taking coats, Mac looming over Jesse, slapping his back, and yelling at him to get out of the house one of these days and go ice fishing with him. Again, the children swarmed by me, pulling a large stuffed dog on erratic wheels. Maureen stood by the table, her glass forgotten, tilting in her hand, and Israfel and Celene were suddenly the center of many startled eyes.

In the kitchen, silence fell. Even Mac's voice stilled. The children had gone. Patty stood motionless. Kevin appeared to have forgotten the coats draped over his arm. My mouth became as dry as dust. Oh, Lord!

Jesse broke the spell, leaping into the breach with a swift summation of the situation. He pounded on Mac's shoulder with a roar of his own. "Go and freeze on some godforsaken lake while drowning some poor worm? Not my idea of fun! Now, meet my friends. This is Len and Rafe."

As introductions were made, manners precluded further staring. The noise resumed: coats were carried away and glasses filled, and shrieks came from the children in another part of the house. Patty turned her attention to the oven and the enormous golden brown bird in there, and I forced myself away from the window and to Israfel's side. I introduced him to Maureen, who gazed at him with huge brown eyes and could find nothing to say, then casually led him and Celene into the living room and made the rest of the introductions there.

This isn't going well, I thought unhappily as again the conversation lulled and the gaze of startled eyes came from every direction. But wasn't this what I'd expected? Worried about? I had walked into this crowded room of down-to-earth people, into this rural community, and had brought two beings with me who didn't belong. They were totally foreign to men in jeans and cords, to the women who thought Jesse the height of local glamour because of his Hollywood connections. Yet here was Israfel, with his dark glasses and shining silver hair, and Celene, looking more angelic than ever, both with a magnetic presence that was utterly compelling. I stood there beside them while all eyes stared, and I didn't know what to do.

Jesse saved us. He came breezing in, filling the sudden silence with shouts of "Merry Christmas," smiling, shaking hands, pressing swift warm kisses, forcing attention onto himself, away from our striking guests. I took the opportunity to draw Israfel down beside me in a far corner of the couch, and Celene followed Jesse to cushions on the hearth. Politeness brought the resumption of conversation, strained and awkward to begin with. Kevin came and took away empty glasses, brought them back filled. A clatter came from the kitchen.

I should go and help, I remember thinking. Maureen was still there, was probably expecting me. But to withdraw what little protection I could give was anathema, even though it was Jesse who had been our saving grace thus far.

Then the trouble really began.

Into the room came Sacha, Roger, and Beth's seventeen year old daughter, slim and lovely, long blond hair hanging in a silken fall down the beak of her satin lemon blouse. Gold lamé toreador pants were gathered below the knees of her long slim legs, immediately attracting attention from these generally rural folk. But she did not see the men's eyes turn to her. She saw only Celene.

About to pass him, she suddenly stopped as though jerked by a rein. Blue eyes widened as she stared at him. "Hi!" she breathed.

Jesse and Celene rose politely to their feet. I heard Jesse introduce them and saw every movement Sacha made as I suddenly understood the meaning of "body language," had it demonstrated right before my stunned and disbelieving eyes. The tilting of the head and the flick of long mascaraed lashes, the slight movements of the shoulder and hips that indicated pleasure and subtle invitation. From where had so young a girl learned such wiles? I heard a caress in her voice. "Are you going to be staying long?"

Celene smiled politely, but I saw her almost reel before its shattering impact.

Oh, God! I suddenly prayed. *No!*

"I suspect so," Celene said.

"Ooh, that's great!" Again, the body spoke volumes, and she produced a smile to nearly match his own.

Suddenly Celene was wary, disdain replacing the politeness, a coldness chilling the brilliant eyes. His head lifted in scorn.

What is it? Israfel's voice spoke clearly in my head.

Look, look at them! Sacha is totally smitten with Celene.

Smitten?

She's enthralled by him, enraptured, and he doesn't like it. But he mustn't show it!

No.

His mind was gone from mine.

I saw Celene's eyes flash toward us, then a semblance of a smile forced back to his face. I threw an appealing look at Jesse.

He caught it and came once more to the rescue. He took Sacha's arm with a firm hand. "You're looking great, Sacha." I could just hear his words. "Oh, hey, you must come and meet Randy."

He steered her across the floor. But she scarcely saw Farrand, did not meet those hypnotic eyes. Her body had become stiff with resentment at being taken away from Celene, and her mouth pouted sulkily. I stared, agonizing, at the empty place Jesse had left beside Celene, had visions of her slipping into it at the first opportunity. I was tempted to go sit there myself, but that would mean abandoning Israfel. And Roger came to me, asking if we'd sold all our young stock.

"All the yearling fillies," I told him, trying to see past him without appearing rude. "We still have a few colts. Six weanling fillies left, but we'll keep them if they don't go as yearlings."

Where was Sacha now? I couldn't see her or Jesse.

"Get all your mares bred back?"

"Seem to be. How about yours?"

Where were they? Roger sat down on the floor, clearing my view. Jesse came from the kitchen, glass refilled, stepped quickly back to his place beside Celene. I sighed with some relief.

" . . . only two," Roger was saying, twirling a glass with ice cubes in it. "Cost of hay last year made me cautious."

"Wasn't a good year. We got most of ours in, but we just happened to hit it right."

Sacha came from the dining room. Jesse promptly engaged Celene in conversation. Sacha sat on the floor next to her father, which put her right in front of Celene. But she appeared to have gathered her wits, was now playing it cool, and scarcely looked at Celene at all.

However, when we went in to eat and found our places at the table designated by neatly scripted name tags, she was sitting next to him.

"Sacha" Patty said in surprise. "Did I put you there?"

The girl didn't answer, glanced up with an innocently puzzled frown.

"Well, it doesn't matter." Patty went back to the kitchen to fetch another dish.

In the ensuing noise of conversation, laughter, the chatter of children, and the clatter of cutlery and China plates, I, seated between Roger and Ted on the opposite side of the table, could not hear what was being said across from me. But Celene's face wore traces of its usual aloof disdain, and his eyes were cold. Several times I saw him shake his head, his lips form the word "No," and Sacha only gazed at him with an increasing admiration.

Israfel, I knew, was tense and alert, and then I realized Roger was also aware of the situation.

"Handsome young man, your friend over there," he said, passing me a dish of roasted potatoes, a sideways motion of his head indicating Celene.

"Mmm. Yes, I suppose he is."

"Sacha obviously thinks so."

I spooned potatoes onto my plate and passed the bowl to Ted. "Oh, well, she's young and impressionable." I tried to shrug casually.

"Cranberry sauce?" He passed me another bowl. "But only last week she was talking so definitively about the beautician's course she's planning to take in Vancouver next year. And she says she's not going to even think seriously about boys until she's at least twenty-five."

"We all say that at seventeen."

"Do you?" He poured gravy over the sliced turkey on his plate, looked across the table at his daughter, frowned at the intensity of her face and the spots of color in her cheeks, the feverish brightness of her eyes. "Laura, who is he?"

My heart skipped a beat, and a dampness broke out on my skin beneath the soft blue velvet of my dress. I swallowed, then turned my grateful attention to Kevin as he leaned over me, poured a frosty white wine into my glass. "Thanks, Kevin."

Israfel's mind reached mine. *Laura, what's rock and roll?*

I tried to tell him but realized Roger was watching me, waiting for an answer to his question.

"He isn't local, is he?"

"Oh, no." I plied my attention to my plate. "He's a friend of Jesse's."

What's disco? Who's Robert Redford? Is he here?

"He doesn't seem to be giving her much encouragement, though, does he?"

I struggled with the questions, the silent ones that had to be answered swiftly and the others so carefully.

"No, he doesn't."

Roger put a forkful of food into his mouth. I did the same but didn't taste a thing.

"First time I've ever seen her so cock-a-hoop over a fellow."

I chewed in silence, my mind racing wildly.

Who's Goldie Hawn? And Darryl Hannah? She's asking him if she reminds him of them.

Oh, Lord! Tell him a little bit of both.

"Blast! I wouldn't be so worried if he didn't look so damned hostile."

I scrambled for words. "Maybe she's coming on a bit too strong, you know. Or maybe he's got a girl." I wished I could change the subject or my location at the table.

Laura, what's wrong?

Roger's her father. He's very concerned. He did not expect this, either.

"I don't want to see her get hurt. She's young, sure, but she's always had her head screwed on right. Never thought I'd see her lose it like this."

"First time for everything," I muttered, lifting my glass and gulping wine.

I don't think he heard me. "Is he in movies? Maybe that's the attraction . . ."

"I don't think so."

What's disco?

Israfel's questions interspersed with Roger's were becoming a confusing tangle. Desperately I wished I'd thought of something like this happening, but it hadn't occurred to me. Again, I regretted coming.

What's a rock star?

She had her hand on Celene's arm. How he must hate that!

A rock . . . I began. My face flushed with embarrassment.

My head was buzzing and all I could do was answer Israfel by showing him an image. I looked longingly at Jesse, wondering how soon we could decently leave. His head was bent attentively toward Maureen. Kevin poured more wine, but I was scarcely aware of it. We had to see this through, of course.

Sacha's shoulder pressed against Celene's arm as she reached to whisper intimately in his ear. I groaned inwardly. *Oh, God, Sacha! Stop!*

Easy, Laura!

Celene smiled politely, shook his head once more.

I drank more wine before I realized what I was doing.

Why is she so interested in him?

It's the way he looks.

That's absurd.

Not to her, it isn't.

"More turkey, Laura? More vegetables?"

Somehow my plate had been emptied. "No, thank you."

"What does he do? Do you know?"

"I think he's some kind of scientist."

"How long have you known him?"

"Not very long."

"I'll bet she thinks he's a movie star . . . "

"Mmm, maybe."

What's a movie star?

Now he was reading my mind without my knowledge. He, at the far end of the table, couldn't possibly hear our words over the general hubbub. I drained the rest of my wine while I answered, my head fuzzy, lacking control, defenseless against his probing.

Somehow, I struggled on with questions and answers, managed to talk to Ted for a while, although it was difficult as the silent questions kept on coming and my attention was constantly drawn to the far side of the table.

Most of the conversation around me was reduced to a meaningless roar until the pies and pudding and coffee were brought in.

"Say," Dan said loudly in the brief lull that followed the initial mouthful of dessert, "has anyone heard anything more about that missing plane?"

Eyes raised and heads turned enquiringly to one another. A new uproar broke out.

"Haven't they called the search off?"

"Sure."

"Nah! The army was all over the Silver Hills last week." Mac's voice boomed this information clearly.

"Yeah. We saw them, Larry and I. We were going fishing up there. Saw them, dozens of them."

"So, how'd you know they were looking for it?"

"They said they were. We stopped and asked a couple of them. Fellers on snowshoes."

"Then why did they say the search had been called off?"

"Damned if I know. But it sure as hell hasn't been."

"Did anyone ever hear who it was on board? I mean, to have the army out—"

"Some fat cat, or a politician they don't want to admit has gone missing."

"Why should that be?"

Questions and conjecture flew around the table. I sat cold and still. Surely someone would notice that five of us – we five – were listening in rapt attention. Even Sacha was forced into silence, Celene not to be diverted from the current conversation by any means.

"They're sure being secretive about it."

"Maybe it was a spy plane."

"Or some new prototype."

"As long as it wasn't carrying any nuclear devices."

"We'd have all been evacuated if it had been."

"You think so?"

"Sure."

"My bet's a spy plane."

"Could well be."

"It may never be found."

"No."

"I don't know, with even the army looking . . . "

"You know how many planes crash and are never found – or not for years and years."

"Yeah, I guess."

"And if they're keeping it so secret, we may never know."

"Hmm."

I saw no one looking with overt curiosity at us as I glanced surreptitiously around the table. Had anyone noticed that our three guests had refused coffee? I didn't think so. That Israfel wore dark glasses in the house had probably been accepted as a Hollywood affectation, his perfect features and shining silver hair regarded as another 'Hollywood' manifestation. And Sacha had turned her attention to her dessert. Maybe we were going to be able to carry this through without further incident.

With dessert finished and the topic of the missing plane exhausted, there was a general movement back to the living room. Sacha disappeared. I helped clear the table, helped load the dishwasher, and stood listening to Maureen, Beth, and Patty talk about a college course Patty was working on. The children were still in the dining room, pulling crackers. Kevin filled a pot with coffee and carried it into the living room, and I could hear Todd telling a joke, the resulting groans and strangled laughter. For the first time that evening I began to relax. Surely, we were past the most difficult part. Everything was going to be all right. Maybe that was all the wine I had drunk talking.

The sound of music came drifting up the stairs. Then I heard Sacha's voice announce clearly, "Dancing downstairs. Come on, everybody, Len."

Israfel's mind flew to mine. *Dancing – what's dancing? She's pulling Celene by the hand.*

I hurried to the living room, flashing images of dancing out to him, not totally conscious of what he had asked me.

"Come on," Sacha was saying to the room in general while her hand still clung to Celene's. "Let's go and dance."

"But Sacha!" Patty protested, coming into the room behind me. "Jesse was going to play for us, and we were going to sing some carols."

Sacha turned to her, wide eyed, smiling. "Can't we do that later? Mark has some super new tapes, just great to dance to. Can't we? Just for a while?"

Again, she pulled at Celene's hand, and he rose politely to his feet but with wary apprehension flashing in his eyes.

Must he go?

I think he'd better.

Show me again.

The images of dancing were becoming difficult to convey as once again a fuzziness filled my head. *Dammit!* I thought, shaking it in an effort to clear it. I must have drunk too much wine.

Doesn't this child realize how different he is? Has she no comprehension that he is far too old for her? Far too sophisticated? Can't she see?

All she can see is his face, I told him unhappily, watching the look of warning flare in Celene's eyes as Sacha drew his arm against her, saw abhorrence in the tight line of his mouth and the stiffening of his body. *But Israfel, she is so very young. Tell him to go along with her in this, but to be careful. And we'll rescue him in a few minutes.*

Again, I tried to fill my mind with pictures of people dancing, felt him absorbing and passing the images on. Sacha and Celene were gone, followed by Ted and Maureen. I moved across the floor to Jesse.

"Love, will you come and dance with me?"

"Best invitation I've had today," he said gallantly, excusing himself from Helen's side, rising, and slipping an arm around me.

"What's up?" he asked quietly as I led him towards the stairs.

"Sacha has taken Celene to dance with her."

"Damn! How he must hate that."

"I know. But he's bearing it – for the moment."

"Never expected anything like that," he muttered as we began to descend the stairs.

"No," I said, pressing a hand against an ache that was beginning to form in my forehead. "And we're going to have to break it up somehow."

Music poured from speakers set to one side of the paneled recreation room. I saw the two fair heads immediately, Sacha whirling so her hair streamed out, her eyes shining but vacant, her face fixed in the dreamy expression I have seen before on teenagers when dancing. Her mouth was curved in a rapturous smile. Celene, registering total unhappiness, moved uneasily around her.

"I'll cut in as soon as I can," Jesse whispered as he swung me onto the floor.

Automatically, my feet moved, following his. Barely aware of the music thudding in my ears, of the jostling as we brushed against other bodies joining us on the floor, of the voices and the laughter, I constantly turned my eyes to Sacha and Celene, her floating hair, his fixed unhappy face.

We circled the floor and came close to them once more.

"Now!" Jesse said. He released me and yelled, "Okay! Everyone changes partners." Then he snatched Sacha and swept her away down the room.

I flung myself at Celene and caught his hand. "Once around the floor," I whispered in his ear. "Then back upstairs."

"What does she want?" he asked, holding me awkwardly, just with his fingertips, carefully at arm's length.

I stared at him. Didn't he know? And Israfel had said he was too old!

I looked at the porcelain smooth skin of his face and neck, at the lustrous hair and the fine line of his jaw, the vivid eyes. Too old? How old was he? He appeared to be about twenty. And no wonder Sacha had fallen so swiftly and hard. He was, as Patty would say with the lively humor of exaggeration, absolutely gorgeous. To a smalltown teenager, he'd be just that.

I questioned him as we neared the stairs. *Israfel, how old is Celene?*

The answer came to me after a brief hesitation. *About twenty-four thousand of your years.*

Twenty-four . . . thousand? The music of Air Supply became a hammering in my ears, and I suddenly stumbled on the stairs.

Yes.

Thousand?

That's what his age represents in your measuring.

I clung to the handrail as the stairs seemed to float. *This,* I thought, my head reeling with wine and shock, *is more than I could even bring myself to contemplate.*

CHAPTER FOURTEEN

ISRAFEL'S MIND CAUGHT ME, HELD me. I felt its strength as my wavering feet moved on, up the stairs.

He met me at the top. *I'm sorry. I didn't mean to shock you like that.*

His strong fingers closed around my forearm, but I drew away in fearful disassociation. If Celene was as old as he said, then how old was Israfel?

All things are relative, he said silently. *In our own lifetimes, we are similar to what you are in yours. Laura, there are so many things in the universe of which you know absolutely nothing. And your own history . . . You know nothing of it, either. You live in a total darkness of your origin and heritage . . .*

Patty saw us standing there. "Anything wrong? Laura, are you okay?"

"Too much dancing after too much wine," I said, trying to smile.

"You want to go and lie down for a while?"

"Gosh, no, Patty. Thanks, but I'll be okay in a minute."

"You sure? Can I get you anything?"

"No, really. It's nothing," I said while my strained nerves felt as though they were going to snap. If stress wasn't coming at me from one direction, it soon came from another.

"Come and sit down, Laura," Israfel said, his hand impersonal under my elbow.

He led me to the couch on the far side of the room. Celene came with us, his face guarded and tense.

That your history has been lost is a detriment, Israfel went on, drawing me down beside him. *One I wish we could rectify. But to do so would be interference, intolerable to established doctrines. Our deaths would be of a greater certainty than self destruction to avoid capture of our scientific knowledge.*

Don't . . . don't talk like that!

Sorry, but Laura, facts are facts. Celene is the equivalent of twenty-four thousand in your years. There's no escaping that. What is, is. Just as there's so much you don't know – what we are, where we're from . . .

This was a tangent of welcome diversion, and I veered into the opportune opening.

That's something we've been meaning to ask you ever since came. Where are you from?

If I told you, it would mean nothing to you.

This brought me up short in an abrupt dead end. Mars or Venus would have been understandable, but of course an unknown, unnamed planet wouldn't tell me anything. I plunged into the next nearest avenue.

And why did you come here? And why, when you have obviously come far, didn't you just land, announce yourselves?

To your first question, I am permitted no answer. You yourself know why the other was impossible.

His mind closed to me, and in the sudden emptiness, the headache that had been lingering earlier now began to pound. He had cut me off, left me feeling disconnected and lonely and that my questions had been unwelcome. But that I should have known.

I sat there, sick and miserable, wishing we could go home – even that Jesse and I would be there alone with only our comfortable, familiar routines, our horses and his music, my pottery, and our privacy.

Laura, you know we wish to be gone as soon as possible.

I turned and looked at him, regretting my selfish thoughts, wishing he hadn't read them.

That wry smile touched his lips. *I understand. I suppose you wouldn't be "human" if you didn't think such thoughts at times.*

Even this was better than no communication at all. I studied his sculpted profile, the shining hair and fine pale skin, wondering if I could face the answer. *Israfel, how old are you?*

His eyes gleamed as dull pewter behind the tinted lenses. *In your years or mine?*

In mine.

Do you really want to know?

I took a deep breath, swallowed. *Yes.*

About thirty-six thousand.

I stilled a tremor that shimmered along all my nerves. *What is it like?*

Greater knowledge, vast experience, time in which to undertake long journeys. Laura, why are you troubling yourself with this? You look so tired, even ill. Could we leave now?

No, Jesse always plays some music when we come. And there's carol singing, and . . .

I heard the other voices, the music, saw almost with astonishment the familiar faces of friends and neighbors – and Sacha. Her cheeks were flushed and there was anxiety in her eyes.

"Len! There you are! Come on. Mark's playing some Fleetwood Mac . . . "

I couldn't take any more. I scrambled to my feet, no longer caring about social formalities. "I'm sorry, Sacha, but I'm not feeling so great. I think I'm going to have to go home, and Len's going to drive me."

Her face fell and she looked at me with crestfallen eyes. "Gee, Laura. That's too bad. But couldn't Rafe take you?"

"He doesn't drive," I said, hoping she wouldn't question that. What grown North American male didn't?

"Then Jesse?"

"He'll stay on and play some music, for the carols."

"I'd better come, too," Israfel said, "or there'll be too many of us left."

He and Celene rose to their feet, and again I saw no one else, heard no other voices. They looked like jewels among pebbles. Couldn't Sacha see? Wasn't she aware of the alien elements in Celene as she gazed at him so avidly? Didn't she realize how different they were? Was she blind? And the others? Surely, they could see how alien Celene and Israfel were, standing there looking like princes out of childhood fairy tales.

Patty came towards us, curious.

"I'm sorry," I gasped, "but I really don't feel very well." I struggled with names. "Len's going to drive me home, and Rafe's coming too."

"Oh, dear," she said. "I'm sorry, Laura. What about Jesse?"

"He'll stay," I assured her.

"So, Len must come back," Sacha said gleefully, "to pick the others up."

I hadn't thought of that. I hadn't thought any further than getting him away from her. How could I have been so damned stupid?

Israfel touched my arm. "He will come back," he said.

Our coats were brought out, and I struggled into mine, feeling like an idiot. We found our boots and said goodbye to the other guests, and I tried not to notice the unspoken questions in so many eyes. Jesse's look at me was followed by a small smile of relief.

The crisp fresh bite of the air outside was welcome on my heated face, but again my stomach lurched as the dogs broke into a frenzy of barking. I called them by name, but they were oblivious to everything but my alien companions. I thought of Celene returning, braving them alone.

Don't worry. Israfel pressed my arm. *They won't touch us. They're afraid, know we are different. That's all.*

"How do I drive this vehicle?" Celene asked me as we reached the truck and climbed in.

"It's easy." I remembered the ease with which he'd learned to read and thought this would be no different.

But Celene, who could navigate a starship across the universe, had the greatest difficulty guiding our half ton up the narrow road.

I sat between them and tried to help him, wished I could go back later to pick up the others. But Sacha would be watching, and I had already pleaded illness as an excuse to leave. My headache even seemed to be getting worse. Israfel, on the other side of me, was silent, his mind closed from me.

By the time we reached the wide white expanse of the hay fields, Celene was managing much better. Familiar with the accelerator and developing a feel for the steering, he was beginning to drive quite well. But still he clung to the wheel and stared anxiously into the pale swath cut by the headlights. He looked so young, and yet, although in a different way, so experienced. Celene, whose age was the equivalent of twenty-four thousand years!

I tried not to think about it, then remembered the look in Sacha's eyes. What would she say if she knew the truth about Celene? And he hadn't seen the last of her. What could I do to discourage her? I feared there was little.

The house embraced me with warmth and comforting familiarity, but how I wished Farrand was here too, that Celene didn't have to go back. How I wished we had never gone in the first place. I made tea and took two aspirins while Israfel and Celene lit the living room fire. I hoped Jesse would effect an early departure and would also be able to come between Sacha and Celene.

The Christmas tree shone and glittered in its corner, filling the room with the resinous scent of fir, and a lamp cast soft rich light on the varnished logs of the walls, the shaggy Scandinavian rugs, and the polished plank floor. Israfel was kneeling on the hearth rug, his face revealing nothing, while Celene stood beside him, still tense, regarding me with worried eyes.

"That girl, what does she want with me? Why did she behave like that? What does it mean?"

I poured tea into mugs, inhaled the minty aroma, and hoped the aspirins would work quickly. "Don't you know?" I handed him a cup.

"No," he said.

"He has never experienced anything like that." Israfel spoke quietly.

"Can you tell him?" I asked. "It's hard for me."

He took off the dark glasses and set them on the hearth, turning his silver eyes on me.

I passed him the tea and honey, wondered what he was thinking. But he gave me no answer. His long pale fingers wrapped around the cup, and he smiled faintly.

"She's a member of your race. You tell him."

I lifted my own cup and curled into a corner of the couch, regarding Celene unhappily while I hunted for words.

"She's attracted to you, Celene," I began, feeling more and more awkward. "She . . . has a . . . a strong liking for you—"

"But she knows nothing of me!"

"That makes no different. She likes what she sees. You must realize that she is very young and impressionable, lives in a small place where . . . well, people as attractive as you . . . just don't happen."

He gazed at me, angry understanding growing in his eyes. "You mean . . . even though she doesn't know me . . . she . . . she . . . " He couldn't bring himself to even say the words. His head lifted and his mouth tightened into its familiar disdaining line.

"And you be careful," I went on quickly, "not to hurt her."

"Hurt her?"

"Yes. She's very sensitive toward you, vulnerable about you. If she thinks you don't care, then her feelings will be badly hurt."

"But I don't care," he said angrily.

"I know." I wasn't doing this well, but my aching head would not allow me to do better.

"You think I'm that uncivilized?"

"How am I to know what you might do in a situation that you haven't confronted before?" I was forgetting that I'd already seen him in that very thing.

"Celene," I said wearily, "I live in constant fear for your safety. This evening has been awfully hard on me, and Sacha was something I never thought of. Most young men I have known have been hurtful, insensitive—"

"I am not as the men you have known," he ground at me.

"I know. I know."

"Do you?"

"Yes. And that's why I did all I could to get you away from her this evening."

"Thank you," he said, his sense of courtesy promptly returning – as it always did when he realized he owed gratitude. "But I am certain I have the ability to handle a child such as that – now I know what her behavior means."

"Then you must forgive me, but I realize how repellant we are to you, know how instinctively you withdraw from us. And I think it's that," I went on, "that makes me worry about Sacha."

He stared at me. I saw how, under stress, his face wasn't as young as the smooth fine skin would lead one to believe. There was a vast knowledge behind those blue eyes, a strongly defined discipline in the lines of the jaw and mouth, exceptional capability in the carriage of his head. Intellectual maturity was masked by the impression of youth.

"Perhaps, if she did get to know me better—"

"And then what? How could you conceal your true identity? And what would happen when you leave?" Foolishly, I plunged ahead, not looking before I leaped, stupidly bypassing a step he had made toward me.

"If she knew me properly then I could tell her. And she would understand why I had to leave."

I pressed my hands to my aching head. "Celene, forgive me again. I spoke without thinking. I probably am underestimating you; I know. But this is a strange world to you. People may not always do what you think they should. And Sacha is very young, much too young to be told the truth."

Silence filled the room. A log on the fire hissed and crackled, but the sound barely intruded as Celene and I faced each other, watchfully, him considering, my head pounding painfully with new stress and concern. I had forgotten Israfel.

When he spoke, his voice startled me.

"Celene," he said quietly, "times here are different now. The child is too young. Our situation here is far more important than a point of pride. You know that."

Celene turned to Israfel, regarding him with curious, almost doubting eyes. They were silent, communicating now in their own way. Celene relaxed and at last turned back to me with his beautiful smile.

"Have no fear," he said. "I shall not tell her – nor will I hurt her."

I looked at the smile, the face, the eyes. I sighed. "Celene, that could be very difficult."

He left soon after, quite cheerfully. I returned to the couch in the living room and collapsed on it with a sigh. Israfel, still kneeling before the fire, gave me a quizzical look.

You see, Laura? In his own lifetime, he is still young.

I pulled a cushion beneath my neck, settled into the soft cushioning of the couch. The extended communication of this evening and our shared efforts had brought a unity, a slight bridging of the gulf between us that I was glad of. The closer he came to us, the easier he would be to live with; the more sociable and lenient he was, the better he could be integrated into the community of our neighbors and friends. The different aspects of his life, even his age, no longer seemed so utterly foreign. The silver eyes watching me didn't bother me at all. I let my aching head fall back, wondered how Celene was faring, what was happening in the house at the bottom of the hill.

Don't worry, Laura. Celene is managing very well. Jesse is playing his guitar, and everyone is singing. A most meaningless song. Something about nature and rocks singing. Farrand doesn't understand it.

I smiled. I never had, either.

The curiosity has faded, and Farrand does appear to have been accepted. But it won't be so easy for Celene and me.

I tilted my head and looked at him.

Wearing dark blue slacks and the light blue and gray sweater I had given him as a Christmas present, he at first appeared insubstantial, slight, little more than an illusion in the flickering light of the fire. But then the power and strength were revealed in the poise of the slender body. Even the unlikely kneeling position couldn't detract from an inherent vigor, a vital energy, the potent life force that was far beyond the human scale. I studied him as objectively as I was able, saw his eyes reflecting glints of flame from the fire, their metallic sheen turning to copper. Unreal. No, the face was not that of any man. He was right. He and Celene would never be anything but alien, not belonging here. And yet to me, now, that wasn't the least disturbing.

He rose to his feet in one lithe movement and stood, looking down at me.

Laura, Celene is also angered by our debt to you. This world offends him, and he resents our dependence on your kindness, your hospitality, even your protection. In his lifetime he is young. I am not. I have learned understanding, but then I've been here before—

What? I was astonished. *When? When were you here before?*

Not very long ago – long ago in your lifetime, but not in mine.

He came a few steps nearer, and I stared at him, my headache again forgotten.

What did you do?

Explored, studied, examined. This world was very primitive then, and violent. We thought its people were young enough to grow, had the potential to develop and learn—

His mind snapped shut like a trap. I saw his lips tighten, his eyes widen for a single moment, then become a hard cold glitter. The mask of stern discipline covered his face, and the sharing was gone.

I pressed. *And?*

His head lifted, turned away from me. His eyes fixed on the Christmas tree filling a corner of the room, its colored lights twinkling, the tinsel and ornaments gleaming among the dark branches. I waited, watching his face.

A warrior. It was the face of a warrior on an ancient frieze from the ruins of a pagan temple, carved in stone by an unknown sculptor who had seen such men-at-arms – or had they been gods? – driving their chariots and fiery horses into wild battles of furious combat. I had seen pictures of such relics, had been drawn to them because of the magnificent sculpting of the horses, horses that looked like those we now bred.

I blinked my eyes in disbelief. What a curious comparison! How could I relate Israfel, this exquisitely civilized being from beyond the stars, to those early warriors depicted in crumbling ancient friezes? But his face, the stamp it bore, was like those. I was certain of it.

Warriors born are always warriors, Laura. His silent voice struck into my mind. His eyes turned back to me, and in them I saw pain. *But I am a warrior no longer. Don't even think it – in any context. I have failed and will relinquish my command.*

Israfel! This was a sharing I hadn't expected, and my unlikely thoughts were forgotten. *You haven't failed!*

I have. My ship is buried beneath the soil of this planet, severely damaged, unusable. My crew and I are stranded here, with no communication, in constant danger. And the blame for that is mine.

But you're safe! I protested. *And so are Farrand and Celene. Your ship is hidden; Farrand is repairing your communicator. You were shot down. How can you feel so blameworthy?*

For a long time, he said nothing, although his mind was open to me. But it was flying so fast I couldn't even catch a glimpse of what was passing through it. His eyes were distant, his face withdrawn, his expression unrevealing. The fire had burned down to coals, and total silence filled the house.

I waited until at last his mind slowed and reached mine. *There are differences between us*, he said, *that are inevitable. Your life is so dissimilar to mine, but we are both what we have come to be. We each must accept that, as I do my failure.*

But you mustn't believe you've failed, I interjected swiftly. *That's acknowledging defeat, and one must go on fighting, or you'll never get anywhere.* I said this last phrase with reluctance, knowing I had no right to push him, remembering his retaliation when I had presumed to attack him before.

He knelt beside me and looked searchingly into my eyes. *That is the distinction of a young, developing life. It has no part in mine because I was born for a purpose – created, if you like, to fill a specific role. Without that I am nothing.*

But you have a brain, intelligence, the ability, surely, to do a thousand other things. Israfel, forgive me for saying this, but we judge people by what they do, and the greats are those who win battles – not necessarily by acts of physical prowess but by overcoming obstacles and getting up and fighting back. That's a form of winning too.

You can't judge me in the same context as you would people of this earth.

Why not? A principle is a principle, and fighters don't quit. No one worth their salt just gives up.

The incompetent resign, if they have a fragment of decency.

You aren't incompetent. You were shot down.

That was my fault.

At an impasse, I stared at him, into the silver eyes – so close I could see the faint rings of purple that marked the edge of the irises. Even the whites were silver, just slightly different in texture. The pupils were black and deep, endless, as wide as a cats' in the soft light of the room. Then he distracted me completely.

Laura, your head is aching. Will you let me take the pain away?

I was as startled by the sudden change of topic as his suggestion.

Take . . . it away?

Yes. I can very easily if you'll let me.

How?

I'll show you.

His hand reached to my hair and there was a quick tightening of my chest, catching my breath. I pressed back into the corner of the couch.

I won't hurt you. Surely you know that?

Already his fingers had found my scalp, were moving, searching, feeling for tiny points that felt like needle pricks as he touched them. Then he was pressing, very lightly, but the bones began to feel eggshell thin, fragile, as sensitive as a bruise.

Apprehensive, I looked at the face I had never seen so close and that now seemed so different. There was a faint drawing of concentration at the inner corners of the fine brows, and the eyes were more black than silver. Such incredible skin, translucent, thin. Farrand and Celene shaved, I knew, but Israfel grew no beard. And his mouth – sensitive, strong, disciplined, and distinctly male. I closed my eyes at the sudden awareness of his nearness and pushed even further into the corner of the couch.

His fingers moved to my temples, and I realized the pain was withdrawing, the tension dissipating, but I kept my eyes closed, afraid now to look at him, to see his face so near.

He took his hands away and the ache was gone.

"That's better," I whispered. "How did you do that?"

By touching the right places, the right way.

"Could you show me how to do it?"

It takes many years to learn.

I opened my eyes, saw he was faintly smiling. *In your years or mine?*

Both.

Still, he knelt there, far too close. I hurried behind a barricade of words, questions with which to deflect the intensity of his eyes.

Israfel, what's your life like? Where you live, do you have a house? A family? I rushed on, aware that he may not like these questions, but I took refuge in them just the same. *Have you any children? Animals? What kind of system do you live in?*

His smile faded. *My life, Laura? My life has never been my own, for I was dedicated to . . . well, more than a vocation or calling . . . my work, if you like. I have no family as such. There are no wives, as you call them, where I come from. It's a very structured, technical society, one I'm not . . .*

His mind veered away, then began to stream along the edge of mine, I think perhaps by accident. For a few fleeting moments I obtained glimpses of faces, extraordinary buildings, great bursts of color and dazzling stars, heard faint trills amid sounds of incredible music, and saw a white pavilion beneath spreading trees amid masses of flowers high on a grassy hill. Then he realized I could see, and his mind closed with its customary abruptness. I was left in empty darkness.

"Don't," I said.

He rose to his feet, stepped away from me. His head lifted, and he again became the alien commander I had first known.

"Please don't."

Don't what?

Don't shut yourself away from me like this.

There are times when I must.

Why?

Again, there was that faint drawing at the inner corners of his brows, and his lips tightened.

Laura, I recognize your sympathy, your concern, even your curiosity. But I have to remember we are of different worlds, that we are really very far part. Because of who and what we are, I cannot give you free access to my mind. Do you understand?

For a long time, I looked at him, at the distance in his eyes, the disciplined set of his mouth, the alien face that was not of his world.

"I think so," I whispered at last.

CHAPTER FIFTEEN

BOXING DAY BROUGHT VISITORS. IT had long been our custom to have friends and neighbors in for drinks and cake, sausage rolls and mince pies, to keep the house open all day long. And our road being generally impassable by then, they come on snowmobiles or cross-country skis, snowshoes or in four-wheel drive vehicles. This Boxing Day proved no exception, and the first to arrive was Sacha.

Celene and Jesse had been uninformative about her upon their return the previous night, Jesse saying he had been too involved with the music to pay her much heed, and Celene giving me a coldly warning glance that prevented further questioning. But in the middle of the morning on the following day, Sacha slid in on cross-country skis.

Her cheeks were glowing and her eyes just as bright. Dressed in a pretty scarlet outfit, her hair streaming from beneath a matching woolen toque, she was a picture of teenage youth and boisterous good health. I regarded her in dismay.

"Hi, Laura! My mom and aunt and the others are going to drive around and then ski in from the road. I guess I beat them, huh?" She was somewhat out of breath.

"Yes, you did. Good heavens, Sacha! Did you come all up the hill on those?"

She was snapping off the skis, her hair falling around her. "Sure. It was kind of hard work," she admitted. "But it'll be easier going back." She leaned the skis and poles against the wall of the house. "Does Len have skis? I meant to ask him last night but didn't get a chance."

"No, he doesn't. I don't know if he even skis."

She stood looking at me with large wistful blue eyes.

The cold air bit into my face. I remembered how chilly it had been when we fed the horses earlier, and I thought of the long steep climb the girl had traversed up the hill. I suddenly felt sorry for her.

"Come in and get warmed up, Sacha. Would you like some hot chocolate or something?"

She followed me into the house and shed her boots and coat in the utility room. What had to be her best white sweater was underneath, and again I felt dismay, wished there was something I could say to deter her from Celene.

The object of her attentions was standing in the kitchen, looking devastatingly gorgeous, as Patty would have said. He gave us both the full assault of his overpowering smile and drew a chair near the stove for Sacha to sit on.

She collapsed onto it, apparently too overwhelmed to speak or even to look at him for long. I put water in the kettle, set it on the range.

"Sacha came up on cross-country skis," I explained to Celene. "She must be frozen."

He said nothing, but Sacha found her voice and spoke in a rush. "Oh, it wasn't cold . . . coming up the hill . . . I mean, I soon got warm."

He stood near the stove, his lofty gaze bent on her, and she flushed, hurrying on. "I wondered, do you have skis, Len? The snow's just great, and it's getting warmer out all the time. Look!" Her eyes turned to the window. "See? The sun's coming out."

Fresh concern caught at me. Did she know how he felt the cold? Had he told her? Could this meeting have been prearranged? Just what was he up to?

Suspicions raced through my mind, and I looked at him with barely concealed anger. The brilliant blue eyes met mine steadily, then turned to Sacha.

"I don't ski, Sacha," he said, quite gently. "I've never even tried."

"Oh, you should!" she burst out. "It's just great fun! Isn't it, Laura?"

If she was hinting that I should lend Celene my skis, she could forget it. I tried to smile noncommittally and turned my attention to mixing a mug of hot chocolate for her.

"I'll come out and watch you," Celene said.

Israfel! I cried silently. *What is he doing?*

Celene had only set foot outside the house twice since we had brought them here.

Let him be. Israfel spoke to me, calmly reassuring. *All will be well.*

But, in spite of his words, my misgivings lingered as I watched them go off together along the road, Celene bundled up in Farrand's coat and boots, Sacha so slim and pretty in her red clothes. Then the arrival of other people made me forget them temporarily – Maureen and Ted on snowshoes, pulling Dennie on a sled and bearing a poinsettia in a pot for me.

Farrand and Israfel came downstairs when they heard the new arrivals and remained in the background as much as they could, but I saw Israfel's eyes light up behind the dark glasses at the sight of the plant in my hand.

Beth and Patty and the cross-country ski party came soon after, filling the house with noise and laughter, and I no longer had time to even think of Sacha and Celene.

He came back alone, just as the guests were leaving, and spoke to them politely at the door while a rush of thoughts concerning Sacha swarmed through my head. Where was she? What had he done with her? What had happened?

"Sacha has skied back," he explained to Beth and a worried-looking Roger. "She said she'd try to beat you home."

Feeling somewhat foolish, I made sandwiches for lunch. He stood by, helping me with a generosity that was surely a form of atonement, and told me what had happened.

"It was very simple," he said. "When she wanted to talk about something called Elvis Presley, I changed the subject to Plato. I asked her whether she agreed with Aristotle's philosophy, what theory she had as to why the Egyptian Kings died so young, whether Charles the second was a good ruler, whether she knew a good ruler, and if she knew where the remains of mammoths could be found. She was embarrassed not to know, so I told her what I thought of the philosophies of Spinoza and Nietzsche, went to great lengths to explain the differences I had found between Kant and Jung, and asked her whether she regarded Einstein as a genius and if the Mayans were clones. I gave her my ideas as to why they had suddenly vanished, and asked her for hers, and was very surprised when she said she had never heard of the

Mayans. At this point," he went on, giving me a sidelong smile, "I think she was becoming somewhat bored."

I stared at him in amazement, barely noticing the juice from a half sliced tomato dripping down my hand.

"Then I asked her what she thought of Karl Marx and his politics, whether he was more influential than Lenin, and if she had ever seen the latter's tomb. When she said no, I asked her if she had seen Edward the Confessor's or Milton's. At this point we reached the small hill on the hay field, and she skied away down it. I waited until she came back, then immediately asked her whether she liked *The Iliad* and Dante's *Inferno*. She said she hadn't seen either, and if she wanted to beat her folks back to the house, she had better leave. I think she was quite glad to get away from me," he added reminiscently.

"Celene!" I exclaimed while laughter and relief boiled inside me. "You're a marvel!"

He gave me another sidelong smile. "No. I am only older than I look. But it is well you showed me how to read your books. Thank you."

Throughout the afternoon, people came, and our three house guests were again the objects of many curious eyes. But somehow, we managed to steer most questions aside, keep Israfel, Farrand, and Celene away from the most curious while still giving the impression there was nothing untoward about them, that we were accustomed to having them here. Being in our own home made it a little easier to do, and the preceding day's dinner party had given them some experience with other people. Then the early fall of darkness sent most of them away, and Jesse played his guitar for Anne and Jason, the only ones left, who could go all the way home on their snowmobile.

The evening was ours, and we spent it grouped around the fire in the closest state to companionableness we had known since they had arrived. I was tired after the exertions and strains of the day. I felt myself letting go now that all the visitors had gone, and I could see Israfel, Farrand, and Celene reacting similarly. Only Jesse was lively and alert, elevated by his music, still riding high on Anne's and Jason's appreciation, the intensity of his devotion to his art.

He threw another log on the fire, poked it until yellow flames sprang into life around it, then added yet more wood. I curled in a corner of the couch and watched the illumination of Israfel's slender form as he knelt beside the hearth, the blue fire reflected in Celene's eyes. Farrand sat quietly in a chair beyond the fireplace, his face in shadow, but I could read the tiredness in his pose, knew what a strain the ordeal of the last two days must have been for him. He concentrated his attention entirely on the communicator, on the tremendous task of repairing it, and I knew how he disliked distractions. But he was too tired to go and work on it this night.

Jesse stretched out in another chair, his eyes on Israfel, but his next comment was for them all. "You've never told us where you came from."

Israfel answered him, and his reply was the same he'd given me. "It would mean nothing to you if we told you."

"No?"

"What would a name convey when it is something you have never known?"

Jesse digested this in silence for a while, then he nodded. "Okay. I see your point. So, tell me this, then. How come you speak our language?"

"It too is universal. All languages were originally. They have undergone many changes throughout the centuries, of course. But by picking up your radio signals from time to time, we have been able to keep up to date."

Jesse was startled. "Our radio signals?"

"Certainly."

"Then . . . " Jesse sat up straight as a new idea came to him. "Why couldn't we radio for help for you?"

Israfel smiled faintly. "It is very unlikely that the signal would be picked up. If it were intercepted and recorded, that it should be collected in the near future is again most unlikely."

I could see that Jesse was beginning to burst with questions, but then something about Israfel prevented him from asking them. And I too could feel a strong force issuing form Israfel's mind, brushing against mine, taking control – not of Jesse but of the situation. Jesse hesitated, uncertainty in his eyes, then he fell back in his chair as though believing that further questions could be impolite or presumptuous.

"Too bad," he said. "Poor Farrand is having one hell of a job with your communicator."

"I know." Israfel spoke softly, and his eyes moved to look at Farrand, understanding and sympathetic.

A bowl of fresh mixed nuts stood on the coffee table, and I began cracking them to distract myself from the atmosphere I could still sense. I passed the kernels around willy-nilly, conscious of Celene's and Israfel's care not to touch my fingers, of the coolness of Farrand's palm when I placed a large Brazil nut on it.

"I'm so limited by what I have," Farrand said.

"I wonder," Jesse said, "if there might be anything . . . well, like radio and television components that you could utilize."

"I'm thinking about bringing the ship up again, seeing if there's anything in there I could use." Farrand sounded tired and depressed, strained and despondent, and my heart moved toward him with sympathy and concern.

"But I don't think you should do that," I said as gently as I could. "It's just all nicely covered with snow."

"I know. It would only be a last report. But I may yet have to."

We declined two invitations to New Year's Eve parties. The Christmas venture had been enough of an ordeal, and I felt I couldn't possibly face another so soon. And each invitation was extended without hesitation to include our house guests. We saw the new year in with a glass of wine before the fire, unavoidably thinking about what it was going to bring.

Two days later, Jesse's agent phoned from Los Angeles with a contract offer for the score of a major motion picture. I heard the immediate excitement in Jesse's voice, saw his knuckles whiten as his hand gripped the receiver hard, and felt a new concern rising in me.

He was scribbling details, his eyes and face intent with concentration, and I knew that I, our alien visitors, this house, the horses, and our difficult situation were all being swept from his mind as it filled with his trust and greater love: his passion for his muse that was his life's blood.

The question reared as a giant. What was he going to do? Everything was different. He couldn't go. But why didn't he say? He was still taking notes, interspersed with *yeah*s and *great*s. Then, to my horror, he looked at his watch, the receiver jammed between his shoulder and neck, and said, "Yeah," again.

"Okay," he finished up at last. "The day after tomorrow. If not, I'll call you." He hung up and turned to me with his eyes distracted but also alive with that familiar excitement.

"Oh, wow! Laura! That's fantastic!" Words spilled, tumbling over one another – about the contract, the movie, the stars, the settings, the director – while he paced restlessly about the room, already impatient to be gone.

"But . . . how can you go?" My voice was tight and grating with desperation and disbelief.

"How can I . . . ?" He left the sentence unfinished, staring at me in astonishment. "Laura, I must go. You know that. You've always known that the music has to come first."

"Aren't you forgetting something?"

"No. What?"

"Our three visitors."

"What about them?" He even looked annoyed. "There's been no trouble. And if there were, my being here isn't going to make any difference."

"I don't really want to be alone with them," I said.

"Why ever not? Farrand will help you with the horses. Christ! I'd have thought you'd be glad not to be alone!"

This wasn't at all what I'd expected. Jesse's reaction startled me. Although I had always understood the priority of his music, had frequently been alone before when he had gone down to LA to work on a score, I thought our current circumstances put the situation in an entirely different light, but it seemed Jesse disagreed.

He stared at my unhappy face, perplexed. "For Pete's sake, Laura! You're not afraid of them, are you?" And when I said nothing, he continued, "Celene and Israfel can't stand to even have us near them, and Farrand is far too honorable a sort to ever suspect of shabby designs. Besides, they need us; their safety depends on us. They aren't going to jeopardize that."

"It's just . . . " My voice trailed away as I knew any argument I offered would seem entirely foolish. And I had always agreed that his music was of prime importance and must always be put first and had let him go without any protest.

"Listen, I'll come back on the weekends if that'll make you any happier," he said.

"All that way—" I began.

"I can't pass this up, Laura. It's far too great an opportunity to miss."

"No, no, of course." I forced a smile, squeezed his hand. "And if I know you'll be back on weekends—"

"And I can do a lot of the work here."

"Yes, I suppose so."

His eyes were turning from me, his mind already occupied with plans and preparations and flights, deciding what clothes to take, which guitar. I had experienced this many times before, but never like this! Never with such trepidation when I thought of what I was going to be left alone in the house with: three beings from another planet.

I drove him to the airport on Sunday afternoon and watched him go in his boots and fraying, faded jeans, in the fringed and beaded jacket and the battered leather hat that invariably brought jaundiced eyes of officialdom on him at airport customs. In these outlandish clothes, with his guitar case slung across his shoulder and a shabby holdall hanging from his hand, he was another variation of the Jesse I knew.

And on that day, I found myself considering another Jesse, the one who went away and left his wife alone in the house with three aliens, with the army hunting nearby for the spaceship he had buried on his property, with the possibility of an explosive situation developing at any time.

It's his music, I told myself as I turned away. *His music is his life, after all. It always has been and always will. I am a separate entity, tied to him by the legal formality of marriage, a partner in the everyday affair of living. I may have his heart, but music has his soul.*

But this explanation did not ease my strong discomfiture at his departure, what he had been so ready to leave me with.

The winter's early darkness was gathering as I drove home, driving slowly at first as I tried to prolong the journey before I'd arrive at the house alone. But then the old anxieties began to invade my so readily troubled mind. What if someone came while I was away? Sunday afternoons were prime times for visitors. Could I reach Israfel's mind from this distance? I called to him but received no answer and began to drive faster along the winding highway. The lakes flowed by me as I passed trackless fields of shadowed gray in the fading light, the hills that ringed them bare silhouettes against a softly glowing sky, with occasional peaks and shoulders gleaming as they caught the last rays of the falling sun, snows tinted to pearl.

But I scarcely saw them as I hurried, urged by the pressure of anxiety that pushed me homeward, by the whistling of the slightly opened quarter vent.

The journey spanned a scant fifty miles, but they seemed like a hundred, with one slow vehicle after another impeding my impatient progress until I could find a place to pass. My hands grew damp on the steering wheel, and all my muscles burned with tension until at last I reached Highway Six, devoid of traffic, and I could fly.

But when I finally turned onto the forestry road, bumped along it between pitch-black trees, and saw only the tracks of our own wheels cutting through the snow, worries about their safety left me, and the only concern I found myself harboring was that I was alone – very alone – with them.

The house was almost in darkness. Only a faint glow from the dining room windows indicated that a lamp was on in the living room beyond. Sally came bouncing to meet me, and when I stepped from the truck into the cold fresh air, into the stillness, I could hear the horses crunching hay, realized they had been fed, and felt a surge of gratitude toward Farrand.

Israfel met me at the door, looked at me with disconcertingly perceptive eyes, and spoke to me in silence.

Welcome home, Laura. I'm glad you're back. Farrand has fed the horses, and Celene has stoked the furnace. I lit the fire in the living room and the kitchen stove. And Laura, we'll do all we can to help you while Jesse is away. You know that, don't you?

My glance passed fleetingly over his perfect face and briefly met the silver eyes before falling in a sudden shyness I thought I had long grown out of. I tried to fill my mind with ordinary thoughts so he would not notice it, visualized potatoes and lamb chops, carrots and green peas, gravy, mint sauce, and cherry pie.

If he realized what my mind was doing, he gave no sign, and he went on, gently reassuring.

Celene is already preparing a meal for us, so you don't have to worry about that.
Celene? Cooking? This was a surprise.

He smiled. *It is not beyond him.*

I hung up my coat, picked up a button that fell from it as I did so, and pulled on my slippers, still avoiding his eyes. But I was very conscious of them on my back as he followed me into kitchen, on my face at the dinner table that night, and throughout the evening as he knelt by the fire, and I tried to sew together the splitting seams of a pair of my jeans.

There was little communication between us, and this served to intensify my feelings, not of isolation but of being out of my depth, abandoned to a sphere in which I did not belong. If Israfel was aware of this – and I was sure he was – he gave me little indication. I could see gentleness in his face and eyes, but his thoughts were not mine to share as his mind remained firmly closed. I felt too awkward to press.

At dinner I had found little to talk about, other than thanking Celene for his efforts in the kitchen and asking Farrand how he was progressing with his tedious and difficult task. It was Israfel who helped me clear the table, deal with the dishes, and clean up while I wished he wouldn't. His presence was disconcerting enough. Almost I would have preferred him to be the aloof and dispassionate, stern-faced and disciplined commander I had first known, as remote and distant as the star he called home. Not this quiet, gentle, helpful being with those too preceptive eyes.

Pleading tiredness, I went to bed early, lay for a long time listening to the silence in the house and the surrounding winter forest, thought of Jesse, gone into his other life, and my three unlikely companions, so uncomfortably close to me in mine.

To escape them, I went shopping in the morning, stocking up on groceries we didn't really need, using the errand as an excuse to leave the house.

At lunch time, Israfel's eyes were constantly on me, distractingly aware, making me feel clumsy and shy and unable to do anything about it. I couldn't find the words to say something that wasn't embarrassing, even if I could have brought myself to try. It seemed best to pretend I hadn't noticed.

But in the afternoon, I went out again and took the long unused Gallant for some exercise in the cold pale sunshine, not knowing that this venture was going to put me wholly into Israfel's hands, make me totally dependent on him, completely incapacitated.

He said nothing when I told him I was going, only looked at me with knowledgeable eyes, a faint smile of understanding on his mouth. This too was disconcerting, and my efforts to appear indifferent only brought an equal expression of discernment. It was with relief that I closed and locked the door behind me, hurrying to the barn.

I took our exit road through the forestry reserve, then turned west and followed the road up the mountain, the one we had come back on after our encounter with Captain Forrest. Gallant was fresh, almost high, tossing his head repeatedly, blowing hard through his nostrils and mouthing the bit impatiently. But the climb was steep and held him in check until we reached the top, the wide white swath cutting across the mountains where the pylons stood so incongruously.

There I gave him his head and let him run, feeling the cold wind streaming through my hair, bringing tears to my eyes, biting into my face with icy sharp teeth as he galloped, snorting at the wind.

The snow on the trail had been packed by snowmobile tracks, but I saw no one, nothing moving except a raven wheeling slowly in the wintry sky.

I took the next road down, the one that would bring me to the western boundary of our property and take me back across the High Meadow. Again, the hill was steep, and I was hard-pressed to hold Gallant back to a safe and steady walk. Fired, he still wanted to run, and his customary eagerness to get back to the barn was also exerting its pressure.

But his steps slowed as we neared the High Meadow roadway, and his ears flicked constantly, back and forth, listening for something he had not forgotten. He mouthed the bit again, uneasy, and tossed his head fretfully as remembered fear preyed on his narrow habit-conscious mind.

His head swung incessantly as we entered the High Meadow and traversed its length, and I could feel his muscles bunched and hard, ready to hurl him into instant instinctive flight. I spoke to him soothingly, patted his neck, and stroked his mane, but he paid me little heed, moving with a stiffly springing step under the control of nervous tension. Foam flew from his mouth as his teeth ground against the bit, and I kept all my attention on him, prepared for him to run away or try to buck me off.

From the corner of my eye I saw that the thick white blanket of snow covering the meadow effectively concealed all signs of what had happened there, of Farrand and Jesse's activities. The snow was like icing sugar, just as smooth, puffing dustily around Gallant's dancing hooves. The meadow looked at it always did in winter: branches of evergreens bent their thick white burdens, sweeping low to the ground while the bare birches held the snow on every branch and twig. There was little color, and the unseen sun was already gone behind the mountain and left the clouded sky dreary and cold, the short winter's day drawing to an early close.

Gallant fought for his head once he was through the gate and on the narrow High Meadow Road, wanting once more to run, to leave this alarming place behind. But I held him back, made him walk. His neck was damp with a nervous sweat, his flanks steaming, and it would be bad to arrive home on a lathered horse, especially on a chilly winter day.

Gallant at last seceded to me, walked more decorously along the road, across the bridge, over the creek, and up the hill beyond.

I relaxed in the saddle, and then knowledge of my imminent arrival home, of the long evening before me, filled my mind and distracted me from Gallant. Reluctance flooded me. Once more I became aware of loneliness, vulnerability, and shyness, of the lack of support Jesse's presence provided, of my discomfort at being alone in the house with them, with Israfel being able to read my mind, and of the closer relationship that had existed between us since that Christmas night.

But darkness was falling and it was rapidly growing colder. I would not linger out here for long, and Gallant was hungry for his evening meal. I could visualize Farrand already in the barn, putting hay into feeders, taking himself away from his crucial work, and wondering what had become of me. I urged Gallant into a trot, and two grouse exploded from the roadside, bursting into startled flight right beneath his nose.

Alert for danger, he wildly flung himself backward, almost unseating me. I wished he had, for a fallen log lay there, across the path of his plunging hooves, tripping him, making him fall sidelong over it.

I heard his gasping snort of fear, felt the furious spasm of all his muscles as they responded to the threatening danger, sensed the panic that was now erupting in his face, and struggled to counter his frantic staggering as he desperately tried to stay on his feet. But his momentum was too great. His weight and his leap from danger carried him on, making him stumble and fall over the log.

Snow-covered branches caught in my hair, tangling and pulling while sharp sticks stabbed viciously into my back and neck. They forced me against the lurching, falling horse, prevented me from scrambling clear of him. Icy snow filled my hair, my eyes, and ran inside my collar while twigs snapped against me and branches cracked and raked me with hard, rough claws. One cut my cheek, narrowly missing my eye, and I heard myself whimpering, "No! No!" I clung desperately to the reins. They were the only hold I had on anything, but needless to say, they did me no good.

Gallant came down with a crash in snow and dead branches, flinging me almost clear as he still struggled valiantly to keep his feet. But my left leg was caught beneath him, and I heard it break with a sickening and horrifying, deep and wrenching crack.

Pain roared through me, thundered in my brain, my whole being screaming silently in terror. For an instant I wondered if the horse would roll over me, crushing me horribly, thought of Jesse, so terribly far away. And Israfel . . . Israfel . . . His name tore through clouding mists of pain, and then everything was gone.

CHAPTER SIXTEEN

I SWAM INTO COLDNESS, DARKNESS, ice and snow and an ocean of pain. And someone was calling me. Although I could hear no voice, my name sounded and resounded throughout my head.

I'm here. I'm here.

What had happened? Where was I? What was I doing lying in this mess of snow and broken branches? What had happened to my leg? And that voice . . .

Laura! Laura!

Jesse! No. Jesse was gone, away. *I'm here. I'm here.*

Something moved between me and the sky. A dark silhouette was framed before the deepening gray. Laura!

He bent toward me. Why were there stars? So close . . .

Laura! What happened? Laura!

His hands touched my shoulders, slid beneath me, began to lift.

No! I tried to scream the word, but my lips were frozen. *Don't move me! My leg! Oh, God, my leg!*

The movement ceased. A cold hand touched my face.

Your leg?

Yes. It must be broken.

My face was held between cold hands, and I could see the silver of his eyes — not stars.

Laura, there is no pain. No pain. Laura, no pain.

The silent voice filled my head with its strength and power, it's incredible influence. The pain ebbed from my leg, leaving it feeling numb. Even the stinging scratches on my face began to ease.

Israfel . . .

Yes. I'm here, Laura. Now be still. I'm going to take you back to the house. But you must keep very still.

I'll need an ambulance. You can't move me. Israfel, you'll have to telephone . . . get help . . . a doctor . . .

No, Laura. Just trust me, please.

But my leg's broken! I almost whispered the words out loud, and terror loomed, fear. Was he afraid to call someone, not wanting any intruders? Was he sacrificing me for his and the others' safety? Didn't he care about what happened to me?

I know. But if you'll keep still, it won't hurt you. And I must get you back to the house.

The hands were slipping beneath me again, lifting me. The ice and snow and hard sticks were slipping beneath me again. Then they were gone, and his arms held me firmly against his chest. The silver eyes were intent on mine.

Don't move, Laura. Don't move.

I was trembling – with cold or shock or fear or possibly all three. But it stilled as his eyes held mine. He walked up the hill and across the snowy fields, carrying me as though I weighed no more than a loaf of bread. I was not very heavy, not very big, but it was a long way to carry someone, and the snow was deep and cumbering. He moved, however, with his customary lack of visible effort while I watched with painful longing for the windows of the house to glow among the trees. I kept my face carefully averted from the one too close to mine in my alarming predicament. It was bad enough that he had to carry me.

Farrand was waiting at the end of the road, but he too looked alien, his eyes blank hollows in the gloom beneath the trees, his slender form spidery and odd against the floodlit snow in the yard behind me. I was alone here, with them, helpless and utterly at their mercy – at the mercy of beings not of this earth.

Israfel's arms tightened, and he spoke to me softly. *Farrand has taken care of the horse. Your steed appears to be undamaged. He has fed the others and brought the young ones in. Don't worry.*

There was the house – but I wanted a doctor, the hospital, Jesse – thought of phoning him in LA and asking him to come back, of getting Maureen or

Mac to drive me to Vernon. Farrand said, "We'll look after you, Laura," and his words didn't reassure me one bit. Then Israfel's mind took total control of me.

I tried to resist, but it was futile, of course. We were in the house, and his hands were undoing buttons, zippers, buckles, taking off my boots. The lamp beside my bed showed me glimpses of his face, his eyes, while I seemed to be drifting within a cloud of floating mist. When I struggled against him, the words, *Don't move, Laura. Don't move,* swiftly stilled me. I tried to speak, to protest, but was stopped again by that silent voice. Then I think I slept.

There was a hand on my shoulder. I could feel it through the thin fabric of my nightgown. A cool hand, for I was warm, a hand that was waking me when I wanted to sleep. I opened my eyes and looked into Israfel's.

"What . . . ?"

My leg felt strange, my body wrenched and bruised. *Gallant . . . falling . . .* I remembered with a surge of alarm, tried to sit up.

His hand pressed me down. *Don't move, Laura. You must keep still.*

"But I want Jesse . . . must phone him. Israfel, help me, let me—"

"No." he spoke out loud, as though the sound of his voice would calm me. It didn't. My heart and my breath all seemed to flutter in my throat. "Laura, don't, please. Don't try to move. I'll get Jesse for you if you really want him. But there's no need."

"No need? I do need him! And a doctor . . . hospital . . . Israfel, you must realize—"

"Laura! I've repaired your leg. Can't you feel it? Does it still hurt?"

I forced myself to subside into a semblance of calm. And it was true. Other than a strange tight stiffness, I couldn't feel any pain in my leg at all.

But you must stay still for a day or so, give it time to strengthen, for the break to completely heal.

I lay still, disbelieving. His hand left my shoulder, and he straightened and drew away. *You see?*

I nodded, weak, but knew what he said was true.

⬡

Sometime in the night I woke, dismayed because I had to go to the bathroom. I wondered what I should do. My leg felt comfortable but stiff, and I knew enough to not move it. The other need was pressing, but I couldn't bring myself to call him. I cursed my helplessness, my vulnerability, nature's determined demand, wished again for Jesse.

Israfel came, unseen in the darkness.

What's the matter, Laura? What do you want?

I had to tell him, embarrassed, my face burning.

Don't let it trouble you. We're all physical beings.

Yes, weren't we! The flush of mortification spreading across my throat, dampening my skin as he drew the covers back, found me unerringly, and lifted my thinly clad body into his arms. The chest I was held against was definitely male, the arms as strong as any man's. My flesh was immediately aware of his hands on my shoulder and hip as the flimsy nylon of my nightgown seemed to have no more substance than woven gossamer. I tried to hold myself away from this intimacy by being stiff and impersonal while the heat of embarrassment seared my cheeks and telltale moisture grew beneath the hand on the bare skin of my shoulder.

He said nothing, put me down in the bathroom, and switched on the light. What felt like a padded vice closed around my leg, just below the knee where the break had occurred, and then the door was closing behind him.

Put as little weight on it as possible, he instructed me from beyond the door, *and I'll come back as soon as you need me.*

My breath was fluttering again, and I stared at the mirror's reflection, at the unbecoming red of my face, and tried to restore some order to myself. I combed twigs and needles and fragments of bark out of the tangle of my hair and washed my face, noticing that the scratch that sliced across my cheek was almost healed.

Regrettably, I had no spare robe in the bathroom, so I switched off the light before I called him. But he had turned on the lamp in the bedroom, and again I felt exposed as he returned me to my bed. However, he didn't seem to notice my embarrassment or the gleam of skin through the pale ecru. Instead, he gave me a look that was comforting in its sympathy. He had brought two glasses of wine and some digestive biscuits. He now knelt on the rug with a glass glowing like a jewel in his hand, his body slender and graceful in the dark blue velour robe Jesse had bought for him. *Relax, Laura. All is well.*

Sensitive, kind, gentle Israfel, who had miraculously healed my leg, was caring for me with warmth, comfort, and security. Sharer of my thoughts, fellow traveler on a different journey, partner in an uncommon enterprise. What did it matter if he was from another world?

Israfel . . . I haven't thanked you . . . I tried to find words that were eluding me, slipping away in a mistiness inside my head. *. . . for what you've done.*

I don't need any thanks, Laura.

He was standing over me, and I hadn't seen him rise. I tried to focus on him, but all I could see were elusive images of a faintly smiling mouth and eyes gleaming through a fog. His hand reached toward me, and I felt the glass slip from my fingers. I drifted away as though I'd been drugged.

⁂

A half glass of wine and two uneaten cookies were on my bedside table, and I stared at them as they brought recollection. Sunlit trees shone beyond the partly opened drapes, and I could hear the harsh cry of a raven. But that was all. I lay still, afraid to move because of my leg, and listened. No other sound. There was a complete and total silence within the house.

Fear gripped me. Had someone come? Taken them? Or could it be that they'd gone away and left me? Was I there alone? What had happened?

Israfel! Israfel! My call was instinctive.

His reply came so fiercely, with such shocking sudden force, it struck into my head like pain. There were no distinguishable words – only a response and a powerful emotion that I didn't understand. I felt as though a hurricane was blowing through my brain, sweeping all thought and reason away, leaving nothing in its wake, not even devastation – only a great blank emptiness.

It was gone as swiftly as it had come. A hand closed around my wrist, drew it from my face where I had pressed it. I looked up into the silver eyes, saw them glittering in the early morning light, his mouth strained and tense.

Thought began to return, but I could find none of his. He released my wrist and turned away, went to the window and pulled the drapes all the way back. I watched him and slowly, insidiously, flowing into the empty places of the brain, came a different nebulous uneasiness.

⁂

Until Jesse's return at the weekend, they cared for me, the house, and the animals with a care and proficiency that I could find no fault in. Celene cooked; Farrand took care of the horses, the cat in the barn, and Sally, and brought wood in to replenish the supply; and Israfel looked after the fires and me. This last task he did quietly and proficiently, with a gentleness and caring that at times touched me and at others renewed that trace of fear. His mind had closed to me, revealing nothing of his thoughts.

What he had done to my leg I will never know. He wouldn't tell me. But at the end of the week, I was able to walk on it with care and was even able to drive to the airport to meet Jesse.

My joy at seeing him brought tears to my eyes. I clung to him tightly, beaded jacket and all, too choked up to even speak.

"Hey, Laura! What's up?" He held me away from him, regarded me with wondering eyes. "Is anything wrong? What's happened?"

I shook my head, brushing away tears with an impatient hand, drew him out to where the truck was parked, and pushed the keys into his hand.

We climbed in and he started the engine, then turned to me enquiringly. "Come on. What's this all about?"

I found my voice, squeezed his hand. "I'm just so glad to see you."

"Okay. Great. But why the tears?"

"I – I don't know. It's just . . . well, it's been a bit rough without you. You see, I broke my leg."

He'd been in the process of shifting the transmission, and now he froze in the process and stared at me. "You what?"

"Broke my leg."

HIs eyes fell to my legs, then shot back to my face. "How? How badly? Why no cast? Hey, come on, Laura. You're having me on."

"No. Honest. Gallant fell on me. But Israfel fixed it."

"Israfel? How?"

"I don't know. He just did."

"And you're out walking already?"

"I have to be careful with it. But it doesn't hurt one bit."

Still, he stared at me, the transmission lever forgotten in his hand. "It really was broken?"

"Oh, yes."

He shook his head in disbelief. "And you don't know how he fixed it?"

"No."

"Good God!"

"Lucky for me he was there," I murmured, remembering the snow and broken branches I had fallen into, the falling darkness and increasing cold. Absentmindedly, Jesse put the truck in gear and drove slowly from the parking lot. I tried to question him about the work he was doing and saw a brief flare of enthusiasm blaze in his eyes, but his answers were short, almost vague. So unlike Jesse.

"Anything wrong?" I asked.

"No. No, nothing." Then, "I just can't get over it. You say you broke your leg. When?"

"On Monday."

"And here you are, less than a week later, walking around without even a cast."

"I know."

"Hell!" he said, then was silent.

In the darkness of the night, I couldn't see his face. And something prevented me from asking why he'd sworn. I told myself it was just an expression of astonishment, refused to consider that he may be angry about something and the possible reason for it if he were.

CHAPTER SEVENTEEN

JESSE STAYED AT HOME FOR almost two weeks. He spent days shut in the music room, working on his score, and was vague and far way when he came out for meals or to sleep. I was accustomed to this, said or did nothing to distract him, and gave him all the support I could – which mostly entailed being silent and leaving him alone.

Israfel too was withdrawn and remote, his mind rarely reaching mine. At times I found his eyes on me, brilliant and perceptive, and at others they were shadowed and unseeing, turned inwards or far away, concentrating on some problem of his own.

Occasionally, I wondered if he still felt blameworthy for their predicament here, or whether Celene and Farrand had been able to convince him of his importance to them. But I never dared to ask, fearful of prying into what I knew to be a sensitive and vulnerable area. Also, I was sure he knew what I was thinking, would tell me if he so desired.

January progressed with its customary cold and snow, temperatures rarely rising above freezing, the sun usually hidden in a dark and gray wintry sky.

Sacha was our only visitor, coming once again – but her enraptured smile at Celene's warm greeting soon gave way to bewildered disinterest when he tried to embark on a long discussion with her about the works of Goethe and Nietzsche.

Farrand continued his painstaking work on the communicator, gradually reassembling it piece by tiny piece, his long and dexterous fingers working with all the precision of the finely honed mind behind them.

Celene flew through every book I brought home for him, and there was an increasing coldness in his eyes, a firmer tightening of his lips. He was always courteous and polite to Jesse and me, but I was certain it was mostly superficial, that the gratitude he expressed was more dutiful than sincere. And I wished our history wasn't so bloody, that the impression he must be gaining of us from the books he read wasn't so condemning.

My leg was as good as ever. Jesse said little about it, other than thanking Israfel for what he had done upon our arrival home that night and asking me how it felt the following day.

Israfel waved his thanks aside. "It was nothing, Jesse," he said. "I was glad to be able to do it."

Jesse studied him with careful eyes, seemed about to say something else, then changed the words. "We are grateful to you," he said.

Israfel smiled, but I sensed a wariness in his mind, a caution.

"There is no need to be," he said gently. "It was the least I could do, for we owe a debt to you."

Jesse hesitated. This was not the Israfel he was accustomed to, the aloof and disciplined commander emanating a constant aura of supremacy. And Jesse, as I, was suddenly on guard, beset by caution, and not quite knowing why.

Then two things happened that once more brought the outside world alarmingly near.

We had become somewhat insulated since Christmas with deep snow isolating us and the pressure of the search shifting away, seeming to center farther east. There was no further mention of a missing plane. Nobody had asked us for explanations as to who our strange guests were, our neighbors apparently accepting them. So, when Farrand asked if he might go with me to Vernon to see if it was possible to obtain parts he could use on the communicator, I agreed with little hesitation. He was also curious about our surroundings and the nearest town, wishing to see more of what was close at hand. I was quite happy to be his guide, so I took him with me the next time I went.

But he was appalled by the traffic and its noise, the close proximity of cars and trucks to pedestrians on the sidewalks, the passage of heavy transports, and the smells of exhaust, and the turbulence of their passing. He clung to me with a desperation that I feared would attract attention, his eyes wide with horror, his face bearing little resemblance to the calm composure of the Farrand I knew. I wondered what he'd do in a large city, what would have happened if they had crashed into one.

He became easier to handle when I drove us out to a mall, and he smiled at me ruefully over his earlier alarm.

"I'm sorry," I said. "I shouldn't have plunged you into the downtown traffic like that. I didn't realize it would be so strange for you."

"I couldn't hear you," he said, "what you were saying. And those noisy vehicles coming so close . . . No, I've never been subjected to anything like that."

Only to space travel, I thought. *How relative things are.*

He did find things he could use while I suffered pangs of nervous trepidation as he tried to explain to curious clerks what he wanted. But his intelligence made him careful, and he limited his questions accordingly.

I took him to the library to get more books for Celene and showed him the buildings of the city hall complex with some pride.

"But I wished it were summer," I told him. "These are fountains, and water lilies grow in this pool here. There are roses and petunias, and these trees are beautiful. Farrand, I wish you could see it then."

"I hope by then we will be gone," he said.

A sudden pain of sadness struck me, a deep regret. It would be a relief to be free of the anxieties they had brought, but there was so much I wanted to know about them, where they were from, what their lives were like. I cared about them, and they were still strangers.

Farrand was watching my face. "It will be better for you when we are gone," he said.

"But there's so much I would like to know about you," I said. "About the place you're from, how you live. There's so much we don't know."

"You should ask my commander," he said, and turned away from me.

Yes, I knew I should. Farrand was obviously not free to answer questions. I looked at his slender body, the jacket Jesse had bought for him hanging loosely, the thick dark hair and his beautifully proportioned face, thought of his warmth and concern, his dedication and caring. To see him leave was going to be far more painful than I had realized. Farrand, so endearing in so many ways. And it was this very quality that brought trouble upon us on the way home.

I found books for Celene, and Farrand waited in the truck while I shopped for groceries and a few items from a hardware store. Then I drove homeward, thankful that nothing untoward had happened. I was too premature in that conclusion.

Trinity Valley Road was mostly gravel, steep and winding, and had been carved from a hillside high above the ravine through which Vance Creek ran. Our house and barn site were separated from the road by this same ravine. It was an old road, leading to one of the earliest settlements in British Columbia but that had never developed into a major center. The valley was still nearly as wild as before my grandfather's days. Deer abounded and bears lived here in considerable numbers. There were coyotes by the score, and mountain lions and lynx lived in the deep woods that massed across the mountains.

The road had been widened from the single trail that it used to be, but it was still narrow on some of the sharper curves, especially at the top of the first long hill. It was on this particular curve that I hated to meet a logging truck, and they were frequent, grinding down the hill laden with giant cedars and fir, bounty from Trinity Valley on its way to the mills of Lumby and Lavington.

I could see one as we came up the hill, its huge square metal front and heavy wheels right across the bend. But it was stopped, the driver's door hanging open, and I slowed immediately, instinctively alarmed.

"Oh, Lord! Now what?"

Then I saw the pickup. It was jammed against the side of the trailer, the trailer that was tipping, spilling huge logs onto the roof of the cab. A man was pulling frantically at the passenger door, trying without success to open it.

I accelerated, wheels chewing into the mixture of ice and gravel that crusted the surface of the road, and slowed to a stop in front of the truck. We both leaped out.

"Christ!" the man was yelling. "Oh, Christ!"

We ran towards him, and he turned and saw us.

"Get help!" he shouted. "I can't open the bloody door, and there's a feller stuck in there."

Even as he spoke, there was a grinding groan of metal, and the logs shifted, settling lower on the roof of the pickup, crumpling the metal and cracking the glass of the windshield.

The man moaned loudly. "Oh, God, what a bloody mess!" And when he saw us still coming on, shouted again. "Go for help, I tell you!"

"Wait." Farrand was beside him. "Let me."

The man glared at him with angry eyes in a face red with alarm and exertion. He was twice the size of Farrand, with hands like great implements, his arms and shoulders bulging with muscle. He glanced just once at the slender white hand extended to the door handle, the delicate form in the loosely fitting jacket.

"Christ!" he swore. "We need help, I tell you. I've radioed, but we need someone closer, fast!"

"Let him, please," I said.

The man turned to me, shoved a peaked cap roughly to the back of his head. "For chrissakes, lady! Don't you see what's happened here? The bloody road's as slippery as hell, and we met on that blasted bend. The guy in there's maybe killed, and you won't—"

There was a screeching, ripping noise from behind him, and he turned to see Farrand step back, the door handle in his hand, a hole in the bulging yellow metal.

"Oh, hell!" the man cried, in anguish and exasperation. "Now what?" He began to beat against the window. "We'll have to break the bloody glass."

"Please," Farrand said firmly. "Be quiet."

The man faced him, desperation bringing angry fury. "Hell!" he shouted. "Don't you see? There's a guy in there either dead or near to it, and you just stand there and tell me to be quiet! For God's sake! Why won't you go get help?" He picked up a rock from the side of the road and began to pound it against the window. The glass starred, went white and powdery, began to crack.

"I said," Farrand repeated, his voice like steel cloaked in velvet, "to be quiet."

The man swung, his face livid, the rock raised in his hand and aimed at Farrand.

"Please," I said imploringly, stepping towards him. "Do as he says, just for a moment. Then I'll go for help. There's bound to be someone at the dairy farm who can bring tools." Already I was thinking of where I could turn around, of the farm at the bottom of the hill, and whether I dared leave Farrand alone with this man.

He stared at me, then at Farrand. He shrugged in a helpless gesture, stood back, and mopped his brow. The logs creaked again, and one slid lower.

I saw Farrand tense, his concentration focused on the monstrous load that was towering over him and pressing down relentlessly on the buckling roof of the pickup. I saw him stand motionless, his hands clenched into fists, the knuckles white and hard. The man, fuming but silent, stood by impatiently. But I heard him gasp, saw him take a step backward in astonishment.

The logs were creaking, scraping, rasping against one another, but rising, lifting, uncannily, seemingly of their own volition, back onto the leaning trailer. Gradually, in an unbelievable slow motion, they settled into place, and the trailer righted itself as they did so. The pickup was released, began to roll, but stopped when Farrand turned his attention to it.

"God!" The man whispered hoarsely. "Bloody hell!"

"Can you stop it?" Farrand asked in tight tones.

I ran for a large rock at the road edge, jammed it against the back wheel of the truck, saw the man, his face now white, staring at us, frozen with shock.

Farrand was trembling, his face drawn with strain, but he went to the pickup door, and the window shattered before his eyes. He put a hand inside, pushed up on the frame, and the door swung open.

"Christ!" the man whispered harshly. "What the hell are you?"

Farrand leaned inside the truck, and I went to help him, to look at the man bent over the wheel. He was bleeding from a deep gash on his head and was huddled beneath the crushed roof, his hand hanging loosely.

"He's alive," Farrand said. "He will be all right." He turned to the other man. "He is all right," he repeated.

The man licked lips gone dry, stared at Farrand almost fearfully. "How in hell did you do that?"

Farrand looked at me in sudden alarm. Our secret was in awful danger. I hurried over to the man, laid my hand on the rough wool of his sleeve, and rushed into desperate, entreating words.

"Please, don't tell anyone what you've seen. My friend has a very powerful gift, but he doesn't want it to . . . to be used." I struggled to find a logical explanation. "You must see how people would try to exploit him, make a circus out of it, or use it for less than honest or humane reasons. It's called telekinesis – you must have heard of it. He has an exceptional ability. That's all."

The man stared at me, white-faced. Then he turned and looked at Farrand, at his trembling slender form and drawn face.

"You can see," I hurried on, "what a strain this has been. And he did it to help you. That man might have been killed, probably would have been." I gazed at him with the beseeching eyes of desperation. "Please, please promise you'll say nothing about my friend here."

The man turned to me again, and he gestured toward the crushed roof of the pickup. "How do I explain that, then?" he asked hoarsely.

I was caught, looked with helpless eyes at Farrand.

His face tightened. "Could one log roll off?"

"I guess so," then man said uneasily.

"Would it do that much damage?"

"I suppose."

"Very well." He urged us away with his hands. "Stand clear."

"What are you—" the man began.

"Please. Be silent."

I stood and watched, barely breathing, saw Farrand summoning his resources. His hands were half lifted, his shoulders shaking as if with strain.

A huge log rose from the top of the load, monstrous in its enormity as it impossibly started to float. It rolled slowly over the pickup and fell to the road with a thudding crash, skittering into the snow beneath the high bank and scattering pieces of bark, flakes of yellow paint, and small sprigs of cedars.

"My God!" I heard the man exclaim. "My God."

"Can you find something to put around that man? A blanket? A coat?" I asked him.

Farrand came towards us, his face white and drained, his whole demeanor one of total exhaustion.

"Yes," the man muttered, eyeing Farrand warily. "Yes. And the ambulance should be here any minute."

"And please." I begged him again. "Promise us you'll say nothing."

His shoulders stiffened, and his voice was rough. "Damn it all, lady! What the hell do you think I am?"

"A man," I said, wishing my voice wouldn't shake so much, "with intelligence and common sense, who should realize the importance of what I'm asking." Farrand reached me and I took his arm. "And who appreciates what F—what my friend has done. That man could have been crushed at any moment, killed . . . "

He looked from me to Farrand, at his pale drawn face and trembling hands, at the partially crushed pickup, at the log lying in the road. He swallowed with difficulty, then sighed heavily and shook his head as though to clear it of unwelcome knowledge. Two spots of color began to appear in the blanched skin of his cheeks.

At last, he looked at me. "Okay. You've got it."

"Thank you." I gave him my best, if somewhat lopsided, smile, hoping, hoping.

I led Farrand back to our own truck, found he was too weak to climb over the high sill, and had to help him up. Then I raced backward down the hill, to a widening where I knew I could turn. I prayed we would meet no one coming up who would recognize me, cause me to be called as a witness. I wondered if the man knew who I was, what would happen if we both should be called. And I was worried what the effort of moving those gigantic logs had cost Farrand. He was leaning his head against the back of the seat, eyes closed, his face pale and still.

Fortunately, we passed nobody I knew. I rushed along Mabel Lake Road and turned up Hurt, heading for the back way home via the Greenaways'. Farrand stirred when the truck began to bump and bounce on the gravel road, on the rutted ice and frozen snow. He looked unhappily out the window.

"I have put us in jeopardy," he said. "I should have remained quiet, not interfered."

"Farrand, you did it out of the kindest motive," I said, clinging to the steering wheel as the truck slewed around a bend.

He was silent. The road straightened, and I could see the Greenaways' house at the foot of the hills ahead of us. "And that man may keep his word."

"Celene will have his doubts. So, perhaps, will Israfel."

"I do too," I admitted unhappily, "but he may not know me. I've never met him before. And he was probably too shaken up to have taken our number."

I slowed to drive through the gateway, and the dogs came racing to meet us, barking with excitement. There was no sign of anyone, so I drove on, locking the four-wheel drive into low range, eyeing the deep snow unhappily. The hill was steep, and the tracks we had made on Christmas Day were long gone. The transmission whined as the truck began to climb, and I forced myself to let it travel slowly, not to push it in my anxiety to reach home. For then the truck could start to buck, lose traction, even stop.

Like a snail, we crawled up the hill, between steep banks thick with snow, in a world of black and white. The sun had gone, leaving a sky as pale as milk, chilled by winter, and the bare branches of the birches were etched as dark tracings beneath their rims of clinging snow. The road was narrow, required all my concentration, and Farrand watched the banks and the bending snow laden branches creep past with equal apprehension, his eyes shadowed with unhappiness.

At last, we climbed the final twisting slope and came out onto a small meadow. "Thank God for four-wheel drive!" I exclaimed fervently, and Farrand turned and looked at me but did not smile.

And what a joy it was to cross our boundary, to be on home ground, to race along our familiar roads and reach the house, our security. But that security was only an illusion, I knew, and as Jesse was quick to remind me.

"He may need you as a witness," he said when I had finished explaining what had happened, telling him how the man had promised not to say anything. "He may be forced to tell."

"Maybe we could still keep Farrand out of it," I said wistfully.

"Doubtful," said Jesse.

"If the man doesn't know you, how would he find you?" Israfel asked.

"Easy enough," Jesse said. "He could ask around until he finds someone who knows our truck."

Israfel was silent. Farrand, after a moment with him, had carried his packages up the stairs and stayed there. Celene stood in the kitchen, where I was haphazardly trying to put a meal together, his eyes cold and mouth drawn into an almost angry line.

"All we can do is wait and see," I said.

"And be prepared," said Jesse.

Two days passed by, and no one came. Farrand worked from dawn until late in the night, his face still drawn and tired, but he was evidently satisfied with his progress. Israfel helped him, and Celene spent a great deal of time standing at the kitchen window, where he had the best view of the driveway approach. Jesse shut himself back in the music room, then took off for Los Angeles a few days later.

I drove him to the airport, anxiety again gnawing at me.

"You worry too much," he told me from beneath the battered leather hat. "And have you thought of this? They're damned lucky to have landed with us. Suppose they'd come down in the ocean or way up the Amazon somewhere. Or at the North Pole, or in the Sahara."

"They might have been safer," I said.

"Not by much. I do admit," he went on, "that it's a bloody miracle that man hasn't yapped all over the place."

"Yet," I added.

"The more time goes by, the less likely he is to say anything."

But I was not convinced. I could still see that incredible rising of those colossal logs, the man's shocked face. And neither was Celene, I knew. His intent eyes at the window, his cold and suspicious expectancy, the angry line of his mouth – all denoted his lack of trust in this race of humans.

So, Jesse left me once again, walked away in his outlandish clothes into his other life, and I drove home through falling flakes of snow with my heart sinking once more as loneliness possessed me, filling me with concern for what would once again confront me, the possibility that something of our secret would reach the wrong ears.

But this very uneasiness brought me closer to them. I found myself joining Celene in his vigil at the window; trying to help Farrand – although no doubt ineffectually – as he worked on the communicator; sharing my thoughts more readily with Israfel. And I was far less conscious of being there alone with them.

A few nights after Jesse's departure, we saw a most astounding television program. It was a special presentation that came on without any forewarning, replacing the scheduled play I had wanted to see, and Israfel and I stared in astonishment. At his silent summons, Celene joined us, and Farrand even dragged himself away from his communicator.

Photographs were paraded before our stricken eyes, films shown, and interviews given. They were all connected with UFOs, with the continuing conjecture that there were vehicles from outer space, ones that were crewed.

I watched in near panic, and Israfel, kneeling on the rug before the fire, put out a hand and gently touched mine.

I was scarcely aware of it, hearing experts with prestigious titles admit the intensive investigation into many sightings had brought no other verdict than "unknown," watching them show astounding photographs that had been subjected to every possible test before being pronounced authentic, seeing a film of a gleaming silver craft flying above a ridge in the clear light of day. There was the usual discussion about hoaxes and sensation seekers, the reluctance in the higher fields of science to accept new ideas, of governments to admit they didn't know. And then, almost casually but very clearly: "The value to us, if we could capture one, would be inestimable, the reward of ineffable value. In fact, the safety of our nation would probably be totally secure."

That was the end. The picture faded away, and there were several moments of silence before the usual crass commercial came on. I moved as though in a trance, crossed the room, and switched the set off. Celene was standing, his face pale and eyes fixed on Israfel. Farrand rose and swiftly left the room.

I, too, stood and looked at Israfel, saw the beauty of his face enhanced by the flickering light of the fire, the cold glitter of his eyes as they met Celene's, felt a silence in his mind that excluded me. He remained motionless, kneeling on the rug, facing Celene calmly, it seemed, but for the hard metallic gleam of his eyes, the total power and strength of his presence.

They remained there for a long while, their minds seemingly locked in an intense but silent battle. Then, at last, Celene turned and stalked from the room, his head held high, his face pale and cold and resolute.

Israfel still knelt, looking after him, and I saw his eyes shade and sadness form on his face. Then his head bent and shoulders curved, and the sense of strength was gone. He looked slight and unexpectedly vulnerable, in incredible contrast to how he had appeared while facing Celene. His customary kneeling pose, for the first time, gave an impression of submission – but to what I couldn't figure out.

Israfel! I went to him, knelt before him, looked anxiously at his downcast face. *Israfel, what is it?*

The eyes were almost gray as they met mine, and his mouth was drawn into lines of regret. *Celene wants me to relinquish my command.*

This was unbelievable, and I stared at him, dumbfounded. *But Celene was the one who worried about you unceasingly. Anyway, why?*

His mind closed to me, and his eyes fell from mine. "I cannot tell you," he said out loud.

Worry upon worry piled on my anxious head. "Did it have something to do with that program?"

"Indirectly, yes. He is certain that we are now in great danger."

"So am I, Israfel. Even more so now."

He did not answer, was motionless there in the glowing light of the fire, his head bending sadly.

What did you say? I asked him silently. *Are you going to give up your command?*

Yes, but not yet, not to Celene's demand. I will only resign before my own commander.

The sorrow in him swept over me, brought tears to my eyes, and carved a deep ache in my heart. I reached out and touched his cold hand, let my fingers lie on it gently, and my gesture – or my tears – brought a surging response from him.

His head lifted, and the eyes shone silver once again. His hand turned and caught my fingers. *Laura, don't. It's hard enough for me. I must cope with failure, with blame, and now Celene and his justifiable demand. He puts duty above all else, will sacrifice himself readily if needs be, and now he knows that I will not. That is another reason why he wants me to resign.*

I tried to understand what he was saying, but his mind was moving too rapidly and on to a different plane from mine.

Please! I begged him. *What are you saying?*

In answer, he lifted my hand and studied it fully, his mind closed. From tear-blurred eyes, I looked at the hand holding mine. Four fingers and a thumb, although his were long and narrow, as were the nails. But his hand was longer than mine, and much finer, the skin unroughened by the handling of hay and clay, curry comb and shovel. The fingers were fine and tapering, but what strength was evident in their quiet sure movements, what hardness of bone and ability of function. An alien hand, cool to touch, but growing warm where it met mine.

"Our common root provides many similarities." There was a softness in his tone, a gentle sadness. But then he rose abruptly to his feet. "I must go and help Farrand. We have to get that communicator repaired as quickly as possible." He went, drawing authority around him like a cloak, arming himself with strength and power as though he were donning metal breast plate and mail. He might claim defeat, but Israfel was very much in command.

Farrand worked day and night, his face was a mask of exhaustion, and there was a grayness to his skin that had lingered since the day of the logging truck. Celene alternated between helping him and keeping vigil at the kitchen window. But no one came.

It was Israfel who helped me feed the horses, clean the barn, and put fresh sawdust down – Israfel, wearing boots and a heavy coat, venturing outdoors for the first time since he had come to find me when I had broken my leg.

Sharing work brought an easing between us, but when I spoke of Celene and the problem that existed between them, his mind would close, his lips tighten, and there would be no further communication until I changed the subject.

A heavy fall of snow had me calling Mac, asking him to plow the road, as I had to get out to meet Jesse when he came home for the weekend. To be snowbound suited me very well, but I couldn't bring myself to call Jesse and ask him not to come home.

The snow clouds retreated to the mountains, gathering there in high-piled cumuli of gray and ivory towers. The sky above was an azure blue, flushed with the lemon gold of the winter sun, and the new snow was a crisp and clean dazzling white.

We worked together on the communicator for most of the afternoon, my job being to polish the glued joints of a myriad broken pieces, to make them as smooth as possible. It was late when we ate a scrappy meal, and darkness had fallen by the time Israfel and I went out to feed the horses. Tired and stuffy after the long day cooped in the house, I was glad for the air and exercise. And the night was beautiful, the sky still clear, a white halfmoon rising from the east, stars glittering with diamond brilliance in the cold.

We turned off the lights, left the barn, and stood looking up into the deep night sky. Israfel's face was wistful, his mind speaking to me softly of vague yearnings, indistinct in their unfamiliarity, of desires on a different plane. He would not elaborate when I asked him to explain, but he smiled faintly at me in the light of the moon.

Would you like the walk for a while? I asked, enjoying the freshness of the air, the moonlit night. *As far as the hay field and back? We can see the lights of the village clearly from there and have a marvelous view of the sky.*

Again, there was the faint smile in acquiescence, but his mind withdrew from mine.

The snow crunched and squeaked beneath our feet, moonlit diamonds sparkling on its surface, and the trees rose, black and silvery gray from deep white drifts. I was warm in my old sheepskin coat, and the freezing air checked its odor. Israfel's coat was dark blue nylon, down filled, chosen for him by Jesse, as were Celene's and Farrand's. Each coat had a fur-trimmed hood, but Israfel's head was bare, his silvery hair gleaming like water beneath the stars.

My old Cowichan toque, adorned with hay fragments, snugged over my ears. But beneath it my hair spread its unruly mass, equally adorned with leaves and stalks, bunching around my collar and scarf. How awkward and gauche I felt, clumping along in my heavy winter boots and worn corduroys from which one knee was threatening to poke at any time. Israfel glided beside me in elegant grace and majestic presence, his face ethereal beside my angular ordinariness, his skin like alabaster while my nose, I was sure, was already turning red.

I tried to ignore him, but his mind brushed mine again with its enigmatic and mysterious yearnings, its soaring flights into realms where I could only vaguely perceive unfamiliar images and strange, incomprehensible figures. Odd patterns whirled by me, shrouded in mists or shadowy in darkness, and elusive melodies echoed briefly from far distances to then be quickly gone. I didn't ask him to explain, knowing that to do so would only cause a swift withdrawal and his mind closing to me once more.

We came to stand on a rise with the field stretching away all around us, tilting upward to meet the forest to the north, slipping away from us to the south. Far below us, the lights of the village glittered and danced beneath the black hills.

He stood beside me, lifted his head, and looked at the stars once more. I felt again that sense of longing, of aching yearning as his mind reached out to mine.

Laura. His silent voice was wistful. *I have so regretted what has happened here, and yet now I'm beginning to see things differently. I have agreed with Celene – that's why he's part of my crew. But now I find myself differing. And I know I could be wrong.*

What are you saying? I stared at him, at the silver eyes that shone with an eerie light as they turned at me.

Laura, I was wished this had not happened. And now I'm glad it has. But it is the wrong time, the wrong circumstances, and if Celene is proven right, then my regret will be tenfold.

Please, I begged. *Explain.*

His mind went beyond mine, racing with his own flashing thoughts. His eyes closed as though in pain.

Then they opened abruptly. *How well do you trust me?* he asked.

I was taken by surprise, unable to think with any clarity, stumbled to find a reply.

Israfel . . . I scarcely know you . . . you're alien to me, different. I want to trust you, I went on lamely, awkwardly, *but you can't expect me to wholly . . .*

He turned away from me, stared out across the valley to the village lights, then swung back to me. His eyes penetrated mine, holding, instilling almost hypnotically. *If a time should come when I demand that you trust me, would you?*

Again, I struggled to find an answer and found it impossible to say yes or no. *How can I know?* I implored him silently. *How can I possibly tell you now, at this minute? Israfel, I wish I could answer you, but I can't.*

Still the eyes held mine, searching, considering, and then he turned away again. Again, the racing mind sped by me with flashing, confusing images.

"Why did you ask me?" I spoke out loud.

He didn't look at me, but his mind slowed, turned away from mine. "I cannot tell you," He said.

CHAPTER EIGHTEEN

JANUARY BECAME FEBRUARY – THE only month I hated. Winter would stir, loosen its hold, and water begin to run everywhere in narrow, hurrying streams. Then it would freeze again, and paths would be treacherous with ice. The mares, heavy with foal, would creep about with anxious eyes and ears laid back unhappily.

Israfel and I spent hours spreading sawdust on all the walkways, only to have it all melt and a new surface of ice form above it, or another few inches of snow would fall, frustrating all our efforts.

Jesse came and went, his mind distracted, spending his days at home working in the music room and hating interruptions.

"A theme," he told me, coming late to bed one night. "I need a theme with a melody that will not only convey the sense of distance on the prairies and great plains but also reflect the labor of the harvesters reaping the grain."

His movements were slow, his eyes distant, and face strained and tired.

"Remember the music from Lawrence of Arabia? How perfect it was for those desert scenes? And all those wild-looking men on those running horses? The enormity of the whole thing? I want something like that, as vast as that, as all encompassing."

"I can't help you," I said sadly.

"I know, hon. It'll come, I'm sure. I just have to keep working on it."

He sat on the edge of the bed to take off his shoes. He needed a haircut, and he even looked as though he had lost some weight.

"I've had several themes that would do for some parts, but not for others. And I want one that can be given variations, that will carry right through the whole thing."

"What does Rex say?"

"Rex? He's just about the damned best director I've ever worked with. He was quite prepared to use the first score I came up with, but when I pointed out what I regarded as its failings, told him what I had in mind, he said he'd wait. They haven't finished shooting yet, anyway."

How pleasant it was to be snug in our softly lit room, talking about our own affairs, to forget Israfel's mind and its strange rushing images, to banish Celene's aloof face and dispassionate eyes, to not think about Farrand working day after day on the communicator. Even though Jesse too was struggling with a problem, it was one we could contend with, deal with on our own terms – not one that had been inflicted on us out of incredible, almost unbelievable, circumstances.

I knew that, to Jesse, his problem was a major one. I sympathized out of a natural loyalty. But it didn't present me with the anxieties our three guests did. For February heralded spring, breakup, the passing of snow. People would begin to brave our road, wishing to see the stallions we stand at stud. And an anxious doubt expanded and grew with the passing days. I was certain it wouldn't be long before the search was underway once more.

The communicator took shape. Farrand still worked until late in the night, stopping only to eat and for a few hours' sleep. There was little we could do to help him at this point, as the work consisted mainly of putting one piece back at a time and fitting the next one to it. Celene would often stand and watch him until Farrand became annoyed and sent him from the room.

Still, the snow kept melting, and there were occasional days when the sky was clear, and we could feel the growing heat of the sun. And Israfel would walk with me after the nighttime chores, saying little, his mind turned far away.

On February eighteenth – I remember it clearly – Farrand came down the stairs very late in the evening. His eyes were shining, and a smile illuminated his face with an excitement I had never thought him capable of. Celene sprang to his feet, his own eyes lighting up like fires, and Israfel rose, went to Farrand, and touched him gently on the shoulder.

"Laura," Farrand said, a tremor in his voice. "It is done. The message is on its way."

I was speechless, stood looking from one to the other, and could find no words to say. Celene was bursting with barely contained joy, Farrand still smiled, and Israfel turned his silver eyes to me, regarding me with a strange mixture of relief and sorrow, and spoke to me softly with his mind.

Laura, why do you say nothing? Are you not glad that these tiresome visitors will soon be gone? Your worries will be over, your life will once more continue without disruption. Unless . . . Laura, if I should warn you of danger, would you trust me then?

Confused, my mind filled with what Farrand had at last accomplished, I stared blankly at him.

Laura, would you trust me?

I brought myself to him, to the silver eyes and perfect face, so alien, so unknown, and my answer was the same. *How can I possibly know?*

Farrand slept for days, a sleep of exhaustion, deep and silent and still. I gave him chicken soup and eggnog whenever he woke up, and even then, it was a state of semi-wakefulness, and I would often find the glass or bowl only half-emptied a short while later and Farrand dead to the world again.

Celene appeared to be almost happy, but he was even more distant from me. He was always polite but ever aloof while Israfel was distant in a different way, withdrawn into a sadness that I put down to his pending resignation. It was only when I sensed a clash with Celene that I saw the stern face of the warrior once more, the disciplined reserve and imperious authority of the born commander. He might be vanquished, but he had not surrendered.

The first foals began to arrive, which meant wakeful nights for me and nocturnal trips out to the barn. But it was only when a mare was delivering that Israfel would appear, reading my mind, coming silently to lend assistance.

March brought a warm sun and the first stirring winds of spring racing high above us in our sheltered valley, sending soft currents flowing down the hillsides. Patches of brown earth appeared on southerly exposed banks and beneath large cedars and firs where the snow had not been deep, and water ran again in wheel ruts and on pathways, down the pasture and the High Meadow Road.

Farrand, apparently restored, began to repair the receiving part of the communicator.

"It isn't that important," he told me. "But it would be nice to know when they're coming. And it gives me something to do."

"When do you think they will come?" I asked. "How long will your message take?"

He was silent, calculating, and then tried to explain to me a complex system of interlocking and intercommunicating quasars, cross references, and pickups. "It depends," he said finally to my uncomprehending face, "on where the base ship is when the message is received and how quickly it can contact another."

"But when?" I asked again. "When might that be for us?"

He went to the calendar hanging on the wall near the phone in the kitchen, examined it thoughtfully. "Possibly by the end of May," he said.

At first my heart sank. Over two months! And then I felt a new pain, a sharp sadness that stabbed at me with an unexpected poignancy. I would miss them, Farrand with his gentleness and consideration, the quality of his kindness; Israfel, and that rare communication between us. And I would always feel regret for Celene, that he had found nothing admirable in the human race.

In less than three months they could be gone, and they would be gone forever. This would be a different parting than those we had experienced when we had left Los Angeles. Those friends were no further than a plane ticket or a number of hours on the road, their voices always in reach by phone. But this was going to be entirely different. This separation would be total and completely permanent with no possible contact. Our incredible visitors would vanish from the face of the earth, leaving no trace, and no one else would ever know. For who would ever believe us if we told them?

"Laura?" Farrand was looking at me with dark and concerned eyes. "Is that bad? I'm sorry it can't be sooner, but I doubt it will be earlier than the end of May."

"I'll miss you!" I burst out. "And I'll spend the rest of my life wishing your stay here could have been better, really, that our world could have welcomed you with understanding and recognition, by all peoples. This has all been so wrong."

"It's too soon," he said quietly. "Laura, Celene is right. This planet is a dangerous place for us because it is too soon for us to be recognized."

"Your history is lost," he went on, "the truth of your origins, the gods, your civilization. Instilled doctrines are difficult things to change, and the threat of new knowledge presents too many dangers to too many people in high places. We would be a menace to too many established systems, and therefore we would be most unwelcome."

I looked at him unhappily, wishing his words didn't sound so logical, that I could deny what he was suggesting. But I knew to do so would be naive and foolish.

He gave me a gentle smile. "Perhaps the time will come when all humans accept further knowledge. I know there are many who do, who would, but it has to be the majority, Laura, and include those in the positions of power and rule."

His words left me feeling ineffably sad, as at the loss of something precious. A great new field of knowledge was on our doorstep, and I had to let the latch remain, the bolts drawn hard against it.

⬡

My beloved Calliope showed signs of foaling late one night. I stayed with her, discreetly out of sight behind bales of hay, shivering with cold and anticipation. This was a special foal, one we had purposely left the mare open for so she could make the long journey to California and the champion stallion I had long intensely admired.

Israfel was suddenly beside me, silent and aware.

Calliope moved restlessly around the stall, pawing the clean straw I had bedded it with, a damp sweat steaming on her neck and flanks. One light in the aisle provided soft illumination, but my vantage point among the bales gave only a partial view.

She lay down and got up again several times, and I waited with my heart grown tight within me. Observed births always seem to take an age, often indicated something was wrong, bringing much more anxiety than I cared to feel. But there was always the possibility of a misrepresentation or the mare getting down against the wall. I had invested too much money and too much time in this foal to take any chances. I was also impatient to see it.

The water bag broke with a gush, and Israfel and I exchanged glances. The foal was on its way.

Calliope stood. I could see her chiseled head and prominent eye, ears pricked as she listened instinctively for danger. Then she turned and lay down again with a loud sigh, and I could hear her straining.

With silent care, we crept from the bales and moved toward her stall. *We must get a separate foaling stall*, I told myself for the umpteenth time, *with a heated observation room next door.* Peeping around the corner of the partition like this was just not good enough.

The first tiny foot began to appear, pale in color, followed by the second. *Soon, soon*, I said silently to Israfel. But I was met with concern. His eyes were fixed on those two tiny hooves.

I stared at them, so small and round, wrapped in membrane – and then my stomach lurched, and my heart tightened with a sickening pain. Despair and anguish rose chokingly in my throat. Those tiny feet were upside down.

"Oh no!" I moaned out loud. "Oh no!" Our vet would have to come from Vernon, twenty miles away, then travel through the snow and ice of our forest road, while I would wait and wait, and the mare would struggle uselessly. I glanced at my watch. Almost 2:00 a.m. What an awful hour to call him. My heart began to pound with fear as I ran toward to door.

"Laura!" Israfel stopped me.

I turned and looked at him, panic rising. "I'm calling the vet. The foal's upside down." I spun toward the door.

Laura!

Again, I halted in my headlong flight.

Come back. Hold the mare. I'll turn it the right way.

You? I looked at him, at his slenderness, at the long white hand already sliding the bolt of the door.

Easily, Laura. Come back.

What could he possibly know of delivering mares, turning a foal? But I went, took a halter from the wall, and slid it over Calliope's damp and anxious head.

She made no move to rise and lay tense and strained in the tumbled straw, her eyes dark and fixed on me in wide alarm. I spoke to her soothingly, stroked her damp neck, saw Israfel bend over her, his hands touching her side with soft, carefully pressing motions. Then I saw him stand as Farrand had stood on the road before the huge logging truck and its looming, leaning load: unmoving, concentrating on the body of the horse on the floor. And I could feel the enormous strength of his mind filling the barn, its power smothering my own mind, centering on the mare before him.

She started, lifted her head, and tried to swing it around. I crouched beside her, clinging to the halter, whispering to her – and saw movement start behind her flank, a flowing beneath the pale hide. She pulled at the halter, once, twice, then subsided with a sigh.

I raised anxious eyes to his.

It's all right. Let her rest. I can do it now.

Cautiously, I released my hold on the halter and straightened from my crouch. He was still standing as before, but now the field of power was narrow, effortless, only a thread to the foal until it slid easily from Calliope's body.

I fell down beside it with a gasp of delight, ripped the membrane from its face, saw the tiny flaring muzzle and the sculpted head, the large wide eyes and long reaching neck of the most beautiful foal we have ever bred.

"Oh, look!" I cried. "Israfel, look!"

He bent beside me and helped me pull the membrane from the wet body and long thin legs. It was the filly we had so badly hoped for, dark, two hind socks, and a star. I was ecstatic, couldn't stop exclaiming over her, thanking him, patting Calliope.

We dried her, supported her as she struggled to her feet for the first ungainly and difficult time, cleaned up the stall, and put more fresh straw down. It was almost four o'clock when we returned to the house. I was too charged up to even think of going to bed, and Israfel was smiling at my enthusiasm.

"I must phone Jesse and tell him," I said as soon as we had shed our coats and boots and had washed our hands.

Israfel began to light the kitchen stove, and I dialed Jesse's hotel in Los Angeles, waking him.

"Calliope has a filly!" I cried into the phone. "And the most beautiful one you've ever seen."

"For chrissakes, Laura," came the irritable and somewhat blurred reply. "Did you have to wake me in the middle of the night to tell me that? What time is it, anyway?"

"Just after four," I said, my spirits suddenly damped. "I'm sorry, but I thought you'd want to know."

"Well sure," he said. "But not right now. Couldn't it have waited for just a couple more hours?"

My excitement waned. "She was upside down, you see—"

"Oh, hell!"

"But it's all right," I hastened to assure him. "She's okay. And—"

"So okay, then. But she's your horse, not mine. And you didn't have to wake me up in the middle of the bloody night just to tell me that!"

"Jesse . . . "

"Yeah? What?"

"Oh . . . nothing. I'm sorry I woke you."

"Okay. Okay. Call me later if you want."

I hung up, feeling crushed. I had expected Jesse to share my joy, the relief of knowing all was well after what could have been a difficult ordeal. His annoyance at me disturbing him took me completely by surprise.

He's in his other life, I reminded myself. *This one isn't that important to him now. That's the one that matters.*

I turned from the phone, met Israfel's eyes, knew he had read everything that had passed.

I woke him up, I told him. *I thought he'd want to know. But I guess it is awful early. And he's so engrossed with what he's doing there. I should've known, realized—*

Laura. He crossed the room to me, rested his hands lightly on my shoulders. *You're tired. It's been a long night. Go to bed and get some sleep.*

His sympathy touched me. And he was also tired. The strain and fatigue on his face was the same as what I had seen on Farrand's after he had raised those enormous logs. Israfel had probably saved my beautiful filly as well as me from the stress of a difficult birthing. I put up my hand to his, found it as cold as ice, covered both of his with mine, and tried to warm them.

Israfel, the filly's yours. I'm going to give her to you, if you can come back for her when she's weaned.

He stiffened, drew away from me, stared at me with startled eyes. *You'd give her to me?*

Yes.

Why?

Because without you I might have lost her.

But you've waited . . . how long? For that foal?

A whole year.

That's a large portion of your life.

I know. But to have lost her would have been so painful. I'd have been heartbroken. And she's just beautiful, Israfel, just beautiful.

He smiled, and his hand pressed mine.

Could you take her? Would there be any way?

No, Laura. I wouldn't anyway. But thank you for offering.

How cold his hand was, but the smile that lingered on his face transformed him. Not so long ago, I reminded myself, I had found this warm and gentle Israfel somewhat disconcerting, almost preferring the one I had first known with his disciplined face and passionless eyes, his aura of regal splendor. But on this night, I welcomed the sensitive being who shared my mind, my long nightly vigils over the cold barn, and my concern for an upside down foal, and who was aware of my distress after my ill-timed phone call to Jesse.

We shared a pot of mint tea, and then I went to bed in an attempt to catch a few hours of sleep. And just before I drifted away, I found myself wondering why I had offered the filly to him.

CHAPTER NINETEEN

A SHORT WHILE LATER, ISRAFEL made the same
fateful choice as Farrand – only this time it was a great deal closer to home.

A clear cold night had frozen the ground to iron, and Israfel and I again
spread sawdust on all the pathways. Maureen had phoned earlier, asking
what the condition of the road was and whether she might bring Deenie over
to see the foals.

It was impossible to put her off. I hadn't seen her since Christmas, and
that was unusual in itself. But I had used Jesse's absence and the foaling mares
as an excuse to not go anywhere.

Farrand and Celene stayed upstairs, and Israfel planned to disappear as
soon as we heard her car.

Ice crunching on the roadway gave us plenty of forewarning, and Israfel
slipped away, going into the house while I waited for her in the yard.

I was happy to see her, to talk to someone at my own level, in my own
sphere, and I realized how much I was missing outside contact. I wasn't even
worried when Deenie ran wildly all over the place in a fashion I usually found
very disturbing.

The mares and foals were in a corral where we had spread sawdust thick
and deep, and Maureen and I stood there, leaning on the rails in the sun
while I excitedly pointed out my new and precious filly, and told her about
the trouble we had delivering her, and how "Rafe" had so ably helped me –
although I did prevent myself from telling her how.

"Rafe? Is he still here?"

Then I wished I hadn't mentioned him at all. "Yes."

"And Jesse's down in LA?"

"Only during the week. He comes home just about every weekend."

Her eyes were on me, conjecture and surprise making her forget to be polite. "Doesn't he mind? I mean . . . well, heck, Laura. Ted would never go away and leave me alone in the house with anyone as attractive as Rafe."

I shrugged, tried to laugh it off. "Jesse isn't the jealous kind, I guess. And besides, I'm not alone. Len and Randy are still here, too."

"Still?"

"They'll be gone in a couple of weeks," I said, telling myself that "a couple" didn't necessarily mean "only two" in the casual idiom of today.

Maureen controlled her face with an effort, but her sense of propriety came to the fore and prevented the stream of questions I could see she was dying to ask.

"We'll miss them," I offered. "They've been so helpful. Couldn't ask for better guests. Oh, look, Maureen! Did you ever see such action as on that little colt there?"

Andante's foal was an opportune distraction as he trotted along the fence like a deer, bouncing and springing in a slow motion that was stunning. Maureen turned to see if Deenie was watching, but the child had gone.

"Deenie! Deenie!" she called. "Where are you?"

There was no reply. I wasn't particularly worried. Deenie never stayed in the same place for more than a minute, anyway, and the doors to the stallions' stalls and corrals were all securely locked. There wasn't too much she could do in the way of mischief, I thought.

But I guess Maureen had enough experience to be concerned, and she hurried into the barn calling her loudly.

There was no sign of her. We went out through the main door, stood in the rutted and crumbling ice of the yard, and looked around with searching eyes. Nothing.

"Drat the child!" Maureen said angrily. "Where on earth has she gotten to?"

"She can't be far," I soothed. "Maybe she's just hiding."

From the corner of my eye, I saw a sudden movement. High above the yard, the hay loft door swung open. "Boo!" Deenie cried and laughed with delight at our startled faces. But the heavy door kept swinging, carrying her out with it, and she hung desperately from the bar that was fixed to the door for closing it. She could only hold on for a few minutes, and her laughter soon faded and became an anguish shriek.

Maureen screamed, piercingly, agonizingly, and horror filled my mind.

It was a long way to the ground. Hay was still piled high in that part of the loft as we had begun to feed it from the other end. There was still enough there for several months. Deenie had climbed onto this pile to reach the door and had succeeded in unlatching it and pushing it open. The ground below was shaded, frozen, promised dreadful injury, if not death.

The force of Israfel's mind responding to mine was a living blow, jarring in its impact. I staggered, stunned, my mind screaming in agony, my eyes blurred by horror. I felt the powerful rush of his control sweep over me.

The child's downward plummet stopped abruptly, and she hung in midair, arms and legs in a blue nylon snowsuit flailing and kicking, her and Maureen's screams a hideous cacophony of sound.

I couldn't move, stood rooted to the ground while the struggling body of the little girl hung suspended, unbelievably, as if at some phenomenal show of magic. But Maureen's anguish and their distorted faces and dreadful screams were anything but entertaining.

I was dimly aware of Maureen trying to reach her daughter, her child's uplifted arms and clawing hands. Israfel raced from the house, flew across the yard, came to a stop beside Maureen. I saw his eyes shining silver in the sunlight, the pale set of his face, heard in a roaring distance the commanding tone of his voice.

"Be silent. Be still."

A deathly silence filled the yard. Maureen, white-faced, her eyes a black torment, stood and stared at him. The child ceased to struggle and hung helplessly with huge wet tears streaming down her pathetic little face.

He reached up to her, and she sank into his arms, her own flinging themselves around his neck as though grasping a lifeline. Fresh sobs burst from her, and she buried her face in his silver hair while Maureen stood like stone and stared at him. Every drop of blood had drained from her face. She was trembling from head to foot but was held in rigid, dry-lipped fascination.

I couldn't move, either, stood frozen to the spot while Maureen stared at the unearthly face before her, the inhuman silver eyes of Israfel.

Maureen. I tried to speak her name, to distract her, but I couldn't summon even a whisper. Deenie was clinging to Israfel like a limpet, sobbing into his neck with gasping choking sounds that Maureen didn't even seem to hear.

Then the silver eyes were on mine, and he spoke to me rapidly, sadly. *Now I have done the same as Farrand. This could be far more dangerous, for this woman knows you, has seen my eyes. But I couldn't let this child die right before you. Celene will be even angrier with me. This could mean trouble, Laura, more trouble for you and for us.*

I knew it, but my own state of shock was preventing me from thinking, of finding any solution to this new and monumental problem. I could only regard him helplessly.

Come, Laura. Come and take this child from me. Maybe that will distract her.

His words released me from my paralysis. I stumbled across the rough ground to him and took Deenie from his arms. She cried all the louder and then saw her mother and reached imploring arms to her.

"Maureen," I whispered hoarsely. "Please."

She turned in slow motion, her eyes dark, haunted and unseeing. She tried to moisten her lips with her tongue, and then she saw Deenie. Her breath caught with a terrible gasp, and then she practically tore the child from my arms. She began to cry uncontrollably, crushing Deenie to her, falling on her knees in the crumbled ice and dirt.

Go, Israfel, back to the house. I'll try to talk to her.

He turned and walked away, and I sank weakly down beside my friend and tried to console her with awkward pats and mumbled soothing words while an inner trembling of my own shook my knees and my futile hands.

But at last, she gained control. Deenie was clinging to her, alive and well, still sobbing, but they were only tears of a lingering fright.

"Maureen." I found my voice. "Come in, now. We'll have some coffee. Deenie's fine. It's okay, Maureen. Come on now."

She turned her enormous tear-streaked eyes to mine. "Laura . . . wh-what did I see?"

"Telekinesis," I said, trying to sound casual and failing dismally.

"Tele-what?"

"Telekinesis. Surely, you've heard of it."

Her eyes became dazed, again unseeing, and she knelt there in the yard looking miserable and lost, her arms wrapped around her daughter.

I patted her shoulder. "Come in, now, and have some coffee. That'll make you feel better. You've had a terrible shock." I stood up and pulled her arm. "Come on, Maureen."

Too shocked to do anything but obey, she struggled to her feet, still clasping Deenie. We stumbled together across the yard, our steps awkward on the frozen or crumbling ruts, knees weak, arms clinging to one another but lending little support.

Inside the house, her eyes sharpened, and she looked around as though she partially hoped and partially feared to see Israfel. But he had disappeared. The kitchen was empty. I guided her to a chair near the stove where she sank down weakly. She was still shaking so badly her teeth were chattering, and her face was deathly white. I filled the kettle with water and a saucepan with milk, set them on the range, and changed my mind about the coffee. Hot chocolate, very sweet, would be better for all of us.

Deenie huddled against Maureen's knees, her face streaked with tears and eyes still wide with shock. She kept whimpering softly, the sound interspersed with frequent sniffs.

The peace and warmth of the sunlit kitchen, with a fire snapping in the stove, the pots gleaming and burnished, and the plants spilling green from the windowsills, seemed unreal after the episode in the yard. And it could have been so much worse if it hadn't been for Israfel. Now he and his crew were again in danger of discovery, for I doubted Maureen could ever keep such a secret.

I wondered if I should confide in her, but no. She was already shocked. Another revelation would be far too much.

"I must th-thank him," she whispered suddenly, her voice tremulous. "Laura, I didn't thank him."

I spooned chocolate powder into mugs, poured hot water and milk, and silently asked Israfel for advice.

I don't know. She's your friend. You know her, what she's capable of. And I require no gratitude.

She's going to wonder about you, inevitably.

Shall I come down?

Not yet. Let me come and get you.

"Laura, he saved Deenie's life. I must thank him."

"In a minute," I said, playing for time – for all the good that would do. "Here. Drink this first."

I passed her a steaming mug and gave another to Deenie. Maureen's teeth rattled against the rim, but she didn't seem to notice. I sat at the table near her, held my warm mug between both hands, tried to steady it by leaning my elbows on the table, and wondered what we could possibly do.

Time did help. So did warmth and the permeating peace of the kitchen. Some color came back to her cheeks; Deenie's tears began to dry.

"Can you imagine," I said at last, "the pressure that'd be put on Rafe if this gets out?" I had to do something, and this was all I could think of.

She stared at me, her eyes wide. "You mean . . . no one knows?" When I didn't answer, she continued, "But that's incredible! I mean . . . a gift like that . . . to be able to . . . Laura! He could make a fortune!"

Had she forgotten how inhuman he looked? His eyes?

"There'd be too much pressure," I said, trying to keep her mind on this aspect of Israfel. "And he doesn't want that."

Still, she stared at me, and I pushed on with this slight advantage, hitting low. "I know it's a hard thing to ask, but if you're really grateful to him for saving Deenie, then you'll never tell a soul about it."

"Never?" she whispered. "How can I never . . . well, Ted, for instance? I'll have to tell him."

"Why?"

"Because I tell him everything."

"So, make an exception."

"He wouldn't tell anyone."

"Maybe not. But the fewer who know, the better."

"Then there's Deenie. She'll tell him."

A child – I was forgetting Deenie. How could I make a child keep a secret? I didn't know.

Silence fell. We were back to square one.

"Unless" Maureen said thoughtfully. "Unless . . . maybe there is a way."

I waited, scarcely daring to hope. Having a problem to tackle had already made her calmer and given her more power of thought. But this was still an awful lot to expect of anyone.

"Let me think for a while," she said. "But I do want to thank him."

I rose, went out to the hall, and called up the stairs. "Rafe, would you like some hot chocolate?"

You ask her, I suggested as he came down the stairs. *She thinks she may be able to keep the child quiet, but she's made no promises herself.*

In the softer light of the kitchen, his eyes weren't as intensely silver as they had been outside in the sun. Anxiety had drawn a fine web of doubt across his face, making him look tired, human. Maureen's own eyes filled with fresh tears when she saw him, and she went to him and took his hand. I could sense Israfel blur her vision so she would see nothing untoward.

"Th-th-thank . . . " she began to stammer.

"There's no need to say anything," he said. "But I do ask you not to tell anyone about this."

Deenie, at the sight of him, began to cry again.

"I'm . . . I'm so grateful," Maureen burst out.

He shook his head and guided her back to her chair, and I saw how tired he looked, how worn – much like Farrand after his ordeal with the logging truck out on the road, weary and depressed. I passed him a mug of chocolate, and he drew away to the window, stood there with his face averted. The child still cried, but Maureen seemed unaware of her, watching him with swimming eyes.

"Your little girl," he said. "Can you stop her from telling?"

She pulled a Kleenex form the pocket of her sweater, dabbed at her eyes, and blew her nose. "I'll try," she said.

She lifted Deenie to her lap. "It was very naughty of you to go up into the loft without telling Mommy where you were going. Now, wasn't it?"

Solemn blue eyes, trailing tears, stared at her. Deenie nodded.

"Daddy will be very cross if we tell him." Maureen glanced from Israfel to me, then fixed her eyes on the child's face. "But you were very frightened, weren't you? Falling was very scary, wasn't it?"

Again, the child nodded, and more tears rolled down her cheeks.

"But if you promise not to go up there again, we won't tell Daddy or anyone else. Okay? It'll be our little secret – yours and mine. Okay?"

"Okay" Deenie whispered.

Maureen's eyes became distant, and she sat holding Deenie to her. Israfel watched her, and I could find nothing to say.

Then his voice drifted across the room like smoke, soft and subtle, meaningful. "Thank you, Maureen."

She raised her head and looked at him, a slight uncertainty in her eyes. He met them, steadily unassuming, and at last I saw her nod.

But could she keep such a secret? Once she was away from here, had time to think . . .

"Let's go to Vernon," I said, "I'll take you out to lunch, and we can go shopping or to a movie matinee or something."

"I . . . I don't feel like going anywhere."

"Neither do I, but it'll be good for us, take our minds off other things. Come on, Maureen. I'll just go and put on something half decent, and then we can go."

She hesitated. She was clearly reluctant to go at such short notice, her mind still haunted by the events of this morning. Israfel's eyes fixed on her face, strong and compelling. She sighed deeply, dabbed at her face with the Kleenex, and asked for a glass of water. Israfel left the room.

Ten minutes later, she had washed her face and Deenie's, and was driving away with me, but she cast one disturbed and fearful glance backward.

⬤

The oppressive atmosphere of the house was palpable that night. Celene's eyes were cold with accusation; Israfel's face was a mask of stern discipline. Farrand avoided looking at either of them or at me, and he excused himself from the table the moment we had finished picking at the Chinese food I had brought home. I had a queer trembling sensation in my stomach and a rotten headache, and I would have gone to bed except I knew I wouldn't sleep. Israfel and I were left alone in the living room, and I wondered if he'd tell me what was wrong.

They're worried, aren't they? I said, watching him kneel on the hearth rug, lifting a log and setting it on the fire as though its weight was too heavy for him.

Celene is angry, very angry. He is demanding my resignation as of today.

I went to the windows, drew the heavy drapes across. *Because of what you did this morning?*

Yes.

But how could you have done nothing when it was in your power to save that child?

I could have. He thinks I should have.

I turned and looked at him, saw that the mask had gone and now his face was only sad.

He thinks Maureen will tell?

He's certain of it.

So, what difference would your resignation make?

His mind abruptly veered away from mine, quickly repressing something he didn't want me to know, and he kept his face clearly averted.

"More difference than I can now permit." He spoke out loud, but the words were barely audible, and they were followed by a sense of guilt, of transgression.

I thought again that it was self-incrimination, the blame he attached to himself for their crash, the condemnation he had surprisingly incurred by Celene. So slight, contrite, his head bent in sorrow . . . how could Celene be so callous? No longer was this an alien from another world, the cold-eyed commander I had first known and feared. This was a friend, near and dear, who had saved my precious filly and jeopardized his safety for the life of a child. His pain became mine, and I knelt beside him and touched his hand.

But he drew away. *Don't, Laura. Please. This is something I must deal with alone.*

I asked him to explain, but he refused.

I slept badly that night. My anxieties about Maureen were magnified tenfold when I lay alone in the darkness, my mind retracing over and over the alltoovivid events of the day. How could she ever keep it from Ted? Impossible. Then what should we do? Tell them the truth? Equally impossible.

Disturbing thoughts of Israfel followed: the struggle he was having with Celene and the distress he was suffering because of it, his refusals to explain.

By morning I was a nervous wreck, with eyes dark and shadowed in a face pale with strain. My companions were all equally pale and visibly depressed, anger still clear in Celene's face.

I phoned Maureen as soon as I was sure Ted had left and listened with growing despair to the phone ringing and ringing in an empty house. Then I put a call through to Jesse in Los Angeles and begged him to come home.

He too sounded weary and despondent. "What's up, Laura? Has something happened? Anything wrong?"

"Well, yes." I hesitated, remembering his irritation on the night I had disturbed him.

"Is it the horses? Or something else?"

It was impossible to relate what had happened over the phone. Privacy wasn't guaranteed, and I was still paranoid about the whole affair.

"We nearly had an accident here yesterday," I said. "And it's kind of . . . I guess I'm still shaken up. And it'd be so much better if you were here." My voice caught on the last words.

I heard him sigh, and his voice was surprisingly subdued. "Okay, Laura, I'll come. I'm not getting very far right now, and maybe I'll do better at home."

My spirits rose swiftly. "Tonight?"

"Better make it tomorrow."

I looked out at the pale sunlit morning. Snow was melting from the eaves, and bare patches lay beneath the trees. What a difference a few words could make in the bright light of day.

But fog rose from the valleys as the sun warmed, drifted up the hills toward us, filtering through the trees, glazing them with an opaque whiteness, and blurring the mountains into gray. Maureen's phone still went unanswered, and my spirits sank once more.

I sought reason, logic. I told myself I was allowing the weather to depress me. What would happen if she did tell Ted? So, he'd be amazed, curious, in wonder, but it didn't necessarily mean he'd call the police or have the army rushing in. Why, then, was Celene so angry and concerned? Because it could lead to that, I supposed, and rescue was a long way away.

Then Maureen phoned form Vernon, said she'd done it, hadn't told Ted a thing. I stood with the receiver pressed against my ear and my rollercoaster spirits soaring upward.

"There're a thousand things I want to ask you," she said. "But if you'd prefer me not to, then I won't."

I hesitated, her words making me cautious. But no. She couldn't possibly suspect. I tried to laugh. "One day," I said.

"Okay. And I bought something for Rafe. Can I drop it off on my way home?"

"Sure. But what is it?"

"Well, I guess it sounds pretty dumb, but I couldn't think what to get. Then I saw these gorgeous orchids, so I bought one. Do you think he'll laugh? Will he think that really pathetic?"

"No. Oh, no. Maureen, how far from the store are you?"

"It's right here. Why?"

"Will you get another one?"

"Who for?"

"Him. From me."

She laughed. "Never thought I'd be buying flowers for a man. Did you?"

"No," I admitted.

"Can you imagine buying flowers for Jesse?"

"No."

"When's he coming home, by the way?"

"Tomorrow," I said with a happy sigh.

"If I have a party, will you all come?"

Again, I hesitated, caution parrying acceptance of any more invitations.

"Or just bring them to dinner, if you'd prefer," Maureen continued. "I want to do something more for him . . . for Rafe."

"It isn't necessary," I interjected.

"But I want to. How would next Saturday be?"

"Can I ask Jesse when he gets home?"

"No." She laughed again. "We haven't seen you in ages, so I'm sure he'll say yes."

"He might, but I don't know about the others."

An operator interrupted, warning Maureen she'd spent three minutes.

"Okay," Maureen said. "I'll get another orchid and see you later."

She was gone, and I rushed to tell my guests what she'd said. Israfel smiled, and the shine returned to his eyes. But Celene remained skeptical.

"What is one day?" he asked me. "One day is nothing. She may yet tell."

"I don't think so," I said, wishing I could be as confident as I sounded.

"You aren't certain, either."

"Nothing is for sure," I said. "Ever."

There was a hard glitter of satisfaction in his eyes. "You see?" he said.

CHAPTER TWENTY

MAUREEN ARRIVED IN THE EARLY afternoon and became nervous and flustered the moment she stepped from the car. She pushed two square boxes into my hands. "You give them to him, Laura, won't you? I don't know what to say to him."

I tried to smile. "But that doesn't matter. Surely you want to give him yours yourself. You don't have to say anything. And don't you want to come in and have some tea?"

"No. And if I see him now, I'm liable to burst into tears. Laura, I'm telling you . . . last night, when Ted came home . . . gosh! I don't know how I did it."

I squeezed her arm. "But you did, and that's just terrific. That's the only repayment he wants."

She hesitated, seemed about to say something, then changed her mind.

"You sure you won't come in and have some tea?" I asked. "It'll only take a minute."

"No." She was adamant, and her eyes flicked almost fearfully to the door behind me. "I'd better get home. But did you ask them about the party?"

"Yes. They'll come if Jesse will."

"Great! Okay, Laura. Call me."

She was gone, driving away into the fog and cloudy gray mist that blanketed the entire place. She left me with an exotic orchid glowing in each hand and a strong admiration for my friend, over which lay only a slender shadow of doubt.

I set the boxes before him where he knelt on the rug by the fire. His face was still and mind far away, his eyes only half seeing me. I sat on the hearth and watched his eyes gain focus and turn from me to the boxes and their exquisite gleaming contents. One flower was creamy white, speckled with gold and purple, and the other orchid was red with an ivory throat.

His eyes widened, shone with sudden brilliance as at an unexpected vision, and his whole body tensed. He lifted one, slowly, and raised the cellophane lid. *Where did you get them?* Even his silent voice was tight with astonishment.

Maureen brought them. One is from her, the other from me.

From where?

A flower shop in Vernon.

She bought them?

Yes. For you.

Fleeting images came whirling into my mind: orchids in a wild profusion beside a pool of glittering water, spilling from pillars and huge white urns, hanging from enormous trees on trailing vines, splayed against a rose-tinted wall. The pictures flashed by me in a dizzying array and a blur of color: purple, coral, lemon yellow and burning orange, soft pink, white, multiple tones of green, flecks of brown and indigo, shimmering gold and mauve. Orchids and orchids, treasured and loved, and joy replaced the astonishment in his eyes. I knew we had given him something he had never expected and that he loved. I hadn't thought him capable of such an emotion.

He lifted each flower from its box, calling Celene.

But there was no softening of the defiance in the cold blue eyes. A moment's astonishment registered on Celene's mouth as Israfel placed an orchid in his hand, but after examining it briefly, he handed it back, his face rebellious. Then he turned and left the room.

Israfel watched him go, then knelt on the rug once more. His face was shadowed with sadness, the earlier joy gone.

Neither of us knew these could still be found here, he told me. *But to Celene, I fear it makes little difference. "They are only flowers," he says, "and nothing compared to the horrors this race of humans is capable of." That, of course, is true. But humans have created beauty in the arts, music, architecture, and I have reminded him of that. But he insists that as long as there exist those who would destroy them, their worth is meaningless.*

This was the closest he'd come to sharing any of his troubles with me, but there was nothing I could do or say, no words to be found that would ease his sadness or make Celene change his mind.

It was with some misgivings that I set out the next day to collect Jesse. Now it seemed I had panicked unduly over the business with Maureen. There was no other reason to call him home, take him from his work, and bring him all that way, and memories of his annoyance when I had woken him in the night still lingered.

I splashed down the hill through running rivulets of melted snow beneath a gray and lowering sky, trying to think of some welcoming words that would make him glad he'd come. Maureen's impeding party was the only highlight I could think of, but I knew this was nothing he would overly appreciate as he was on the guest list of a large number of Hollywood hostesses, most of them begging him to bring his guitar along and often imposing on him more than he felt due. Maureen too had made the same request.

As I turned at the stop light in the village, I could hardly believe what I saw at first, then I felt my stomach turn over in dread. There were no less than ten army vehicles standing in the supermarket parking lot across the way – large, dark, ominous, gathered together in a block and surrounded by officers in uniform. Two Jeeps were among them with long silvery antennas waving about their roofs, and I could just make out an officer in each wearing a set of headphones.

"Israfel! Israfel!" I cried it out loud in desperation. "Can you hear me?"

Yes.

His voice came to me clearly as I completed my turn. I tried to keep going as though I had seen nothing untoward.

I filled my mind's eye with those sinister shapes, the men, the Jeeps with their swaying antennas.

Keep watching, Israfel. Listen for the sound of those engines. If they come, you should hide in that place upstairs. I'd come back, but I have to meet Jesse's plane. Oh, Israfel! Are they looking again already?

I don't know. Surely word would have slipped out by now if they are.

So, you think they don't know?

I wish I could be certain that they don't.

But we can't be, can we?

No.

I had to hurry on as three cars and a truck were piling up behind me.

Don't worry. Israfel's voice came to me again. *We can hide. And if they do come, it's probably better if you're away. Then you won't have to confront them and undergo the difficulty of talking to them. We'll manage, Laura.*

So, I drove on, praying that Jesse's plane wouldn't be late. At least I was now justified in having him come home, even though this threat had only come after I'd asked him to.

Clear skies greeted me when I came down into the Coldstream Valley, and above Vernon and the lakes it was virtually cloudless. But I saw two small planes flying, one following the ridges to the south, the other heading north slowly, its wings catching silver in a shaft of sunlight.

An ache of despair seemed to crush my very bones. I was positive the search was in full motion once more – very close, uncomfortably close to home.

Jesse, dispirited, lines of fatigue drawn onto a face worn with frustration, was less concerned than me.

"You can't be sure," he said, flinging his hat onto the seat and letting his head fall back with a sigh. "And you worry far too much."

"You're always saying that," I said in sudden irritation, jamming the transmission lever into drive.

"Damn right I am! Because you do. You're like a long-tailed cat in a room full of rocking chairs. Never a moment's peace."

We drove from the parking lot in an offended silence.

My annoyance with Jesse and anxiety to get home made me throw caution through the window. I slewed the truck out onto the highway, dangerously close to a heavy transport vehicle that I should have waited for but had no wish to be caught behind, and tramped the accelerator to the floor. We roared and rocked along the road, the window on our passenger side whistling at the quarter vents. We swooped down a hill onto a pair of glowing taillights and streaked past a sedate black sedan.

"You trying to get a ticket?" Jesse asked, clutching at the case of his precious guitar.

"No. Get home." I spat the words out while braking with a screech behind another slow moving vehicle.

Israfel! Israfel! I called to him again and again, but there was no reply.

Jesse sat in stony disapproval, nursing his guitar and silent resentment as the truck fled along the road, tires squealing in discordant protest as I didn't slow for bends or curves, engine roaring violence at every car and truck I passed. Israfel did not answer my call.

I ignored the posted speed limit signs on the long downhill into Vernon, fumed as a car before me didn't turn at the light, cursed out loud as the next set of lights too went red.

"What in hell's the matter with you?" Jesse broke the silence angrily, and I was suddenly ashamed of my reception of him.

I stretched a hand out to him, but he didn't take it. "I'm sorry. I'm just awfully worried, that's all." I tried to make some amends. "Are you hungry? There's a nice big pot of chicken cacciatore waiting for you."

The light turned green, and the truck leaped forward.

"If we make it in one piece," Jesse said darkly.

I ignored his comment, took advantage of the small amount of traffic on Highway Six, and raced along it as fast as its twists and bends and narrow surface would allow.

It began to snow, and I bit my lip, tried not to let my anger at this show, kept the truck running as fast as my visibility permitted, straining my eyes before the big white flakes that streaked toward us.

At Lavington, Israfel answered my call. I gasped out loud in relief and was unable to prevent a smile as I poured my anxieties out to him.

No one has come, Laura. All is quiet.

Immediately my foot eased on the accelerator, and I relaxed on the seat with another sigh.

Jesse noticed. How could he not have? He stared at me with narrowed eyes, a tight wrinkle standing vertically on his forehead. I held a swift debate with myself as to whether I should tell him or not.

Two things prevented me. First, he would wonder why I hadn't told him before, and second, I didn't think he'd appreciate such an exclusive connection between Israfel and his wife. He didn't like Israfel, irked by that sense of superiority. Even though Israfel had changed considerably, first impressions do last, and Jesse had always resented authority. He had belonged to several radical groups during his college days, took part in marches and organized protests, subscribed to a number of leftwing magazines and newspapers.

He had mellowed with maturity, but the aversion to officialism remained. His frequent confrontations with customs officials were something he took an almost malicious glee in, flaunting his long hair and fringed and beaded jacket in their faces, the battered hat with its wide feathered band from which a much longer feather rose most distinctively. He never wore these particular clothes at any other time.

No, I decided. *Better not to tell him. Any enmity between Jesse and Israfel must be avoided at all costs.*

I went through a small pantomime of flexing my neck and shoulders as though to ease them, taking a breather from my frantic drive, then I leaned forward to peer through the falling snow, and floored the accelerator once more.

"Would you like me to drive?" Jesse asked, his eyes suspiciously on me.

I eased off the gas, tried to give him a capitulating smile. "You're right, hon. We wouldn't be any good to them at all if we were in the morgue, would we?"

We went on through the darkness at an easier pace, but any attempts at a normal conversation failed. A prickly atmosphere surrounded us, and it hampered talking while silence made it even more evident. And, when we at last turned onto the forestry road and I saw it was smooth and untracked beneath an inch of fresh snow, I realized that I hadn't told him what had happened with Deenie, Israfel, and Maureen. And by then it was too late to tell him about that misadventure, just as it was too late to tell him that Israfel and I could communicate telepathically. But the knowledge that I hadn't told him was disturbing and disconcerting, and it served to erect another small barrier between us.

Jesse had to agree with me that a search was again in progress. A large airsea rescue helicopter passed slowly overhead the very next morning, its heavy beating drone intruding loudly, alarmingly. And fresh tracks marked the snow on the forestry road, although we saw no vehicles and had heard nothing. The news broadcasts did not mention anything that could possibly be related to the returned military presence, but we kept the radio on all day. The only item of news that did draw our immediate attention was the evening report of a UFO sighting in Idaho. The next day there was another, due south of us near Omak in Washington State. Such sightings were so rarely reported that I was immediately alarmed.

"Are they real?" I asked Farrand. "Are they your people possibly looking for you?"

"I don't know if they are," he said.

"What? Real?"

"Yes, and my people."

"You think they're hoaxes?"

He was thoughtful, frowning, his eyes dark. "I don't know what to think."

To drive down to Omak, to try to find the people who had reported the sightings, would take me from the house for far too long, and I put the idea aside even as it formed. The apparent intensity of the search in our own vicinity kept me constantly wanting to be here, sleeping fitfully, always listening, starting at the least untoward sound, expecting my fears to be realized every time a strange vehicle approached or a small plane or helicopter passed overhead.

To distract myself, I went down into the cellar and tried to arouse some enthusiasm for my clays and glazes, the long-idle wheel and kiln. But the windowless aspect of my workroom there, its isolation from the rooms upstairs and the view from the kitchen window, soon put an end to any incentive, and I returned to the upper regions of the house. Emptiness greeted me. The only sounds were made by Jesse, fingering his guitar in the music room, and by the small hurrying winds rushing through the tops of the firs and pines around the house.

There was no sign of our guests, and I began to wonder if I was the only one who suffered these anxieties, this constant, nagging, nerve-straining worry. I went out, saddled Andante, rode up the forestry road on the mountain to the west, and ran into Captain Forrest in an army Jeep on a sharp bend near the top.

The shock of suddenly seeing the Jeep right in front of me was almost painful. Andante stopped abruptly with a loud snort of alarm and moved uneasily as I was too stunned to even speak. The Jeep was parked with two men in it, but then one got out and came marching toward me, and my shock turned to dismay as I recognized the military precision and pale smooth dispassion.

"What are you doing here?" I asked, trying to smile. When he gave no answer, I said, "You really gave me a scare. I thought I was all alone up here." I pressed a hand to my chest in a gesture to conceal my nervousness and steadied Andante, who was already receiving my signals of alarm.

"Mrs. Tremayne?"

"That's right. We live just down—"

"Yes. I know."

A gust of wind swept down the mountainside, shaking the bare branches of the birches, soughing through the dense needles of fir, blowing my hair and Andante's mane, and sending cold fingers sliding down my neck. I shivered, pulled up my collar, and wished I had worn my toque.

Impervious, the cool eyes of Captain Forrest studied me, with what I, in my current state of mind, was only too willing to imagine was suspicion. I rushed into what I hoped would be logical words.

"Are you still looking for that missing plane?"

"What I'm looking for," he said, "is a spacecraft."

His answer paralyzed me. I stared at him wordlessly while the forgotten wind's icy fingers tugged at my hair.

"It's most crucial that we find it," he went on. "It's a question of security."

Numb, speechless, I still stared at him while whirling thoughts formed a pandemonium in my brain. *He knows! He does know! That's why he's here, why they're searching . . . and he has told me, admitted it!*

Desperation gave me a moment's cunning. "Y-you m-mean," I stammered, "it's . . . Russian?"

"Shall we say of a foreign power? It's better if no names are spoken," he went on. "Politics, you know."

My heart was pounding, thundering in my ears, and I could hardly breathe. With an effort, I forced my face to be as controlled as his.

"And," he continued, "it's better if you say nothing, Mrs. Tremayne. The only reason why I've told you is because you live nearby, and we're certain it came down here somewhere."

I stared around me, at the thick and tangled trees and the banks of snow, at the muddied and frozen ground, at the distant pale blue mountains far away to the east. "Here?"

"Yes."

It was silent except for the scurrying of the wind and the creak of my saddle as Andante shifted her weight, scraping with an impatient hoof at crumbling ice. What could I say now? What should I say that would be logical, acceptable, divert the suspicion I presumed he had?

"Is . . . is . . . could it be . . . dangerous?"

A trace of a smile softened his mouth. "Probably not, but I'd recommend staying away from it if you should see it. Until we've had chance to examine it, we won't be sure."

"Radioactivity?" I suggested, my mouth so dry I formed the cumbersome word with difficulty.

"As I say, we won't know until we can examine it properly. Or . . . it could be wrecked." He hesitated, as though he might have said too much. "Whatever the case may be, it's vital that we find it. So, if you should see anything at all . . . "

"But don't touch."

"No. Get hold of us right away."

The encounter was coming to an end. I longed to turn Andante and head for home. I tried to remember a nearby alternative route that would take me in a circle. The Jeep was facing up the mountain, west, which meant that if we both went on we'd be traveling together. Those close eyes were watching me with their composed perception and the steadiness of authority. There was no trace of the brief bending I had glimpsed.

Again, the cold wind blew, and Andante tossed her head fretfully. Her teeth ground on the bit, and again she pawed at broken ice. A few of the previous year's dead leaves scurried across the road like small brown mice, uncertain of their destination but hurrying just the same. Winter, whirling down from the mountain top beneath a leaden sky, still clung with grasping fingers to the bare stark bones of the birches, slashed at cedar boughs, and moaned among the firs and bending pines.

I shivered, knew I was close to trembling, and felt the wind's keen bite and Andante's uneasy movements reflecting my own disquiet. "Winter hasn't gone yet," I said.

"No," he agreed, watching me still.

"I suppose I can tell my husband," I said, adopting a Jesselike slouch in the saddle. This man must not recognize my nervousness.

He nodded. "But ask him to keep it to himself."

"Was anybody on it?"

There was one brief blink of the pale eyes. "We aren't sure."

"But . . . this cold . . . " I huddled my coat higher around my neck, let my words trail away as though that was all that was needed.

He didn't answer.

"It's freezing up here," I said. "I think I'd better go back."

Surely that was suspicion drawn in those faint lines on that cool and unsmiling face. Surely, I should say something else, or ask one more logical question at least. What would a normal reaction be under these circumstances? I, who had been subjected firsthand to that very thing, should be in a better position to know than anyone. But my mind was as frozen by the cold surmising of those eyes as my body by the wintry wind sweeping down the mountain.

"No way to get warm on a horse," I said lamely. "And if that thing crashed last fall . . . how could anyone survive the cold up here?"

"We don't know."

What didn't he know? But I dared not ask, longed to be gone, to race homeward with my disquieting news, share my additional anxieties, warn Israfel of this very-present danger.

"So, if you see anything at all," he went one, "even if it's only a fragment, let us know right away."

"Okay." I turned Andante. "Now I'm going home to warm up."

There was that slight gesture, a small stiff raising of the hand, and I rode away with the cold wind and dead leaves hurrying after me, and a new fear going with me. Captain Forrest did know what he was looking for, and he was much too close to home. And why had he told me? That must be against policy, or we'd have heard before. Had he perhaps resorted to a desperate means of his own? And Jesse and I could be so easily silenced.

They received my news in silence, the words uttered awkwardly from my frozen lips while I huddled, shivering, before the fire.

Jesse concealed any surprise he may have felt and regarded me with thoughtful eyes while Celene received my information as though he had expected it. Farrand and Israfel's faces remained inscrutable. Only in Israfel's eyes did I see concern, and his mind touched mine with a shared anxiety, a quiet certainty that danger was near. But then it wrenched away from me into another fierce conflict with Celene.

"I think you probably said the right things," Jesse said, unaware of the battle beginning to rage within a few feet of him. "And then there's this. Who knows how anyone would react to such a statement?"

I scarcely heard him. All I could see was Celene, the anger burning in his eyes, an insistent demand, the force of invisible wrath directed at Israfel.

"It could bring any number of different reactions, depending on who you are, how you feel, what you believe." Jesse was going on, still oblivious. "There's no tangible reason I can think of why you believe he's suspicious."

The power of Israfel was filling the room, subduing even the flames of the fire to a flicker. His eyes stabbed at Celene like knives, and the light of the lamps was only a feeble glow beside their blaze. Even the walls of logs seemed frail.

"What you said sounds quite logical to me." Jesse's voice came to me as from a distance. My senses were imprisoned by Israfel's strength as physically as Celene's were, for I saw him try to move and fail.

I trembled, remembering how I had been enmeshed by that power on the night Israfel had awoken. But Celene? What strength did Israfel possess that he could hold even Celene as motionless as that?

"It's probably just his attitude." Jesse, totally unaware, went on. "Typical officialdom, all tied up in red tape like any pretty bureaucrat, and brainwashed to boot."

Celene began to crumble before my eyes. His face paled and his eyes fell from Israfel's. His head turned away in frustrated resignation as the power of his commander defeated him. I almost pitied him. But then Israfel released him, and Celene walked away without a backward glance – another sign of challenge – and without a glimmer of apology.

Farrand, after a sympathetic glance of complicity at Israfel, followed Celene from the room.

"Are any of you listening to me?" Jesse asked.

Israfel was hiding a pain I could feel. He hadn't wanted to hurt Celene. "Jesse," he said, "I fear we may yet bring trouble to you."

Jesse shrugged. "I don't mind fighting the establishment," he said.

The silver eyes studied my husband. "Rebellion is the forte of many young men, it seems."

Was he also making an excuse for Celene? But then Celene couldn't really be called young! If he was trying to divert us from Celene and Farrand's abrupt and unexplained withdrawal, he was succeeding.

"Have you ever rebelled against anything?" I said, suddenly curious.

"Not back then. I was brought up to be what I am, to follow a chosen course. I never questioned it."

And now you want to resign, I said silently.

I have to. I wish to.

"You've never told us very much," Jesse said, throwing more wood onto the dwindling fire, "about where you're from, your civilization. Or why you came here," he added, dusting off his hands before sprawling into a chair beside the hearth.

These were questions we should have asked long ago, but although Israfel met Jesse's inquiring eyes, I could read reluctance and a quick and ready caution in the racing of his brain.

"It might be easier for you if you don't know," he said.

I was certain Jesse would say he'd sooner know than have things made easier, but something stopped him. Like me and Celene, he was brought under Israfel's influence. I knew he didn't want to, but he nodded in acceptance of Israfel's words.

CHAPTER TWENTY-ONE

I WAS DOING A LATE-NIGHT check in the barn when Israfel found me and offered some explanation.

In the soft light of the aisle, amid the rough planking of the stalls, on the sawdust littered floor, he looked foreign and dislocated, and his eyes were distant. I leaned against Andante's door, uneasy. His racing mind was troubled, wanting to explain but being careful just the same.

I know you're puzzled, he began, *about the difficulty Celene and I are having.*

You don't have to tell me—

But I think I should tell you something of it. You have the right to know because it may affect you quite directly.

Israfel—

No. I want you to have some explanations. Laura, Celene is certain that the danger to us is increasing and is as equally certain that I am wrong.

His eyes were unfocused, unseeing, and my uneasiness grew as I watched him.

Today he tells me that, on this morning's news broadcasts alone, he heard of dreadful acts of terrorism, of a man beating his two-year old child to death, of twenty-three bodies found in a common grave on a farm in France, and of an elected government official convicted of accepting bribes and punished with nothing more than a small fine. He tells me he is sick of this earth, the corruption and violence of its people, its arrogance and hypocrisy, its cruelty and greed. He tells me over and over that its little culture, its art, music, and architecture, are minuscule against its horrors, its history of torture and war, treachery and murder, slaughter and cruelty, crime and corruption.

Laura, how can I argue against that? I've tried and tried, pointed out the humanity of the people we have met – of you and Jesse, Maureen – the beauty of this planet, the striving for decency by so many. But he insists they are irrelevant when there is the greater danger of the wickedness of humanity, lack of probity in high places, such selfishness and greed that jeopardizes all we have worked so long for. Laura, I fear he may be right, and I wrong.

He has said this all before— I began.

I know he has. But now he may have stronger grounds on which to base his judgment, for mine is clouded in more ways than one. He is certain, too, that my pending resignation means I have abstained from my obligation. He insists I am now putting self before duty, my own desires before responsibility, and that my refusal to relinquish my command is causing the failure of this mission.

But you were shot down, I protested. *You were hurt, your craft wrecked. You weren't able to go on.*

His mind closed to me like a door slamming in my face. His eyes became even more distant before, and then he turned away from me.

Israfel?

He didn't answer, standing there in the pale light, taut with tension.

Around us were all the sounds of horses in the night: the scrape of hooves shuffling straw, the fluttering snort of nostrils, the crunch of teeth on hay. The air was redolent with the aromas of the barn: horse, hay, sawdust, grain. But they were only vague impressions at the far edge of my consciousness. There was another greater presence, an aura of something disturbing, a power of emotion that wasn't only alien because he was from another world but foreign in other aspects.

Israfel?

He did not turn and spoke out loud. "I have asked you before if you could trust me. Do you yet?"

I stared at the slight figure in a down-filled jacket, the flowing silver hair, tense shoulders and poise of head. *I . . . I don't know.*

"There are times when I feel I could trust you," Israfel continued out loud. "You've done nothing to make me think otherwise. But then there hasn't been any great demand made of you. Oh, yes. I know having us here, concealing our identity, has been a trial. But it hasn't put you into any personal danger. If

I were to tell you that letting us go when the time comes could put you into very great danger, would you still let us leave?"

"What are you saying?" I whispered. "What are you telling me?"

"I'm not telling you anything, only asking what I presume is a difficult question."

"How can I answer it?" I said, feeling obtuse, inadequate, hopelessly young and incapable. "It isn't a fair question."

Then he turned back and looked at me, and his eyes were brilliant, focused, and his face as I first remembered it. I pressed against Andante's door, my heartbeat quickening, my muscles tightening with alarm.

He smiled. *If I am wrong and Celene right, then I do have a solution I hope you'll come to accept. But there's time, Laura, and Celene may learn patience.*

His eyes were on me, but I didn't think really saw me. His head was filled with racing images that flashed by me at their usual lightning speed. He smiled again. *And never, Laura, never did I think I'd experience the emotion of hope.*

I had no clarity of thought throughout the rest of the evening. Immediately upon our return to the house, Israfel went to his room and closed the door. Jesse remained behind that of the music room, and Farrand had apparently joined Celene in their room upstairs.

I attended to a pile of correspondences in what must have been a very haphazard manner, for I would later receive two replies asking me to explain what I had written. I filled out registration applications for the foals and kept my precious filly's paperwork aside, determined that Israfel at least name her. There were stallion bookings to attend to, and it was with a shock I discovered that the first visiting mares were due to arrive the very next day. This meant having stalls ready for them and brought the customary concerns about the condition of our road.

But constantly intruding in my mind were Captain Forrest on the mountain and Israfel's strange words, his mention of danger, the difficult questions he had put to me.

In the surrounding silence of the house, in its warmth and glowing walls, it was often hard to remember there were three aliens beneath our roof, beings from another world. But on that night, I was very conscious of them, remembering again and again the anger in the eyes of Celene and Israfel's words out there in the barn.

I sealed all the envelopes, tidied things away, and went quietly to bed. Jesse came a short while later, and I clung to him, holding on to the security of his warm arms and strong body, the familiar feel of him. But I said nothing of the disquieting conversation I had had with Israfel.

All the extra work involved with visiting mares and another foaling kept me fully occupied during the next few days. I had little opportunity to talk with Israfel, and when his mind sometimes reached out to mine in the night or during some brief interlude in a busy day, it was only to present a brief image, a fleeting concern or passing idea, and his mind would close once more.

Celene, pale, silent, and unhappy, appeared only at mealtimes while Farrand, also distressed, continued to work on the receiver with an engrossment that I was sure was only an excuse to keep him away from the barn or to avoid conversing with the people who brought the mares. Israfel might as well have not been there for the little I saw of him. He came sometimes for meals but ate very little, strain evident in every line of his face, his eyes rarely meeting those of Celene.

At times I longed to go and talk to him, but his door was always closed, an invisible barrier drawn firmly before it. And the shutters across his mind warned me too against intruding. Then there would be more phone calls, arrangements to make for other mares or information to give on the stallions we were standing, and I would be involved in my own life once more, our alien guests temporarily forgotten.

Then it was the night of Maureen's party, and Israfel stunned us all, and me even more.

We went down together, me driving with Israfel and Celene in the front while Farrand gallantly volunteered to ride with Jesse in the back. It wasn't very far to go, and the evening was mild with the approach of spring. Wrapped in warm coats, Farrand and Jesse joked about the differences between traveling across the universe faster than the speed of light and riding in a farm pickup, sitting on bales of straw. Neither Celene nor Israfel joined me in the laughter, Celene appearing unhappy as usual and obviously not looking forward to an evening out. Israfel was still withdrawn, seemed preoccupied and far away, and said nothing at all as I drove the truck out through the forest and down the hill to the valley below.

Ted and Maureen's stone, glass, and cedar house glowed like a jewel amid its surrounding trees. We were not the first to arrive. Kevin and Patty as well as Anne and Jason were already there, sitting before a blazing fire with glasses gleaming in their hands. Maureen, with a quick touch of Israfel's hand drew us into the warm, softly lit room. Celene drew away into a shadowed corner of the room, and Israfel, the dark glasses concealing his eyes, slid unobtrusively into a place near Jesse by the hearth.

Others came, Mac and Helen, Sarah and Todd, the Campbells, who had not met out house guests and looked at them with the customary response of politely restrained but curious eyes.

The evening began typically, with Todd making his terrible jokes –which most of us laughed at because they were so bad.

"Hey, Jesse!" he shouted merrily. "Know what you get when you pour boiling water down a rabbit hole?" When Jesse resignedly said, "No. What?" Todd answered, "A hot cross bunny!" The exchange brought the usual mirth from all of us, except Israfel, Farrand, and Celene. But only I seemed to notice their reserved responses as glasses were filled again, bowls of chips and dip passed around, and Maureen slipped in and out of the kitchen as she tended her roast of beef.

"Hey, Randy!" Todd cried. "Can you name three inventions that have helped humanity get up in the world?"

Farrand glanced at me, puzzled.

"The elevator, the escalator, and the alarm clock!"

Farrand's wondering eyes turned back to Todd, who slapped him on the back and chuckled gleefully.

"Here's another for you. What do you call a person who puts you in contact with the spirit world?"

Israfel, I said silently, *tell him a bartender.*

"A bartender?" Farrand asked innocently, uncertainly, before his questioning eyes turned to me once more.

"That's right!" Todd shouted, slapping him again. "You've heard it before, by George!"

I could see that Farrand was about to deny that and passed another swift message to Israfel.

Farrand smiled, and Todd, bested, mercifully changed the subject. But I saw Maureen glance curiously at Celene, sitting apart in his darkened corner, his face pale and set, his head high and aloof. She went to him and sat beside him, and I watched anxiously as she tried to draw him into conversation. I saw the courteous smile appear that I knew to only be a mask.

"You did bring your guitar, didn't you, Jesse?" Anne asked.

"Sure. It's out in the hall."

"Cleared any more of your land, Ted?"

Normal conversation resumed. Maureen was still talking to Celene, Farrand was listening politely as Kevin told him about a movie he and Patty had gone to see the previous night, and Jesse was stretched out in a chair in his usual casual pose, telling Anne about his score. Beyond him, Israfel was quietly attentive to their conversation, his face in shadow and eyes enigmatic behind the dark lenses.

I relaxed into the warmth of the room and the harmony of my friends, and drank deeply of my wine. Surely here we were safe before Ted's steady eyes and Maureen's great depth of gratitude to Israfel. Surely the smile on Celene's face was one of genuine appreciation for her consideration in not leaving him alone on the far side of the room. And Farrand must recognize how all these diverse people not only accepted them but were willing to extend a helping hand toward their friends.

The wine was rich and heady, the fire hot. I sat on a cushion on the wide slate hearth, my long blue skirt wrapped cozily around my legs, and listened to the voices and laughter. How warm, how secure this house was; how familiar those faces – so far from that cold mountain trail and the military bearing and the cool dispassionate face of Captain Forrest, from the strange craft buried beneath the soil of our High Meadow.

Sometimes I wondered about it, what it contained, how it was powered. I had never really seen it properly.

Maureen went out to the kitchen and did not return, and the clatter of dishes drew me to help her.

"Laura." Her face was still tense, slightly pale. "Why is Len sitting there by himself? I tried to make him join the others, but he said he preferred not to."

"He's a bit of a loner," I said lamely.

"He wasn't like that at Christmas," she said, lifting a huge roast of beef from pan to platter.

I steadied the plate for her and tried to think of something else to say. But the wine and the warmth had fuddled my brain, left it woolly and thick.

She put the pan on the stove and began to make gravy. "I feel so inadequate," she said, stirring rapidly with one hand while making a despairing gesture with the other.

"Inadequate? Good heavens! Why?"

"They're so goldarned superior. And it's not that they're egotistical or opinionated . . . nothing like that." She peered into the pan, added water from a kettle. "They make me feel like a dope."

"Oh, come now, Maureen," I said, although I knew what she meant.

She turned and looked at me, a flush stealing across her cheeks. "Rafe, now. I want to say a million things to him, assure him of my gratitude over and over, and I can't even bring myself to ask him if he'd like another drink."

I could only smile as though she wasn't serious.

"It's true, Laura. Stupid, isn't it?"

"Just don't let it bother you. Really, they're very nice when you get to know them."

"I didn't say they weren't. It's just that—"

She broke off as Ted came into the kitchen.

"I smell food," he said. "Want me to cut up that meat?"

Maureen dragged her attention back to the roast on the table, the gravy on the stove. The color faded from her cheeks, and she found a knife, gave it to Ted, and went to the refrigerator.

I spooned pickles from a jar into a dish, wished I had drunk less wine and that Maureen hadn't been so perceptive, and wondered if Celene had said anything untoward.

Israfel spoke to me in silence. *He said very little, Laura. Your friend is overly sensitive about us. She senses something different, and it troubles her.*

Could you come and talk to her?

Now? When she's involved with what she's doing there? It would only make matters worse.

Again, I cursed the wine, my inept head. I tried to attend to the neglected gravy and split rolls, and find extra knives while Maureen set dishes out with her eyes avoiding mine. But she had wanted us to come. Ever since the Christmas dinner, I had been reluctant to take our guests anywhere. Then, while we were all milling around the table, Larry Campbell dropped a bombshell.

"Say," he said loudly. "You know what I heard the other day?"

With my ever-ready anxiety, I should have been prepared. But I wasn't.

"My brother George – the one in the RCMP in Winnipeg – well, he was here for a visit, and he said it wasn't a plane they were looking for around here last fall, but . . . " He paused dramatically, and his words fell into an expectant silence. "A spaceship!"

My insides lurched horribly, and the floor seemed to vanish beneath my feet. The silence lingered, potent and ominous.

"What kind of spaceship?" asked Jason. "You mean a satellite?"

"Uh huh." Larry grinned and shook his head.

"But we'd have heard if one'd crashed."

"Not necessarily."

Ted ceased to carve the roast before him, and Maureen stood with a jar of salad dressing forgotten in her hand.

"You mean it was Russian, then?"

"But surely we'd have heard!"

"Not," Larry said, with another dramatic pause, "if it was alien."

There was a long silence. I dared not look at Israfel, who I knew was standing close behind me.

"I shouldn't really be telling you this," Larry went on suddenly. "It's supposed to be top secret. But . . . " he shrugged his shoulders. "Rumors have sure begun to spread."

"You're drunk!" Todd said abruptly. "You must be blind drunk!"

Larry laughed. "Not that drunk. I know what I heard."

"You mean to say you believed such a cock and bull story?"

"Just a minute," Anne interjected. "Are you saying it came from Mars or somewhere like that?"

"That's right."

Todd snorted, continued to spread butter on a bun.

"Why," asked Ted, "is it believed to be alien?"

"It was shot down, that's why."

"Argh!" Todd exploded. "Flying saucers and little green men from Mars – they've all been hoaxes or tales told by someone on the pipe. We all know damn well there's nothing out there."

"Have you been?" Ted asked politely. "Have you seen?"

"Christ!" Todd swore. "Okay. So maybe we don't know everything, but all those stories have been hoaxes, just a load of bunk. You know that as well as I do."

"But I don't."

"You mean to tell me you believe in flying cups? Or maybe pots and pans?"

"I said I don't know that all those stories are hoaxes."

"But there's no proof, none at all! Have you ever seen any?"

"No," Ted said. "But I've never seen an albatross or a submarine, either."

"But you can see bloody pictures of those things."

"So, you can of these," said Jason. "We saw some on TV a short while back."

"Star Wars stuff," said Mac. "You know what they can do on film these days. But anyway, if they say they shot one down, then where is it? Huh?"

"That's what they're looking for," Larry replied.

"Probably just a bloody meteorite."

"With windows? That takes evasive action?"

"Then it must have been Russian or maybe Chinese. We don't know what the hell they've got."

"The food's getting cold," said Ted.

"And they wouldn't let on if they had satellites flying in our airspace," Todd said.

"Satellites don't fly. They orbit," Ted said. "Come on, Todd. Forget about it now, and let's eat."

I stole a look at Farrand, saw him move as though in a trance toward the table. Jesse was across from me, studiously arranging slices of beef on a bun, his eyes cast firmly down.

Israfel, I said silently. *They all know now.*

No. The answer came back softly. *They won't really believe it until they have tangible proof. There's always a small barrier of doubt when the premise is only theory to anyone with a reasonably logical mind.*

Ted carved more meat, and Sarah, ahead of me, began to put salad on her plate. But the conversation did not die. Todd was still denying loudly that he could believe "that crap."

"Comic book stuff," he said. "Horror movies." He spread a large slice of pickled cucumber. "Show me a little green man whose paint won't come off, and then . . . maybe . . . I might say okay." He shoved the pickle into his mouth and speared another.

"So, what would you say if they do find something?" Larry persisted.

"That's if we ever hear anything more about it," Jason said.

"I'll bet we won't," Mac said.

"You mean another coverup?" Anne asked.

"Nah," Todd grated through a mouth full of pickle. "Just another cock and bull story."

I felt I must say something or the silence of the five of us would become noticeable. "How can you be so adamant," I said to Todd, "over something you know nothing about?"

He glared at me. "I just don't believe in any such garbage, in fairy tales. Besides, if there are these things flying around, little green men and all, then why don't they come down and introduce themselves, eh? Why all the mystery? No," he went on, slathering mustard on his beef. "I won't believe any such thing until I see it standing right in front of me."

I looked at Farrand's thick dark hair, so close to Todd where they stood at the table. I felt Israfel's laughter respond to mine, and for one wildly hysterical, wine-inspired moment, I wanted to tell Todd, tell him what was standing right there before him. But I bit my tongue and put on a polite smile, helped myself to salad with careful concentration, aware of Israfel's caution as the conversation dangerously went on.

"So why was the army all around here last fall, eh?"

"How the hell should I know?"

"They were supposed to be looking for missing plane."

"Some plane!"

"They don't get the army out for nothing."

Celene retreated to the now empty living room. Farrand quickly followed, with Jesse and me close behind. Israfel came in a few minutes later, and we huddled together by the fire, united by the turn of events, the threat of revelation brought by the spread of knowledge, the rumor that held so much truth.

"But it had windows!"

"Says who?"

Something unintelligible.

"There are people who . . . "

"Bunk. Nothing but bunk!"

"I don't think they'd have . . . "

Snatches of sentences, bits of arguments came to me from the kitchen. I half listened while the rest of me longed to get away from here, be in the secluded security of our own home, away from these people who now represented danger.

But we couldn't leave, of course. Questions would immediately be asked, curiosity aroused. Jesse had promised music, and the party was being given, in the main, for us.

Maureen came and joined us by the hearth.

"Crazy bunch," she said, sinking down into the rug beside me. "Helping to spread wild rumors, if you ask me." She bit into her bun, glanced at Israfel sidelong. "Anything for a good story, I guess."

I nodded noncommittally, tried to appear casual.

"But you were out hunting for that plane, weren't you?" Maureen was caught up in the story, in spite of her doubt.

Again, I nodded, saw Jesse's eyes on me, a small frown between them.

Her eyes followed the direction of mine. "Gosh, Jesse! What would you have done if you had found it?"

His eyebrows rose quizzically. "A plane?" he asked.

"Whatever," Maureen said.

Jesse shrugged in that magnificently offhand way he has. "Who knows?"

"Well, anyway . . . " Maureen's eyes shone in the firelight. "I do think Ted's right. How can we possibly know if all those stories are hoaxes or not? I mean, there must be hundreds that we never hear about."

Helen and Sarah came back into the room and, to my intense relief, succeeded in changing the subject. And before long, coffee and cake were served, the fire stoked up, and Jesse asked to play.

Bit by bit, I was able to relax. Israfel and Celene were inconspicuous in the shadows beyond the hearth, and Farrand sat with Helen and Jason in apparent belonging, fitting in as he so easily did. Maureen was regarding us with pleasure, enjoying having us there, and Larry seemed no longer anxious to pursue his hot topic.

Jesse's amazing hands began to draw music from the strings of his guitar, and Ted rose quietly, went to the piano, and played a soft accompaniment. I closed my eyes and gave myself up to the pleasure of listening. This was what I had so long loved: Jesse's music by a fire and a circle of appreciative friends with nothing to intrude. I could forget Captain Forrest's pale eyes, the army Jeep on the mountain where the cold winds of winter still hunted between the trees, and relax in this warm house and the security of my friends.

Jesse played on, the guitar singing in his hands, and Ted's muted harmony played perfectly in the background. Anne got up and sang a few of the more popular songs, her clear sweet voice matching the sounds of piano and guitar, and the rest of us listened in a deeply appreciative silence. Only Maureen and Celene had the hazy look of distraction.

At last, Jesse, obeying his own stringent rule, laid down his guitar and shook his head at the outcry for more. "I've never tired you out yet," he said, smiling, "and I don't intend to start now."

Loud protestations greeted him, but he was adamant. "Always leave them wanting more" was a philosophy he lived by and from which he never wavered.

Ted, knowing this, closed the lid of the piano and returned to the fire. Maureen brought in fresh coffee and refilled our cups, and Israfel, with a quiet "May I?" lifted Jesse's guitar to his knees and examined it thoughtfully.

Lazy in the warmth, my head still filled with music, I stirred my coffee and watched him with only half an eye. He was sitting near the corner of the fireplace, beyond Jesse who sat opposite to my place on the hearth, and shadows fell across him, muting the silvery hair, masking the perfect face. But I could see his mouth drawn into thoughtful lines, the considering bend of his head over the guitar.

Subdued by the music, sipping coffee, we were mostly silent, only Sarah and Helen picking up some thread of conversation. But they broke off abruptly when a few sudden incredible notes came from the guitar.

All eyes swung to Jesse, to his hands empty except for a coffee cup, to his equally startled face. Then they all tuned to the shadowed figure beyond, the long pale hand moving so deftly over the strings.

The notes began to flow, then pour in cadence after cadence – lifting, falling, soaring, singing – exquisite, unearthly, ethereal, totally unlike anything I had ever heard before in my life. My skin crawled as cold shivers passed up and down my spine in a constant, ceaseless procession, and my heart turned over with a twist of pain. I was dimly conscious of Jesse's face frozen into incredulous disbelief, his eyes fixed on Israfel in amazement. Then the music filled the room with a flood of sound that swept away all awareness of time and surroundings, of the people gathered at the hearth. There was only a vast sky filled with dazzling stars that swirled in continual motion so controlled it was relentless, yet it moved with all the beauty of a disciplined dance, executing perfect forms. And the music was almost mathematical in its precision, the repetition of a haunting melody that would reverse and change keys only to meet the theme again in a perpetual pattern.

I knew only what Jesse had taught me about music, which wasn't very much, as I preferred to listen to what I liked without knowing all the technicalities of its execution, but I recognized the perfection of this piece, its exquisite harmony, the flawless structure of its form. So did Jesse, sitting there dumbfounded.

Another sound joined that of the guitar: his voice, like shining crystal. Israfel's.

At first, I listened with the same frozen concentration of those around me, shivering as the eerie fingers crept on my scalp and down my back. But then I heard the words and was numbed by shock, could scarcely believe my ears. This couldn't be. What on earth did he think he was doing? Was he out of his mind? What had possessed him?

The words rand out, as clear as glass, and each one was a bruise on my heart.

"*To touch the stars,*
The dancing moons,
And walk on distant crystal shores.
To move through time,
Beyond the spheres

Of a farflung glittering universe.
The blazing suns,
The frozen snows
Of endless spinning galaxies.
To search, to find,
Through space and time,
A mind, a heart, a soul
As mine."

Then he was only humming, another source of music, and the guitar's song became muted, the haunting melody distant. But the words echoed and echoed, were written indelibly on my mind, and would never be erased. I saw Maureen gazing at him, her eyes wide pools of tears, and Jesse sitting as motionless as me, struck dumb.

The notes faded, became only the theme of the melody as it lingered, and then both voice and guitar were silent.

No one spoke. Everyone but me sat staring at the figure in the shadows beyond the hearth. I looked at Celene, saw his face was white, his brilliant eyes gazing at Israfel in shocked disbelief. Farrand was also pale, frowning in apparent doubt. So was Ted, and Larry's eyes were narrowed and wondering.

Anne at last broke the silence. "My God, Rafe!" she gasped. "Where in the world did you learn that?"

"I didn't."

His reply was calm and quiet, but I cringed even further as I construed its meaning.

"You don't mean you wrote it?" Anne's voice was breathless.

"I haven't yet."

There was another silence, but one that shouted at me with questions and emotions, doubts and conjecture.

Still Anne was the only one able to speak. "Are you saying you just made that up? At this minute?"

"Not really. It's been running round in my head for a few weeks."

Ted spoke cautiously. "Would you play us another?"

Israfel smiled and shook his head, passed the guitar back to Jesse – who appeared to take it without seeing him. "That isn't my instrument, and I think I've subjected you to enough for one day."

Maureen, her voice trembling with emotion, said brokenly, "Rafe, that's the most beautiful thing I've ever heard!"

His head bent briefly, and he smiled again. "Beauty in exchange," he said, and then he turned to me. *Laura?*

Why did you sing that? I screamed at him in silence. Those words! Those reveling words! *What were you thinking? Israfel, what on earth are you doing? Are you out of your—*

I have my reasons.

His words halted my tirade.

And you're avoiding their other intent.

His mind was distant, blurred, but the eyes behind the dark glasses were so bright and intent I could see their metallic gleam. I turned away.

Laura.

No . . .

Laura, the song was for you.

CHAPTER
TWENTY-TWO

IT COULD HAVE BEEN A simple token: the acknowledgment of our ability to communicate in silence, or gratitude for the extent I had gone to protect him and his crew, even recognition of a form of friendship that had come to exist between us. But I believed it was none of these. There was a fervor in his words, but one so strong and deep and purposeful that it wasn't an emotion familiar to me. A profound certainty, so unequivocal that my denial meant nothing to him, was a passion of its own.

Israfel, no. Don't. Don't.

What is, is. Laura, don't you realize that by showing me a new life, you are part to it?

No.

Yes. I can't change that any more than you can the past. What's done is done.

No. Your life has nothing to do with me.

But it does. Without you I wouldn't have one.

I'm married to Jesse . . .

I know that, and even that can't change what is.

I turned my mind away from his. Maybe I was misconstruing his words. If he thought I was part of his life while understanding that mine belonged to Jesse, perhaps that was perfectly acceptable to him, and I was overreacting. After all, he was an alien from another world, and what did I know of his mores, his relationships? Besides, I was as distant from him as a bird. Weren't my horses part of my life? Of course, they were.

He was letting me have my privacy, even though he was waiting for me to say something further. I forced my attention to the startled faces and wondering eyes around me, to Jesse gazing with total abstraction at the floor, Maureen looking shocked at the far side of the hearth, and Celene, in his own shadowed corner, glaring with furious eyes at his commander.

Mac and Helen got up and began to say awkward goodbyes, and Sarah and Todd promptly followed suit. I saw Jason touch Anne's arm in a gesture that checked any further questions and indicated they should also leave. The party was obviously over, and we followed the others, Jesse almost forgetting his guitar, Maureen staring at us with eyes full of questions as we pulled on our coats and boots.

My relief at escaping into the night was short-lived when Celene refused to even be close to Israfel in the truck. He vaulted into the back with Farrand and Jesse, one killing look making his reason very clear. Israfel and I were alone in the cab, nothing between us on the seat but Jesse's guitar.

However, his mind didn't touch mine as I drove home. He left me to my private distraction, my uncertainties, and my compound of anxieties. I wished I could find the courage to ask him what he'd really meant. But I selected a cowardly incertitude over the possibility of his scorn.

Upon our arrival at the house, Farrand and Celene slipped away upstairs, Israfel went to his room and closed the door, and Jesse blew his stack.

"What the hell does he think he's doing?" he roared, hurling wood into the kitchen stove. "Damn it all! Why doesn't he just stand out on the street and shout who he is?"

"Jesse," I pleaded. "He'll hear you."

"I don't care!" He poked savagely at the wood. "What the hell can he expect?"

I paced about the kitchen, unable to be still, too distraught to put my mind to anything.

"Here we are," Jesse went on, slamming down the stove lid, "bending over backward to help them, keeping a terrible secret, and he goes and opens his mouth and tells the whole world!"

"Hardly," I said, suddenly defensive. "Only a few of our friends."

"Only a few? Dammit all, Laura! You know how gossip spreads in a small place like this. How long do you think it'll be before the story's as big as a house? And coming right on top of Larry's alien spacecraft!" He threw his hand in the air. "I give up."

"He must have his reasons," I said, still on the defensive.

"For chrissakes, stop making excuses! As if we haven't got enough problems already. I'd just like to know what in hell he thinks he's doing."

"So why don't you ask him, then?" I burst out. "Instead of taking it out on me."

"Ask him? And have him look down his bloody nose at me in that damned superior way he has—"

"That's all in your mind."

Jesse's face was a red burn of anger, his eyes a furious glare. "It isn't in my mind! It's right here on my bloody doorstep! And I'm pissed to the teeth with the whole bloody works!"

"I wish you wouldn't swear like that," I said plaintively.

"It's how I bloody well feel. And if you felt the same, you'd bloody well swear, too."

I caught my tongue, aware of the sudden, disconcertingly dangerous ground. Could this overly exorbitant anger be fueled by jealousy? My defense of Israfel could seem unwarranted. Had Jesse recognized the form of alliance that existed between Israfel and me? Then why hadn't he said anything before?

"Okay, okay," I said swiftly. "But there's no point in getting angry about it. It isn't going to do any good."

"Like I said – it's how I feel."

"Would you like some tea?"

He scowled. "You have some if you want. I'm going to bed."

He managed to stomp from the room, even though his feet wore only socks. He left me shaken and upset, aware that for the first time in our marriage, he had damaged our relationship by walking away from a break.

I followed him, unhappy and fearful. We undressed in a hostile silence and lay far apart and alone while an even deeper loneliness came to me from beyond the bedroom wall.

⬤

In the morning, Jesse began to make arrangements for an immediate return to Los Angeles. I watched him in dismay. He didn't apologize for his anger the night before, but he did make some amends, smiled, and made a joke about Todd's disbelief in flying saucers.

I didn't want him to go but accepted that I couldn't stop him. Nor did I want our parting to be strained by ill feelings, so I made my own amends, drove him to the airport in the afternoon, clung to him with willing kisses, and told myself all was well. Jesse was over his spat; Israfel had meant nothing more than an appreciation for an unlikely but small friendship he hadn't expected to find. And weren't the words of many songs quite meaningless?

But I was disconcerted to find that Israfel avoided me.

This I had not expected. His eyes looked through me or beyond me when we met. He was aloof, distantly polite when he had to speak, and his mind was securely locked.

To my astonishment, I found this deeply distressing. It was as though some unknown part of myself was reacting without any control, responding to something unseen, hurting when no wound had been inflicted.

Israfel disappeared in the evening and vanished again as soon as breakfast was finished the following morning. Farrand and Celene were equally distant, and I'd never felt so isolated in my life. I did the chores alone, mechanically and automatically, with my mind suffering a loneliness I didn't want to feel, thinking constantly of Jesse's abrupt departure, his anger after Maureen's party, Israfel's disturbing song, whether he was hurt, and if so, why? Could I find the courage to ask him? Then I had to forget about it as a vaguely familiar pickup drove into the yard.

It's someone we met in connection with the horses, I thought, trying to remember the names of the two men who got out. One was fairly young, with a pale, tired face beneath unruly black hair. He wore the customary jeans and a scarlet plaid shirt of wool under a down-filled jacket. His eyes were wide and brown and filled with a curious apprehension as I went to meet them. His companion was large, burly, dressed the same way, and regarded me with a diffident caution that didn't belong on his ruddy, open face. His hands were more implements, also familiar, his boots typical loggers' wear. But I couldn't recall where I had seen them, or that yellow truck.

"Mrs. Tremayne? I guess you don't remember me, or us."

I frowned, still trying.

"Last time you saw us was over there on the road."

Yellow pickup. Enormous logs leaning over it and on it. Farrand. This man.

"Of course!" I exclaimed. "I remember . . . "

"I'm Gus Peterson," he said, enveloping my hand in his colossal clasp. "And this is the guy I damn near killed."

The other stepped forward, shook my hand. "Colin Webb."

They had taken me completely by surprise, and I couldn't think of a thing to say. There was a difficult silence, during which Colin Webb's gaze flickered beyond me to the open door and windows of the house.

"Do you have a moment?" Peterson asked at last. "We'd like a few words with you."

Oh, Lord! What words? "Sure," I said, trying to sound far more positive than I felt. "Would you care for some coffee?"

"That'd be great."

They followed me into the house, shed their heavy boots and coats in the utility room, entered the kitchen, and searched it rapidly with their eyes.

"Nice place you have here."

I waved them to the chairs at the table, filled the kettle, set it on the range, and told them how my grandfather had built the house and I happened to be his only heir. But they paid me little attention. Their ears were constantly listening for other sounds, and their eyes wandered from me to the door and back again.

I poured the coffee, passed the cream and sugar and a plate of cookies, and pulled up another chair. "Now," I said, steeling myself, "what was it you wanted to talk about?"

There was another silence. Gus Peterson stirred his coffee as though it were the most important task in a heavy day while Colin Webb ate two cookies and watched the door. This, I figured, was shaping up to be trouble.

At last Peterson took a deep breath and plunged in. "Mrs. Tremayne—" he began.

"Laura, please," I said.

"Okay. Laura. Have you heard any of these rumors that are going around? About a spacecraft crashing here? And that it's alien?"

I tried not to swallow too visibly. "I've heard something."

"We didn't take much notice at first, thought it just some kid's dreamedup story. But Colin here works for the Forest Service, and he was up in the woods north of here last week, saw the army searching there. Dozens of men, Jeeps, even dogs."

I tried to appear mildly interested.

"Now, we figure they're not there for the good of their health. Frost's just coming out of the ground, mud everywhere . . . hell of a time to be in the woods."

I nodded, sipped my coffee without tasting a drop.

"Your friend still staying here?"

The question came abruptly, took me unawares. I stared at him; my lips suddenly frozen. How was I to answer this?

He had his answer, of course, just from reading my face.

"Colin here figures he owes your friend his life," he went on. "And so do I."

Coffee stuck in my throat like a lump.

"There's no need for you to say anything, Laura. But if you want any help at all, of any kind or in any way that we can provide, just call us. We're both in the book, and if we're not home, our wives will make sure one or the other always is. They can quickly reach us. Okay?"

Dumbfounded, I could only stare at him.

The huge hand lifted, palm out, fingers spread in a gesture of understanding. "We'll be glad to help, any time. Now we'd better be getting along."

They rose to go while I sat in stunned bewilderment. Had I heard him correctly? Had I understood his meaning? But surely, I had. What else could he possibly be saying?

Awkwardly, I scrambled to my feet and followed them back to the utility room, watching as they hauled on boots, zipped up coats.

"Thank you," I mumbled as they turned to the door.

Again, a short wave of the huge hard hand, a smile on the ruddy face.

Colin Webb said, "Tell him thanks for me, would you?"

I nodded; my throat suddenly aching. Other hands had come to help, genuine hands, bearing a debt of gratitude.

"Okay?"

"Okay," I whispered, watched them walk back to the yellow pickup. They were the first we'd gathered to our side.

Celene, always skeptical, couldn't understand why I was so pleased.

"So now they know we're here," he said, poised as though for flight at the top of the stairs while I stood on a lower step still brimming with good news.

"But they've promised to help!"

"How do you know they weren't just confirming suspicions? How can you be sure it wasn't just a ruse?"

"I don't think they're like that."

"But you don't know them. You have no idea what they're like. They could very well be just like most humans: greedy, selfish, unscrupulous—"

"Celene! You're being most unfair! At least give them a chance, some benefit of the doubt."

"And how much will they give us? What chance will we have if they go to your police, your army, tell them they know we're here? What chance, Laura?"

I looked at him despairingly, and then at Farrand. But his eyes also harbored doubt and a darkness of distress.

"Farrand! What do you think? Don't you believe they meant it? You've seen them. You know how Gus Peterson kept quiet after that accident on the hill."

But he shook his head. "The circumstances are different now, Laura. The story is spreading. It can come far more easily to the wrong ears. And if those men do know we're here, we can't be sure of their silence."

The sharp prick of reality deflated me. My joy and relief left me. Again, I felt isolated, abandoned to an old and lonely anxiety once more.

"Where is Israfel?" I asked Farrand. "I want to tell him about it."

"He's out in the woods. You'll be able to find him."

I stumbled back down the stairs and pulled on boots, my sheepskin coat. At least I had a reason to approach Israfel, and maybe he'd be more receptive to what I still wanted to believe was a genuine offer of help.

I slipped through the mud on the road past the corrals. Colin Webb's pickup had left deep ruts in the melting ground. Breakup. Trucks and trailers hauling visiting mares in this soft and slippery mud became more of a problem every year. The original gravel was breaking down.

Israfel, where are you?

There was no answer.

I struck into the forest beyond the corrals, tripped on the slash that still lay on the remains of an old logging road, tried to dodge a branch that deposited a shower of icy drops onto my already straggling hair, moldering leaves and rusty needles squelched beneath my feet, and patches of snow, grainy and stained, lay beneath the low branches of hemlock and cedar, small saplings of evergreens and birch.

I passed a gigantic larch, still bare, clambered over a fallen log, stood still, and listened. But there was no sound, no answer to another silent call. I went on, apprehension growing. Why didn't he answer me? Or had I, with my initial presumption at his song, his words, embarrassed him, and was that why he was avoiding me?

Israfel, please answer me. I have something to tell you.

He materialized so suddenly in front of me, a gasp of alarm tore at my throat. He stood looking at me, cool and remote and very alien on the rough trail between the weeping boughs of evergreen. So unbelonging, his eyes a gleaming chrome in the pallid light, his face a pale smooth cameo incongruous amid nature's random trees. I scrambled into the refuge of words and told him, my voice gabbling once again, of Gus Peterson and Colin Webb's visit, the promise they had made.

"Celene and Farrand don't believe," I said, my tongue stumbling and eyes vainly trying to meet his. "They think you're in greater danger."

"Hmm. I'm wondering if my gamble might pay off. What do you think?"

"G-gamble?"

"That's what you call it, isn't it? A game of chance, doing something that may or may not have the desired effect. Weighing equal probabilities against one another and taking a chance that the one you wish to come about will tip the scale in your favor."

"Ch-chance?"

"You have a saying: 'When in Rome, do as the Romans do.' " He took a step away from me. "Thank you for coming to tell me, Laura."

"Are . . . are you saying . . . that you intended this to happen?"

"Not intended – hoped." He laughed softly. "Don't tell Celene. He doesn't believe in hope. I never did before . . . "

But I scarcely heard him. My ears echoed with his incredible music, the words of his song. "Is that why . . . "

"Yes. But the song was also for you. Facts are facts that have to be accepted. However, I'll say nothing more about it if you're more concerned with keeping our friendship on its former basis."

"I am," I whispered, staring at him fearfully.

He smiled. *If that's the way you want it, Laura.*

"I do. I do." I hadn't even noticed that he'd spoken in silence.

And will you tell me what that noise is?

Noise?

Yes. Listen. It sounds like an engine.

I stood, confused by this sudden change of topic and the equally sudden reestablishment of our earlier relationship. I was also relieved, grabbed at what I presumed was a proffered friendly hand.

That isn't an engine. It's the waterfall.

Waterfall? Will you show me?

Beyond the treetops, the sky was paling with the sun, flushing gold across a spreading blue, clouds that were only mist. There was a softness in the air, a touch of the warmth of spring. I didn't want to go back to the house, to Celene's accusing eyes and angry face, to the demanding work of horses and household chores.

I'll help you. I'm sorry I didn't earlier, but I thought you'd be more at ease without my presence.

I gave him a regretful smile. *Okay. Let's go and look at the waterfall.*

I don't think he intentionally manipulated me. Maneuvered me, maybe. But out of embarrassment, the near drowning of our relationship. I led him on through the woods, overjoyed as he shared with me his pleasure in seeing a squirrel, a midnight blue Steller's jay, and then we came to the water running white in slanting patterns down faces of rock, coursing through narrow channels between wet and gleaming boulders, splashing and foaming into the creek bed far below.

There's a waterfall in our creek too, I told him. *Not like this one, and much more difficult to get to.*

Will you show me?

Tomorrow, I promised.

But it was not to be, for the follow morning, trouble came upon us with lightning speed.

CHAPTER TWENTY-THREE

THE DEPRESSION THAT HUNG DARKLY over Celene and Farrand couldn't dampen my own euphoria. I was for once trying to look on the bright side, ready to accept Gus Peterson and Colin Webb's promises, even if only out of hope. And Israfel sharing his own optimism with me lifted me way above the clouds of the others' skepticism and doubt.

In the morning I hurried through the chores, Farrand and Israfel both helping. The day was clear and bright. There was heat in the sun, and Israfel also seemed eager to have the work done so we could be gone.

The phone was ringing when we went back to the house to wash. I picked it up without thinking, my mind out in the sunlight in the woods.

"Laura!" Maureen's voice breathed rapid anxiety in my ear. "Listen! I'm at Helen's. There are a bunch of army vehicles and a police car heading up Hurt, and another group has gone on along Mabel Lake Road."

Euphoria vanished. Anything that went far enough up Hurt Road would eventually come onto our property.

"Now listen," she was going on. "I won't bother you with questions now, but could they be hiding at your place?"

"Yes." I had to say it, even if it meant confirming suspicions Maureen must have been entertaining.

"What do you want me to do?"

I tried to think, frantic, while Israfel's eyes watched me as he read every thought passing through my mind. There was a hiding place upstairs, but it wasn't that secure. It was also in the house, and if they were coming here, we could be trapped between the two groups. If the one on Mabel Lake Road came this way . . .

"Laura?"

Here was my friend offering assistance, because she must know . . .

"Yes. Maureen, could you pick them up at Trinity Valley Road? If I sent them down through Vance?"

"Sure. Whereabouts?"

"You know where our boundary crosses the road? Just below there, an old logging road comes up to the bank. Be sure no one sees you before you stop. Blow your horn if it's clear."

"Okay," she said quickly. "I'll be there in less than ten."

She was gone, and I turned to see Farrand and Celene standing beside Israfel, brought by his silent summons. Celene was as white and as stricken looking as on the day they'd arrived, and Israfel was again the imperious commander, aloof and stern.

"Hurry," I said, "down into Vance. Farrand, remember where the logging truck was? Just down the hill from there is an old logging road, and it comes out at the bottom just below here. Maureen will pick you up on the road, but wait until you hear her blow her horn."

"Maureen?" Farrand stared at me, and even Celene looked startled.

"Yes. It seems she knows. But you must go now. Quickly."

Celene dashed up the stairs, and I heard him locking the panel to the hiding place while Farrand pulled on his boots and coat, and Israfel stood and looked at me with the trace of a small mystifying smile.

But I immediately turned my attention to removing all traces of them from the kitchen, taking all but one place mat off the table, emptying the dishwasher, and putting things away.

Celene returned, carrying something under his arm, and then they were hurrying through the utility room door. I saw them disappear into the trees, and then I raced up the stairs and stripped Celene's and Farrand's beds, smoothed the spreads over them, and ran back down again. I shoved the linens into the washing machine and turned it on, then rushed to Israfel's room and stripped his bed also, grabbing the extra towels from the bathroom and adding them to the wash.

I had just finished putting the blankets away when the police car drove into the yard. Actually, it wasn't a car but a four-wheel-drive blazer, and it carried five members of this country's once-famous constabulary.

Four got out and banged on the front door. There was no sign of any army vehicles, but I was certain they weren't far away.

"Mrs. Tremayne?" They stood there with unsmiling faces, neat in their dark uniforms with the yellow strap prominent on each trouser leg.

"Yes?" I tried to gaze at them with the customary curiosity and suggestion of alarm that most people exude when confronting an unexpected visit from the police.

The one nearest held out an official looking document, his face severe. "This is a search warrant. We have reason to believe you are concealing a spacecraft and possibly its occupants."

I laughed. What else could I do? And wasn't that what most people would do when offered such a preposterous suggestion? And I was pleased at how natural my laughter sounded.

The officer's face pinkened at my laugh but there were no smiles from him or the others.

I stepped back, still laughing, ushered them in. I wondered if I dared to make the usual comments about little green men from Mars and mysterious UFOs but opted for safer discretion. And when their large, uniformed bodies filled my entrance hall, a sense of outrage began to form.

"You've got to be kidding!" I said, offended by the eyes that were instantly probing my surroundings, intruding impolitely into my home.

"I wish we were," another said, and the tone of his voice ended my attempts at jocularity.

They stood, purposeful, authoritative, and I was forced to retreat, offer them the freedom of the house with a helpless gesture while sudden tears burned my eyes.

"Mrs. Tremayne, Captain Forrest gave us to understand that he had told you what we're looking for." This one had a heavy dark face and eyes that were chilled from having seen too much. Tears would never affect him.

I swallowed, forced my chin high. "Yes, he did. But I thought he meant some kind of satellite."

"No."

I stared at the hard black eyes, and a chilling thought dawned. Why had they come here like this, even with a search warrant? They must have had a good reason to obtain the warrant. Had somebody given us away? They must have. My stomach turned, and I could feel the blood draining from my face. Someone had betrayed us. But who? I wondered about Celene's doubts over our visitors of the previous day. I had been convinced of their sincerity. But had I perhaps been gullible? Grasping at straws out of loneliness and despair since Jesse's anger and abrupt departure? Even Farrand had shared Celene's doubts. And this entourage of police officers had arrived the very next day, knowing what they were looking for.

The tears welled again, scalding. I turned away. "Go ahead and search, but you'll find nothing here."

"We have to look in your outbuildings, too."

"As long as you don't disturb the horses, I don't care what you do."

I walked away and left them. I went into the kitchen and dried my eyes and blew my nose, then busied myself with washing the floor. But all the while I listened to their footsteps on floors and stairs, to the opening and closing doors, to the rumble of voices. I held my breath as a pair of feet passed overhead in Farrand and Celene's room, wondering what I would do if they discovered the compartment hidden there and it's curious contents. And I gave thanks to Maureen and her remarkable behavior, also to the good fortune that had taken her to Helen's at such a crucial time. I wondered too how Israfel, Farrand, and Celene had fared on the steep slopes of the ravine, in the snow that lingered long in its depths, in the tangled wilderness that cloaked its sides, and whether Maureen had picked them up without incident.

Still the feet trudged about the house. I squeezed out the sponge and let the dirty water run away. A figure appeared in the doorway.

"Is there a basement?" the dark one asked.

I gestured to the door near the utility room, heard the washer spinning, and hoped they wouldn't look inside.

He gazed at the wet floor he would have to cross, then at me with suspicion. "What do you have in the basement?"

"Cellar," I corrected him. "The furnace and the kiln and pottery wheel. Freezer, jars of preserves, firewood, tools, garden furniture . . . The usual kind of stuff."

Again, his eyes went to the damply gleaming floor, and I realized that to wash it right then hadn't been the wisest choice of tasks. I forced a faint smile.

"It's okay. You can walk across it. I still have to rinse it."

He did so cautiously with stockinged feet. The cellar was searched.

When they found nothing in the house, they went out and checked the barn. I followed them, determined not to have my precious horses and the visiting mares disturbed. Justifiable indignation rose at the mere idea.

They looked in the feed room and tack room, into every stall and loafing shed. But it was the hay and the loft that interested them the most, and they moved every single bale. I sat below on some straw near the ladder and watched them as impassively as I dared.

With fragments of hay clinging to their uniforms, they finally reached the floor and glanced at one another in frustration.

"Why are you searching here?" I found the courage to ask. "Are you doing this everywhere?"

"Not everywhere," one said evasively.

"So why have you picked this place?" I demanded, feeling justified in asking.

"Because of information we received," came the terse reply.

"From who?"

"We don't usually name our sources."

He turned from me and began to restock the bales.

"That doesn't matter," I said. Now I only wanted them to go.

But they hung around, reluctant to leave without finding anything. I tried to think of natural questions to ask, but I was too impatient to see them gone. I was also worried about the army vehicles, that they could be exploring the High Meadow. The longer they stayed, the more fearful I became. What if they searched the house again, thinking they must have missed something? What was happening up in the High Meadow? To conceal my anxiety, I took a brush to Shadrach and tried to put a gleam on the heavy winter hair.

By the time they did drive away, my nerves were strained to a breaking point. I waved aside their apologies for disturbing the hay. It didn't matter how the last of it was stored. I only wanted them to go, to find out where the army vehicles were, and to call Maureen.

I stood in the yard, listening to the sound of the retreating engine and drawing in deep breaths of soothing air. The day was gray and still, but the sunshine was gone. Trees stood motionless, having shed their loads of snow, and were waiting patiently for the benison of spring. I stood waiting, too, until the sound faded. I could hear nothing else, so I went back to the house and called Maureen.

"They're here, Laura," she said. "They were just coming up to the road when I got there. Now, I'm making lunch, and then I'll bring them back, shall I?"

I hesitated. Now that the house had been searched, its privacy intruded upon, it was no longer a secluded solid fortress within the silent woods. It was now as open and vulnerable as a crystal glass. A single piece of paper had made it so, and somebody we knew had said enough to instigate the search. Larry had believed the story of the spaceship, and then Israfel had played that unearthly music and sung that revealing song. There were also Gus Peterson and Colin Webb . . .

"Laura?" Maureen was waiting.

"I . . . I'm just anxious about the place now," I said. "The police had a search warrant, looked everywhere . . . "

I heard her long exhalation of breath. "Oh, Laura!"

"They can stay here for a while, if you like," she said.

"But what about Ted?"

"He knows."

A small pang of curious dread began to hurt deep inside me.

"After the other night," she went on, "he kind of guessed. And then . . . I'm sorry, Laura, but I told him about Deenie."

"So, what did he say?"

"Not too much, but he kind of gave me to understand that he sympathized with the predicament you were in. Then he said he would've done the same."

"He did?"

"Sure. So, you don't need to worry about Ted. And if you think they'd be safer here for a few days, then that's fine by us."

But the pain of dread had become an ache. "There's one thing, Maureen. Somebody must have told them, given us away . . . "

It was her turn to be silent. Then she said softly, "Who, Laura? Who would have done that?"

"I don't know, and I can't possibly ask."

"Well, it wasn't us," she said staunchly.

"No, I know, Maureen. And a million thanks for your help today."

"Gosh, Laura. It was nothing. I just wish there was more we could do."

"If you could keep them for a couple of days, until I'm sure that the heat's off here."

"No problem. It's the least we can do."

The words provided some relief, but after I'd hung up, the aching dread increased tenfold. Our alien guests were in very great danger. And where were those army vehicles? Up on the High Meadow?

I went out and saddled Andante.

The police car had left deep ruts in the road, but up on the high field was a morass. The army vehicles must have passed through while I had been cleaning the kitchen floor, and the noise of the washing machine must have prevented me from hearing them. There were footprints in the mud at the road's junction, as though men had waited there. I followed their trail across the field and down to the creek with one burning question searing my mind. Had they taken the road up Copper Mountain that would bring them across the High Meadow?

Andante moved at an easy walk, and I forced myself to keep her at that – not to hurry in my rush to see which way the tracks had come from. For although there was no sign of anyone, suspicion had been laid right on my doorstep, and if someone should be watching me from the forest, they must derive the impression that I was out for little more than an afternoon ride. Though I let myself gaze in dismay at the condition of the roads, caused presumably by trespassing vehicles. Being angry at the destruction would be natural. Jesse was going to be furious when he saw it, the ruts churned wide and deep.

Snow still lay in broad white sheets across the field, thick beneath the trees on the hillside going down to the creek. A thin runnel of water ran on the road, little more than a token of springtime thaw and breakup.

Andante's hooves thudded on the timbers of the bridge and squelched in the soft wet mud of the lowest part of the road. Here a vehicle had obviously slipped sideways, skidding into the ditch Jesse had so painstakingly dug, in an attempt to handle the waters of the creek when they overflowed during particularly heavy runoffs. There were more deep footprints and elongated holes where wheels had sunk. Mud had sprayed from the spinning wheels as another vehicle had pulled it out. Jesse was most certainly going to have harsh words to say.

But I didn't linger to survey the damage. Just over the next rise was the junction of High Meadow Road. I urged Andante to a trot.

The tracks came down the High Meadow Road. I let the mare go, her feet splashing in the water and crumbling patches of lingering snow. The ground was stonier here, harder, and the wheels had left only tread marks. But the trail was still clear, and it ran along the high side of the meadow where the ground was bare, away from where the craft was buried. I saw with relief that snow still lay thick there. Trees shaded the area from the low-angled sun, and there wasn't a single footprint.

Feeling somewhat easier, I went on and rode up the familiar trail on Copper Mountain. But when I returned home – darkness falling in the forest, the horses waiting impatiently for their evening feed, and only me there to do it – despondency returned.

The rutted tracks across the hay field were too vivid a reminder of Captain Forrest, the men and machines he had at his disposal, the frightening proximity of the search. When I went into the house and closed the door, I found it was no longer my warm, strong sanctuary. For it had been invaded that day with the prying eyes of unknown officers looking behind every door and with a legal right to do so. Now, the house's sense of emptiness came from more than just my solitude within it. The searchers seemed to have stripped it of its substance, its essence, leaving only a shell that was cold and bare. Everything I touched, from the food in the pantry to the handle on the bathroom door, had been tainted by the gaze of probing eyes or the touch of suspicious hands. My privacy was gone, eliminated by words on a piece of paper, and the house seemed to no longer be mine.

I accused myself of being silly, but the feeling persisted, following me on silent feet wherever I went. I tried to lose it in the oblivion of sleep as I curled into a knot, pretending that Jesse was with me, that Israfel was just beyond the wall, and that Farrand and Celene were upstairs. But the sound of silence drummed in my ears with the echoes of other feet, and to pretend otherwise would be childish and futile when I knew that Jesse was in Los Angeles and the others all at Maureen's.

Mist pressed at the fragile window. The doors were closed only by bolts that would have to be opened when authorities demanded. Jesse had gone and left me to face men with search warrants. Danger to Israfel Farrand and Celene had arrived, literally, on our doorstep. I was too young, too inexperienced, and too unworldly to cope with all this, and the tears of loneliness, self pity, and helplessness rose achingly in my throat. I sat up, fumbled with a Kleenex, and decided I'd call Jesse and beg him to come home.

It was Israfel's mind that came to mine, flashing swift thoughts across the distance that separated us. *Laura, why are you so troubled? They were only officers. Your home is as it was before. Please, Laura, don't be so distressed. The blame is really mine. Blame me, Laura, it's my fault, for all of this.*

No, no, it's okay. I was just upset by those men and knowing that someone must have given us away. I'm okay.

But it's my fault, and at times like this I wish you had just let me die.

Israfel! The tears spilled from my eyes, ran in hot streams down my cheeks. *Don't say that!*

Why do you weep? I know you only did what your ethics make you believe is right. But you don't realize . . . Don't know . . .

Then tell me! Israfel, tell me.

His mind veered away from mine, leaving me in darkness. But I could sense he was still near. I waited for a long time, tears trailing down my face, the lonely emptiness of the house pressing against me.

Laura . . . Laura . . . When at last he spoke to me again, the voice was soft and hesitant. *I'm going to ask Ted to bring me back. You shouldn't be there alone. It isn't safe for you here.*

That doesn't matter. It's too lonely for you there. And I'll try to tell you . . . soon . . . Laura, I'm coming back.

He was gone, leaving me with drying tears and a house that no longer seemed so empty.

I turned on the light, and the phone rang. It was Ted.

"Rafe wants me to bring him back, Laura," he said. "He doesn't think you should be left there all alone."

"All right," I whispered.

"You think it's safe? There's no one around?"

"I haven't seen anyone. But I don't know how safe it is."

"Then . . . shall I bring him?"

"Does he really want to come?" My voice was constricted, my anxiety struggled with my loneliness, and I was afraid that I was putting Israfel in danger, being selfish in letting him come.

Israfel, answer for me. I want you to come.

"He seems to," Ted said.

"Okay." My mouth was suddenly dry. "Then bring him, Ted."

By the time the car drove into the yard, I had washed my face, built up the fire, and made a pot of tea. I tried not to think about anything else.

Ted paced around the kitchen, looking worried, and was reluctant to leave.

"Call us instantly if anything happens," he said at last from the door. "We'll do whatever we can. You know that don't you?"

"Thanks, Ted." My voice was still a tight whisper, my whole being conscious of the one who stood behind me. "I will."

"Okay. Hang in there." The door closed behind him. The car drove away into the night. Silence fell.

I turned and looked into the silver eyes, saw them clouded, his face drawn and pale. *Israfel, you shouldn't have come. It's too dangerous.*

I don't care. There's little left for me to care about. What matters, Laura, is that you cease to be troubled, and that Farrand and Celene are safe.

What about you, Israfel? What about your safety? And there has to be something you care about.

There was. But not anymore. I now realize that my hopes had just been wishful thinking. Something I let myself indulge in now that my career is gone.

I gazed at him sadly. *Now, you mustn't give up! You can't just accept defeat. Anything worth having is worth fighting for.*

His eyes glittered strangely, and he took a step toward me. *Laura, I don't think you know what you're saying.*

Well, I guess I don't understand the principles of your life, but I still don't think you should quit. Even if you do have to resign from your command, there's still your music. Surely you can do something with that.

That's my recreation. It isn't what I was born for. It isn't what I want. But no more now, Laura. You're tired. Go to bed, and we can talk again tomorrow.

Sleep came quickly with him just beyond the wall. We planned to go down to the creek in the morning, and my mind was diverted from troubles. Once again, the house harbored me with strong stout walls and a wide sheltering roof, and the silence surrounding it spoke of freedom from danger.

But only for a while – so short a while!

CHAPTER
TWENTY-FOUR

IN THE STREAMING SUN OF one of the unexpectedly beautiful mornings we sometimes have in March, Israfel followed me and Sally down the steep and narrow path that traversed the bank to the west of the house.

It was made by horse loggers years ago, I told him, trying not to trip over a lace that had come undone. *They must have cut it by hand, then dragged hundreds of logs up it.*

With horses?

Bigger ones than ours. Belgians, Percherons, Clydes. I stopped and tied the lace, not wishing to go sprawling clumsily before his elegant surefooted grace. *Our machine age is relatively recent.*

I know.

We still use the word "horsepower."

I've noticed.

And the trees were huge.

Only a few stumps remained, the last remnants of the giants that had stood here long ago, now dark with age and slowly rotting. The path was overgrown with Indian paintbrush, yellow arnica, mosses and lichens, and sprawling kinnikinnick. Nature swiftly reclaimed. But this path and those lingering stumps had endured to this day.

Israfel's mood was hard to read that morning. His face was expressionless, and his mind revealed nothing more than an interest in our planned excursion. I, responding to the warmth and brilliance of the sun, to the absence of droning planes and pounding helicopters, away from the house and its depressing recollections of the previous day, was relatively lighthearted and went on down the path with a joyful step. And when we reached the creek and stood beside the rushing, splashing, sunlit water, I saw Israfel's eyes light with pleasure and a smile touch his lips.

We slowly moved upstream where fallen trees and low hanging branches impeded us. We had travelled more easily on the trails left by those old-time loggers and kept open by deer. The creek chattered beside us as it poured over stones and twisted between rocks and the reaching roots of trees, falling over shallow falls and boiling in eddies and pools.

In a clearing filled with slanting rays of sunlight, we stopped. A few green shoots pierced the leafy mold beneath our feet, released from the snow and drawn to the warmth of the sun.

Spring is coming. I pointed to them. *Look.*

He stood and looked around him, at the gleaming, splashing water hurrying between sculpted banks, at the wet stones glistening and reflecting the light blue of the sky, at the trees stretching graceful branches and standing dense and tall, at the evergreen of cedar and fir. And then a clear sweet song came to us, trilling, delicate, and musical. He turned to me with wondering eyes.

What's that?

The song of the wren. It's down by the water there. Come quietly. Maybe we'll see it.

We picked our way between fallen sticks and twigs while my eyes searched for the minuscule brown bird that owned that exquisite voice.

There! See? I drew Israfel beside me. *On that branch above the water.*

The wren flitted to another branch on small wings, raised its head, and sang the song again. Israfel was entranced. He stood and gazed at it, enchanted by every note.

Laura! That's unbelievable! If only Celene could hear that, see this place . . .

A darkness shaded his thoughts, and he hid them from me. I tried to dispel it.

Wait until you see the flowers! All wild. Violets growing along the creek: purple, white, and yellow ones. Forget-me-nots of the most beautiful blue, columbines, lilies. There are lupins up around the house, and we even have some pentstemon and calypso orchids.

His attention came back to me. *Orchids? Wild?*

Yes.

His mind began to race, too fast for me to follow. I had to wait for him to realize.

I had no idea – his mind slowed with an effort – *that this earth could contain so much beauty.*

But you say you've been here before.

Not here . . . not here, in this cold northern hemisphere.

The mind was rushing again with strange memories I wished I could see. And there were questions he was trying to answer, the consideration of new ideas. Then there was an overweening sadness, a poignant sorrow, and I saw pain in his eyes, knew he was thinking again of what he regarded as his failure and blame.

Israfel, I pleaded with him, *why don't you stay here? Why go back if there's nothing left for you? You say you must resign from something you also say you were born for . . . that you have nothing left. Then stay here, with us.*

I met only astonishment, a complete disbelief.

Please. Think about it, Israfel. You say you've been here before. Then live here again. You can find beauty here, and it's much, much better in the summer. Please stay, I finished lamely.

Why do you ask me this? The question stormed into my head.

I gazed at him, biting my lip, suddenly awkward before the penetrating glare of those metallic eyes. *Because I wish you would.*

His mind closed to me, and he turned away, the silver eyes unseeing. The sun was rising above the trees, flooding us with yellow light and gentle warmth, casting gold on the pools and ripples of the rushing water. It caught his hair, lit the perfect contours of his face, illuminated him against a backdrop of dark cedar and fir. Alien, yes, but no longer to me. I knew how very empathetic he could be. And now I feared I had spoiled the bright moments of this beautiful morning with a ridiculous suggestion.

Laura. He swung to look at me intently. *I have learned much from you and Jesse, from your friends. I'm now disposed to look at you with a very different perspective because of the loyalty I have found among you, the willingness to protect us in difficult circumstances. But, Laura, you know very well I can't stay here.*

I stared back into those strangely colored eyes, saw them brilliant in the sun, and then noticed a gentle ruefulness on his lips.

Shall I show you, Laura? Shall I show you what I would go back to?

Still, I stared at him.

He stepped behind me, laid his fingertips gently against my temples, held me still.

There is my music, Laura. I can go back to that. But it is only secondary. I could go and tell them about you, the humanity that exists on this earth, the integrity and loyalty that can be found. But I have no wish to without this.

The fingers pressed.

Close your eyes, Laura, and I'll show you what I mean, for I don't think you have understood me yet.

Obediently, my heart trembling with a deep trepidation, I let my eyelids fall. Gone was the world around me, the one I knew. I stood on a grassy hillside, on a lawn as fine as hair, as soft as velvet, beside a white stone pathway that was edged with flowers. But they weren't like any flowers I'd ever seen. Great flaring heads of pink and gold were splashed with indigo and a red as rich as wine. There were delicate yellow trumpets tipped with orange, other similar ones of rippling magenta flecked with white. Small blue flowers spread in masses, mingling with others of yellow, white, and mauve. And from a nearby trellis hung orchids with blossoms larger than my hand, white streaked with red, long yellow stamens protruding like tongues.

Then my eye was caught by something I had seen before, although that had been only a fleeting glimpse. At the crest of the hill, framed by vast spreading trees, stood a shining white pavilion. Solitary on the hilltop, amid a profusion of those incredible flowers, it was an exquisite structure harmonized to its surroundings by a beauty of stone and walls of glass, by a shallow roof that seemed to float above the low and graceful lines that blended with the hill.

I was guided by an invisible hand onto that white pathway, stepping in brilliant light between those unearthly flowers. And beyond me I saw movement. Toward the pavilion at the top of the hill came a horse, gray, vaguely familiar. And on its back a rider with thick dark hair, a woman, again slightly familiar. Then both were lost to sight among the trees.

I went on along the path until a broad flight of shallow steps took me up towards what was apparently the entry. And I heard the music, drifting through the open doorway, played on an instrument I had never heard, so beautiful every note struck pain.

A smooth terrace lay beneath my feet, and I crossed it as if in a dream, passed through the wide doorway, and found myself in a space that was too beautiful to be real. Where was I? I looked up at the ceiling that was like the sky at night, dusky and deep, silvered with stars. Walls were iridescent with light, trailing vines smothered with flowers, while the floor was a mosaic of delicate colors, swirling in patterns that were too intricate for the eye to follow. And all around me was that music, beautiful beyond compare and moving me to tears.

Through an archway to my left was a room filled with light. A wall so clear it could have been open bounded the room between massive white pillars, and far away I could see a dazzling sheet of water.

My eyes glazed with tears. I saw Israfel rising from a strange ivory and silver instrument, and the woman I had glimpsed earlier was running into the room, smiling with joy as he took her in his arms.

I stood still, frozen, the music echoing and echoing in my ears, tears beginning to fall from my eyes. My head reeled and my heart beat painfully. No wonder the horse out there on the hill had looked familiar. It was Calliope. And the woman, too . . . for she was me.

The vision swam before my eyes, blurred, faded, drifted away in a mist. The pressing fingers left my temples, and I saw again the dark wild tangle of cedar and fir, heard the water now roaring in the creek. The yellow sunlight shone like diamonds in my eyes and was just as hard, splintering into stinging tears.

"Israfel!" I whispered out loud. "Oh, Israfel!"

I turned and looked up at him, saw his face pale and still, the silver eyes muted.

Now you know, he told me silently.

My heart felt as though it were breaking, being torn apart. I struggled to gather the pieces of myself together, thought of Jesse, my home, the life I had built so carefully. This other being was my friend, the companion of my mind, even of another world. There could be nothing else.

I tried to tell him. *Israfel, it cannot be. I'm married to Jesse, married to him . . . you know that.*

An expression of pain passed over the beautiful face, and it hurt me even more.

Israfel, why?

Why? The silver eyes met mine. *You should know that much. Why Jesse? Then that should tell you all.*

But it doesn't. Not now.

This puzzled me. *Why not now?*

What does being married to him mean?

To stay together forever, to love one another, for richer, for poorer, for better, for worse. I quoted the words blindly, made a despairing gesture with my hand.

If those vows should be broken, then isn't the marriage also?

To this I could find no answer, tried to turn away.

Laura!

His mind held mine, using its power, its force.

Laura, vows I make to you will never be broken. And they would be of love – which means everything, in every way, from respect to freedom, from passion to unending care. I would give you the immortality that is my life span, the freedom to always be as you wish, a life devoid of pain or sorrow, anxiety or despair. And there would be something you can do – bring a gift to the society of mine, where perfection has dulled the concept of loyalty, where a surfeit of beauty has blinded the eyes to the delicacy of a flower that grows wild, and the music of the spheres deadened the ear to the song of a bird. Laura, we can go no further there as we are. That is why we came here – to see what people who are still learning are making of their world. But you could show us a different road . . .

No.

A sad smile touched his mouth. *Work for you, Laura. Challenge. Example. And the beauty of my home—*

Israfel, stop. Please.

Why? I can't expect you to follow me blindly, away from what you know, where you feel safe, have roots.

I can't go with you anywhere.

But still the voice came to me, penetrating, strong, and with a sense of passion more powerful than anything I had ever known.

There is one thing I ask of you – that you come because you want to be with me. It mustn't matter that you're curious about something you've never seen, that I can grant you what is prospective immortality, or even for the reason that I love you. You must only come because you want to be with me – not Jesse. And if you are as true to yourself as I believe, then that will be the reason.

Numb, I tried again to turn away, but his hands caught my shoulders, held them with that same overwhelming, passionate strength.

Laura, I hate to see you distressed like this. I'll say nothing more about it until the ship comes for us – unless you want to talk about it. And Laura, remember this. If you come with me, then wish you had not, I shall bring you back.

His fingers moved to my cheek, brushed away the tears.

"Israfel," I whispered. "If it weren't for Jesse . . . "

I let the words trail away as his eyes suddenly blazed before mine, and then I felt a tremor in the fingers touching my face.

"Please," I went on shakily. "Say no more. Israfel, it can never be."

But the eyes shone like stars, and the fingers moved into my hair and held me.

Laura, you are what you are, and time will tell. However, as you wish . . . we shall say no more until the ship comes. But, till then, don't turn away from me. Don't fear me or what it is I am. Please give me days like today. Give me that much at least, for in my lifetime they are only minutes.

This was yet another Israfel, and one I was afraid of. This was a being who could be as passionate as he was strong, who contained a power beyond anything I had ever encountered and come closer to me than anyone I had ever known. He was an alien from another world, as diverse in his ways as Jesse but entirely different. And I knew he was rocking the foundation of my life by saying he loved me.

There were times when I knew I'd sooner die than let anything happen to Israfel, see him fall into the hands of Captain Forrest or those unsmiling police officers with their guns and dehumanizing uniforms. But there was Jesse . . . Jesse, for richer, for poorer, for better, for worse . . .

I drew away, afraid to look at him, knowing I was always going to be fearful of him, that I would forever see the passion I now knew lived behind those silver eyes and that perfect face, remember his words, the vision he had shown me, here by the creek on this sunlit morning.

He let me go, stood lightly on the bank, his face pale and set, and his eyes shining with a strange brilliance, polished by the sun. I glanced at him quickly, just once. He was so slight. Surely a strong wind would blow him away. An illusion, I reminded myself, catching my breath. A dangerous one.

I turned from him blindly, glazed with unseeing eyes at the sprawling branches of maple and hazel, a rotting, fallen log that lay across the clearing. The voice of the creek pounded in my ears, and Sally stood poised before me, ears cocked, staring intently upstream.

Coyote? Bear? Cougar or deer? The thoughts flashed instinctively. There was movement beyond the sweep of a cedar branch, a glimpse of a button, brass catching the sun. An eye, an ear, the barrel of a gun.

Israfel! There's someone with a gun! Quick! Get away!

Sally stepped forward on stiff, cautious legs, muzzle raised, ears straining. I spun around. Israfel was no longer there.

I'm up here, in the tree.

Sally sprang forward as a stick snapped. Her sharp barks rent the air. I jumped away from the thick green cedar that Israfel had so silently disappeared into. Who was this stranger? What were they doing here? Had they seen us?

Branches swayed and another stick snapped while Sally barked furiously. I did nothing to stop her. A face appeared, red with exertion. Startled blue eyes stared at me in genuine surprise. A rifle swung forward, clear of the branches, and a dark uniform came into view, heavy boots soaked with water.

I glared at him, apprehension giving way to anger. Here was one of the authors of those muddy ruts all along our fragile roads, a trespasser in my woods.

"Ma'am?" The voice came to me faintly through Sally's barking. "Ma'am, can you silence you dog?"

Why should I? I thought angrily. He was an intruder, a threat. Let her bark. Let her deafen him.

"Ma'am, please."

Reluctantly, I called her to my side.

"What are you doing here?" I demanded. "Don't you know you're on private property? How dare you come tramping through here like this!"

His face flushed into an even deeper red, and Sally muttered at him beneath her breath when he made an awkward gesture with the gun.

"Sorry, ma'am. Didn't know I was on private property. Jesus! You don't know where you are around here. I was just following the creek, this ravine . . . "

"Don't you have a map? Aren't you keeping track of where you are?" I wanted to ask him what he was doing here, decided I'd better not. He must be assuming I knew.

He shifted his wet feet on the rough ground, and his mouth tightened. "The captain does," he said. He pulled a walkie-talkie from his belt, drew out the antenna. "Sir? Sir? Roberts here, sir. It looks like this is private property, sir."

There was a staccato crackle from the set, a distant tinny voice.

"Yes sir. Captain asks, would your name be Tremayne?"

I nodded stiffly.

"Yes sir, it is."

Another metallic chatter, then he switched the set off, pushed it back into his belt. "He says he'll be right here, ma'am."

My heart sank. I knew intuitively who his captain was going to be. And Israfel was only feet away, imprisoned in a tree.

Trying to keep my expression one of annoyance and disapproval, I moved away from that tree, close to the rotted fallen log. I felt it as though I was looking for a place to sit, anticipating an irritatingly lengthy wait. But the log was pulpy, saturated with moisture, most uninviting. All I could do was lean against the trunk of a large cottonwood with as much affronted dignity as I could summon and wait with studied patience.

The man, Roberts, mopped his brow and gazed at his wet boots with a look of self pity. But little sympathy came from me.

Sally barked again as the snap of twigs and the sway of branches heralded the arrival of another intruder. And I wasn't surprised to see the smooth pale face with its neat mustache, the cold clear eyes, and the unsmiling mouth that were becoming too familiar.

He gave me a stiff nod of acknowledgment. "It appears we're on your property," he said.

"Yes, you are," I said, warning myself not to antagonize this man. Be helpful, willing to assist. Anything to avert suspicion.

"I'm sorry," he said, "but it's so thick and wild in here, so easy to lose track of where you are. Have you searched this creek area?"

I hesitated. We hadn't, of course. But I didn't want him to.

"Captain Forrest," I said unhappily, "my husband is going to be most upset when he comes home and sees the condition our roads were left in yesterday."

To my astonishment, a faint flush of embarrassment tinged his cheeks. "I'm sorry about that, too," he said. "But we had no idea when we came through that the road would be so soft in places."

"And I would have appreciated being asked for permission."

He was silent, watching me coolly, his composure restored. Then he said calmly, "We came to back up the RCMP in case they needed reinforcements."

A coldness settled over me, a clamping of the iron teeth of authority. There was no escaping those. And someone had told them, brought them to my home with so much confidence, they'd even obtained a search warrant.

All my anger was pushed aside by the cool, usurping, official tone of his voice, and I was left without defense.

The pale eyes saw. "May we search on down the creek?" he asked, taking advantage.

I could only make a surrendering gesture, as I had to the searchers of the house. "Go ahead."

"Will you show us the best way?"

I turned without a word, fighting despair, biting my lip. They were intruders, just like the others. Every heavy footfall behind me seemed to tramp my soul, crushing leaves and fallen twigs where Israfel and I had walked so softly. The wren's sweet song had ceased. All I could hear was their feet.

"Mrs. Tremayne." Captain Forrest drew abreast of me in another clearing. "I'll send equipment in to repair your roads."

"Tell that to my husband," I said narrowly, not looking at him.

He didn't speak again until we emerged onto the road just above the bridge. There he stopped, assumed a kind of aggressive, stiff-legged pose. "Mrs. Tremayne, I don't think you appreciate the serious nature of this situation, of what we're looking for."

"You say that," I said, trying to keep my voice even and under control, "when I have the police on my doorstep with a search warrant, coming into my house saying they've been told we're hiding a spacecraft and its occupants."

"I still don't think you realize how serious that could be."

"Why?" I asked, fighting down a choking lump in my throat. "In what way?"

A slight frown appeared between the cool eyes, a look of caution. *Oh, God!* I thought despairingly. *He's just as suspicious as the police. Israfel! What can I do?*

Hold on, Laura. Hold on. Remember your anger. Attack can be the best defense, but only when you're certain he's about to attack you.

"Could we go to your house and talk for a few minutes?" Captain Forrest managed to arrange his face into a smile. "Both Sergeant Roberts and I got our feet wet in your creek, and we'd sure appreciate the opportunity to dry our socks."

Once again I was caught, imprisoned in the trap of authority.

"Of course," I had to say. "There's a fire in the stove, and I'll even give you a cup of coffee." Perhaps that would allay some suspicion. I couldn't hope it would banish all of them, not after the extreme measures they had taken the day before.

I led them up the path we called the Cat Track. We had seen a wild cat there one day. I didn't want them to see the path Israfel and I had taken. I wanted to keep it known only to us for as long as possible.

Sergeant Roberts was breathing heavily by the time we reached the top, but Captain Forrest showed no sign of distress at all. *Probably does thirty push-ups every morning, and purely out of vanity*, I told myself viciously.

In the kitchen, I filled the kettle and put it on the range, asking Israfel silently to contact Farrand and make sure Maureen didn't phone me. I ground coffee beans, put out cups and saucers, filled the cream jug – all done under the constant scrutiny of the discerning eyes of Captain Forrest as he pulled off his socks and hung them by the stove, all done with as easy an air as I could possibly summon – each of us playing out the small charade on which so much depended, each of us with an opposing goal at stake, and each of us convinced that we were in the right. Was I really? At times, that nibbling doubt came to nip at me with the sharp teeth of uncertainty.

Laura. Israfel's voice reached me, reassuring, soft. *Laura, hold fast. You aren't wrong where I'm concerned. Laura . . .*

But I could no longer listen. Captain Forrest – his large bare white feet stretched before the fire, his arm hooked over the back of the chair so his well-formed chest was clearly displayed – began to question me with professional expertise.

"Mrs. Tremayne, you must realize the importance of what we're looking for."

I rummaged noisily in a drawer for spoons. "If you'd all be more specific, then maybe I would."

The kettle boiled, and I poured water into the coffee filter, glad for these tasks that I could focus my attention on.

"The police have been told you're hiding a spacecraft, concealing it's occupants."

I gave him a fleeting glance. "I'd like to know by whom."

There was the indication of a shrug. "Do you know anyone who might . . . well, have a grudge against you?"

"No," I said. "I'd like to think nobody does."

"But someone told them. And you don't know why?"

"I don't know why anyone would tell them that . . . to get at us. I didn't think we had any enemies at all. And I don't like the idea of it when my husband's out of town."

"Let me ask you this, then. Do you know anyone who could be hiding it and was perhaps trying to transfer suspicion?"

I put cookies on a plate and spoke cautiously. "I'm certain none of our friends are."

He appeared unconvinced. "You do realize, of course, what a terribly dangerous thing it could be to do."

"Dangerous?" I tried to meet his eyes.

"Well, yes. In the first place, what was it doing here? If its mission was peaceful, why didn't it just land and make its intentions known? Second, it could have brought some dreadful disease with it. Third, it represents an awful danger to our security."

"Wait a minute," I interjected. "Are you telling me this thing's from another world?"

He swallowed, eyed me coldly. "We're not ruling out any possibilities. This is in the strictest confidence, of course."

I stared at him for a moment longer, then brought the coffee from the range and poured it into cups while I thought rapidly of what I should say next.

But he went on. "It's very likely that it just crashed, anyone on board killed. And searching these mountains and woods is one hell of a job, of course. It may not be found for years."

I passed the cream to him.

"It's very odd, though" – the pale eyes fixed on my face, now near his – "that someone would call the police and say you're hiding it."

"Yes, it is." I tried to agree as calmly as I could, offering him a choice of honey or sugar, wishing those pale eyes wouldn't look at me like that.

I took the cream to Sergeant Roberts, wondering how much longer I'd have to put up with them. But the wet socks hanging before the stove showed no tendency to dry at all. They were thick, well woven, obviously army issue.

"Shall I put your socks in the dryer?" I inquired. "They'll take ages to dry like this."

They were obviously in no hurry to leave. Captain Forrest, with his nose close to the scent of his quarry, was going to follow the trail for as long as he could. I whisked the socks away before they could stop me, carried them to the utility room, and set the dryer rolling.

"What would you have done if you had found it?" he asked me when I returned to the kitchen. His voice was quite conversational, relaxed, but I knew it was only a ploy, that I had to retain my guard.

I sat down, stirred my coffee, forced a vague smile. "It's difficult to know how one would react to such a circumstance. I mean, it would depend on how you felt at the time, whether it was dark or daylight, what the thing looked like, what came out of it."

"You seem to have given it considerable thought."

It was my turn to shrug. "The subject came up at a friend's house the other night. There're rumors going around the village. But I don't think many people are taking them seriously."

"Do you?" he asked, those penetrating eyes holding their cool and steady gaze.

"I do now," I said, then filled my mouth with a cookie so it would be impossible to speak.

But he persisted. For the rest of the morning, obviously dissatisfied with my answers, he pressed questions and warnings onto me. My head spun. The difficulty of giving evasive answers that were plausible without telling an outright lie twisted me into knots. I wished I could tell him I didn't have to answer his questions – and I knew I had the right to. But the danger of being uncooperative was obvious. And he kept his tone of voice conversational, so I had no choice but to go along with him.

Retrieving their socks when the dryer shut off gave me a moment's respite, and I remembered Israfel's advice.

"Why are you being so persistent?" I asked on my return to the kitchen. "If you haven't found anything, think it's probably wrecked, why go on like this?"

"As long as there's a chance . . . " Again, the almost negligible shrug.

"But what this must be costing! Taxpayers' money," I added a shade darkly.

"Being an American, why should that concern you?"

Good God! What else did he know about us? "We pay taxes here, too," I snapped.

"Of course," he said quickly, placating me, and I wondered if perhaps he might be as fearful of antagonizing me as I was of him. I was a prime suspect, and my cooperation might prove valuable. He pulled on the dry socks and summoned a smile. "Thanks, and for the coffee. Now, if you're ready, Sergeant, I guess we'd better go on with the search down the creek."

"I trust," I said, as coldly as I dared, "that you'll keep your vehicles off the place."

He gave me a look to match my tone of voice. "I'll arrange for them to pick us up over on the road. I suppose we can get up to the road from down there?"

"Yes, you can. It isn't easy, but it can be done."

"Then that's what we'll do."

Even the way he put on his coat was military, the way he walked, the erect bearing of his shoulders and head.

"Where are your vehicles now?" I asked.

"Up in the forest."

I shouldn't have asked. Surely that was suspicion in those unwavering eyes. And when I said, "So they needn't drive through here again," even the sharp shake of his head didn't loosen that pale stare.

They moved toward the door, and he turned there and looked at me imperiously. "Remember, Mrs. Tremayne, if somebody is hiding that ship, they could be in very great danger, in many more ways than one. So, if you wish to tell me anything, you know where to find me."

"I do?" I tried to gaze at him in complete innocence.

"We're at the army camp. Leave a message if I'm out. They'll contact me by radio."

Again, the semblance of a smile, another penetrating look from those cold blue eyes, and the two men walked away across the yard toward the road and the Cat Track down the bank.

CHAPTER TWENTY-FIVE

REACTION SET IN, NERVES FRAYED by the abrasion of Captain Forrest's questions giving way, and I sat in the kitchen shivering with emotional exhaustion, reliving every vivid moment of this racking morning.

And how would I know when they were gone? That it was safe for Israfel to leave his hiding place and return to the house? They might come back, hoping to catch me unawares, and would see him. To watch them, observe their progress down in the ravine, was practically impossible, and if they should happen to spot me . . . In my worn and frazzled state, I had little resistance to anxiety fed by unanswerable questions. What on earth was I to do?

Laura. Israfel spoke to me gently, reassuring. *Hold on. We'll wait.*

"I'm trying," I whispered, rubbing my aching forehead. "I'm just a bit worn out."

I know. You did fine.

No. I knew I hadn't. Captain Forrest was still suspicious, would surely be back.

Then I had an idea. I pulled on my boots and coat and hurried outside. From the barn loft, I could see the road, watch for those vehicles, and know when they went down. Sally, left in the yard, would bark if the intruders returned, and my presence in the barn could be easily explained.

For nearly two hours I sat on a hard bale of straw in the gloomy loft, my eyes glued to the dusty window, the short distance of road visible, straining my eyes in a fixed focus, listening constantly, nervously, for Sally's bark. And my fevered mind kept whirling with Captain Forrest's warning words, the question of who had betrayed us, and over and over again Israfel's shattering revelation from the morning.

The condition of my nerves didn't improve, and when at last I saw a dark shape move across my narrow field of vision, to be followed by another and then another, relief left me shaking as tension released. I sat there on my bale with my hands pressed to my face and shivered as though cold.

Laura. Hands lifted me, turned me toward warmth and strength and caring. *Laura.* Arms wrapped me and held me close to soft wool and a slow thudding heartbeat. *It's all right. They've gone. Laura . . . please. Don't.*

I shuddered against him, crushing my face to his chest. "They were so close. Israfel, they were so close! They had only to look up—"

But they didn't. His hand stroked my hair with long soothing motions. *And they've gone.*

My eyes scalded, threatening tears, and my throat was a throbbing ache. "He kept on and on, asking me, warning me . . . and I couldn't take any more . . . "

His arms tightened. *I know. I knew what you were going through. Laura, I felt it all. And it hurts me as much as it does you. But they're gone. It's over.*

"II'm sorry," I mumbled. "Don't know why I went to pieces like that." I drew away from him, tried to hide my reddened eyes and running nose. All I had to wipe it on was my sleeve, which was definitely grimy, no doubt smudging my face most unbecomingly. "I'm a mess," I muttered. "Israfel, go . . . don't look at me like this."

Do you think I care what you look like? Cool fingers brushed my face. *Laura, I'm sorry you've suffered this. But there was nothing I could do.*

I know. You did help me. He was just so . . . so relentless. I didn't think he'd ever quit. And I don't think he's ever going to give up. He'll be back, I'm certain. We're going to have to be very careful, watch all the time—

Don't think about it anymore. He turned me toward the ladder. *Put it from your mind for now.*

But I couldn't. The impressions were too recent, too powerful and vivid. And they weren't only of Captain Forrest and his persistent questions.

I watched Israfel surreptitiously as he knelt before the newly lit fire, where we had brought tea, crackers, and cheese for a belated lunch. I knew I should send him away, but how could I? Where would he be safe? At Maureen's, but for how long? She and Ted had already taken them once, were still harboring Farrand and Celene. I couldn't expect more of them.

But he was no longer the companion of my mind, sharer of my thoughts. He had told me he loved me, asked me to go with him. Everything was different now, changed by that very knowledge.

Laura. He lifted sad muted eyes to mine. *I'll respect your wishes and won't speak of that again until the ship comes. Won't you trust me now?*

How can I? After this morning—

Especially after this morning.

I kept my eyes on his. *But I can't, for I still don't know you.*

There was a brief glitter in his eyes, but then he turned away, and his mind closed from me.

Never had I been so conscious of the house's silence as it fell around us like a veil, or of the nearness of his slender, graceful body against which I had so recently been held. That we were there alone took on enormous portent as I remembered his words and what he had shown me, the strength of the passion I had seen in his eyes.

"I don't want to hurt you," I whispered. "But you must understand."

There was no reply. I sat there wishing Jesse would call, say he was coming home, or that Farrand were there – even Celene, with his mutinous eyes and angry face. But the phone remained silent, and I would not call Jesse. Farrand and Celene were safer at Maureen's.

Probably not. Israfel intruded abruptly into my thoughts. *They'd be safe here now. The house was searched, the army here today. Would you be happier if they came back?*

I bent my head, embarrassed that he had read my thoughts, and admitted that I would.

I phoned Maureen and offered to pick Len and Randy up, but she insisted they'd bring them over.

"It'll look better that way," she said. "If we should run into anyone. Sooner us than you."

"The army was here today," I said.

"The whole army?" She gave a short laugh. "That sounds pretty horrendous."

"Captain Forrest is as good as a whole army."

"Then we'd better make it later," she said. "Just in case he's still around. I've got dinner ready for us all, anyway."

"Okay," I said, suddenly avoiding Israfel's eyes. "Come for coffee and cake after, then."

Farrand appeared happy to be back, but not so Celene. News of the house having been searched, Captain Forrest's presence that very day, obviously disturbed him. Ted saying that this house was probably the safest one to be in did little to thaw Celene's chilly eyes or allay his constant skepticism.

"And now," said Ted with a glint in his eye, "I have an idea."

We sat around the fire with coffee, mint tea, and chocolate cake, and looked at Ted expectantly.

"It isn't very much," he began, "but I do keep wondering who gave Laura and Jesse away."

"What could we do about it if we did know?" Maureen asked.

"Not much, I guess," he admitted. "But we can lay a trail of red herrings."

The eyes of Farrand, Celene, and Israfel all stared at him nonplussed. And it was only then I noticed that Israfel had foregone his tinted lenses. Ted and Maureen seemed to notice nothing untoward, and I wondered what had transpired between them when they had been together at their house.

Ted smiled. "Never thought I'd be suggesting this at my age and weight, but if somebody tipped the police off about this place, why not have someone tip off ours?"

Still, we all stared at him.

"And then the Marsdon's, and then the Fielding's." He chuckled. "That should give Todd something to shout about. But by then they should think the whole thing's a practical joke and forget about it."

A faint smile began to play around Maureen's mouth. "And who's going to do all this tipping off?"

"Never mind!"

"Ted!" I exclaimed. "Can't you get into trouble doing something like that?"

" 'All's fair in love and war,' " he quoted. "And when the army comes, when they're trooping through my friends' property, that's a form of war."

I gazed at him with misty eyes.

"But they're not that likely to dismiss it as a joke, knowing what it is they're looking for. And the army, too," Maureen said meaningfully.

"No," Ted agreed. "But they could dismiss that someone here is hiding them. It's only a small diversionary tactic," he added.

"And anything for some of those," I said fervently, remembering once more Captain Forrest's questions from that morning, the police officers' thorough searching of my house.

"Anything's worth a try," Ted said, stretching out in his chair, his eyes preoccupied.

Gratitude welled in me. I seized any small measure as a means to ease the burden that at times I feared would crush me. "Ted! Maureen!" I burst out. "How can we ever thank you? You've done so much . . . "

But my words trailed away as Ted held up a warning hand.

"Laura, what we've done has been relatively little. And don't count on us too much. This situation could become more than any of us can handle. Matters might be taken entirely out of our hands, leaving us totally helpless, you know. You must consider what measures you'll take in the event of an extreme emergency – which is what this could very well become."

His words came back to me after I had gone to bed, lying sleepless in the darkness with my mind going over and over the events of the day. And they included Captain Forrest's words of warning, his constant assertion of danger. Had he been trying to scare me? I presumed so. And Ted's warning, although of a different nature and intent, was as equally disquieting.

I was forced to consider whether Jesse and I had been overly rash in taking these aliens into our home. For we did know nothing of them, their background, their purpose. And what might we be bringing on ourselves by concealing their sovaluable craft? We were hiding it from the army that we ourselves supported, who worked to defend the country we lived in. *Would there come a time when we would suffer for the folly of our actions?* I wondered. And I was to blame far more than Jesse. He'd wanted to call the proper authorities right away, and it had been I, impulsive perhaps, who had rushed headlong onto this dangerous ground where surely even angels would fear to tread.

Israfel's thoughts pierced mine. *And what do you think angels are, Laura?*

My mind somersaulted over this unlikely question while I wondered, with a sinking of my heart, if he had read every one of my thoughts.

Angels, Laura. Your ancient histories speak of them, and there are books today that still refer to them – although they have become little more than myths from an age whose true history has been lost or distorted by time. Have you never wondered about them?

Sometimes, I told him, hesitantly, uncertain. This sudden change of drift had taken me entirely by surprise.

Messengers of the gods.

I digested this in silence, disturbed by the distraction he had presented, suspicious of his motive.

Israfel, I was thinking about your purpose here, the dangers of this whole situation.

I know you were. The answer came back gently, softly, but I tensed against him. *And you were also thinking perhaps how foolish you've been. How you could be wrong.*

There was no denying it, of course. I waited, uneasily, for him to go on.

And you're avoiding the subject, I protested.

Not at all. Do you think I don't appreciate that we owe our safety to you? The efforts you have made and trouble you have gone to? Laura, what do you think I am?

That's what I don't know, I told him painfully. *How can I? You're beyond the grasp of my comprehension.*

I'm not to blame for that. But nor do I blame you. We are what we are, and you have eyes to see, the ability to reason, the standards you live by. Those are also my standards. They stem from the lineage of our heritage, a distant common root. Humanity didn't just happen on this earth. No such thing is possible within the irrefutable laws of nature. What I am saying is this: we aren't so different, you and I, Jesse, Farrand, and Celene. It's only the directions we've taken that are. Humanity has been crippled by the destruction of their knowledge, the dreadful persecutions of the Dark Ages in which the greed of a few brought darkness to the eyes of multitudes. Inevitably, this led to overpopulation and starvation, cruel laws based on ignorance, and ignorance bred a form of total irresponsibility, which, combined with cruelty, has written the hideous history of this planet in the annals of the universe. And we, who could change this, would only fall victims to that same greed, silenced forever for the sake of those who stand to lose. Celene is right in that respect.

I lay still, listening to him with a strange dampness breaking on my skin.

But Laura, as long as there are those who refuse to stand by and let corruption ride over justice, who will not betray their friends but are loyal to the point of selfsacrifice, then there is hope. It may be small, but even that must be considered in the final summation—

Israfel, I broke in. *What are you saying?*

His mind began to race, too fast for me to follow. Then it slowed abruptly. Laura, as long as you are loyal, you are in no danger from me – not at all – until the ship comes. Then I shall speak again, as I have promised. But now, trouble yourself no more. The house is safe. All is still. We have allies now, Laura. Rest in peace.

His mind drew away, left me feeling even more confused than ever. But I was exhausted after the day's trials. Sleep claimed me and blurred all the memories, his words, into one cloudy problem that hovered in my sky that only the passing winds of time could blow away.

CHAPTER
TWENTY-SIX

IT WAS APRIL, BEAUTIFUL, TEMPESTUOUS,
promising, stormy, rampant April – when the sun poured warmth from a
delicate sky in which high white clouds gathered, suddenly turning gray,
bringing quick, abrupt stinging showers. Butterflies swarmed, winging
haphazardly about the patio on the south side of the house. I celebrated
by setting out the garden furniture. They were made of redwood, and we'd
brought them from California. I was scarcely able to believe that this time
had finally come. Even Celene appreciated the warmth of the days, the
sunny pleasure of the patio and its cushioned furniture – although he would
rarely sit there in Israfel's presence. It was when we were gone, walking in
the woods, searching for the first violets, that Celene would go out there and
soak up the sun.

Jesse came home only rarely, and then I think more out of a sense of
duty than anything. He was withdrawn, almost taciturn, and would talk only
reluctantly about his score. It was still proving difficult, he admitted to me
when I pressed him, but he was making some progress. Then, having assured
himself all was well, he would fly away again.

I tried not to let it bother me. I had gone through this before, knew he
would return, the Jesse of old, once the final bars were done. And I was busy
with visiting mares, breeding our own, and managing the ever-worsening
conditions of our road.

Thaw was full upon us, with the corrals turning into quagmires and every
gateway knee-deep in mud. Water ran everywhere in thin bright streams, and
the roads were only passable at night or before the temperature rose above the

freezing mark in the early morning. Vehicles carrying horses were forced to use them then or the animals would have to be led in from the road.

Farrand and Israfel, in jeans and gum boots and sweaters smelling of horses, helped me, quickly understanding what had to be done. I asked Israfel if there were horses in his world, and he smiled faintly and said there were.

But Farrand, I told him. *He had never seen a horse before.*

No. Farrand comes from a different world where everything is very technical and automated. It just happens that he had never had occasion to see one.

Other than showing me that telepathic glimpse of his home, it was the first time Israfel had given me any such information. I was hoping he'd tell me more, but already he was changing the subject to something else, and I knew immediately he had no wish to divulge anything further.

I shall never forget those days in early April. The joy of soaking in the sun, of seeing the snow and hardpacked ice vanish from the earth, of spotting slender green shoots pushing from the soil and the first hint of new grass flushing the slopes of the pasture. The pleasure was made all the more intense by the departure of the searchers, a sense that our place was now safe.

Ted and Maureen's house was searched, as was the Fielding's, much to their incredulous consternation. But we heard of no other searches, and Captain Forrest and his officers had again moved further east.

Farrand was still laboring industriously on their broken receiver; Celene enjoying the sun; Israfel searching for the first spring flowers.

Although I could never feel totally at ease with him, the fact that he kept his word about not asking me to go with him again, along with his generally aloof and quiet demeanor, somewhat reinstated our earlier relationship. I think it was mostly due to his efforts, for I was wary for a long time, reluctant to be alone with him, always apprehensive of what he was about to say. I knew he was hurt by my distrust, but I reminded him of his own words, "What is, is," and he looked at me with the sad and rueful smile that was becoming so familiar while his mind closed on a torrent of words. Nothing more was said, and I began to breathe more easily, found an increasing pleasure in our explorations, the quiet gentleness of his company, the sunlight in the silent woods, his own delight in the butterflies and robins, the first mauve violet found on a sunny bank.

The car, its wheels embedded in deep holes on our road, was an unpleasant surprise.

We came upon it while returning to the house via the road across the hay field, and my heart leaped to my throat at the sight of it. Where was the driver? Had he seen us out there on the wide open expanse of the field?

Footprints in the mud indicated he had gone on toward the house. Had Celene heard him coming? For I had grown lax in recent days, let Sally go with us on our wanderings, leaving the house unguarded.

The car was gray, plain, impersonal, the kind salespeople use and rental agencies provide. There were no cushions, toys, magazines, or bumper stickers that distinguish the private family car. Who was it?

And then anger boiled. What fool would have ventured in on this kind of road in the middle of breakup? No wonder he was stuck in the mud! More damage to our already-suffering road. More work for Jesse. And – more pressing – how were we going to get him out?

I began to hurry in the wake of those muddy footprints, then remembered Israfel. I swung around, but he had vanished.

He spoke to me from the forest beside the road. *I'll make my way back, Laura. Go ahead – see who it is. Don't worry. Celene is dealing with him. He says he's from a newspaper in San Francisco.*

What?

I was astonished, stopped dead in my tracks, then broke into an awkward slithery run.

The sound of voices drew me to the back patio. The visitor was lolling in a chair. He was young and fair, had an intelligent face alive with enthusiasm, and was tanned to a color that was quite foreign in North Okanagan at this time of year. *Probably uses a sun lamp*, I thought spitefully. His neat gray slacks were splattered with mud, his fine leather shoes caked, and the expensive sports jacket he was wearing had also managed to gather pale brown flecks that didn't match its tweed. A large notebook lay on our redwood table, very conspicuous to my immediately suspicious eyes.

My own muddy jeans, my jacket that had managed to retain one button but was losing both its pockets, and my hair unruly and adorned with pine needles drew a dismissive look at first. Then he saw my angry face and rose politely to his feet. He smiled, but I did not. He was an intruder, another destroyer of our road. But Celene's presence made me bite my tongue. This man was from a newspaper – dangerous ground. How long had he been here? What had Celene told him?

"Mrs. Tremayne?" His voice was uncertain, but he held out a grubby hand. "I'm Tony Roth. I just came up from San Francisco. I'm a feature writer—"

"And you're stuck in the mud on our road, in the middle of the hole you've made," I said caustically.

"Well, yes. That's a pretty terrible road you have there—"

"At this time of year," I said, each word as sharp as a knife, "all back roads around here are like this. And if you'd only phoned, I would have told you and saved you the cost of a tow truck."

He gave me a smile – one that was undoubtedly effective on other people, I told myself viciously. He could no doubt use charm like an oilcan, greasing locks, opening doors, soothing bitchy women.

"I did phone, but nobody answered," he said, blue eyes bright in that unnaturally tanned face. "And if I may use your phone to call one, I certainly don't mind paying for a tow truck."

My cutting mood persisted. "That will be messing the road up even more," I said, then knew a sinking feeling as he studied me with a waiting politeness. So what else could be done?

"Gee," he said, lubricating me with a youthful smile filled with very white teeth. *Are they capped?* I wondered. "I sure am sorry if I've damaged you road. First time I've ever been up to these parts, so I really didn't know."

"And why are you here?" I asked while my mind ran furiously over the problem of getting him out. It was hours before the sun went down and the road would freeze. Our tractor had starting problems that only Jesse knew how to deal with.

"Like I said – I'm a feature writer. I work mainly in the San Francisco area but do some freelancing as well."

I flopped into a chair, took a quick look at Celene.

Tony Roth drew in his cheeks, bit his lip, and tapped a pen against his teeth. I knew he wasn't planning an article about Jesse or the horses by his obvious uncertainty. His eyes flicked from me to Celene, then came back to me. He sat down again. "I guess I'll just have to come out and say it," he said with a sigh, "but there are a bunch of rumors going around . . . that there's a crashed spaceship or UFO here somewhere."

"Yes, there are," I said.

His face became expressionless. "I heard from a friend, who heard it from someone else, that you're hiding it."

"Me?" I stared at him in what I hope was amused and stupefied astonishment.

"That's right."

"Where on earth did you get that idea?"

"I told you. From a friend."

"All the way down in San Francisco?"

"Uh huh."

I let a small, incredulous smile play around my mouth. Celene laughed, it was the most expressive laugh I had ever heard. Amusement, ridicule, and humor combined rang out clearly, eloquently, saying far more than any words. Tony Roth turned and looked at him. Celene, lounging easily in a chair, his hair ruffled, in casual jeans and a shirt with sleeves pushed back to the elbow, was managing to look remarkably human.

The inquiring eyes came back to me. "Your husband's not here, Mrs. Tremayne?"

"No. He's down in LA working on a score."

He nodded. "I know who he is." He waited, inviting explanations.

"This is Len," I said offhandedly. "I can't run this place by myself during our busiest time of year."

Again he nodded, slowly, his news-conscious mind finding a story. But then he must have realized it was one of little consequence to what he had come looking for. I was no celebrity; Jesse was not overly in the public eye. And if our hired hand was a devastatingly handsome young man who lounged about on the patio and laughed loudly at my visitors' comments, then okay. Small potatoes to a crashed and supposedly hidden alien spaceship.

There was silence. I knew I should say something else, that it would be only normal to do so. But getting him and his car out were foremost in my mind.

I can move it. Israfel's voice came to me. *But how would we explain it?*

I don't know. I don't know.

And those curious blue eyes watched me, the inquiring mind waiting, the seeds sown of one scoop of a story – if it were true.

"Have you been to the police?" I asked. "They could probably tell you something."

"I have," he said. "But they couldn't – or wouldn't – tell me anything."

"Oh."

Again, there was silence.

Celene rose to his feet. "I'd better go and check that mare," he said and walked away.

He gave me the trace of a sidelong smile as he passed me, and I was surprised. Celene was the one who had been so anxious.

"A mare arrived this morning," I explained. "She bruised her knee in the trailer. We have to watch it, make sure it doesn't swell."

"I see," Roth said politely, not interested in the least. He tried to return to the topic that did. "What rumors have you heard exactly?" he asked.

I shrugged. "The usual kind of nonsense. Nobody seems to be paying much attention." I wondered if he had heard that the army was out looking and that our house had been searched.

"So why," he said, pushing the point hard, "does somebody give me your name?"

"It could be because someone did the same thing here, called the police and gave them the same story."

"But why?"

Again, I shrugged. "We must have an enemy we don't know about."

He was obviously disappointed, probably could see his exciting lead turning into another silly hoax. And he had come all this way, got his car stuck and his fine clothes all plastered with mud. A moment's pity for him ticked through my mind.

"Mr. Roth, what kind of story did you plan to write?"

"Whatever I could find," he said.

"Why?"

"News," he said shortly.

I swallowed a biting reply. Ask a silly question. "You said," I began again, "that you got our name through a friend."

"Yes. And he heard it from someone else. But I don't know where he got it from."

"Strange," I said.

"I guess so. Why it should turn up as far away as San Francisco . . . There's been nothing in your local papers?"

"No. Not a thing."

"That's odd, too." The blue eyes narrowed. "Unless it's the usual coverup."

"Maybe," I said, wishing I could think of some solution to the problem of his car imprisoned in its muddy berth, wondering if I should call a tow truck for the sake of expedience and let the road suffer. But the tow truck might just as easily become stuck, and we'd have an even greater problem.

Israfel, where are you?

In the trees beyond the house. I can slip in through the front door if you keep him where he is for a few minutes.

Okay.

"Mr. Roth, you can't have come all this way just because of a few words of the friend of a friend."

"I've gone further for less." His eyes watched me carefully. "That someone like your husband could be hiding an alien spacecraft . . . far too great a story not to investigate it. And I sure am curious as to why it came up in the first place."

"So am I," I said.

"I'll try to find out when I get back."

"I'd appreciate knowing, too. And I'm sorry you've been disappointed."

"I'll keep asking around. Rumors aren't always unfounded."

"And there's still the problem of your car."

"So how do you get in and out?"

"Four-wheel drive, and when the surface is frozen."

"I see."

He showed no inclination to move, hesitating like a dog before a hole in which he's certain he saw a rabbit disappear.

"Mrs. Tremayne, have you any idea who might know more about this?"

"The RCMP, I guess."

"Well, other than them."

"I think you'll find that most of the people in the village think it's only a hoax, some story that started in the beer parlor or the Legion Hall."

"Do you think it's a hoax?"

"What would you do if it weren't?"

He displayed his dazzling teeth. "Send the best damned story possible out over the wire service, that's what. But why do you ask that?" The smile was gone, the eyes sharp and attentive.

"I just wondered."

"And I'd make damned sure the truth got out – that there'd be no coverup."

Temptation reared its shining head. Here perhaps was another ally – and a very useful ally. This one held a most powerful weapon: the freedom of the press.

He was watching me, reading my face with experienced eyes.

"Mr. Roth, it isn't a hoax. The army are searching all through these woods – have been through here. And the police have been with a search warrant to a number of houses, including this one."

He made a sudden grab for his notebook, his eyes alight and his whole pose one of alertness.

Israfel spoke. *Careful, Laura.*

"They haven't found a trace of anything," I added quickly, while Tony Roth scribbled wildly. "And you can imagine the difficulty of searching these woods." I waved my hand in an all-encompassing gesture, saw the intent blue eyes follow it briefly before concentrating on his notes once more. "And we're only at the edge of them," I said. "They go on for miles."

"The army, eh?" The dog had found a new scent, and I was beginning to regret having given it to him. "Wonder if our guys know about it . . . "

I tried to make light of it. "Who knows? But I doubt they'd tell you."

"That's for sure." He scribbled some more. "What else do you know?"

"Mr. Roth," I said, feeling mushy ground beneath my feet, "that's all I can tell you."

"Please," he said, the smile intended to be disarming. "Call me Tony. And may I use your name?"

I shrugged. Let him think I didn't care.

"Great!" Such enthusiasm, but then his eyes narrowed again, studied me thoughtfully. "Laura, it seems to me that, what with all the coverups and outright putdowns there've been, if a person were to be hiding a UFO, or whatever, they sure wouldn't tell just anyone who happened along, would they?"

"I guess not," I said, wondering again how I was going to get rid of him.

"Unless the person who happened along could show pictures, give names, tell the whole story so everyone would know." He let a trace of excitement creep into his voice, the blue eyes crinkle. "Then there'd be no way they could cover it up."

I looked at him with the first considering interest. I had had the same notion. But what could this man prove to be? Friend or foe, ally or enemy?

You don't know, Israfel spoke to me again. *Be careful, Laura.*

The sun moved behind the trees on the west side of the patio, and immediately the air was cold. But it would be hours before the temperature dropped to freezing and the roadway surface firmed. Israfel regarded my unwelcome visitor with fresh annoyance.

"Right?" he said.

"I don't know, Mr. Roth. Who can say? Now, I have horses to see to and chores to do, and there is still the problem of your car."

"Could I get a cab?" he said, trying to conceal disappointment. "I can walk out to the road." I looked ruefully at his muddy feet. "And then I'll have a tow truck come up first thing in the morning to get the car out."

"Sure. You can phone for one right away."

I rose to my feet, indicating the interview was over. But he hesitated, loth to give up such a tantalizing story.

"You do understand what I'm after, don't you?" Hopeful eyes fixed on my face.

I was wary, cautious, studied him carefully. Had he offered help? Or was he only after a story? I really didn't know. I let his words echo in my mind, flow out to Israfel.

Take care. The answer came back swiftly, just as warily.

My hesitant pause made Tony Roth curious. I could see it in his eyes.

"You're looking for a story," I said.

"Yes."

He waited expectantly.

I shrugged in an imitation of Jesse's offhand way. "And I have work to do. So if you'll excuse me . . . " I began to walk away. "I'll show you where the phone is."

Determined not to leave him in the house alone, I busied myself basting a roast while he used the phone. Immediately above his head, Farrand and Israfel waited, listening in silence. *If only he knew*, I thought, *how close he was to the story of the century, to one of the most astounding headlines that have ever been.*

He put the phone down, and I closed the oven door. Again, the smile was meant to be disarming. "He'll be there in an hour," he said.

An hour! It only took twenty minutes to walk the road. He was still showing no inclination to leave. And the portent of some of his words also lingered. If the world did know . . . surely Israfel, Farrand, and Celene would then be safe. Surely interest would run so high that no harm could ever come to them. Could this young man be our greatest ally yet?

"I have to feed my horses," I said, heading toward the utility room door. "Would you like to see them? You have a few minutes before your cab comes."

"Sure."

He followed me, notebook clasped firmly in hand.

Israfel, ask Celene to stay in the loft. He can put hay down through the slots to the feeders. This man is one of those reporters with an inherent nose for news.

"How did you ever find this place?" Tony Roth asked conversationally as we walked across the yard. "What brought you way up here?"

I explained how my grandfather left it to me, and the observant blue eyes missed nothing while he still managed to convey the impression that he was giving me all his attention. And the possibility of the help he could provide taunted me constantly. He was the owner of the mighty pen, able to draw millions to our side with the aid of public opinion. I wondered how ambitious he was, if he possessed the selfishness of all overly ambitious people, the readiness to sacrifice ethics and integrity for the sake of advantage or financial gain. Our onetime proximity to the Hollywood press had caused me to regard them as ghoulish, determined to publish everything involved. But the press was also responsible for uncovering corruption in high places, the revelation of scandals, of crimes and injustices that would otherwise have never been revealed.

I measured grain into pails while Tony Roth hovered at the door of the feed room, his nose practically quivering at the scent of something else.

"Of course," I said suddenly, "anyone who could be hiding it might never tell."

The eyes fixed on me, intent and purposeful. "You could be right," he said.

"Would you blame them if they didn't?"

He considered his reply long and carefully. The time he took convinced me that he was very certain I knew far more than I was telling him, that his reply could either open the door to his story or see it closed firmly in his face. His cab was obviously forgotten, and I went back to mixing my feed, wishing I hadn't asked such a blatant question, that I had kept my impulsive mouth shut.

"It would depend on why they didn't," he said at last, slowly, his voice thoughtful. "If they were being threatened, held hostage in some way, then you couldn't blame them for staying silent."

I stirred molasses into a pail, did not look at him. "I'm sure nobody around here is being held hostage," I said.

"That was a difficult question you asked me," he said. "Difficult for me to answer. Don't forget – my job is to get the news, tell the people. And a story like that would have to be told."

I loaded as many pails as I could carry on my arm, moved past him into the aisleway. Celene was dropping hay into the feeders.

"Your cab may not wait if you aren't there," I said.

He followed me and made a motion as though to help me but drew his hand away when I shook my head.

"Mrs. Tremayne, I've been perfectly honest with you—" he began.

"I should hope so," I said tartly, setting a bucket down outside Calliope's door.

"And all I ask is that you are with me."

I turned on him in angry exasperation. "Mr. Roth! There is nothing I can tell you. Now, if you'll please excuse me, I have work to do. And your cab will be waiting." I moved on, buckets clanking from my arm.

"Mrs. Tremayne . . . Laura! Please."

Once more I faced him.

"I could leave your – anyone's – name out, if I could just have the story."

I was about to order him away. Then Israfel spoke quickly. *Careful. Don't antagonize him. He could make things very difficult for you.*

"Look," I said. I put the buckets down in the aisle. "Give me your number, and I'll call you if anything comes up. Okay?"

Darkness was falling outside. The bulbs in the aisle ceiling cast little light, but I could see his eyes widen, flare into brilliance.

"Promise?"

"Sure."

He fumbled a wallet from an inside pocket, dropping his notebook in his haste. He extracted a card and thrust it into my hand. "Anytime. Call me at any time. Leave a message if I'm out. Okay?"

I nodded, pushed the card into the pocket of my jeans, wondered if I'd ever use it.

"Thanks, Laura. Gee! Thanks a million."

"Your cab," I said.

He smiled at me radiantly, scooped his notebook from the floor. "You won't forget, hey?"

"No," I said.

He hurried away at last with several parting waves of his hand. And I watched him go with an uneasy feeling. Friend or foe? Ally or enemy? I still didn't know.

CHAPTER
TWENTY-SEVEN

ISRAFEL'S HANDS RESTED LIGHTLY ON my shoulders. *I think our days of solitude are soon to be over.* The words drifted into my mind on a wave of sadness. *Word is spreading. The man who was here today will not give up readily. His very questions could provoke more rumors, sustain the subject that is falling into an increasing number of minds.*

He knelt before me on the rug by the hearth, where I sat with my legs folded under me, a second cup of coffee held between my hands. In the light of the fire, his face bore a resemblance to the one I had first known – the pale and resolute warrior, calm but quietly determined. And the flames reflected from the silver eyes burnished them to copper.

I was at once wary of his hands, for he touched me rarely. And I was still fearful of the passion I had glimpsed, the strength that I knew lay behind it, the revelation of his words not long before.

We were alone in the early hours of the evening, Farrand and Celene having gone upstairs to work on the receiver as soon as the dinner things had been cleared away. Tony Roth's visit had been the subject of extensive discussion, and it was only Celene who took it lightly – at first.

"He doesn't know anything," he said. "He thought I was just your hired hand."

"No, he didn't," I interjected. And when Celene stared at me in surprise, I corrected the statement. "Not just the hired hand. He immediately suspected there was something between us."

The surprise turned to astonishment. "Between you and me?"

"That's right."

An icy rage possessed Celene that made my blood run cold. He went white, rose stiffly to his feet, and looked from me to Israfel and back again with eyes that were filled with murder.

"He knew nothing of me or of you." The words flew from his lips like chips of ice. "He had the audacity to suspect us – US – of some base activity in your home—"

"Celene," I pleaded, "he's a reporter. People like that look for stories everywhere."

The iridescent eyes blazed at me. "Don't make excuses, Laura, for such an animal! Creatures as that should be—"

The power of Israfel's mind swept across the table, froze the words Celene was about to say as though he had been struck dumb. I felt it too, its slamming, shocking force. I reeled back in my chair, looking nervously from one to the other.

"Celene," Israfel spoke out loud, the vibrant tones of his voice breaking the cold and angry silence that had fallen. "You know no more of that man than he does of you. You're as guilty as he is of reaching conclusions. And you can't condemn him for doing what he is employed to do."

The rage in Celene's eyes did not diminish. He glared at Israfel in continuing silent but eloquent fury, another condemnation of his own.

The silver eyes met the incensed blue ones undeterred, dispassionately, while I watched them with increasing trepidation, wondering again exactly what this bone of contention was that lay so violently between them.

I was tempted to ask him, there before the hearth, while his hands touched my shoulders in a gesture of regret. But the face of the warrior prevented me. And the eyes were still dispassionate. Israfel was a difficult being to ask questions of. Yet, in the few days of solitude that followed, his mind opened to me in constant communication. I felt as though he was using every passing minute because time was running to an end and the hours left could be counted.

Usually his mind was racing, a swift flight of images, sounds, colors, ideas, and resolves too alien for me to ever understand, fleeing across the surface of my consciousness at a speed too great for me to catch and hold a single one. But when we walked beneath the trees or beside the rushing creek, the thoughts were clear as he discovered beauty in the mosses and lichens that spread their green velvet cushions or featherlike fronds beside our path, in butterflies dancing in the sun and thin streams of water running down from the hills. The soft hazy mists and the turbulent skies of April – when white clouds massed into purple gilded with gold, climbed into the blue above us to wash the earth with rain to then scatter beyond the mountains and leave the sun to shine once more – brought him a pleasure he'd never thought he would find.

At night, by the fire, he told me of many things I still could not understand. He did speak of his music, and of Jesse's after I had played some of Jesse's recordings for him one evening. And there was a different sense of discovery and a new application as his mind sped by mine on a voyage of its own. But still he shared it with me.

Sometimes I wondered if he ever slept at all on those nights, for he spoke to me instantly if I woke. I couldn't bring myself to ask him, though. He rarely invited questions. But I didn't really mind that, not when he was communicating with me so openly and freely. And he never appeared to be tired.

I wished those enchanted days of solitude would never end, that the new elements of beauty he was finding would not cease but go on and on, that a magic spell could conjure time and more time. *There's so much more to come*, I told him as he stood beside the first yellow violet we'd found on the bank of the creek. *So many you will not see.* And I tried to show him images of the lupins and wild roses, the white drifts of moon daisies in the grass of the fields. *But I know you'll be gone before they bloom. You'll miss the honeysuckle and the wild clematis, the lilies and the columbines . . .*

The silver eyes darkened, and the pale lips tightened. His head lifted, and the being who only moments before had been sharing joy of finding another flower with me the, a deep kinship with the earth, became alien, mystical, and strange.

You are denying before you know, he said silently. *You wish for more time, and then tell me what I'll miss. You know I want the far greater things that can be, but you disclaim truth, bury yourself in your surroundings without considering the potential that you are seeing this as it is.* His eyes burned into mine, and he spread his hands in a wide gesture. *You aren't looking at what it has done and can do, not only the physical reality, but what it can mean.*

I didn't want to listen, for I knew what he was referring to. I didn't want to think about his impossible request, only of the here and now, the beauty of the morning sky, that the sun was warm on my neck and he had been sharing my pleasure. I wanted these days to remain beautiful, a memory of something precious and rare. He had no right to ask more of me, for there was no other place for him in my life – as there could be none for me in his distant world.

Laura, haven't you a limitless horizon?

No, Israfel, of course I haven't. My marriage and the life I've made are my boundaries. They have to be. Don't you see that?

Once my vocation had been mine. But you yourself have shown me that life is for living and to be used. Without challenge there is no achievement, without opposition there is no winning.

A marriage isn't just an achievement.

No. But success is.

Jesse and I are making our own successes. Israfel, you can't ask more of me.

But Laura, I have to. Don't you realize how hard it is for me to adjust? For me to change from what I am to what I'm going to have to be? You've given me life; don't you know that? Without you, I would have died and died anyway. But you showed me a new way, the value of challenge. You've given me a new life, so you are an intrinsic part of it. How can you expect me to give you up? What did you tell me about fighting and winning? Forgive me for turning your words back on you, but I'm fighting now . . . for you.

"Don't," I whispered, turning away from him, hugging my arms across my chest in a feeble protection. "Israfel, don't." I stared blindly into the water of the creek. "If you care about me at all, you'll forget this idea you have—"

Care about you? Laura, you're only the woman I've ever wanted, the only one I've ever loved . . .

"Don't!" I said again, my voice rasping.

Don't? How can I not?

"You mustn't . . . "

What is, is.

"You're always saying that when you know it can never be."

I know what exists, what you keep denying.

I whirled to face him, no longer able to speak. I couldn't feel the sun's warmth, couldn't hear the splash of water, couldn't even see him clearly beside the blurred boles of birches. I lashed at him with silent, angry words. *What exists is my marriage to Jesse – that you have no right to try to destroy! What your society has become is no responsibility of mine. It's for you to deal with. I can't help you. I must stay here. Israfel, I don't want to hurt you, but don't you know that love is also letting go? So forget it. Forget it! There is no other way . . .*

I ran out of words and, shaken by my outburst, stood with chest heaving and hands twisting together with nervous agitation. God! How was he going to react to that? But he stood staring at me, telling me nothing.

Was he angry? Hurt? Had I wounded his pride? His vanity? All I could think were questions as a tangle of confusion wound around my thought processes, preventing any reason. Had striking at the superiority of his intellect again made him condemn me as a deficient creature of poor comparison, unable to control even a simple emotion? And why did this notion trouble me?

Somehow, he was before me, and I hadn't seen him move. His hands touched my shoulders, featherlight.

Laura, I'm not angry or hurt. I haven't that kind of pride or vanity. I treasure everything you are because your motives are not at fault. I understand your emotions now. But come, put what I said from your mind, and we'll go on as before.

The metallic eyes shimmered before mine, and I regarded him with wary anxiety. Could we just go on as before? I didn't think so. Nor could I simply forget his words. And was he now deliberately avoiding the situation he himself had created?

But . . . do you understand what I mean? I asked him, trying to keep my eyes on his.

Oh, yes. Yes, I do. His hands left my shoulders. *There. I'm letting go. Now, what else can we find?*

Nonplussed, I stood there, uncertain, still confused. He was letting the matter drop far too easily. He said he had understood – but had he? He wasn't angry or disappointed, not even regretful.

Laura, don't worry. I do understand. But let's go back to this beautiful morning, to the sense of magic in which you find security, to this journey of small discoveries that means so much. Forget everything else.

For his sake as well as mine, relieved and grateful that he was making such an effort to reinstate our earlier relationship, reciprocating by trying to do the same, I hid my cowardly head in the sands of delusion once more. Within an hour, I thought we'd recaptured the magic as we stood at the edge of the forest and watched a coyote trotting across the hay field.

Wild, I told him as his eyes shone and his mind responded to the foxy face and brushy tail, the extraordinary ease of gait. *Totally wild, really a pest, but I must admit I love to see one.*

And it lives here, like this?

Yes. You've heard them singing on the mountain.

I hadn't been able to put a face and form to that particular voice.

Those tense moments beside the creek were forgotten, dismissed from my mind as they seemed to be from his. Once again there was magic in the delicate sky and the sun's yellow light, in a blue haze on the mountains and the soft scented air, delight in seeing a wild creature clearly before our eyes.

Self-delusion, of course – that I chose to regard as enchantment. For in that containment there was a perseveration of my rare communication with a being from another world and escape from the realities I didn't want to accept.

When Maureen broke the spell that night, finally and conclusively, the breaking was cold and hard and shocking.

"Have you seen today's paper?" she asked me over the phone.

Here came the outside world, and I faced it reluctantly. "No. Why?"

"Ted just brought it home. You'd better read it."

"I haven't been out to pick it up for days. Why, Maureen? What's in it?"

"We'll come over after dinner, bring it with us."

"Okay."

I hung up, resenting the intrusion, a newspaper that obviously meant trouble. The evening was beautiful, and we'd planned to go out and look for deer. Now we were faced with a probable end to our days of magic, solitude, and peace. Israfel watched me with resignation in his eyes, in his mind. He had known it couldn't last, that the danger to him and his crew would be here for as long as they were. And there were probably still six weeks left to go.

We were a somber group at the fireside that night. One look at Ted and Maureen's faces was enough to cast a pall of depression over all of us. Pots of tea and coffee stood neglected on the hearth as Ted unfolded the newspaper and passed it to me in silence, his face grim. Maureen sat motionless in a chair, her eyes wide and dark as they watched me while I read. And the still faces of our alien guests surrounded me in an apprehensive waiting.

The paper was thick, felt heavy in my hands, and the black headline stared at me.

UFO DOWNED IN CANADA. POLICE AND ARMED FORCES SEARCHING FORESTS AND MOUNTAINS FOR WHAT IS BELIEVED TO BE AN ALIEN SPACECRAFT.

The article was on an inside page, placed there no doubt by an editor who didn't want to risk ridicule by putting it on the front. But the caption was large, eye-catching, and the article long. Tony Roth had done his work well.

A numbing dismay spread over me as I read. He had seen right through my thinly veiled questions, my hinted-at statements, but his words gave me no recourse against him.

I read out loud, trying not to reveal the despair into which I was sinking.

He started with a brief explanation of "where," then went on with "buzzing rumors and conjecture, army vehicles and helicopters, but no one in authority wants to talk."

Residents, however, had revealed that a search had been in progress since the previous fall. This search had led to Jesse. The article listed the familiar songs and scores of motion pictures Jesse had composed before turning to the crucial details.

" 'A visit to the Tremayne residence,' " I read, " 'proved most interesting. Laura Tremayne corroborated the story of what the army is reportedly looking for, admitted that her home had been searched by the police, but was very reluctant to discuss the matter in any great detail. Too reluctant, it seems, for one who had nothing to hide. Obviously, she knows more than she's telling. But why is she remaining silent? Whatever the reason, it should prove most interesting. Or is this all just part of another coverup? Or yet even prove to be a hoax? Is the army on maneuvers, as they claim? Are the police just looking for an escaped convict? I don't think so. There are too many rumors, too much reticence from those in authority, and too much suspicion about Jesse and Laura Tremayne.

" 'Is the reason for all this secrecy obvious? The Pentagon has shot down every UFO reported in figurative flames. Responsible people, such as airline captains, police officers, and reputable citizens, have been made to look like fools or idiots or even worse. To find a UFO right on our doorstep, complete with crew, could prove embarrassing, to say the least – if it were publicly known, that is.

" 'Reliable sources have revealed that the US Air Force has been given instructions to bring one down at any cost, for any government that has a UFO could possibly have an ultimate weapon. Something that could reportedly outfly, outmaneuver, and outdistance anything we own, defy gravity, turn at an abrupt right angle, and operate in total silence while holding the key to simple, economical space travel. These are big stakes. Is it a big coverup? It's tempting to think so.' "

The words blurred on the page but not in my mind. They stood there sharp and clear, their careful intent, the implication of Jesse and me that opened the way to a storm of further questions and suspicion.

I left the paper fall, looked at Israfel with heart-wrenching anguish. I had failed to handle the first reporter who had come, and I'd put him and his crew into far greater jeopardy than they had ever been. Now the word was wide, national, had perhaps gone even further. There was no safety for them here. And our days of solitude were no more.

But there was no accusation in his eyes. Only a vague sorrow lay behind their steady depths, and if his face wore a frown, it was only one of faint regret. Then he gave me what could only be meant as an encouraging smile, but his mind was closed and remained so.

"So there we are," Ted said. "And now what?"

"They'd better come back with us," Maureen said.

I was numb, unable to think, sat staring helplessly at Israfel.

"Thank you, Maureen," he said. "But one of us must stay here. Laura shouldn't be left alone."

"Maybe Jesse . . . " Maureen began tentatively.

Surely Jesse would come home now, I thought. *He must realize the predicament we are in, the necessity of his presence here.*

Israfel was watching me, understanding and aware. My heart ached with a numbing regret. Again everything was different.

"Yes," I said. "I'll call him."

But I didn't move, remained fixed in my chair, watching the reflection of these days fade from the darkening mirror of his eyes.

CHAPTER
TWENTY-EIGHT

JESSE CAME HOME – UNWILLINGLY, I knew – two days later. Farrand and Israfel went to Ted and Maureen's while Celene stayed on. Having been identified once by Tony Roth as the hired hand, there seemed no reason not to leave him as such. I had no time to do anything or to even think, for the phone began to ring and hardly ever stopped.

Some of the calls were obscene or from fanatics and obvious cranks. Most were from the media, requesting information and interviews or simply asking if the story bore any truth. And people came in droves. The curious as well as reporters and photographers, a crew from the CBC television station in Kelowna, crackpots and cranks, people with obscure faces who tried to question us without revealing who they were.

They attempted to drive in during the day, transformed our roads into deeply rutted furrows oozing moisture and spewing gravel, dug deep holes with spinning wheels before abandoning their vehicles and begging to use our phone to call a tow truck.

I phoned Mark, and he put a "Road Closed" sign across the entrance for us, only for it to promptly be pushed aside by a group of longhaired youngsters in a minibus who insisted they could get through. They bogged down when they had gone less than a hundred yards, followed by a journalist from Vancouver in a rented car and a religious fanatic in a large black Dodge plastered with stickers telling us "The End of the World Is Nigh."

I had to phone Jesse and warn him to take a cab and walk in. The road to the house had become impassable, and Celene and I and the visiting mares were virtually prisoners.

Celene, for the most part, was able to avoid the questioners. With his hair rumpled or covered by an old hat of Jesse's, in grubby jeans and a shirt with a rent in the sleeve, a halter or pail hanging from his hand, he stayed among the horses or in the hay loft of the barn and was readily dismissed as only the hired hand. I was the one they wanted until Jesse came, and my refusal to answer questions only provoked them more. Then the road became so bad it was barely passable on foot, and they began to ask questions elsewhere.

Jesse had to have the cab drop him at the Greenaways' and walk up from there. That road too was a mess. Several washouts and two enterprising reporters who ventured up it in rented cars soon wrecked it. Kevin and Patty kept their gate closed from then on.

My relief at having Jesse home was shadowed by worry.

"The roads are awful," I warned him, grinding coffee, casting worried glances at his face. He was already tired after walking all the way up from the Greenaways', where he'd finally had the cab leave him, then hiking up the Cat Track laden with his carryall and guitar. That draining journey should have put him firmly into a state of irritable resentment.

But he shrugged and slouched lower in his chair at the table. "To be expected, I guess. Next year, we'll have to have them re-graveled or splurge and go for blacktop."

I shook the coffee in the filter, still prepared for wrath. "You wouldn't believe the phone calls. Some of them are just sick."

"I guess."

"And I worry about Farrand and Israfel at Ted and Maureen's. They've no place to hide there."

"They shouldn't need to. And you worry far too much." He sighed and ran a hand through longer-than-ever hair. "I'll just be so goddamned glad when this whole bloody mess is over."

I bet my lip, said nothing more. At least he hadn't flown into fury over the damage done to the roads and our lack of accessibility. Even the constant ringing of the phone didn't overly trouble him. He answered all questions with a firm, "I have nothing to say. I'm sorry," and hung up.

Then we had a brief respite. Tony Roth suggested a cover up, but the radio and television newscasters began to treat the whole affair as a joke. They showed pictures of cars and trucks and a rival television network's van wallowing in our mud, the futile efforts of the drivers as they tried to get out of them. Wheels spun and muddy splatters sprayed over those who pushed to the strains of "If I Can Help Somebody," and as other vehicles slid into the holes left behind an industrious tow truck, "My Elusive Dream" floated on the airwaves.

When the weather suddenly turned wet and cold with all the capriciousness of spring, they had a field day. Shots of our muddy rutted road in pouring rain were offered as though this were an advertised tourist attraction. "Come and enjoy our sights and sun." Someone concocted a poster with "WANTED" printed above a bad reprint of a photograph that could have been of Jesse James, and this was shown while Waylon Jennings sang, "Don't You Think This Outlaw Bit's Done Got Out of Hand."

Tony Roth must have been furious. I was delighted. The visitors departed as rapidly as they had come, and the whole thing died away. No doubt the tow truck driver was disappointed as well as those in the village who had enjoyed a sudden boom in business. But I could only welcome the peace that descended on us. Israfel and Farrand came back; Jesse returned to Los Angeles; Celene shed his grubby garments with relief; and I didn't care at all about the cold and the rain.

But then four men came on foot early one morning, and it was only Sally's warning bark that saved us, sending Farrand and Israfel from the breakfast table and up the stairs, plates and mugs caught up swiftly in their hands.

Faceless men, unsmiling, with cold and searching eyes, the quiet aura of power that supreme authority gives, in discreet gray suits with conservative shirts and ties, unnoticeable in a crowd, distinctly uncomfortable to have in my kitchen.

They were polite, but there was no mistaking the iron within the velvet. They apologized for disturbing me so early, but the words were empty.

I tried to stay calm, distant, unimpressed, to conceal my alarm, my feeling of defencelessness. They were far older, matured by a life very different to mine. Their air of ruthless authority forswore the validity of any rights I might try to stand on.

One of them, with a thin and hollow face, showed me an official identification, and my heart hit the soles of my shoes. He said they were from the Defense Department, but I immediately thought of the CIA, and my apprehension was a trial to hide.

I invited them in before they could demand admittance, offered them coffee, introduced Len, "Who looks after our horses."

"Today's his day off," I explained. "So, if you want to go, Len, feel free."

Israfel, tell him to go to your room as though it were his, make the bed, then take his coat and boots and go out. And you and Farrand had better strip the beds there, hide everything behind the wall. But don't make a sound! These men mean business.

"Are you all alone here, Mrs. Tremayne?" Polite urbane voice, cool and penetrating gaze. There would be little deceiving men such as these.

"My husband is down in LA working on a score. I have Len to help me here."

"I see." The cool eyes studied me calmly.

I brought cups and saucers to the table, put the kettle on to make fresh coffee.

"You're up early."

"When you have animals to care for . . . " I left the sentence unfinished, wished desperately that Jesse was here. He wouldn't take any flak from even this level of officialdom.

They seated themselves around the table, exerting authority by not waiting for my invitation. They had already dismissed me for my youth, my obvious lack of experience, my faded jeans and ancient sweater that clumsy laundering had left too big around the waist. And they were the kind of men who lived in man's world where women had little place.

"There was a very disturbing newspaper article about you a short while ago, Mrs. Tremayne." The man who spoke had shoulders so square they had right-angled corners, and a mouth like a shark's: no lips and lots of teeth.

"Yes," I said shortly, measuring coffee beans into the grinder. "It sure was. And it brought so many people up here, our roads are now completely wrecked and are going to be a terrible job to repair. I wish I could sue them," I added, slamming the lid on the grinder and plugging it in.

"Why don't you?"

I pretended not to hear, pressed the button so the deafening noise of the machine prohibited any further questions.

Israfel, Israfel. Help me. Listen to my mind, help me, Israfel.

Be calm, Laura. You're doing fine.

"I said," he repeated, as the machine ran down into silence, "why don't you sue?"

I shrugged. "What good would it do?"

"You might get your road repaired."

"And a lot more publicity I don't need."

They digested this in silence, watching me with considering eyes, waiting for me to make the slightest mistake as I shook the coffee into a filter.

"Don't you like publicity, Mrs. Tremayne?" Such cool tones, such careful questioning.

I shook my head, tried to smile. "That kind I can do without."

"Aren't you curious why we're here?" asked another, a bulky man whose quality suit looked ill at ease on the plebeian body beneath it.

"Of course I am," I said quickly. "But I figured you're here because of the same rumor."

"Rumor? You're saying it's just a rumor?" The question was sharp in spite of the velvet tone of the voice.

Israfel warned me, *Laura, take care.*

"No," I said. "There's a Captain Forrest who's been searching all around here. He told me what it is they're looking for."

"So why did you say it was a rumor, then?"

"That it could be an alien spacecraft seems to be."

Not one of them blinked. Four pairs of unsmiling eyes watched me steadily, coldly.

"We would like to know," Square Shoulders began, "why your name has been linked to this matter." His words were spoken as a demand, with an increasing note of authority creeping into the voice.

"So would I," I said.

"You have no idea?"

"Somebody," I said, trying to hold my voice steady and failing, "seems to have a grudge against us. They caused the police to come here with a search warrant, even. And then a reporter came all the way from San Francisco."

This was obviously not news to them. They watched and waited.

"That makes me feel very uncomfortable," I went on. "My husband is away. We have all these valuable horses here. And I have no close neighbors."

"So what are you doing about it?"

The kettle boiled, and I poured water into the coffee. "What can I do?" I asked.

"You have no idea who this person is?"

"I don't know why anybody would even have a grudge against us. Everyone we know here we regard as a friend."

"You're American, aren't you, Mrs. Tremayne?"

"My mother was Canadian," I said. "She married an American. They're both dead now."

There was no sign of sympathy for me, regret that my parents had died while still relatively young. Cold callous men, bound by ambition or duty or a combination of both. I wished them quickly gone.

"We're treating this affair as a matter of security." The last man to speak had a gravelly voice and thick white fingers that moved constantly on the table edge. Both his voice and fingers repelled me. I stood by the range, waiting for the teapot's steam to begin, feigning polite interest while my insides twisted and tangled into uncomfortable knots.

"And we don't mind telling you," the gravelly voice went on, "that we'll take any measures necessary to secure possession of this craft."

"Mr. . . . ?" I raised my eyebrows in a question. Dammit! If he was going to speak to me in this fashion, at least he could tell me his name.

"Harcourt."

"The police have already searched this house. The army damaged our roads, considerably." I made no acknowledgment of his name, fighting for every little advantage that I could. "Captain Forrest and Sergeant Roberts have been right through here, and my husband and I spent many uncomfortable hours in the saddle last fall, assisting the search in the forest. Since then, an incredible story has been printed, using my name without my permission. And you have seen for yourselves what our roads have been reduced to because of it. They are ruined. We have other people's mares here and others yet to come, and getting them in and out is now practically impossible. I sure don't appreciate any of this one bit."

I took the coffee to the table and poured it into their cups, my hand shaking with what I hoped they'd think was anger.

None of them spoke as they attended to their coffee, but the eyes still kept me under surveillance the whole time. I resumed my place and regarded the last piece of my breakfast toast with distaste as my churning stomach rebelled at the very thought of eating it.

"One of the newspaper stories said you obviously knew far more than they'd been led to believe," the thin-faced one said, stirring his coffee automatically.

"One of them? You mean there are more?"

"Any number. I'm surprised you didn't see them."

"I haven't been able to get out," I said as sharply as I dared.

"Well, that's neither here nor there." The spoon was dropped into the saucer, and his attention riveted itself on me. "Do you know more than you're telling?"

"About what?" My tongue moved stiffly in my mouth.

"This supposedly hidden UFO."

"Captain Forrest," I said unevenly, "told me he was looking for a spacecraft, and he asked me to keep it confidential. That's what I've tried to do. He hinted that it might be dangerous, warned me to keep away from it if I should happen to find it. Jesse – that's my husband – and I rode for miles in the cold and the snow – when we thought it was a plane – and saw nothing."

"And you haven't seen anything since?"

"We haven't been out again. Nobody asked us to. And he's been away, working, and I've been busy here with the horses." I took a mouthful of coffee and realized too late I had put neither honey or cream into it, and I couldn't rectify it while those watchful eyes considered every move I made.

"Mrs. Tremayne." It was the gravelly voice again, his fingers scurrying about his cup and saucer like fat white grubs. "Don't you think it odd that with all the army personnel who've been searching – the helicopters and other aircraft, not to mention people like yourselves – that nothing's been found?"

"Mr. Harcourt," I said. "Have you been out in the forest around here? Have you any idea what it's like? It's a jungle, and it stretches for miles."

The white fingers did a little dance on the table edge, and all the eyes watched me unflinchingly.

"Those are trained officers, Mrs. Tremayne. They've been over all those miles of forest. They've flown over it and searched it. And they've found nothing."

"Maybe they're looking in the wrong place," I said.

They didn't even attempt to argue. Expressionless, the faces showed nothing – like cameras, recording everything they saw, dispassionately, filing it all neatly in the boxes of their brains.

They're machines, I thought. *Not human*. And the thought of Israfel, Celene, and Farrand in their hands was horrifying. "Or," I went on, determination stilling the tangling in my stomach, "how do you know there's a craft at all?"

"Because it was shot down."

"Then maybe it's wrecked," I suggested helpfully. I took another swallow of hateful black coffee, kept my face composed despite the bitter taste.

"Then there'd be wreckage."

"Well . . . " I glanced meaningfully at the clock on the wall. "I'm sorry I can't help you."

"We're not convinced you can't," the one who had first spoken said.

I turned and looked at him, at the iron gray hair and thin firm mouth, the corded ropiness of his throat. There was a trace of a military man in the lean face and straight back. I tried to meet his glacial gaze.

"If you want me to go out on a horse again, I can try to fit it in."

"No. Not that. Have you noticed anything strange at your friends' homes? Or any of your neighbors'? There'll be a reward," he added, "that would be kept quiet, strictly between us and its recipient."

A sick anger threatened to inflict my miserable coffee back on me. I swallowed hard, tried not to choke. "If you think—" I began, then broke off abruptly. All those calculating eyes were watching me, waiting for such a reaction. "That any of my friends know something, then why don't you ask them?"

"You're the one whose name's been mentioned publicly. You're the one who was first brought to the attention of the RCMP. And you're the one we're not convinced is telling us the truth."

"I most certainly am!" I said hotly.

They weren't in the least affected by my flash of anger.

"Then," the miliary type went on, "perhaps you'd be good enough to tell us, have you seen anything the least bit suspicious at any of your friends' homes?"

"Not a thing," I said adamantly.

"And you are telling us the truth?"

"You're damned right I am!" I snapped, my anger overflowing. "And I'll tell you this, too. I'm sick to death of being hounded like this. I'm fed up to the teeth with people walking into my house, invading my privacy, ruining our roads, taking up my time, and harassing me with this kind of questioning!"

The four pairs of eyes did nothing but narrow slightly.

The bulky one spoke, his nondescript face still quite expressionless. "Mrs. Tremayne, if you recognized the seriousness of this situation, understood the necessity of our questions, I'm sure you'd offer more cooperation."

"All I can see," I said, my voice shaking with emotional stress, "is the damage done to our roads, those men with a search warrant prying through my house, and the people who've been treating me like a public property ever since some . . . person – and I wish I knew who it was – went to the police with a story that most people would regard as mere fiction!"

"But you forget. It isn't. The police know as well as us what it is we're looking for. And in a matter involving such a high level of security, every single lead will be followed."

I drew a deep breath, tried to gain control of myself. "Security? Why do you keep saying it's a matter of security?"

The iron gray head turned briefly to his companions, then the cold eyes fixed on mine again. "We don't know where this thing has come from, or what it was doing in our airspace. It could be some Russian secret weapon, for all we know. Or it could be highly radioactive, even toxic. Until we can locate it and examine it properly, we don't know how dangerous it might be. Now surely you can appreciate that."

I swallowed, nodded. "Of course. Yes."

"So, any information at all that you might have could be useful."

I let myself sit and think for a few moments while those waiting eyes watched every muscle of my face. Then I shook my head. "The rumors I've heard are no doubt the same ones you have. But I will go out on a horse again and look, if you like."

The bulky one made the first show of impatience. He banged down his cup and shoved his chair back, a flicker of annoyance passing across his eyes. The others didn't move. Only the thick white fingers of the one with the gravelly voice turned his saucer in constant rotation on the table.

"It's information we need," the military one said coldly. "These woods have been thoroughly searched. Now we need responsible citizens to act in a sensible manner and use their heads. If anyone is hiding this thing, they could not only be in extreme physical danger themselves, but they could also be jeopardizing everyone else's in the surrounding country. Behaving bloody foolishly, in fact. So, you think about that. And if there's anything you want to tell us, you'd better speak up."

I gazed at him with hot eyes, controlling a rising rage by sheer physical effort, trying to keep my hands lying easily on the table instead of clenching into fists. "I've absolutely nothing to tell you," I said as calmly as my fury would allow. "And if you think any more search attempts by us would be wasted, then that's just great. I've plenty of other things to do." I pushed my chair back and stood up, waiting for them to also rise.

They did so, not out of politeness but in an attempt to convey that they too had no more time to waste. The white fingers of the one played for a moment more with the saucer before he too rose. He looked at me with open contempt.

"We must remind you, Mrs. Tremayne," he said, his voice oozing unctuously, "that if we hear anything more about you to increase our suspicion, then we'll be back."

"As long as you don't drive over our roads," I said.

"We'll do whatever's necessary." The threat in his voice wasn't even veiled.

"I'd advise you to think about it," the military one said as he began to move towards the door. "Try to be sensible."

Patronizing, sanctimonious chauvinist! I thought savagely as I followed them into the hall. Biting my tongue, I stood with my chin raised in defiance as they pulled on muddy overshoes and coats. The vigilant eyes still managed to watch my face while they dressed. I gave them no further words at all and let Sally bark at them the whole way across the yard and out to the muddy road, watching them from the window until they were out of sight. Then anger and strain and the snapping release of tension reduced me to tears, and I stood in the hall, shaken by a helpless sobbing, barely resisting the temptation to beat on the door as though it were their retreating backs.

Laura.

I was turned into a sympathetic embrace, held against a lean hard chest.

Laura, I'm sorry. I'm sorry. Don't let this anger hurt you, for it isn't for you to bear. Don't cry. I hate to be responsible for these tears. You did so well, my dearest one. We're all impressed, and very grateful. Laura, please don't cry.

I let myself lean against him, press my face into the soft wool of the sweater I'd bought for him, feel the incredibly slow heartbeats behind it thudding against my cheek.

It . . . it was that they tried to bribe me, and almost threatened me, and treated me as though I were a stupid child.

His hand smoothed my hair with a touch as light as air, but I was immediately aware of it, its soothing quality. *I know, Laura. I know.*

They were so dangerous, and so close to you.

Don't think about it anymore.

Never, I thought fiercely, as the strong arms still held me, the slow heartbeat against my face, would I let them take him. Never, never, never! What danger could he represent? Other than that, he wished to take me from my home. And what danger could that damaged craft hold, buried beneath the soil of the High Meadow? Oh, God! How little I knew! How terribly unaware I was!

CHAPTER TWENTY-NINE

RAIN AND THE RUINED ROAD caused us to be left in peace for several days. The weather did create extra work with the horses and bringing mares and foals in through pouring rain and knee-deep mud was no pleasure. Cleaning up the sheds in which they constantly sought shelter was a never-ending chore for Celene and me. But he, realizing how precarious their position here had become, was ready to forget his differences and do whatever was necessary, use a shovel or fork, halter or pail as needs be, resigning himself to shabby clothes, the rain, the mud, the horses, and their work, with a forbearance that was quite admirable.

Farrand was still laboring over the receiver, and Israfel, in a new distress I was powerless to do anything about, either helped him or braved the rain soaked woods with me in an attempt to recapture the enchantment of those few days we had known.

But a cloud lay over us that wasn't just the gray of the sky above. The brilliance of the remembered sun was darkened, and the magic spell broken by those four men with their threats and warnings, the unwelcome visitors after Tony Roth's article, and the spread of newspaper publicity. I was constantly alert, knowing that Israfel shouldn't be out here in these woods where we could run into anyone, from the simply curious to Captain Forrest or others of his ilk. And there was little pleasure in the cold and rain.

Then the skies cleared and the sun beat down once more with brilliance and warmth, and the hand of spring again touched the budding leaves and flushing grass, brought violets in profusion and the first bright sprigs of paintbrush to the sloping sides of the Vance ravine.

The creeks swelled as the snow melting on the mountains traveled through a myriad springs and water courses to join them. And their voices began to roar like distant jet planes, echoing through the trees until we could hear them from the patio behind the house.

Parts of the road dried up, but others remained churned and rutted quagmires with pools of water gleaming in deep holes. It was still impassable to traffic, and Jesse stayed in Los Angeles – making progress, he said.

At the end of April, there came a day so beautiful it more than compensated for the rain and mud of the cold gray anxious days that had dragged so slowly by. It was heralded by a hummingbird, ruby-throated, shrilling across the patio where we were lounging in the sun after doing the morning chores. Farrand had even joined us, the beauty of the morning drawing him outside for a brief respite. Israfel, too, was responding to the heat, the clarity of the sky, the fragrance of the sun-warmed earth and growing things, smiled as I celebrated with small ceremonies: setting the first vase of a few wildflowers on the redwood table and filling a feeder and hanging it from the eave. Then we all sat and watched as the jeweled creature hung on the air, its throat glowing in the sun and miraculous wings whirring. Even Celene was impressed, I could see. And Israfel's mind flowed into mine with the renewed sharing of an exquisite wild thing.

I left them there, saddled Andante, and rode out, up the mountain on the forestry road, to cut back across the slope on an old trail, down again to join the road where I had first known something strange was happening by Gallant's odd behavior. I followed the edge of the main pasture, passed into the High Meadow, and stopped to listen. But all I could hear was the creek and birds singing in the forest, the robins and thrushes, and the shrilling of another hummingbird. No planes traversed the delphinium blue of the sky. No helicopters pounded up the valley. No tracks marked the forestry road or trails. I cantered Andante homeward, calling to Israfel. There was one thing I wanted him to see that we might just find.

He unsaddled the mare while I changed. Sandals and a dress – what a pleasure after the long winter months to feel the air against bare arms and legs, the softness of it, and the warmth of the sun. It was still too cool for Israfel to shed the woolen sweater, but he smiled when we saw me and again later at my determination to find what I sought.

The groves of cedar beyond the corrals were usually the most probable places, but on this day they yielded nothing. We turned and followed our northern boundary. Here the forest was thick. Tall, ragged firs met the sky. The branches of the birches were still bare, but the occasional larch wore a faint flush of green. We walked a few trails but were forced to the edge of the hay field when the trees became too tangled and thick.

Far below, the valley was glazed with a soft blue haze, and the mountains ringing it were misted and ethereal. The sun in that low trajectory caught the tips of fir trees on the ridges, tinted them with russet and gold, and gilded them as though by an artist's brush against the gray blue velvet folds and steeply falling shadowed slopes.

"How beautiful," I breathed, thinking this would be some recompense if we didn't find the flower I sought.

Yes. Israfel's silent answer was rich with appreciation.

The enchantment was surely returning. All around us was sunlight and the song of birds, green growing shoots and small unfurling buds, the sweet fragrance of spring. Now, if I could only find . . .

The land began to fall away toward the creek, and the insistent voice of rushing water came to us through the trees. An old logging road traversed the slope, and we followed it, climbing over fallen trees and branches, stopping at times to listen and search the way ahead. For it was in this vicinity that Sergeant Roberts had so suddenly appeared, and our memories of such incidents were long.

A splash of pink caught my eyes. Incredibly it was growing in the middle of the roadway: one perfect solitary calypso orchid. I caught his arm, the delight of triumph surging in me. *Look!*

He knelt in the leaves, in the fallen needles and twigs, and stared at it, motionless, his mind racing too fast for me to obtain a single thought.

I stood still and watched him – and found it hard to believe that this was a space traveler, a self-proclaimed warrior, the commander of an alien ship with a mind more powerful than I could ever understand. That slight and graceful being with silvery hair shining in the sunlight, now kneeling before a tiny flower in this deep wild forest, was from another world?

Impossible. He was my friend who talked to me of many things, shared my joys and concerns, my pains and sorrows, held me with strong arms in times of need – and asked me to go away with him, I reminded myself uncomfortably, to that other world.

He knew what I was thinking, and in one smooth movement was on his feet and looking at me. The silver eyes shone with sunlight, but his face was pale and set.

Yes, Laura, and I shall ask you again. But for now, we have another day in which to enjoy the sun and find beauty such as this. He made a motion with his hand to indicate the orchid at his feet. *There is no need to think of leaving at this time . . . unless you want to discuss it. Or this day can be what you choose to think of as magic, when you know as well as I that magic is an illusion. If those days were as real to you as they were to me, then there was no magic, no illusion, but only the reality of a positive truth, and one in which no rain or clouds, gray skies or unwelcome visitors need ever intrude again.*

He took a step toward me, and I could see the passion in his eyes again, a silver intensity as they drove into mine.

Laura! His hands gripped my shoulders. *Laura! Why don't you see?*

Alarmed, I wrenched myself away from him, and he let me go as though I had burned him. An expression of sadness passed across his face, shaded his eyes, and etched his lips with lines of pain.

Israfel! Please! I touched his hand, his sadness becoming mine. *I don't want to hurt you. But you must understand. I'm committed here to Jesse, to the life we've built together, that we share.*

The eyes flared into brilliance so suddenly I caught my breath. *Is that why you fear my touch?*

I stumbled before that dazzling gaze. *I . . . I guess so.*

A faint smile replaced the look of pain. *Then I am not so hurt.*

Bewildered, I stared at him. He laughed softly.

My poor Laura. So confused by your loyalties and ethics, the imprints of your culture, tenets often blinded to common sense. Like so much of your architecture, the foundation and structure are hidden by a facade that is often false, and what is seen is believed more readily than that which is not.

He smiled at my barely-comprehending face. *You fail to see how that applies to you? Of course you do. But forget it now, Laura. At this moment, it is less important than the warmth of this sun, the blue of that sky, and this exquisite flower you have gone to so much trouble to find. If you believe in magic, you can conjure it if you wish.*

He turned away. *Shall we look for another orchid? Or is there something else you wish to find?*

Yes. More about you.

Again, he laughed. *You know as much about me as you need. Ask me more if you wish. But not now, Laura. Later, this evening, when the sun has gone and we can no longer walk in these lovely woods and find flowers such as this.*

We went on, back along the creek. Its roar precluded anything in my mind, and his had closed to me.

There was no magic for me in that day, beautiful though it was. What he had said about reality made fancifulness seem childish and immature, and I found myself wondering how he could possibly want me to go with him when his intellect was so vastly superior to mine.

At the foot of the Cat Track he stopped and turned me to face him once again. *Have no misconceptions about me, either, Laura. The level of your intellect is on an entirely different plane to mine. But it's your loyalty that matters to me, the loyalty you have maintained in the face of great difficulty. I don't care what you look like or that you have little comprehension of the universal laws that are as basic to me as riding on a horse is to you. It's you that I want, and what I know we could share. My life will be only existence without you because music can't be all. I still have to work for something. And I can now, but I need you to help me.*

My eyes burned as I looked at him, but I couldn't speak. I shook my head and went on.

There were killdeer crying on the pasture that night. After the evening chores were done, Israfel told me he'd like to see them. So, we set off down the narrow pathway behind the house, through darkening shadows between colorless trees.

There had been little communication between us for the rest of the day, our time taken with the repair of a broken fence rail and the breeding of one of the visiting mares. But I was very conscious of him, of his soft footfalls behind me as we went down the steep hillside in the cool still air.

The first stars were appearing when we reached the pasture. They shone brightly in a deep green sky. To the east, a few bands of purple clouds lay above the mountains' dusky silhouettes. Copper Mountain to the west rose in a dark shadow while the horizon to the south was only faint, blending into a hazier sky.

I saw him look up wistfully, as he always did at night, at those distant shiny stars so very far away. But then the cry of the killdeer came again, and we climbed up the hillside in the short spring grass until we saw them, their pale wings and rapid flight. They circled around us, their voices ringing plaintively in the stillness of the evening, their ghostly shapes gathering in the dusk.

On our way back, I saw a deer on the road but caught little more than a flash of white as it sprang away into the trees. I was distressed and wished he had seen it more clearly.

I saw it, he told me. *Laura, I see more than you realize.*

Darkness had fallen by the time we reached the house, and it was growing colder. The fire on the living room hearth was welcome, the softly lit room inviting. Celene and Farrand had apparently gone upstairs to work on the receiver, and the coffee and tea pots were still hot on the side of the kitchen stove.

I carried in another cup of coffee, studied Israfel cautiously as he knelt before the fire, and wondered what more I could ask him – as he had said I could.

Your parents, I began tentatively.

Yes? The silver eyes flashed toward me.

You do have parents?

Yes. Although I wasn't born the way you were.

I was astonished. *You weren't? Then . . . how?*

Very simply. I was removed as an embryo, raised in a perfect environment, and went back to my parents when I could function on my own.

I stared at him. *Good grief!*

So were Farrand and Celene.

I digested this, or tried to.

I realize now, he told me quietly, *how much I missed, and I imagine my parents did also. Seeing Maureen with Deenie, the children at the Christmas dinner . . . life, Laura. Real life.*

And . . . have you ever been married?

No.

Do you have marriages?

Not as they are here. A vow made is a vow kept in total freedom.

Israfel, tell me about your life, please. What it has been, what it's like.

He was silent, watching the fire with unseeing eyes, and his mind sped by mine so fast it was only a streak of light.

I can't follow you, I told him. *Israfel, please . . . did you go to school?*

School? His head lifted, turned so the silver eyes were on mine once more. *I was taught by a very great being, a master of the universal laws. He took me everywhere, showed me everything, even brought me here. I was fortunate to have him, not only as my teacher but as my friend. It will grieve him deeply to know that I have failed.*

The words came to me, short and sharp, and the last ones were painful.

"You haven't failed!" I said out loud, my voice vehement with the anger of disappointment. This self-blame was not in character with the powerful being I knew.

Laura, you are kind to say so. But as long as I am convinced I have, then for me it is so.

I set my cup down on the hearth, went to the window, and drew the heavy drapes across. When I turned, he was standing, watching me, poised as though waiting.

Okay. So, I know I don't understand your laws. But I'd have said it was an accident. After all, you didn't want it to happen, did you? You weren't stupidly careless.

I should have seen it, that fighter plane, and taken evasive action in time to avoid it.

"Should have" is only "too late."

He regarded me thoughtfully as I went back to the fireside, put out his hand, and stopped me when I was about to sit down again. I was immediately wary, gathering myself for defense.

Laura, why do you fear my touch?

I . . . I told you that this morning.

But have you told yourself?

The same reason.

Because you're married to Jesse?

Yes.

Is that a reason?

Sure.

Think about it. How can that be a reason?

My apprehension growing, I tried to move away from him.

Don't, Laura. Face up to it, and to me, please.

I took a deep breath, wondered why a tremor was starting deep inside me.

Okay. You're alien . . . different, and a danger to me, my marriage, everything I've established. I care about you, Israfel, but I'm married to Jesse. I love him, and always will.

Then you have no cause to fear my touch at all.

But I do!

So, you still don't know the reason.

One step brought him close to me. His arms swept around me and held me tight. *Laura, is this it?*

The world vanished; everything I knew ceased to exist. Except Israfel – and a passion so vast, so powerful, it was tenderness and gentleness and a total love and a desire that was shattering in its violence, inescapable in its demand, a fierce and wild fury that left me as nothing.

The slow beat of his heart was a drum inside my own; the feather touch of his lips on my face a brand that seared right through to my brain. And his mind filled mine with a rush of wanting and caring, of desire and loving, the promise of ecstasy and a fulfillment that I could almost feel as my senses quickened, burned, then raged. His wanting was mine; the aching of his heart a pain in my own. There was the glorious warmth of his body, the marvelous strength of his arms and touch of his hands, the sheer excitement of a vital maleness that sprang into life as he called to me, body and soul, heart and mind.

The responding core of my womanhood answered with a desperation, an ecstasy, and a fevered delirium that shocked me. I had never known this, felt this wild heat, the aching yearning, this possession of my senses and them turning into something quite apart from me. Jesse's lovemaking was quiet, gentle, comfortable, and I received him with tenderness and warmth. This was entirely different, a losing of self, of identity, of any direction, and I tried to pull away before I was lost completely.

The effort was only in my mind, the only part of me of which I still had any control. My body was yielding to him, helpless with desire, resenting the covering of clothes. I moaned as the searching mouth found mine.

No. Israfel, no.

Dazed, gasping, my bones liquid, I floated back to strong arms holding me and silver eyes-only inches from my own. So close, I could see the texture of those extraordinary irises, their strange metallic gleam polished to a shining brilliance. They reflected the light of the fire in a bronze and copper sheen that sparked with gold as the flames flickered.

"What are you doing?" I whispered. My lips trembled, were still throbbing form the touch of his.

Showing you something of me, and something of you to yourself. And Laura, does it matter so much that I'm an alien?

"Don't ever do that again!" I said hoarsely, feeling my legs wavering beneath me and my heart thudding to distraction.

The silver eyes did not flinch, met mine steadily with all their glow and glitter. *Laura, does it matter to you that I'm alien?* he asked again.

"Jesse does," I said weakly. I tried to find the strength to break away from him.

He held me with his hands. *I know he does. And I won't do that again until you stand beside me on my own land, free of everything that binds you here. And you still haven't answered my question.*

Strength was returning, desire fading, my head was becoming my own again. I kept my eyes on his. *No. It doesn't trouble me that you're alien.*

Only what I just did?

Wordlessly, I nodded.

But you weren't afraid of me?

No.

I heard him sigh, felt him touch my cheek in a gentle gesture. *Laura.* He knelt on the rug before the fire, drawing me down beside him. *Laura, there are times when the truth is painful, I know. But illusion is delusion and self-betrayal. Truth must be confronted, even if it hurts.*

You're so much stronger than me, I told him unhappily. *And your mind can rule mine so easily.*

But I swear I'll never use that to take advantage of you.

You just did.

No. Only to tell you something.

My cup of coffee still stood there on the hearth, a thin trail of steam rising from it. I was amazed to find that it was still hot. It seemed as though an eternity had passed since I had set it there, that I had aged, grown old. My hands shook slightly as I lifted it, held the warm mug between them. I forced myself to look at him once more.

So slight, so graceful, kneeling there before the fire, its flames illuminating his perfect face and reflecting in those alien eyes. But he was closer to me than he had ever been, and I was astounded to realize it. Even though the passion that had flared had lasted only seconds, it had forged an intimate link between us because I had lost my fear of him. He had stopped, only shown me what could be. I knew he had won an advantage over me, forced me to admit I no longer found him alien, but at last I did feel I could trust him.

CHAPTER THIRTY

APRIL BECAME MAY, AND I turned the calendar page with
very mixed feelings. This was the month they expected the rescue ship to
come. Our ordeal could soon be over, and I would rest again in peace. Israfel,
Farrand, and Celene would be safe, that craft gone from its hiding place
beneath the earth of the High Meadow, and our lives once more our own. I
tried not to think about the pain of parting, the sorrow I dared not let myself
contemplate. They would be gone, their secrets with them. And I would lose
Israfel, the close companion of my mind, be left to days of emptiness and a
silence that would be hard to endure.

The roads were dry, and Captain Forrest kept his word, had a grader
brought in to repair the damage done to them. I felt somewhat guilty at this,
knowing that what harm the army had done was slight when compared to
the damage that had come after them. But I salved my conscience by paying
for the work done on the road to the house and inviting him in for lunch.

After my encounter with the Apocalyptical Four, as I always thought of
them, I found Captain Forrest almost human, considered him as at least an
acquaintance. After all, he had taken me into his confidence at one time, even
if he had only done it out of an ulterior motive and he'd had his own interests
at heart. The lack of searchers and questioners during the last couple of weeks
had also served to lay a veneer of confidence over my anxieties, and I was so
grateful for the respite that I was willing to spread largesse. We were even able
to joke about the vehicles stuck in our mud and the tongue-in-cheek attitude
taken by radio and television newscasters, while above his head our alien
visitors waited in silent amusement for him to go.

They too, with rescue now close at hand and the lack of disturbance in their place of refuge, were becoming more relaxed. The once-close dangers seemed very far away, and the days, warm and sunlit, passed by with a smooth serenity that made us feel all the more secure. So it was harsh, shocking, when the whole affair was blown into the open, especially as the wind of revelation came from an entirely unexpected quarter.

Young and impressionable, not-so-easily forgetting Sacha put two and two together from newspaper reports and the rumors in the village. She came up to ask if our four visitors were the beings she now presumed them to be. And she didn't come alone.

Two visiting mares had just departed, and I was in the barn with Celene, clearing up the stalls to prepare for the next arrivals due the follow day. Israfel was in the house with Farrand, working on the receiver, and I was not alarmed at Sally's barking or at seeing Sacha ride into the yard on a gray pony. She looked pretty in jeans and a lavender blue sweater, her hair shining in the sun. And the two other girls and two boys, all mounted, weren't particularly alarming either. It was a lovely day for a ride, and the old logging roads that surround us were popular trails.

That Sacha was slightly pale, her eyes enormously wide, didn't strike me at first, either. I received her cheerfully, thinking they were only passing through, had come to the house to see the foals or to tell me they were using our roads. I didn't even expect her to dismount, so I was slightly surprised when she did. One of the boys followed suit, passed his reins to the other, and one of the girls also slid to the ground and took the reins of Sacha's pony as though this had been prearranged.

Sacha stood before me. "This is Gary Peterson," she said, indicating the boy who had come to stand beside her.

The first jangle of a warning bell sounded in my head. Gary must be the son of Gus Peterson, the trucker who had seen Farrand's powers at work. He was about eighteen years old, tall, towheaded, and blue eyed, with hands and shoulders he had obviously inherited from his father.

Sacha took a furtive look around. "Laura, can we talk to you for a minute?"

"Sure," I said, an unpleasant apprehension rising. "What's up?"

"Well . . . " She wet her lips, scuffed a booted foot in the dirt. "It's . . . it's about Len."

"Oh? What about him?" My voice sounded tight and strained, and I tried to smile to mask it.

There was silence. I could hear no sound from the barn, I wondered where Celene was, and my inner voice warned Israfel: *Danger! Danger!* The gray pony shook its head, jingling the bit.

The Peterson boy spoke. "Mrs. Tremayne, Sacha's told me about him. There's been all this stuff in the paper about you. And I think my dad knows something, too."

"Oh?" I tried to look politely curious while my heart was pounding and my ears ringing, and the faces before me became all eyes – all-seeing, all-knowing eyes.

Israfel! Israfel! Help me now. What can I say to them?

Call Celene. The answer came immediately.

"Len!" I called toward the barn. "Would you come here a minute, please?"

He appeared in the doorway, and I scarcely saw the stained shirt and faded jeans, the shovel held in his gloved hand. The fair hair looked like spun gold or silk, the iridescent eyes as infinite as the sky, the incredible face far more beautiful than any of Botticelli's angels.

"Yes, Laura? Hi, Sacha. Hi," he said casually to the others.

Sacha had gone even paler, standing and staring at him as though dazed.

"Yes, Sacha?" He gave her his beautiful smile, looked at her with those amazingly blue eyes.

"Len," she whispered painfully. "We think . . . We think we know who you are."

Israfel! Now what?

Wait, Laura. Let him handle this.

"Yes?" Still, he smiled, but I could see it didn't touch his eyes. They were cold, wary.

Sacha kept staring at him, and then her eyes began to examine every part of his face, slowly, and her lips moved in small silent gestures.

He forbore this scrutiny, waiting and watching, while I felt as though my breathing would stop, that my heart hammering in my throat would choke me. The eyes of the others were fixed on him, too, with varying expressions that ranged from disbelief to admiration. I could feel Israfel's mind close to mine, tense and waiting.

Sacha suddenly spoke, her voice low, the words falling over one another in haste. "I wondered why you were different – thought it was just because you were so smart. I couldn't understand what you were talking about most of the time – and why you've been here so long – you and those others." She glanced around the yard, then her eyes fixed on him again. "Len, why didn't you tell me? You could've. Then I'd have understood you better, realized why you were different, what it is . . . If only I'd known . . . " Her voice trailed away, and she gazed at him with sorrowful beseeching eyes.

"Sacha." He sounded for once uncertain. "I don't know—"

She broke in quickly. "We could've been real good friends, gone out together, had a good time—"

I saw the abrupt lift of his head, the disdain leap to his lips. It was my turn to break in. "Sacha, you're too young to be involved in this. It'd be much better if you'd just forget it. For you and for us."

Her enormous eyes turned to me, filled with pleading. "But we want to help," she said. "Gary and Sue, and Moira and Rick here. We want to know all about it, see the spaceship. We're really interested, Laura. Honest."

It was too late for denials, and we'd never fabricated a story for this kind of emergency.

"Sacha," I said as gently as I could, "you must realize that's impossible. This is something you mustn't become involved in, really."

"But we want to," she said obstinately, her eyes again on Celene. "This's just the best thing that's ever happened around here. And Len . . . well gosh, Laura! I'd never have guessed."

"Then pretend you never did," I said desperately. "Sacha, this can bring too much trouble on all of us – you included."

"Oh, we won't tell anyone," She said quickly.

Gary Peterson said, "Honest, Mrs. Tremayne. We want to help."

"Then the best thing you can do is forget the whole thing."

Crestfallen, they stared at me. Then Sacha's head lifted defiantly. "Forget Len? No way, Laura!"

Israfel, now what do I do?

They're just children. They don't realize what they're confronting. They're zealous, naive, want it their own way. Laura, this is trouble.

Didn't I know it? I gazed unhappily at their determined young faces while I searched in despair for some other means to deter them. But my mind met only blanks, and the five pairs of eyes faced me with indomitable purpose and intent. I turned to Celene in despair, saw the uncertainty lingering in those soblue eyes.

"What if I asked you to?" he said.

Sacha shook her head. "We know what we're doing," she said.

"But do you?" I cried, my voice breaking into ragged pieces. "How can you know? You've no idea what's involved here."

"Sure we do. You're hiding a spaceship, and Len's one of the crew. We think that's cool."

"Cool! Cool!" I shouted, my voice startling the horses so they tossed their heads and backed away. God! I was becoming hysterical. "Sacha! Oh, hell!"

Laura! Israfel's voice reached me. *Easy. All is not lost. Try and swear them to secrecy.*

I took a deep breath, looked at them with new eyes. The integrity of youth, so zealous at that age. Were these youths like that? Could they be trusted? What could I offer them in exchange for their word?

The truth. Israfel's voice was calm.

"Put the horses in the corral," I said wearily. "Then come inside and we'll talk about it."

They sat around the kitchen table, eyes bright with excitement, while Celene hovered near the stove, and I faced those eager young faces with the utmost trepidation.

"Look," I said in one last attempt. "They'll be gone before too long. How'd it be if I called you when the ship comes for them? And in the meantime, you all put the whole thing from your minds?"

Sacha's face fell. "Going? Are you leaving, Len?"

"Yes, Sacha."

"But . . . when?" Her eyes widened with distress.

"Near the end of the month, we suspect," he said.

"Oh, heck! That's gosh awful!"

"No, it isn't," I protested. "They're in danger here. It isn't safe for them."

"Danger?" Her eyes became even wider. "Not safe? Laura, how?"

They were naive, for all their confidence and assurance. They were too young to bear such knowledge.

"That's why I don't want you kids involved," I said.

Gary Peterson spoke. "Mrs. Tremayne, we're not that young. We're not kids any more."

"Okay," I said desperately. "So, you're not kids – but you are too young to get all tied up in something like this. Really. But if you say you'll forget it for now, I promise I'll call you when the ship comes."

Five pairs of eyes studied me, considering. The eyes of one of the girls – Sue, I think it was – kept going from me to Sacha to Celene and back again while those of Gary Peterson reminded me more and more of his father. And he was one of my suspects, someone who may have given us away.

"And miss all the fun?" Sacha suddenly burst out. "Laura! No way!"

"What fun?" I demanded sharply. "If you think it's fun Sacha, then you are too young to know what you're talking about."

Abashed, she stared at me. Then her eyes turned to Celene. "Len, that isn't true, is it? About you being in danger?"

His eyes glittered. "I regret to say that we are."

"Oh . . . oh, wow!" She regarded him unhappily, her forehead wrinkled in a puzzled frown. "But . . . but why should you be?"

There was a silence. I could feel Israfel's mind racing beside mine, knew he was communicating with Celene, that they were debating whether it was wise to explain. I too tried to decide but couldn't.

"Sacha," Celene said softly. "When you're older you will understand. But for now, realize that our craft is valuable to your armed forces, to your government – as it would be to that of any nation. And that it is too soon for most people to accept us."

Indignation flared in Sacha's face. She drew herself up in her chair with a gasp. "You're not too soon for us! Is he, guys?" she said to her friends, who all shook their heads solemnly. "I think its just terrific that you're here! Gosh! It's more exciting than . . . than . . . " she searched futilely for a simile. "Than anything!" she finished vehemently.

"But you do see why you mustn't tell, don't you?" I pressed for an advantage.

Indignation was still strong in the wide blue eyes as they met mine, and a hot spot of color glowed on each cheek. "No!" she said angrily. "If everyone knew, then the army couldn't do anything. They wouldn't dare!"

"But they might," I interjected. "And for Len's sake, you must keep quiet."

This was hitting below the belt, I knew. But I remembered Ted's words – "All's fair in love and war" – and this was a combination of both.

"Okay," she said at last, reluctantly, the anger fading. Her shoulders slumped, and she looked at Celene with sad regret.

But Gary Peterson rose to his feet, and there was still determination in his eyes. "You will call us if there's anything we can do to help, though, won't you?"

I regarded him unhappily, remembering the similar words of his father and our subsequent betrayal. And what could a small group of teenagers do for us?

"And phone us when the ship comes," the boy named Rick said.

I nodded, feeling defeated. I had done the best I could – so had Celene. But there was an obstinacy in the face of Gary Peterson, in the eyes too like his father's. The other two girls had said scarcely a word, sat there silently taking everything in, eyes filled with wonder and admiration every time they looked at Celene. There was nothing else we could do, though, but let them go and watch them mount their straggly ponies and gallop excitedly away from us along the road, carrying our secret in too-hot heads, on too-young shoulders, with little hope that that was where it would stay.

⬡

They talked, of course. Sacha denied that she had, and I believed her. Gary Peterson made the same denial, but I was somewhat skeptical. Sacha blamed Sue, said she had been unable to avoid hinting that she knew something when the topic came up at school. So, rumor ran rife once more, the phone began to ring, and before long, I was inundated with reporters and other news hounds.

This time they were more persistent. Now they were certain the rumors were founded, and determination was strong on every face, in every voice. I had a story, and they wanted it. They used every means at their disposal, from a ceaseless barrage of questions to offers of exorbitant sums of money for an "exclusive." Cameras and microphones were shoved in my face at every turn; vehicles jammed our roads; and the phone only stopped ringing when I left it off the hook.

A hot dry spell tuned our roads to dust that rose in constant clouds behind the traffic. It drifted over the corrals, annoyed the horses, coated the trees and fences with a powdery film, sifted through the windows of the house, and made my temper even shorter. Furious cries of "Leave me alone!" "I have nothing to say!" and "Get off my property!" helped. Hysteria was becoming easier and easier to feign, and often my desperate tears were genuine. Then Jesse came home, much to my relief, and stayed. He turned the people away far more deftly than I had and was even amused by this incredible publicity.

Radio and television newscasts only reported briefly on the further developments at our home and didn't elaborate in any way, as though their earlier attitude still stood and this was merely a rehash scarcely worth looking into.

But many paid attention. And then the most extraordinary convoy arrived. A luxurious motor home pulled into the yard late one afternoon and found a space between two reporters' rental cars and a sports car from Wyoming bearing an amateur photographer who insisted he was going to publish a book about the whole affair. Jesse and I were trying to do the chores while ignoring the retinue of pencil waving reporters that followed us up and down the barn and tried to avoid tripping over the pails we purposely set down in their path.

The motor home bore Californian license plates, and the driver was a tall, distinguished man with graying hair and a neatly trimmed beard. He was wearing well-tailored trousers, a white turtleneck sweater, and a fine silver chain around his neck from which hung a strange pewter symbol. He stood back and waited until the three would-be writers eventually gave up and left. Then the reports came back, said there were so many vans and trucks blocking the road, they couldn't get out.

"I'm afraid those are ours," the gray haired man said politely.

Jesse and I were locking doors and dusting off our clothes, preparing a means of ridding ourselves of the latest visitor and wondering if we could manage to have an evening's peace for once.

The man bowed to us with foreign courtesy. "You must forgive us for coming unannounced, and if you don't want us here, we'll most certainly leave."

I bit my too-quick tongue.

"We're the Flying Saucer Club of California, and we'd like to offer our help and support."

Jesse and I both stared at him in astonishment.

"I know." The man smiled, made a deprecating gesture with his hand. "You think we're another bunch of crackpots." His alert bright eyes twinkled. "Some of us may be a little odd, but our intentions are the best." He held a hand out to Jesse. "Miguel Sands, at your service."

Jesse, as speechless as me, took the proffered hand.

"Only thirty of us were able to get away – seventeen vehicles of a varied assortment. But we're all self-sufficient," he hastened to add. "And if you could just direct us to a suitable place to camp . . . We'll be no trouble, leave no garbage, and do whatever we can to enable you to protect our alien friends."

Still, we gaped at him.

"You are the Tremaynes, I trust?"

I nodded weakly. People, allied with us! Thirty of them! And a dazzling thought dawned. "You're welcome to camp on our High Meadow. But for how long will you be here?"

"Until you tell us to go," he said with another bow.

Jesse was staring at him with disbelieving eyes. I walked across the yard, looked beyond the Wyoming sports car and the two rentals, saw another motor home, trucks with campers, a van, a few people standing – metal, headlights, windows, roofs – a veritable convoy all along the road. My heart filled with an absurd joy.

Israfel! Oh, Israfel! Look at them all! People, friends, allies! Isn't it terrific? Oh, gosh!

I went back. Jesse and Miguel Sands were discussing how to turn the convoy around while the two reporters were busy scribbling away about this new development, and the Wyoming photographer took pictures of the line of vehicles along the road.

"There are three with trailers still out on the main road," Sands said. "We didn't know what it would be like for turning around in here. I'll radio them, if you'll give us directions to your meadow."

There were even three more! My cup was overflowing.

CHAPTER THIRTY-ONE

THAT NIGHT, IN THE BEAUTIFUL long light of evening, Israfel slipped away with me, down the steep and narrow path behind the house, and up the road to the High Meadow.

The sun, still low, had gone behind the mountain, and deep blue shadows lay across the slopes, the trees, the short grass of the field. The camper trucks and motor homes, the vans and trailers and cars all gleamed faintly in the evening light. They were parked in an orderly row along the slow incline near the road that edged the meadow. Some had lights turned on, windows glowing warmly, and a group of people stood around a large hibachi, sizzling steaks. They glanced at us curiously as we passed, smiled, and said "Good evening," but did not stop or question us.

Miguel Sands's motor home was parked halfway along the row. He opened the door when I tapped on it and gazed at us at first enquiringly, then with startled recognition.

"This," I said quietly, "is Israfel."

All his ready eloquence fled as he stood there in the doorway, his eyes fixed on the silver ones that met his, the perfect face before him. Then he almost fell down the steps, touched Israfel's hand in a brief gesture of respect, and hunted futilely for words.

I laughed softly at his sudden loss of equanimity, his startled face, and his smothered speech. But then it all broke loose in a torrent of words.

"Oh, God! I'm delighted! Never did I think . . . I've hoped . . . So long . . . Always believed! Oh, God, I'm so pleased . . . What a thing this is! What can I say? You've taken me so by surprise. Oh, my . . . " Then he gathered himself together, pushed the door wide open. "Please! Please come in. Will you have coffee? I have a pot full. Do come in. Please."

"No." I caught his sleeve. "Miguel, we must go back. I just wanted you to know . . . that your journey hasn't been in vain."

His aplomb was returning, his elaborate courtesy. "My dear Laura, I never dreamed for one moment that it was. One must believe. And now . . . You've made my day complete. Oh, my . . . yes!"

Israfel smiled. "Thank you for coming," he said.

Miguel Sands was overwhelmed, pressed his hand to his heart in an emotional gesture. I swear I saw a tear in his eye. "The pleasure is all mine. All mine . . . oh, a hundredfold! I can't tell you . . . " He made another excessive gesture with his hand. "You must excuse me . . . I get carried away."

"I know how you feel," I said sympathetically and saw Israfel turn and look at me. "But now we must go, and yes, thank you all for coming."

<hr />

They were just the forerunners, the vanguard of a voluntary legion. And those who came attracted more.

A similar organization to Miguel's arrived the very next day – a hundred and eighty members of a group from Montana – to be closely followed by fifty or so from another such club based in Alberta. And to their accompaniment came dozens more – from the merely curious to the dedicated UFO buff. Young people on motorcycles with a pup tent strapped to the back; families in cars with tents or trailers; and a steady stream of motor homes, camper trucks, and vans.

They soon overflowed from the High Meadow and were diverted to the main pasture and a small meadow at the foot of the hill. We began to have misgivings about the hay field, wishing to keep that clear, but wondering, as they kept coming and coming, if we were going to be able to. But we did welcome them, even though we realized some were merely curious, attracted only by the large gathering. And some reminded me uncomfortably of my Apocalyptical Four, but we had no power to do anything about them.

Miguel and others of the Californian group did station themselves at the entrance to give directions, and they noted those who looked suspicious in any way, tried to keep them under some kind of surveillance.

"The RCMP were here today," he told us a few evenings later as we sat in the kitchen over coffee. "They came to inspect the camp but couldn't find any irregularities. But," he went on, his face clouding, "they're bound to come back. Even their deadpan faces couldn't hide their surprise at the number of people here, the obvious waiting for something."

And waiting we were, all of us, with excitement and longing, anticipation and anxiety, and many other emotions.

The patience required for waiting! For resigning to the slow beat of time, the measure of the marching sun and slow cadence of stars, the unalterable ticking of the clock. For Celene, those days were intolerably slow – as they were to the people camping out there on the cold wet fields of spring. For me, they were the suspense of uncertainty and the pain of torn emotions.

Farrand still worked on the receiver, exhibiting no impatience, either with his slow progress or the knowledge that rescue could be near, and only the completion of his work would confirm just how near that rescue was. He remained calm, undisturbed by the people who moved constantly about the property and often came to gaze curiously at the house. But Celene, always alert, on edge, expecting danger everywhere, watched the roadway and sky with straining eyes and an unhappy desperation.

Israfel was silent, waiting in his own restrained fashion, visibly untouched by any emotions, the warrior I had first known, at the helm of his command for as long as duty demanded.

It was Jesse I did not understand. Secretive, uncommunicative, he told me little of his thoughts or anything about his score.

"It's almost finished," was all he would say when I asked him.

He was obviously looking forward to the arrival of the ship, the departure of our guests, and the withdrawal of the crowds from our fields. But he looked at me with a trace of scorn when I said what a tragedy it was that our alien visitors must leave this earth no richer for their presence here, that it must end this way.

He shrugged in his expressive offhand way. "That's our fault," he said, and then refused to discuss it any further. "There's no point," he said firmly. "They'll soon be gone, and that's that."

And I struggled to hide my feelings, my regret and relief, the pain of loss, and a desperate fear that something terrible would happen yet. For those apocalyptical men were still in the camp, with others like them arriving daily. The RCMP patrolled regularly, and the stillness of the media, its waiting silence, seemed to my ever-suspicious mind like the calm before the storm, the deathly period that precedes an attack.

The army had become invisible, was waiting . . . where? Even the small planes and helicopters had ceased to fly by, and an empty sky yawned constantly above us, traversed only by the fast-flying, billowing lavender and the cream colored clouds of spring.

The sun was hot, but the nights were cold, and fires burned on the High Meadow and pasture fields, their smoke aromatic in the air, the dark shadows moving around them another army in defense. *But what could these men, women, and children do*, I asked myself, *against soldiers with guns, helicopters, and other machines?*

There was little sleep those nights. Although Miguel had watchers patrolling constantly, ready to raise the alarm, this very fact kept us in a constant state of listening. We in the house were always maintaining a vigil, especially Celene. He hardly ever slept, and then only when Farrand took watch.

But it was Celene, restless, pacing in the yard late on the night of May twenty-first, who saw the light in the far northern sky. His pounding feet and the slamming of the door brought me from the bed where I had been only dozing and took me out into the hall with Jesse close behind me. Israfel was already there, Farrand leaping down the stairs. Wordlessly, we ran after Celene and out into the yard, gazed upward in the direction of his pointing hand.

"I see only stars," I said.

"No. Look." Celene's voice was trembling with excitement. "There, Laura. That is not a star."

Across the indigo darkness, a myriad of stars glittered in silver points. To the north, the sky slanted away, tinged with gray, a glaze upon its face that masked the constellations. One did shine more brightly than all the rest, but it was still only a pinprick in the dusky velvet fabric of the night.

"I don't see anything," I repeated.

Israfel spoke, in silence. *It's the ship, Laura. It's there.*

Farrand said, "I can see it. You're right, Celene. It's come."

"When?" Jesse asked abruptly. "When will it be here?"

A slight frown touched Farrand's face, but his eyes were bright and his lips smiled. "Late tomorrow night or early the following morning," he said.

And suddenly the days had become hours, the time could be counted – the time that was left. I turned and looked at Israfel, saw the silver eyes meet mine, and knew he was still waiting.

Tomorrow, he said silently. *Forget about it till then. We have a busy day ahead of us, and you must sleep. Laura, tomorrow I shall ask you again.*

I can give you my answer now, I said. *Israfel, it had to be no.*

I will wait.

Distressed, I turned away from him, stared once more into the northern sky. But the stars blurred into shimmering dust, and the one had become no brighter, seemed to be no nearer.

It would be so much easier, I told him, *if you would just let me go.*

No. Love may be letting go, but it is also holding on, no matter what. You yourself have taught me that.

So I have to hold on here, and let you go, alone.

And he said again, *I will wait.*

CHAPTER THIRTY-TWO

JESSE AND I WENT BACK to bed but lay awake for a long time. It was impossible not to be excited at the ship's arrival, to anticipate the impending event as history on our doorstep once again. But deep within me was pain, and my heart wept the tears of loss.

Above us, soft sounds went on throughout the midnight hours as our visitors assembled their equipment and got ready to leave, and I heard a soft thud from the outside door: Celene returning to his sky watch.

Jesse slept at last, and I dozed, unevenly, with strange dreams that were so vivid I was sure they were reality. Israfel standing and looking at me reproachfully while loud voices shouted and heavy fists thundered at the door.

I woke with a start while the dream echoed and a voice was calling and the front door reverberated before heavy blows. Jesse was stumbling across the floor in the dim dawn light, pulling on a robe, and I leaped up with terror snatching at my throat.

Israfel! Israfel! What is it? Is this danger? Where are you? What can we do?

I couldn't find my slippers, and my dressing gown seemed to have lost its sleeves. I struggled to right it, scrambled into it, scarcely hearing him in my haste.

. . . one man. Have let him through . . .

Jesse was opening the door as I rushed into the hall. Through fear-filled, sleep-blurred eyes, I saw the wide shoulders, large ruddy face, and shrewd blue eyes above the red plaid shirt, heard the voice I remembered clearly and that had echoed in my dream.

"You must be Jesse. Hi." The ham-like hand extended, took my husband's in its massive grasp. "And Laura," he said as I poised, barefoot, on the cold slate of the entry floor. "Now listen. I've blocked your entrance road, and a whole bunch of the other guys have closed off your top road and the one up through the Greenaways'. Now, tell me, real fast, if there's any we've missed and where."

"Blocked our road—" Jesse began in angered disbelief.

"Damn right we have!" Belligerence was in the big voice, darkening the high-toned face.

Dismay sharpened my voice to a screech. "Why?"

"Because there's a bloody great army convoy heading this way, that's why! Now quick, what other roads?"

This was the man I'd suspected of betrayal, and his sudden appearance in the dawn hours, his announcement of having blocked our roads, made it hard at first to realize his intent.

"Other roads?" Jesse was still barely awake.

"Yes. I've got six more guys waiting out on Trinity Valley."

"What with?" I asked feebly.

"Logging trucks, loaded." The reply was terse, impatient.

I sat down weakly on the hall chair. "For goodness' sake, Jesse, ask the man in," I said, grasping at the first glimmer of understanding. "His name's Gus Peterson, by the way. And I think he's come to help."

Gus Peterson came through the door and filled the entry hall with his massive body and energetic presence. "Where else?" he asked.

"You say our road?" Jesse began, closing the door. "And the top road?"

"That's right."

"What about the forestry road?" Jesse was wide awake now.

"I figured that's the way they'll come, and I've sent one guy up the hill a way. He'll stop anything coming down from the power line."

"How?" Jesse asked. "Where?"

"One of the guys saw the convoy just on the other side of Lavington, radioed me, and told me about it. So I figured you're the target, called all the guys in the area with loads, and we all came straight here."

I gazed at him, overwhelmed, bitterly regretting the suspicion I had harbored. "Mr. Peterson," I began, "how can we ever thank you?"

He waved me aside with his huge hand. "Never mind that. Have we got all the roads?"

"There's the one down to Vance on the other side. But the only way up from it is on foot."

"Okay. I'll have it checked."

"And there's the remains of an old trail out to the forestry road halfway up our northern boundary. It's very overgrown and blocked by fallen trees, but it could be made passable."

"Probably best if we just block the whole road right off. Only thing is, you folks won't be able to get in and out for however long it takes."

"Mr. Peterson," I said, managing a smile, "the ship has come. It'll be here either tonight or tomorrow morning to take them home."

The shrewd eyes stared at me while his lips pulled into a wry smile. "All these crazy stories are true, then?"

"Some of them," I said.

He grinned. "Figured what I saw wasn't quite human. Okay, I'll get going. We'll do what we can to keep the blasted army out, anyway." He went toward the door. "Oh. I saw some Spanish kind of feller up by your entrance." He turned and looked at us once more. "I told him what the score was. He's moving a whole bunch of campers up to the top of your pasture, says that's the most vulnerable area on the place. Christ! It's like a bloody war, isn't it?"

Jesse laughed shortly. "Only thing is," he said, "we're all totally unarmed."

"Couldn't do anything even if you were."

"There are other weapons than guns," I said, thinking of all the people now supporting us.

"But nothing so permanent," Gus Peterson said and stomped out into the rising morning.

Fully awake now, I hurried up the stairs. Celene and Farrand's room bore all the signs of immediate departure. The equipment had been moved from the hiding place behind the wall and was stacked near the door. The communicator stood on a table, a strip of light flickering rapidly on part of its face, presumably emitting some kind of signal. Celene was not there, was no doubt still watching the sky, and Farrand was making up his bed while Israfel stood and looked at me with sorrow-filled eyes. I noticed at once that they had put on the ivory and gold clothes they had been wearing when they'd come. And while Farrand's movements were quick and hurried, Israfel stood motionless, still waiting.

I told them about the convoy sighted on the highway, Gus Peterson's attempts to block the roads, and the combined efforts of the other drivers who were taking part. Farrand smiled. Israfel waited still.

I left them, went down the stairs and out onto the small lawn in front of the house. It was with apprehension that I looked up into the northern sky. What would I see? What would this craft look like? What would it bring? But, to my astonishment, I could see nothing. The sky was clear, shot with the golden light of the rising sun, a few fluffy white clouds and wisps trailing away to the south. That was all.

I hurried back into the house, found Celene and Jesse in the kitchen making coffee.

"Celene!" I burst out. "There's nothing there! Has it gone?"

He turned to me, and his face for once was almost friendly. "No, Laura. You just can't see it in the daylight. And the rotation of the earth has put it close to the horizon. Wait until this evening. Then you'll see it."

"And when . . . when will it be here?" My emotions were mixing painfully again.

"Most probably in the early morning tomorrow."

"Oh." I turned away, went back to our room to dress. One more day, one more night. And that was all.

Israfel called me just as Jesse and I were finishing the morning chores.

It was surprisingly quiet in the barn. With only the familiar sounds of horses, grain flowing into buckets, the rustle of hay, it was hard to believe there was an army convoy near, logging trucks jammed across our roads, and hundreds of people on our property.

"I'm going to check what's going on," Jesse said as we left the barn at last.

And Israfel's voice came to me clearly. *Laura, I must speak to you.*

There's nothing to say, I said silently, watching Jesse trudge away along the road. I was dreading this confrontation with Israfel.

There is more than we can ever say, came the answer. *Laura, if you think anything of me, you will come.*

And so I went, my chest tight and hands clenched, my teeth pressed hard together. But my words would be the same.

He was south of the house, standing amid the paintbrush and first blue lupins on a wild grass lawn between the firs and pines that grew there. The ground fell away on both sides, and the voice of Deafies Creek rose, a steady murmur on the one side while the more insistent voice of Vance echoed in the canyon on the other. But I hardly heard them, scarcely saw the flowers beneath my feet. There was only Israfel, ivory, silver, and gold in the sun, the companion of my mind, the dweller in my heart, an alien from another world who had come so close to me in mine.

He took my hand between his long cool fingers, regarded me steadily with those silver eyes. And I looked back at him and thought this was how I'd remember him best – shining in the sunlight, tall, slender, and ethereal, but with all that strength and power revealed in the fine structure of his face, the stern yet gentle mouth, those brilliant metallic eyes.

There was so much I would never forget. Him nearly dying and his lack of hope, and then the subsequent rise above the failure he had been so ready to accept, him finding a new life in the challenge of living on this earth.

I would always remember the way he had healed my broken leg and saved Deenie's life, the hours he had spent with me out in the barn, the support and the strength and the caring he had given me. And how could I ever forget our telepathic communication, the sharing of his mind, his friendship – even that vital passion? Never, ever, for as long as I should live.

But now these improbably ties, treasured and valued for their rarity, were being severed. My determination to stay had weakened the links, was disconnecting us from the unlikely chain that had bound us in our strange alliance. He was about to leave, alone. I could stand here and know this was how I'd remember him most vividly – looking like that, close to me but going away into another life. I didn't want to think what my last impression would be: the paining hurt of his departure, the last sight that would be forever.

But now, as he stood there in the ivory and gold of his investiture and looked at me with those extraordinary eyes, I could feel a certain disassociation. I had to stay here where I belonged, and he was going on into a new life, to a world I could never even wonder about.

Then . . . Won't you please come with me? he asked silently, and for a brief sharp moment, the ties became as strong as iron, pulling against my resolve with the fierce tug of love. There was so much gentleness in his voice, such a deep and fervent longing, my heart seemed to stumble inside my breast, responding to him with all its caring and the portion of my loyalty that had been his for so very long.

To my dismay, tears swam into my eyes, and when I tried to speak, my throat tightened into such a swollen knot I could hardly even breathe. I spoke in silence, and still the words tore through my chest as pain.

I can't. I must stay here. Israfel, I can't go with you.

The fingers holding mine gripped harder, but his expression didn't change. *I'll wait for you, I promise. Before I leave, I shall give you something with which you can signal me. There'll be a trail of relays kept between us. I'll come for you. But I do ask you, as I have before, that you only use it because you want to be with me. Don't come for any other reason, please.*

His free hand lifted, brushed a tear from my lower lashes.

Laura, if you are what I think you are, that would be your reason for coming, wouldn't it?

His face was a misty blur, his eyes a million dazzling stars reflecting on the tears in mine. The ache in my throat was intolerable, and my whole body felt physically beaten. Not since the untimely death of my parents, when I had been a young and vulnerable seventeen-year-old, had I been so racked by grief and anguish.

Laura. Again, he brushed away a tear. Don't let this distress hurt you. *I know what you're feeling, and it makes my leaving you a little more tolerable in that I know there's hope, and that you will come for the right reasons if you do. But please, Laura, don't suffer now.*

I can't help it. Israfel, I hate to see you go. But you do see why I must stay, don't you?

From your point of view, I do. And I'm caught in the trap of loving you for your loyalty, the very loyalty that's making you stay. However, you have to reach your own conclusions, make your own decisions. It's only hard for me to go away and leave you here, to the dangers of this earth, and to be without you when all I want is you.

Please! Don't say any more. Israfel, I'll always remember you, treasure the days I've spent with you, miss you fearfully when you're gone. But I can't leave Jesse.

Blindly, I stumbled away from him, through the orange paintbrush and mauve lupins, to where the shining windows and stout log walls of my home stood waiting. And masses of exotic flowers beside a green and velvet lawn swam before my eyes, a white pavilion gleaming on a hill between vast and spreading trees.

I turned and looked back at him, saw him still standing there in the wild grass beneath the pines. And I knew the images hadn't come from him but were my own, that they too would forever haunt me.

But I walked away, to the house that was my home, to my husband and my horses, to the life I had built and the vows I had made, in loyalty to my ethics and the substance of their fulfillment, and I dared not look back again.

Farrand was there alone, and he regarded me with sympathy and understanding. "Laura, I will say nothing. Any decisions you make must be your own. Israfel too would have it so."

"I know," I said brokenly. "I just wish this hadn't happened."

"We had wished at one time that none of this had happened," he said. "But now there are reasons for which we must be glad that it did."

I went to the sink, splashed my face with cold water, drank some from a glass. "Farrand, don't get me wrong. This has all been an unforgettable experience for us. Really, we wouldn't have missed it. Many will envy us, wish they could have shared it – all those people out there in the field, for instance. I just wish it could have been better for you and not have ended this way for Israfel."

"We will never forget, either," he said. "But Laura, Israfel—" What he was about to say I don't know, for at that moment we saw uniforms, the sun catching bright brass buttons, the dark trousers with the yellow stripe of the RCMP – Captain Forrest and three police officers marching into the yard on brisk determined feet.

Farrand was gone, upstairs. I had no idea where Celene was, wondered with sharp agitation if Israfel was at that moment coming around the corner of the house, if he would walk right into them. I warned him quickly but was unable to listen to his answer as a fist thumped on the door.

I took a deep breath, tried to pull myself into one functioning piece, and opened the door.

Captain Forrest's face was white and set with an anger he was visibly trying to control. The police officers regarded me with a combination of annoyance and stern caution that I found as disconcerting as Captain Forrest's simmering rage.

"Mrs. Tremayne," he said, the forced even tone of his voice fraying at the edges, "where is your husband?"

"Out somewhere. He went to see what's going on."

"And do you know what's going on?"

"I haven't had time yet to go and see."

"Well . . . " He drew a ragged breath. "Your roads have been blocked by loaded logging trucks, sabotaged, no less. And nobody knows who or where their drivers are. There's a bunch of self-appointed security people at your entrance who refused to let us in unless we disarmed. And we'd like to know the meaning of this."

"Do you have a convoy out there, Captain Forrest?" I asked, as calmly as I could.

"Yes, I do. And if those trucks aren't moved quickly, something will be done."

"Those trucks are not on a public highway," I said. "Our place is crammed with visitors. And we don't want a bunch of army vehicles driving through."

"What you want may become irrelevant," he said coldly. "Under these circumstances, with national security being threatened, as I've warned you before, measures can be taken – firm measures – that will see the end of this situation in hurry."

"What situation?" I asked, as innocently as I dared.

"We're positive you're harboring aliens, concealing a spacecraft that could be highly dangerous. Not only that, but with all these people here, you're in a situation that could get quickly out of hand."

"And if we weren't 'harboring aliens,' as you put it – concealing something to which the government has no right – what would we be doing wrong?"

He blinked, and then his gaze intensified.

"You could be charged with any number of things," one of the officers practically barked at me. "Threatening national security, concealing illegal immigrants, obstructing police officers in the performance of their duty, public mischief, to name just a few."

Another spoke, far more gently. "There's something else you may not know about, Mrs. Tremayne." He smiled in a disarming manner. "May we come in for a few minutes and discuss this quietly and calmly?" He turned briefly to the other who had spoken, smiled again. "I'm sure there's no need to advise Mrs. Tremayne of such charges at the present time. Surely, once she knows the facts, we can discuss this sensibly." He turned back to me, old eyes in a young face beneath neatly trimmed light brown hair. "And if you could get your husband, Mrs. Tremayne. He should be in on this too."

"I don't know where he is," I said wearily, wondering when this questioning would end. And the sky beyond those four intent faces was still an empty blue. Where was the ship? If only it would come now.

So, I had to lead them into the kitchen, make coffee, again try to act as though there was nothing untoward.

How large they were, how young, strong, powerful. And those carefully trained, observant eyes that missed nothing, the firm mouths that only smiled when it behooved them, the officious uniforms that cloaked any humanity. Captain Forrest, the anger replaced by determination, cold, dispassionate, watched me with accusing eyes. And before those watchful faces, I made coffee, put out cups and spoons, cream and sugar, knowing that they knew, were only waiting. There was no sign of Jesse.

I poured the coffee, passed the cups around, and sat down at the table with them. I looked at them expectantly. "Okay. What else is it we should know?"

The brown haired one stirred his coffee slowly, and his eyes never left my face. "There's something up there, very, very, very high, far out in space, but coming closer at an enormous speed."

I said nothing, sat watching his face with careful curiosity.

"And there's some kind of signal being relayed to it . . . from this house."

"How do you know that?" I asked stupidly.

"Never mind how we know. We're not that dumb, you know. But your lack of cooperation could go badly against you now, unless you want to change your mind and make what we've come for go nice and quiet and easy."

"Oh? And what's that?"

The first one who had spoken went furiously red. He glared at me with blazing eyes. "Mrs. Tremayne, do you want to be arrested, too?"

I lost my temper. All my long-held restraint snapped as a rotten thread, unraveled into loose wild words.

"If you think I'd give my friends up to you, you'd better damn well think again!" I shouted at them. "When all those people have come hundreds and hundreds of miles to help? No way! Never! Not for all your threats! Not for all your bribery! Send me to jail! Go ahead! I don't care. Do what you like. But I'll never give them up. Never!"

My voice broke on the last words. I drew a harsh breath, sat staring at them in a rage of blind fury. My whole body was trembling, and my hands were damp, clenched tightly on the table's edge.

They weren't the least bit moved by my outburst. Only their eyes narrowed slightly, and Captain Forrest's face was a tight frame for the satisfaction my revelation had brought him.

"Then we'll bring in helicopters," he said brusquely. "We can shoot that thing down as soon as it reaches our airspace, bring troops in here on foot and by helicopter, and tie the whole thing up."

"I would advise," said a quiet voice near the door, "that you bring no aircraft near, of any kind. Either here or to that approaching vessel."

The few words were spoken quietly and calmly, but the tones of the voice were carrying and clear, the note of authority unmistakable. They turned as one and looked at Israfel.

He came a few paces closer, moving with his effortless flowing tread, and the ivory and gold of the clothes he wore, their sheen, the closefitting golden boots, were terribly out of place in our rustic kitchen.

His face was completely that of the commander, disciplined, undoubting, unyielding, and strong, and the silver eyes steadily met those of the four men facing him.

There was no doubting what he was. He stood there before them, ethereal, slender, beautiful, unearthly in every aspect, and – I had to admit it – dangerous.

Captain Forrest made an instinctive snatching motion to where his gun should have been. Israfel ignored it. One of the police officers began to rise, but at one flash of those strangely metallic eyes, he sank back into his chair. The others sat transfixed, like rabbits staring at a snake. And I was as motionless as them.

The quiet voice went on. "It's for your own benefit I tell you this. Those machines of yours would be useless against the forcefield they'd encounter.

You would suffer, not only their probable destruction but the considerable loss of life. So, send no aircraft here and keep them away from that ship."

Captain Forrest swallowed. "Who are you?" he tried to demand, attempting to display his own authority, his military strength. But it lay over him with no more substance than a web, transparent, of fragile strands that would break at a touch beside the inherent commanding presence of Israfel.

A faint smile touched the stern lips, the silver eyes. "One of whom I fear you have spent much time searching."

Captain Forrest turned to me, defeat bringing a show of quick retaliatory anger. "You lied to me," he snapped. "Over and over again."

"Never!" I retorted hotly. "I agree I misled you, but never have I lied."

"Captain Forrest!" The words rang out, commanding. Captain Forrest leaped automatically to his feet, almost stood at attention before that being from another world. "Leave her alone," Israfel said. That sense of danger was even stronger.

The outer door opened and closed, and Jesse came in from the utility room.

"Laura," he began, "there are people from—" He broke off abruptly as the men at the table came into view, Captain Forrest standing and Israfel beyond him.

"Oh, boy!" he said, his eyes going from me to them and back again. "Oh, hell. Now what?"

Captain Forrest pounced on him with words. "Mr. Tremayne, maybe you realize the severity of this situation, what trouble you're in for, and will see reason . . . "

Jesse's head came up and his eyes narrowed. Captain Forrest pushed on, trying to regain his dismantled dignity, his authority.

"Before you get yourselves into any deeper trouble, I suggest that you surrender these aliens and their craft to me at once. In fact, I demand it."

"Do you now?" Jesse drawled with studied insolence.

"As I've told your wife, we're prepared to take whatever measures necessary."

"Such as?" Jesse raised one quizzical eyebrow and leaned causally against the kitchen counter. His hands thrust deep into the pockets of his jeans and his shoulders hunched beneath his hair.

"The Emergencies Act, if needs be."

"Is that so!" The other eyebrow raised. Jesse's aversion to officialdom was alive and well and living in our kitchen. "Well," he drawled again. "There's one hell of a bunch of people out there you'd have to get through first."

"Then you'd better clear them out."

"I don't think they'd go."

"Then we'll have to do it for you."

"I wouldn't advise it," Jesse said. "There's a TV crew from Seattle and half the village out there now."

A flush of anger spread across the pale face. "So you're refusing to cooperate?"

"Damned right I am!"

"Jesse," Israfel said. "Please don't bring further trouble to yourself because of us. Captain Forrest, why don't you just leave it and avoid the trouble, for tomorrow we'll be gone."

Captain Forrest's jaw tightened, but then loud knocking on the door interrupted whatever he was about to say. Jesse went to open it, slouching across the floor in his socks. He admitted a sergeant with an embarrassed face and shuffling feet.

"I must speak to the captain," he began awkwardly, hovering just inside the threshold of the door. "Sir, there's trouble out on the road. There're people there, telling us to go home."

"Sergeant, aren't you able to handle a few civilians?" Captain Forrest, still flushed, drew himself up to his full height, glowered with withering eyes at the sergeant.

"Well, sir," he said diffidently, "not this many. There are . . . hundreds, sir."

"You see?" Captain Forrest turned angrily to me. "The situation's quickly getting out of hand."

"It was fine until you came," I said.

Again, the anger faded. "We have no alternative," he said.

"Yes, you do," Jesse interjected. "Just go away and leave us alone. You heard what he said. Tomorrow they'll be gone."

"I have my orders," came the stiff reply.

"The hell with your orders! Just get out of here, off our property. Dammit all! Isn't this supposed to be a free country?"

"This is a matter of security."

"Nothing's happened for six bloody months, and now you're worried about security?"

Again he repeated, "I have my orders."

They glared at each other, two so entirely different men, diametrically opposed from the way they looked to the occupations they lived for. And yet Israfel was able to be both soldier and artist, warrior and musician.

He was standing back, watching them intently, the implacable face revealing nothing, the silver eyes going from one to the other with an intense curiosity. The three police officers were motionless in their chairs, spectators. But I could see by their faces, the poise of their bodies, that they were just waiting for a chance to participate, to do what they regarded as their own duty. The sergeant had moved back into the entry hall, was standing there indecisively, unsure what to do.

"I don't care about your orders," Jesse said with heavily feigned boredom. "I care about our home, our privacy, the life we choose to lead. So if you'll kindly go back to where you came from . . . and after tomorrow, we can forget the whole thing."

"You'll be hearing from my superiors," Captain Forrest warned, snatching his cap from the chair where he'd left it, facing Jesse once more with tight lips and coldly raging eyes.

"I'd sooner not," Jesse said, still bored.

Captain Forrest spun on his heel and marched out, flinging one last glaring look at Israfel as he went.

"You too," Jesse said to the three RCMP officers.

The brown haired one rose slowly to his feet, his eyes hard. "Mr. Tremayne, you must be aware of the trouble you're bringing on yourself—"

Jesse waved his words aside. "I asked you to leave," he said. "And as you have no authority to be here, I'm telling you to go. Right now."

The officer sighed, studied patience replacing his watchfulness. "We can get any authority necessary," he said. "And if the War Measures Act is invoked, you won't be able to do a thing."

"You're kidding!" Jesse said, his voice spilling scorn. "War Measures!"

"A declaration is already being prepared . . . in the event you should refuse to cooperate."

Jesse glanced swiftly at me, at Israfel, before his eyes returned to the waiting ones that were hard again. "Look," he said. "Tomorrow they'll be gone. Can't you just forget it? They're doing no harm, have caused no trouble . . . "

"No trouble!" The other, his face flushing with fresh fury, burst into angry words. "Only wasted thousands and thousands of dollars of taxpayers' money, time and fuel in a search that's gone on for months—"

"That wasn't their fault," I was swift to point out.

The angry face turned to me. "They have no right to be here. They're aliens, here for what purpose? Do you know?"

I hesitated. I had no definite answer to this question. It was one I had sometimes asked myself.

He hurried on. "You're both in trouble, Mrs. Tremayne. Deep trouble, believe me. But if you'll just let us carry out our duty, show us where the craft is, and let us take them away quietly, it'll go a long way to making things easier for you in court."

I stared at him, my stomach heaving with a sick disgust. "I told you," I said, my voice shaking, "that I won't take any bribes. Now just get out of here! Leave us alone!"

He shrugged, the motion transferring all responsibility for their subsequent actions onto me. "If that's the way you want it," he said meaningfully, "then you'll just have to take the consequences." He began to move towards the door, and the others rose and followed him, casting condemning glances at Jesse and me as they did so.

The brown haired one, wary and apprehensive, faced Israfel, looked at him with nervous, curious eyes. His voice was tight in his throat, as though it was an effort for him to speak. "If you realize the trouble these people are in for concealing you, and I said that the charges against them could be dropped in exchange for your surrender, would you come with us?"

Israfel, his mind racing, communicated with me silently. *What charges, Laura? What does he mean? What could happen to you?*

He's bluffing, I told him. *He's doing everything he can to make us let him take you. Israfel, they can't do anything to us. And you're only safe here.*

"I will do what my friends advise," Israfel said, the silver eyes fixed steadily on the uneasy face.

The officer spun back to us. "And if you've any sense, you'll tell him to give himself up."

"No," I said. "Never."

"There's nothing to stop me from arresting him right here and now."

"There's plenty," I said. "For one, if he doesn't want you to touch him, you wouldn't be able to, not in a million years."

There was a distinct paling in the young face. He had, for some reason, believed me. No doubt the steady gaze of those strange metallic eyes helped convince him, for he turned away, his lips tightening.

"Then I'll go and get a warrant and reinforcements," he said. "And then we'll be back."

They went, but their departure gave us no relief. They had left us with new fears, additional disquiet, and Jesse cursing softly, "Damn! Damn! Damn!"

CHAPTER
THIRTY-THREE

THE REST OF THE MORNING passed in a tangled turmoil
of people and worries, of rushing about, trying to find Miguel Sands and
Celene, and dealing with an ever-increasing influx from the village.

Ted and Maureen arrived, tired from having to walk for at least two miles
from where they'd been forced to park their car, but bemused and excited
by all the people, the sense of something about to happen – although the
emptiness of the sky still gave me grave doubts every time I looked up into
the barren blue.

"I've been talking, Laura," Maureen told me, her face flushed and eyes
enormous. "I've been telling anyone who'd listen what's going on here.
Because now, with the army out there like that, we're the only ones who can
protect Rafe and the others."

"I didn't think so," Ted said. "But when I saw all the cars and trucks,
the people out there telling the army to go away and those logging trucks
blocking the road . . . well, gosh! Maybe we can."

"And a rescue ship will be here tomorrow," I said.

"So if we can just hold out till then . . . " Maureen's eyes too lifted to
search the blue. But only a few puffs of white drifted on an invisible wind.

I told them about the recent visitors, the threats of the War Measures Act,
and the police who had gone to obtain a warrant, and then we split up to go
in search of Miguel Sands and advise him of the latest dangers.

The easiest way to get around, we found, was by horse. I saddled Andante
and went out to the entrance while Jesse took Astra up to the High Meadow.
And I stared in disbelief as I rode.

The roads flowed with people, an unending stream of men, women, and children moving with steady purpose in the dust and the sun – a long straggling line of pilgrims on their way to a "happening." They were burdened with coats and picnic hampers, cameras and thermoses, babies and rugs, cushions and tents, transforming our mountain hideaway into a dust-hazed fairground.

Many had no doubt come because of the attraction a crowd draws, an event in this otherwise quiet community. But they had come – more eyes to see, ears to hear, voices to tell the world.

Some faces I recognized, and they questioned me eagerly. "Is it really true?" And when I nodded, began to press with more questions. But I had no time to stop and talk, hurried on after a few words of apology.

The logging truck blocking the road just beyond our gateway was massive. Its great metal front filled the narrow space; the high-piled logs rose between the trees as a monstrous barrier. A group of men stood between it and the gate, but Miguel Sands was not among them.

"He's up on the hill," one of the men told me, "Organizing the folks over there." He was tall, tough, and efficient looking, with a tanned face and expensive sunglasses, well-cut clothes and a no-nonsense manner.

"Are you part of the California group?" I asked him, and when he said he was, I went on to explain about the police and their warrant, the measures we were being threatened with.

He regarded me steadily from behind the dark glasses, his well-booted feet planted firmly in the dust. Three of the others in the group came forward and listened attentively.

"Okay," he said when I finished speaking. "We'll keep the cops out from now on."

Apprehension and uncertainty lay coldly within me. "How can you?" I asked. "If they come with a warrant, take such drastic steps as declaring war measures . . . "

He stood there unyielding in the dust. "They can't put three thousand people in jail," he said. "Women and little kids. Not for protecting ones who are guilty of no crime."

"Three thousand?" I asked, incredulous.

He smiled, showing very white teeth. "That's about it, we reckon. And there are hundreds more out on the road, trying to get rid of those army guys."

So many! Brought mostly by a rumor. Where had they all come from? What would they be able to do? And what about the army still out there on the road?

I couldn't get Andante past the logging truck, and the trails in the reserve were difficult to travel on a horse. They were also now crowded with people making their way in. I had to abandon the mare, tie her to a tree, and ask the tall Californian to keep an eye on her for me.

Again I was bombarded with questions as I hurried along the crowded trails, but I pleaded haste and went on.

An extraordinary sight met my eyes when I eventually emerged at the junction of the forestry road and Trinity Valley. The usually empty road was jammed with cars, trucks, and people. The dark colored army vehicles in their midst were at the center of attention, and the shouts aimed at their occupants could be heard far into the forest. Gus Peterson was near the turnoff, waving his huge fists while the roar of his voice rose above the noise of the crowd and the rumbling engines. I saw Colin Webb thumping the hood of a dark green Jeep, and Sacha and Rick, Gary Peterson, and a dozen more boys were shouting with the rest of them. About twenty men, heads down, backs bent, legs straining, were literally forcing the lead vehicle on along the road, pushing it while its braked wheels skidded in the gravel.

Then, as I watched in astonishment, the convoy yielded to the determination of this throng of people and began to move.

There was no room to turn around. Another great load of logs filled the entrance to the forestry road, and the vehicles parked on both sides of Trinity Valley left only a corridor for any traffic to pass through. They had to go on – which they did, in a cloud of silvery dust and to the accompaniment of an enormous cheer.

I fought my way through the crowd, the dust, the parked cars and trucks, trying to reach Gus Peterson. There were the police still to deal with. This exultance over the departure of the army could be too soon. We weren't out of trouble yet. Gus Peterson, when I finally reached him, listened to my hurried words of warning with his lips tightening and a glint appearing in his blue eyes.

"Leave it to us," he said. "Sergeant Mann's a pal of mine. He'll listen to reason."

"Sergeant Mann may not have much to say anymore."

"Then we'll just have to keep all these people here and as many as possible around your house and other entrances."

I left him marshaling the "forces" and hurried back to Andante with my heart brimming with gratitude to the people who had turned out in such numbers to protect aliens they didn't even know.

But the suspense during the early afternoon was agonizing. Israfel, Farrand, and Celene stayed upstairs. Their equipment was again stowed behind the wall, and they kept the door to the hiding place open in case the police did manage to come back with the promised warrant.

And still the people came, setting up camps on the pasture or in small glades in the forest, with dogs and children, camp stoves and sleeping bags, and sometimes little else. Neighbors began to drift in. "Wish you'd told us sooner," was the general complaint. But they all accepted our explanations as to why we hadn't.

"Knew it was true," Larry Campbell said, grinning with satisfaction. "But never would've guessed that was who your friends were."

More and more members of the press arrived and were told very little by the watchers at our gates, but they stayed as the great number of people was already telling a story.

I, ever anxious, went out and looked into the sky again. If only the ship would come soon, take them to safety, away from Captain Forrest and his army, the police who wouldn't give up that easily. I imagined a fierce winged vessel swopping down, snatching Israfel, Farrand, and Celene in some sci-fi movie fashion, spiriting them away from under the frustrated noses of troops and police in a daring – but naturally successful – rescue while we and three thousand plus cheered and waved.

The emptiness of the sky brought depressing reality. There was nothing there. And would I cheer and wave? For Israfel would be gone, and this ache of regret bruising my heart would become the torn wound of parting, the pain of loss, a torture I was going to have to somehow hide, for it was my own fault. I was the one to blame, allowing myself to conjure magic when there was no such thing, hiding reality behind a screen of delusion. I had gone on blindly, secure in the armored shell of loyalty and integrity, ignoring all the warning signs along the way, and fallen headlong into the fatal quicksand of love.

CHAPTER
THIRTY-FOUR

THAT NIGHT, JESSE TURNED OUR last dinner
together practically into a gala. He brought a bottle of Lachryma Christi
from the cellar – one he had been hoarding for several years – and poured it
into glasses he had chilled in the freezer. He had even gone so far as to discard
his jeans and looked very debonair in dark green slacks and a cream-colored
cashmere sweater.

Maureen had cooked, insisting she wanted to, and had taken extreme
trouble, preparing chicken in wine with herbs and a selection of vegetables
she had rummaged out of the freezer. She made a blue cheese dressing for
the salad, hot garlic bread, and a delectable strawberry cheesecake. But we
were a somber group that gathered at the table, and our appetites were
generally scant. Only Jesse was loquacious, humorous, and cheerful, making
the threats of the army and police and the departure on the morrow at times
seem far away.

He rose to his feet at the head of the table, his hazel eyes and brown hair
shining in the light, and raised his glass. "I'm going to propose a toast," he
announced. "In fact, several. First, Maureen, for cooking this excellent meal.
To Ted, for his support and assistance. And to our guests. May you have a
safe journey home."

I could see Israfel's eyes on him, considering, contemplating him with
thoughts he would not share with me. For when I asked him silently what he
was thinking, he said, *I cannot tell you now.* Then he rose also, stood behind
his chair, tall, graceful, and palely ethereal in the soft light. The silver eyes
turned to me with all their strange intensity, and he smiled.

"And I would propose a toast also," he said. "Yes, to Maureen for this. And to all of you for sheltering us. May success be the outcome of every endeavor, and the decisions made always the right ones."

It sounded innocuous enough, but the silver eyes glittered at me over the rim of his glass. He spoke to me swiftly, in silence. *Laura, my beloved, remember what I have said. Think carefully, clearly, and independently of traditions and mores. Let logic be your guide, and when the truth is obscure, search diligently for the answer. When you find it, and you know it's right, then loyalty belongs more to the truth than it does to false virtue. Be true to yourself, Laura, and you will never be able to live a lie.*

He resumed his seat, and I sat numbly, was bewildered, oblivious to Jesse's joking and Maureen's responding laughter. I passed dishes, put salad on my plate, tried not to think about words whose meaning I could barely comprehend.

Israfel.

His eyes immediately turned to me.

I raised my glass, let my eyes fall from his. *My toast to you – I wish you every happiness.*

Only you can make it so, was the swift reply.

I hope you'll be happy without that.

Warmth came from him, a soft pleasure. *Then, Laura, I shall wait.*

There was no more I could say. I forced myself to speak to Farrand, to Ted, to offer more salad, compliment Maureen on the dressing she had made, and watch Jesse being charming and delightful, the perfect host trying to make everyone feel at ease. This was a rare side, seen all too infrequently, but its appearance was opportune on this particular night, so welcome. Jesse, with as many facets as a diamond, his long soft hair and magic hands, his talent and his courage, his skill and his dedication. Jesse, the man who wrote "When Laura Smiles" just for me. Jesse, the man who worked beside me on cold nights in the barn and in the hot sun of the hay fields, who shared my interests and my home, around whom the structure of my life was built. Jesse, my husband, always. I did not look at Israfel.

Darkness began to fall, the sky deepening to green beyond the black silhouettes of trees. The chill of night descended. Jesse lit the fire in the living room and lingered beside it with Ted and Farrand. Pots of tea and coffee stood on the hearth, but Celene beckoned me away, drew me outside. At the center of the lawn, he pointed upward.

"There, Laura. Look."

This time, there was no mistaking it. That was no star but a dazzling light. It hung in the northern sky, white and brilliant, glowing with a touch of fire against the darkness, something from another world.

"But it isn't moving!" I exclaimed.

"It is," he said with a touch of triumph. "It will be here in the morning."

I shivered. The night air was cold, and I hadn't put on a coat.

"Tomorrow," Celene said with satisfaction. "Then the lordly Israfel will be my commander no more."

I turned to look at him curiously. Light flooding from the house touched his hair with gold and the blue of his eyes with a shimmering iridescence. The shape of his uplifted face was as beautiful as always, and I felt a new sadness. Unhappy Celene. He was so eager to be gone, would leave with no regret, remember us with little caring. The times I had come close to him were so few and far between that they were entirely insignificant. Even Sacha, lovely Sacha, had been unable to move him at all. Yet his care for Israfel at first had been far more out of love than duty. He had stood by his unconscious commander with a dedication far beyond the bounds that he felt now, I was certain. And I wondered again, why?

We went back to the house and met Israfel, Farrand, and Jesse in the hall.

"Israfel wants to go up to the High Meadow, thank the people there for coming. We're going in the truck. You want to come, Laura?"

I saw Celene stiffen at Jesse's words and look at Israfel with barely concealed angered astonishment. The silver eyes fixed on the blue ones, hard and intent. Celene subsided visibly.

"Of course, I'll come," I said. "But we'll all need coats."

Celene's anger was palpable, seething, his eyes mutinous and face pale. Farrand came willingly, but it was only Israfel's will that forced Celene outside and into the back of the truck with them. Jesse and I rode alone in the cab, Ted and Maureen insisting that they stay behind and do the dishes and clean up.

There were people everywhere, some wandering along the road across the hay field, others carrying pails of water up from the creek, and many standing in clusters looking up at the strange light in the sky.

Fires burned all over the High Meadow. The campers, tents, cars, and trailers were parked closely together, and up on the pasture more fires burned and windows glowed. Dark shapes moved between them, silhouetted against the flames or illuminated with a rosy glow. But there was an odd silence. We noticed it as soon as we had stopped and gotten out of the truck near the gate into the High Meadow. The waiting stillness I had heard existed before a battle. The light in the sky wasn't visible here, hidden behind the trees that rose tall and thick from the creek ravine, but the people knew they were on the eve of a momentous event.

A group, attracted by our headlights, came towards us, and I was relieved to see Miguel Sands among them. But when he saw who was with us, he immediately became silent.

Even though they wore down-filled jackets over their gold and ivory clothes, their differences were immediately recognized. Their bearing and effortless grace as we moved from group to group, fire to fire, distinguished them at once. And Israfel's face and eyes struck awe and sometimes fear.

"Thank you for coming," he said over and over again. "Thank you very much," And stunned faces turned to watch him while others paled, and shocked and frightened eyes gazed after him.

Farrand and Celene followed him, but it was Israfel who commanded the attention, the perfect face and flowing silver hair, the metallic eyes reflecting copper from the fires. The people must have been hoping that they'd see something of them, but they hadn't expected to suddenly find a being like Israfel in their midst. Rumor became reality, fantasy was fact, and they reeled before the shock of truth.

I shall never forget that night. Israfel moved across the rough grass with a step as light as thistledown and as majestic as an ancient king's. He smiled but was untouchable; he spoke softly and kindly, and yet people stood away from him in awe. He looked ethereal and yet so strong: alien and unearthly and altogether real. Israfel, as beautiful as his music but still the commander he was born to be. I suppose it was inevitable that he would invoke jealousy

– and yet Jesse's motives were not the ones I had considered, feared, done everything I could to counteract.

A hum of excitement had replaced the silence on the High Meadow by the time we left. And many followed as we drove out to the pasture and up the hill. Figures hurried behind the truck in a thick dark mass, and I began to share Celene's apprehension. Many of those camped were suspect, men who had come alone or in pairs. They were so nondescript as to be faceless, and Miguel had taken careful note of them. But what could he do now, out in the darkness amid these crowds?

From the high open space of the pasture, the light in the sky was clearly visible. Our headlights leading an enormous crowd warned those camped up there, and they left their fires and campers, their tents and trailers, and gathered near the crest of the hill.

Israfel, stepping down into their midst, took them by storm. I don't know what they'd been expecting, but it hadn't been this. Again the alien presence and the metallic eyes brought a shocked silence, stunned disbelief, incredible stares, and a frozen stillness.

He smiled and held out his hand, thanking them for coming, but no one moved. I went and stood beside him, but no one saw me. All they could see was that perfect face and the alien eyes, a being from another world.

A young man broke the spell. He couldn't have been more than seventeen or eighteen years old. Eager with enthusiasm, bold with the courage of youth, he suddenly stepped forward and took the proffered hand. He tried to say something but was rendered speechless by the enormity of the moment. But his eyes shone and the expression on his face said far more than any words could, and when he backed away as quickly as he had come, another came forward and also shook Israfel's hand.

Before I could realize what was happening, Israfel moved into the crowd that closed around him in sudden wild excitement. Celene was beside me, his eyes anxious. Farrand tried to push his way through the crushing throng and was just as quickly swallowed.

Israfel! Israfel! I called him in silent anxiety. *Take care! Be careful. So many people . . .*

But he paid me no heed, was moving easily beyond the press as they made way for him, the crowd to packing in behind him and following him as he walked.

I struggled to keep up with him, and Celene and Jesse followed close behind me. A man's body cut me off, his heavy wool coat grazing my wrist. Two women crushed against me, their heads lifted high as they strained to see. Celene and Jesse were carried away from me, and I was being swept along by the sheer mass and weight of the people around me. Israfel was gone.

I tried to fight my way through, elbowing and pushing, making no apology for treading on toes. *Israfel! Israfel!* I called to him again and again, but still he paid no heed.

The crowd stopped, stood tightly packed, and I could no longer move. Standing on tiptoe, I could see only the silhouettes of heads against the glowing blaze of a fire, a surging sea of knobs – hair, the outline of a cap, or a woman's scarf. There was no sign of Jesse, Farrand, or Celene, and Israfel had vanished. I thought fearfully of the faceless ones somewhere in the crowd, and fear brought anger. This was my property. It was my pasture we were in, my grass beneath my feet. I was being denied the right to move at will on my own land. Israfel might be in awful danger, and these people were preventing me from reaching him.

Blindly, I struck out, crying, "Let me through! Let me through! Please!"

"Wait your turn, lady," someone said.

"I live here!" I shouted. "This is my home."

There was a muttering of voices, a turning of heads, curious eyes peering at me through the darkness.

"It's Laura Tremayne," I heard someone say. And then they began to fall back, allowing a narrow pathway. Hands urged me on, encouraged me, patted my arm as I went, while many tried to question me, and I also saw envy in some eyes.

Israfel was standing beside the tall and leaping flames of a blazing fire, his eyes golden in its light.

Why, Laura? He was almost laughing. *Why are you so fearful for me when these people are all friends?*

Because some of them aren't. I was breathless, and the heat of the fire was searching for my cheek, the crowd pushing us too close.

So I am gambling again. He was definitely laughing. *This game of chance is getting me into trouble, Celene. But it has been worth it, Laura. And surely the more friends we have, the better. Your authorities will not be so easily deterred.*

I stepped away from the heat of the flames, and he turned with me, became a slender silhouette before a rush of sparks blazing skyward. I could no longer see his eyes. Behind me, the crowd was a great breathing mass rippling with excitement.

So, you're doing this out of ulterior motives.

His mind checked sharply, and the laughter ceased. *Positive motives, and not only for us but for you. And I do wish to thank these people for coming, for what they are doing.*

I was having to brace myself against the pressure of those behind me. They were beginning to push, people at the back becoming impatient. Again, I was fearful for his safety. He was only one to their thousands; Farrand and Celene were lost in the crowd. I, too, was only one, and what could I possibly do against the potential dangers lurking in the darkness? Hidden in that great anonymous mass of humanity, the obscurity of numbers.

Laura, the greatest safety lies in love.

At first, I could scarcely believe what he had said. Surely, he, with his vast intelligence and superior intellect, couldn't be that naive! Hadn't he learned anything of humanity during his sojourn here? Didn't he know?

But his mind was steady with conviction as it met mine, and I felt his smile. Then he was gone, back into the crowd.

An innocent? How could he possibly be? And yet I knew he was . . . and in even greater danger of trusting too blindly, a child among savage, hungry wolves.

I rushed after him, my heart pounding so frantically it made my whole body shake. Nervous sweat broke hot and damp across my back and down my sides, and the nails of my fingers bit into my palms as my hands clenched into desperate fists. He was an innocent. An innocent and could be walking straight into danger at this very moment.

The crowd parted at my furious rush and let me through, but I couldn't break into the circle that had surrounded him. I was confronted by a solid wall of determined legs and impenetrable backs, ears that were deaf to my pleas. Again I strained on tiptoe, and then there was a gap. I could see his head bending, hear his voice. I saw a woman touch his extended hand, another draw fearfully away. A man reached out and touched his sleeve, a child stared up at him in awe, and something prevented me from intervening.

He went on, and the following crowd carried me in its wake. And gradually I began to realize. He walked in the very protection of that extraordinary innocence. He gave trust and received it back again. If I had imposed myself then between him and the people who wanted to see him, I would have broken that fragile link, nullified what he was courageously and openly building.

I fell back, worked my way to the outer edges of the crowd, kept pace with Israfel at a distance.

It was working. I had to admit it. He emerged from the midst of the excited multitude with a look of triumph in his eyes. He had won, won their hearts as well as their support, and made the greatest gain of all.

Many told me later that just seeing him go so trustingly among them made their long journeys and cold waiting wholly worthwhile, that the experience was one they'd never forget.

Jesse, Farrand, and Celene were at the edge of the crowd, near the truck, and I hurried over to them. Celene still looked anxious, Farrand bemused, and Jesse quite enigmatic as we observed Israfel's progress towards us. The crowd was spreading out, and I feared that the truck would be surrounded and urged Israfel to hurry.

Easy, Laura. These people are our friends.

But there are so many . . . and Israfel, there are others among them . . .

They are few.

But he did get into the back of the truck, and Celene and Farrand joined him. A tide of people swept down the hill and around us, and my heart took up another hammer beat.

"Quick, Jesse. We must get them away."

We scrambled into the cab. The truck started and began to roll, and I watched fearfully as people milled in the path of the headlights. But they moved aside as the truck gathered speed and bumped down the rough hillside on creaking springs. I could hear every sound it made as I listened with anxious ears to the noise of the crowd following us. Above us, the brilliant light shone even brighter. It had drawn perceptibly nearer and could be seen between the trees when we reached the road and ran down to the creek.

I huddled on the seat, still shaking with tremors. I was certain they wouldn't be safe until they were on board that mysterious vessel shining in the sky.

⟨⟨⟨⟩⟩⟩

There seemed to be little to say that night. I was drained after the ordeal out there one the pasture but was too tense to sleep. Israfel too appeared tired after his earlier excitement, excused himself soon after returning to the house, and went to his room.

I helped Maureen make the bed up in the other spare room upstairs, as she and Ted wanted to stay. Deenie had been left at Ted's mother's home. Farrand and Celene were doing something with the communicator, making adjustments and changing the signal, and Jesse and Ted had gone out to make sure the crowd wasn't coming up to the house.

Maureen glanced at me occasionally with inquisitive eyes, and I was careful to act as though I was entirely pleased that our ordeal was almost over, that our alien visitors would soon be gone. She was too polite to ask whatever it was she was thinking.

We made tea and toast and sat by the living room fire in an uneasy quiet. Farrand and Celene came down and joined us, Jesse, and Ted from outside. But Israfel did not come and remained alone in his room with his mind closed to me. Later, however, with Jesse and Ted outside again, the others retired, I did go to bed, and Israfel talked to me with silent hurrying words long into the night.

Laura, I could show you things you have never dreamed of, take you to places too wonderful to ever describe. I could show you pictures, but it wouldn't be fair – to you or to me, for then motives could fall into doubt. Laura, I have seen stars shatter and galaxies form, new suns form, and old ones die. I have seen treasures of precious stones, diamonds beyond compare, birds and flowers and trees such as you could not even believe. I have heard the music of the spheres, so beautiful it would make you weep. I have walked on shores of crystal beside water so pure, so green and clear and warm, that to bathe in them is a delight to all the senses. I have a company of friends with such a scope of hearts and minds that to know them is an experience in itself.

And yet here I have found more pleasure in those small wildflowers than you can imagine. I would sooner walk with you by that tumbling creek than by all those marvelous lakes, on those mossy banks, than on those shores of crystal. I'd sooner see you smile than look at all the jewels in the universe.

Never, Laura, had I dreamed. Imagined, yes, but the course of my life was long destined. A starship was my ordinance, to protect the laws of the universe my decree. It was inherent at my conception. It was my heritage, my future, unquestioned and absolute. My music was my inner self, the balance to my duty, the foil to my discipline. In it, I was unbeholden and free.

Now everything has changed. Tomorrow I shall resign my command and show that I can take on another life. I shall prove the value of freedom of choice. But it won't be enough. You and what we can achieve together will be my next life's work.

I dream, Laura, for making this choice has also made me free to do so. I dream of the day when the ship touches down, the one that will bring you to share the life you have given me.

No, I implored him. *Don't dream of that, Israfel. It can never be.*

It can be, and as long as the possibility exists, then so shall I dream.

Don't. Not that.

What is, is.

That's a dream, and dreams rarely come true.

They don't when they're only fancies with no logical foundation. But when they're based on possibilities, eternally springing hope will give birth to dreams. Now I'm free to indulge, and I know the likelihood exists.

No.

Yes. Laura, think how it will be to have your life joined to mine. There would be no closing of our minds. Every thought would be known and understood. We would be as one entity, and loneliness would cease to be. Can you imagine a more complete love? A more total passion? And I vow to make your life worthwhile, and if you aren't happy, to bring you back.

But Israfel— I began.

I know. You say you can't come with me. I know you can't – not now, not while you believe that. I just want you to understand more of me. I don't expect you to come blindly.

I can't come at all. But I do wish you could stay here.

I know that too. But it's impossible in this day and age, at this level of civilization. Two thousand years ago, it was different, and perhaps in a hundred years' time it will be possible. But not now. But that isn't what I want. I want you, all of you. So, you will have to come to me, to my home.

I stared blindly into the darkness, heard Ted and Jesse talking in the distant kitchen, the silence all around the house. *No, Israfel. I never will.*

You only think you won't. I know differently. But don't trouble yourself now. It's time you slept, for tomorrow will probably be another hectic day.

And it was going to be a shatteringly painful one. I pulled the bedclothes up around my ears. Tomorrow I was going to watch him go.

I couldn't stop myself from saying one more thing to him. *You know I'll miss you, don't you?*

Yes, he replied.

I tried to turn my mind to my own life, to the shows we'd be going to, how marvelously well my beautiful filly should do, to the dinner service I wanted to make . . . Jesse . . .

Go to sleep, my dearest.

His last words came to me softly, laying like a velvet cloak over my seething brain and painful heart. I scarcely heard Jesse come into the room and must have been asleep before he lay down beside me.

CHAPTER THIRTY-FIVE

VOICES AND VEHICLES WOULD NOT wake me. The sounds of trains and planes, even a thunderstorm, could pass by and leave me undisturbed. But the sound of frightened horses in the barn always brought me from the depths in seconds.

So, it was on the morning of May twenty-third. I was instantly awake, sitting up, and listening to the distant thudding of uneasy hooves, a faint but anxious whinny. In less than a minute, I had pulled on a robe and slippers, and was running from the house in the first gray light.

Our horses were uneasy, wide-eyed, listening for strange sounds. But the visiting mares were frightened. They paced their stalls, anxious foals clinging to their sides even though their mothers kept bumping against them. I turned on all the lights and the radio we kept there, and I spoke to each one soothingly and tried to calm them down. But they wouldn't listen and soon turned away from me. Two of them were sweating.

I climbed up to the loft and dropped hay down into feeders. Soon their preoccupation with eating stilled them to an extent, and I began to breathe more easily. The mares were valuable, entrusted to us, and it would be awful to have one injured while in our care. Then, with a stomach-lurching jolt, I realized what it could be that frightened them. The ship! It must be the ship! It had come.

What would I see? This was the unknown, and it was with nervous apprehension that I went to the door and peered out.

Dust lay pale in the early light and the corral fences sparkled with a fine dew. Nothing moved; there was no sign of anything. I went out and looked up.

At first, I thought it was a cloud. Across my narrow sky between treetops and barn roof, a great silvery gray mass extended, high, misty, catching a tint of gold from the sun still far down behind the eastern mountains. I could see nothing else, walked away from the barn toward the more open lawn, and looked up again.

It was not a cloud. The most colossal thing I could ever imagine hung motionless in the sky, one end of it partially obscured by a few clouds that were drifting in from the west, the other above a point that must be at least one mile east of us. There were no wings, no fins, no projections of any kind that I could see, and it was too high to make out any details. But its sheer size was overwhelming, the silent ease with which it remained so still. My throat constricted to shout, and I stared at it, and then I was running to the house trying to shout, "It's here! It's here!" and managing only a croak.

Israfel was in the hall, all silver, ivory, and gold, his face alight but lips drawn. Jesse came stumbling from our bedroom, sleepily rubbing his face. Celene and Farrand were hurrying down the stairs.

"We know," Celene said eagerly. "Hurry! We must go!"

Ted and Maureen appeared at the top of the stairs, and a hard fist pounded on the door once more.

I opened it at once and gazed in blank dismay at Captain Forrest; at his pale, triumphant face; at a wide chest bearing distinguishing marks of gold; at the hoarse-voiced, slug-fingered member of the Apocalyptic Four and his three comrades in plain clothes; at their stony faces and hard eyes and that unmistakable air of authority.

One of them stepped forward, spoke brusquely. "Mr. Tremayne, we have a court order entitling us to search your house and take into custody anyone we deem necessary." He stepped into the doorway, wide shoulders filling it. "Now, please don't give us any more trouble."

The others crowded behind him, and then I heard, coming through the still morning air, the advancing beat of an approaching helicopter. Israfel gave me a swift warning.

"Captain Forrest," I said. "There's a helicopter coming."

He nodded. "Reinforcements. Just in case . . . " He let the words hang meaningfully in the air.

"I said," Israfel spoke from the far side of the hall, "that you must bring no aircraft near."

"I heard you," was the cold reply while Captain Forrest twisted his hat between suddenly nervous fingers. "But what are we supposed to do? Stand back while heaven only knows what trespasses in our airspace?"

"I know what that is out there," Israfel replied. "It's not heaven."

Celene, I could see, had gone very white. Maureen and Ted came to the bottom of the stairs and stood there uneasily while Jesse, now fully awake, regarded the new arrivals with increasing distaste.

The leader of the Apocalyptical Four spoke, his hoarse voice like gravel in his throat. "If you don't want us to blast that thing right out of the sky, you'd better just come with us, right now, and make no more trouble."

Israfel smiled, but it was a dangerous one. His eyes glittered like icy fire. "You have already tried to 'blast it out of the sky,' as you put it. And we have no intention whatsoever of going with you."

"We have a warrant," came the leader's sharp reply.

"That doesn't apply to us. We are not citizens of this planet. We are beyond your laws."

"Oh, you are, are you?" The voice ground like stones.

"Indeed. But I will advise you to turn that helicopter around before it finds itself in serious difficulty."

"No way!" Captain Forrest snapped. "It's bringing reinforcements right here – and it does appear that we're going to need them."

"You'll keep them off our property," Jesse said abruptly.

"We've a court order," Captain Forrest immediately rejoined.

"Stuff it!" Jesse said.

Blood suffused the face of the man with the insignia. He glared at Jesse with a look that must have destroyed many a subaltern. "Young man," he rapped with a withering voice, a frown like thunder storming on his brows. "You're headed for bloody serious trouble. You know that? Bloody serious."

"So is that helicopter," Israfel interjected.

Captain Forrest turned and looked at him, aware of the authority in the voice. "You mean it? It really is?"

"It is."

"We can't turn it around. We've no means of communicating with it from here. Your road is still blocked." Captain Forrest turned to the other army man. "Sir, I think he means what he said."

"Then he'll be held responsible," the leader said.

"I warned Captain Forrest yesterday," Israfel said. "But while we're standing here arguing, it's getting closer."

Captain Forrest turned on the step and strode out onto the lawn. We all followed, immediately aware of that gigantic object in the sky. Now it was beginning to shine as the rays of the sun grew stronger.

"Good God!" I heard Jesse say, and Maureen took a sharp intake of breath.

The noise of the helicopter had become a roar, and it came into sight from beyond the trees, flying low over the top of the main pasture. It was a Chinook, the kind that could carry many men. The two large rotors whirled above its roof.

"It's too close," Israfel said angrily.

Beneath it was the gleam of chrome and glass, the rising smoke of early fires. The encampment on the pasture was already bathed in sunlight. Above it, the helicopter swung, looking for a place to land.

Suddenly it lurched, staggered, and tipped. The front end lifted as though it were about to climb. The sound of the engines changed. Captain Forrest swore loudly. From our distant vantage point, we could barely see the helicopter, and it was being tossed like a toy in a playful hand. The engines faded into only a muttering sound, and the rotors slowed, catching the sun as they tilted toward us. The machine swayed, tipped again, and began to fall toward the mass of shining metal clustered on the pasture.

I felt the strength of Israfel's mind as an enormous force. It brushed past my horror. I saw Farrand leap to his side, both of them tense as they stood there, immobile, all their concentration on that swaying, turning, falling object that was not a toy, but a vehicle filled with helpless young men, and below it were campers and tents, women and children, civilians who had come here to help. A great cry of horror went up from the encampment on the hill. We could clearly hear the women's screams, the men's hoarse shouts.

The sound of the engines died altogether. The rotors sagged uselessly.

"Bloody hell!" Again, Captain Forrest swore.

Maureen started to cry, covering her face with her hands. Ted put his arms around her, pressing her head into his chest as though to muffle the dreadful sounds we were all waiting for – all but Israfel and Farrand.

Jesse groaned. "Oh, God!"

I thought desperate, frantic thoughts of calling for ambulances, our blocked roads, what medical supplies we had in the house, if there would be a fire . . .

At a crazily drunken angle, the helicopter began to move again, slowly, upward and away. Before thousands of incredulous eyes, the impossible happened. Where disaster had been inevitable, a hideous crushing crash, was silence. A nolonger functioning machine was defying all the laws of gravity, inexplicably being moved by another invisible band away from danger and dreadful destruction and death.

Israfel and Farrand were both shaking under the strain. Their faces were tense and hands trembling, and I felt my own body trembling with theirs.

Slowly but steadily, the helicopter turned up to its normal attitude, and suddenly the engines coughed into noise again. The machine still swung as if from an invisible chain. The rotors began to spin, supporting it once more, and then it was in flight, traveling back the way it had come.

Israfel fell to his knees in the grass, white and shaken, and Farrand beside him looked like a ghost. Captain Forrest, his fright turning to anger, whirled on them in fury and shock. "My God! Damned lucky for you it didn't crash! I'd have you . . . "

"Don't you realize," I screamed into his face, "that they stopped it? Didn't you see? Are you blind?"

He turned and gaped at me, his eyes disbelieving. I was shuddering with the release of tension, my teeth chattering with cold and fear. I could say no more, only stare at him with blurring eyes. He looked at Israfel, fallen to the dewwet grass, at Farrand's drawn face and hollow eyes, at his superior officer, to the thing in the sky, and back to me again. His shoulders sagged and he shook his head.

Jesse, also breaking under the strain, suddenly whirled on the senior officer. "Get out of here!" He literally snarled. "Get back to your vehicles and call off—"

"Just a minute, mister!" This man was unaccustomed to being spoken to in such a fashion, and he must have possessed nerves of steel. He didn't appear in the least affected by what had almost happened on our pasture. He made a brief gesture to indicate the huge craft overhead. "Our business here isn't finished. We still have to deal with that, with the situation here. We have our duty to perform."

"The hell with your duty!" Jesse continued, undeterred. "And I don't give a damn for your business. Just get the hell out of here and be grateful you don't have a mess of dead people to explain."

The fierce eyes didn't even flicker. "If you want to avoid any more unpleasantness, you'll let us carry out our duty."

Jesse's eyes moved beyond him, to the road at the far side of the lawn. He almost smiled. "You might find that kind of difficult," he drawled.

The road was thronged with people. Some were those who had guarded us so diligently, and others I recognized as people from the village and the groups from California and Alberta. Some were looking at the incredible craft in the sky, but most had their eyes on the group on the lawn. Israfel was still kneeling, and the army man made a defiant move toward him, a last attempt to exert his authority.

A dangerous throaty rumble came from the road. Four men stepped onto the lawn.

"You see?" Jesse said with mock cheerfulness. "I don't think they'll let you. In fact, maybe you'd better get the hell out while you still can."

Those men had tight faces and steady eyes, and it was only the leader of the Apocalyptic Four who showed any apprehension. His thick white fingers moved against one another with increasing agitation, he cast a furtive glance back toward the others with increasing agitation, and he threw another glance back toward the house. Celene saw it, went to stand between him and the doorway, and exchanged a brief look of complicity with me.

The crowd came closer. Israfel rose to his feet, and the army man took a sudden backward step, then another as the silver eyes fixed on his. He didn't stop until he'd reached the center of the lawn and had put at least ten yards between himself and Israfel. He appeared to have changed his mind about his duty.

A sound was nibbling with irritating teeth at the edge of my subconscious, but my attention was on the tableau on the lawn. Then I saw Israfel start, turn to Captain Forrest.

"Planes, too?"

Echoing in the valley was the sound I had been hearing. The whine of a jet engine. Oh, God!

"As I said – we have our duties. And that thing is trespassing in our airspace."

Israfel sighed audibly. "I can't do any more," he said. "You were warned. If that helicopter had been any further away, it would have been beyond our power to save it. That plane is."

"Planes. There's a whole squadron." Said Captain Forrest.

"Then do something about stopping them." Said Israfel.

A missile shaped fighter plane came streaking out of the western sky trailing vapor. The morning sun caught it, flashed gold from its wings as it banked and turned, curved away to the north.

"You'd better hurry," Israfel said. "Next time he might come closer."

Captain Forrest turned uncertain eyes to his superior officer. And another plane came, whining up the valley from the south. It was lower than the first one, partially obscured from our sight by the trees south of the house. But we could hear that it was flying in our direction, coming much closer to the area below that huge craft in the sky. Then the engine cut out and in again before it seemed to choke.

I caught a glimpse of the plane as sunlight glanced off the wings, saw it go tumbling sideways as though struck by an enormous fist. There was a high-pitched scream from the engine, and then Captain Forrest cursed again, loudly, frantically. He turned and ran towards the house.

The rest of us stood frozen on the lawn, catching glimpses of the wildly spinning plane as it hurtled across the valley. But it was going away from us, away from the force field extending from the alien vessel high above us. Miraculously, the engine roared into life again, but it seemed an eternity before the pilot brought the plane back under control. But by the time it had straightened and stabilized, it was far away in the east and heading for the distant mountains. It did not come back.

"He's telling the others, "One of the men said behind me.

"They have their orders!" the army man barked.

"The helicopter left," Israfel pointed out.

"It'll be back."

"I can't stand any more of this," Maureen said suddenly, her voice thin and awash with tears. "And it's cold out here. I'm going in."

Her words made me realize how cold I was, too. My slippers were soaked, my feet felt like ice, and I was shivering in my nightgown and thin robe.

"I'm coming with you," I said. I glanced at Israfel and Farrand, and saw they were both still pale and strained. *Israfel, come inside, and we'll make something to drink. Bring Farrand. Perhaps then these men will go away.*

They came with us, Celene following, and the men on the lawn stood and watched them go with suddenly helpless eyes.

Captain Forrest came from the house as we reached it. "I've phoned," he said, his voice tight. "I've stopped them."

Behind me, I heard Jesse call, "It's okay, Gus. These . . . gentlemen . . . are leaving."

We stoked the kitchen stove, and Maureen filled the kettle and began to set out mugs. I went to our room and dressed. My hands shook as I buttoned my blouse and pulled a sweater on over it. My teeth were still chattering. From the window, I could see the crowd beginning to disperse and no sign of Captain Forrest and company. That enormous vessel still hung there in the sky.

Jesse was backing the truck up to the door when I returned to the kitchen and came in with Ted and Gus Peterson. We gathered around the stove, hot mugs in our hands, suddenly strangely silent. Our time left was almost gone.

CHAPTER THIRTY-SIX

DRIVING ALONG THE ROAD BESIDE the corrals with our alien guests and their equipment in the back of the truck, I felt disconnected and unreal. Maureen was next to me, her face pale, and Ted and Gus were riding in the back. Jesse alone seemed in ebullient spirits, and I wished I could share them with him, feel the same apparent relief that rescue had come and our vulnerable visitors would soon be safe. But I sat staring blindly through the windshield at the people standing in excited groups or hurrying along the road, and dismally saw them only as vague, indistinct figures quite distant from me and my presence here. Pain seared my mind and was tearing my heart to shreds. *Israfel, Israfel . . . you will soon be gone. What shall I do without you? What will I do with my lonely days when my mind is mine alone, my thoughts unshared, and I have no way of reaching you?* I could see little else.

Jesse, I realized as he drove, was unaware of the suffering that was rending me, and I knew a strange sense of disloyalty to Israfel that this should bring a faint touch of gladness. After all, it was my fault.

The clouds moving in from the west had thickened, piling up into lavender and ivory masses that partially obscured the ship, making it seem less vast, less ominous. I could only obtain glimpses of it between the passing sunlit billows, but those limited views revealed it glowing like molten gold in the morning sunlight, so dazzling it hurt the eyes. I found I couldn't bear to look at it at all.

A solitary figure was standing near the junction of the roads. He was familiar – too familiar – and I felt my stomach tighten with apprehension. He moved to Jesse's side, waved us to stop.

"No way," Jesse muttered beneath his breath, and would have driven on, but the face of Captain Forrest was not as I remembered it, and his military bearing was bending beneath a weight he was obviously unaccustomed to.

"Just a minute, Jesse. Maybe he has something important to say."

Jesse braked reluctantly, sat back in his seat, and stared stonily ahead.

"Mr. Tremayne . . . Mrs. Tremayne . . . " He spoke diffidently, and there was a dazed look in his eyes. "I've just resigned my commission—"

"So?" Jesse said impatiently.

"Yes." He tried to straighten into his usual erect carriage. "The general had gone to order more planes and the helicopter to return. And there are troops waiting somewhere in the woods. There are too many civilians here . . . there's too much risk . . . and I came close to making a grave mistake back there." He spoke with an effort, his lips stiff with reluctance. "I wanted to capture these . . . at any cost. So does the general. But I no longer do. I've sent another message, warning headquarters of the risk here. And I've resigned," he said again.

Israfel leaned over the side of the truck, extended a hand. "Captain Forrest, will you ride with us?"

He blinked up at the figure in ivory and gold, at the silver hair and silver eyes, looked nervously at the long pale hand.

Careful, Israfel, I warned quickly. *Maybe it's a trick.*

Laura, my Laura. The man is not armed. And what better way to gain his trust than to give him ours?

"Please do," Israfel said out loud. Was he an innocent – or as clever as I knew he had to be?

As a man walking in a dream, Captain Forrest moved toward him, raised a cautious hand to the one held out to him, and was swung up into the back of the truck.

"Well!" Maureen exclaimed, twisting around to peer through the window. "Imagine!"

The truck rolled forward again, and Jesse's face had become noncommittal while I resumed the struggle to hide the pain that gnawed at me, to force back the onslaught of loneliness that was already biting with long hard teeth.

Across the hay field, now studded with clumps of people, their faces turned skywards or quickly toward us, the truck moved relentlessly. Down the hill between the so-familiar trees – here was where Gallant had fallen and I had lain in the ice and snow and tangled branches until Israfel had found me. The bridge rumbled. There was the creek, its water like crystal in the sun, and on its banks we had wandered in sunshine and rain, and he had shown me what he wanted and the beautiful place in which he lived.

Everywhere there would be memories: beautiful, unreal, enchanted memories that I knew were not an illusion. And a dreadful one yet to come, that was and never would be anything but a harsh reality.

Up the High Meadow Road – here was where I raced on Gallant, my heart pounding and mouth dry, on the cold November afternoon that was now as distant as eternity.

"Tomorrow," Jesse was saying, "we'll be wondering if any of this really happened."

"I won't forget," Maureen said at once.

Nor I, I thought. *Never.* The times I had thought too magical to be real would always live, now. The absence of Israfel in my mind was going to be a void I could never ignore.

And how different the High Meadow was on this day in May to the cold damp gray one of last November, with patches of sunlight and drifting cloud shadow, the glitter of chrome and the shine of polished paint and windows, and excited people everywhere.

Miguel met us near the gate, surrounded by his friends from the Californian group. They opened a way for us to the area where the craft was buried. The campers had been cleared away from the grounds surrounding that area in the center of the meadow. Jesse drew the truck up to the edge of the opening and stopped.

He and Celene jumped out with alacrity, but the rest of us followed more slowly. Captain Forrest still looked dazed, Farrand was crouched over the communicator in the back of the truck, and Israfel stood there shining in the sunlight and looking at me with hurt and tragic eyes. Above us, through a widening gap in the clouds, that vast vessel shone with its molten glare, and all around us a great crowd of people moved and watched and breathed excitement.

I wondered briefly where the faceless ones were, the troops Captain Forrest had mentioned. But I was too wrapped up in the pain for it to be more than just a passing thought.

Celene was watching the sky and, inevitably, all our eyes were drawn in the direction of his gaze. From there would come the next act in this incredible tableau, and it was a play none of the spectators had ever seen before, one with an unknown script.

Some, I could see, were fearful, watching us, the sky, the empty space of young green grass with considerable trepidation. Many had drawn back as far as they could while still being able to see, and others had cameras ready. The Seattle television crew were right in the forefront. I was somewhat surprised to see that they were the only ones. I would have thought the great ship in the sky would have brought media photographers in by the score. But my anguish again prevented any further consideration.

They came, three smaller crafts slipping down from the clouds with a faint fluttering. They shone a shimmering opalescent silver, a band of gold spinning around each's central dome, and alighted on the grass as softly as butterflies. It happened so quickly; most were taken unawares. At one moment the clearing was empty and bare, and then the three silvery craft were there on the grass.

I heard a gasp from the crowd, and there was an instinctive pulling back. But I only had eyes for Israfel. I watched numbly as he walked away from us and toward them, tall and ethereal and as out of place as those strange craft, his hair and the gold of his tunic reflecting the sun as an alien light. There was a door, a ramp, and a silver figure standing before him. And then the other two craft rose smoothly into the air again and moved away until they were poised above the place where the wrecked craft was buried. Two slender rods came down from each and pierced the ground with a soft humming sound, and the surface began to crumble and lift into small pieces.

Celene, a piece of their equipment in his arms, hurried across the grass to the other craft and disappeared through the open doorway. He promptly came out again, walked back to us with Israfel, and carried another piece away. Israfel stood before us again, regarding us all sadly with muted eyes and only the trace of a smile.

Beyond him I saw the wreckage come rising from the ground, plastered with damp earth and clinging tufts of grass and a few tangled roots. The two craft set it down and landed beside it, their doors sliding open. Several silvery figures emerged and began to clear the earth and debris away.

Israfel's eyes met mine again, glazed with pain and sadness.

"Laura, Jesse," he said out loud. "Maureen, Ted. Our debt to you can never be repaid. We just hope you will suffer no serious consequences from our visit. We regret the trouble we have brought on you and wish it could all have been so different."

Except for one thing, Laura. What I have found with you I'll never regret.

Celene hurried backward and forward, transferring their equipment. Farrand was still doing something with the communicator.

Maureen broke away from us, ran to Israfel, and embraced him fiercely. "We're so fortunate to have known you," she whispered, her voice choking. Then she let him go. I saw his eyes soften as he looked at her and then at Ted as he stepped forward and silently wrung his hands, to be followed by Gus and Miguel.

Then, to my astonishment, Celene was before me, taking me into his arms and holding me close for one fraction of a moment. "Thanks, Laura," he said. Then he turned to Jesse and pressed his hand into Jesse's.

My eyes filled with tears. The sands of time had run down to the last few grains. Other arms held me. I looked up into the dark eyes of Farrand and saw them through a mist of helpless tears. I clung to him desperately, aching with sadness and regret. Dear, precious Farrand. Kind, gentle, dedicated Farrand. So selfless and industrious, so warm and sincere – even Jesse had liked him, I knew.

"I wish you would come back one day," I whispered painfully against his chest. "Farrand, my dear Farrand."

His arms tightened, holding me with all gentleness. "One day, Laura, I hope. Like Israfel, now I too dream."

I let him go, my eyes scalding. I saw him take the communicator from the back of the truck and begin to move away. Celene was already halfway to the ship. Israfel still stood there looking at me with a thousand glittering eyes. But then mine cleared.

There was sudden activity on the far side of the clearing near the road and the trees that edged the ravine. Men were there – the faceless ones, drawing back. I saw black helmets, dark uniforms, the bright gleam of buttons, weapons. They had come from the ravine, somehow going unnoticed up its steep wild banks, and met the men in the crowd we had not trusted. I saw walkie-talkie radios, a raised barrel, heard the hideous staccato cracking of gunfire. And Farrand sank in silence to the ground.

Israfel's fury! It raged all around me like a killing storm. There was thunder echoing in my head, and lightning flashed across the meadow. I saw a gun fly from a suddenly nerveless hand and another body fall.

Then I was screaming in horror at the sight of Farrand, the dreadful stain spreading across the ivory and gold, his dark hair in the grass where it should not be. Maureen's screams joined mine. I heard Ted's shout of anger and Celene's single terrible cry of rage. Then a wild frenzy of screams and shouts blurred into a pandemonium of noise.

Ted, Jesse, Captain Forrest, Gus, and Miguel went running across the clearing, and I fell to my knees beside the figure on the grass, screaming his name, touching him with frantic hands. Maureen was beside me, and beyond I had a glimpse of rushing people converging on the armed men who had come so terribly. A madly trampling mob hid the uniforms, helmets, and guns, a mob screaming a fury of anger and dismay, horror and shame.

Someone knelt beside me, and long white hands reached to the dark hair. *Laura, he is not lost. We can save him. Laura, please, be still. Farrand is not lost.*

A shadow fell over us, and Celene bent beside us, his eyes blazing like blue suns in the whiteness of his face.

Israfel turned Farrand over, revealing an even worse stain, the face as pale and waxen as death. His eyes were closed, the lids tinged blue, and I fell into a despair that had no end. Farrand! Oh, Farrand!

Israfel lifted him in his arms, rose to his feet, regarded me with compelling eyes. *Laura, he will be all right. On the ship—*

His mind cut from mine as though severed with a knife. Celene had risen with him, was gazing at him with unleased fury, an implacable and defended anger, justification for it in his eyes. Once again, the battle raged between them, and then Celene broke away, turned, and began running toward the wreckage of the ship.

I saw that it stood there alone, abandoned in the sudden emergency. There was no sign of the silver figures, and the doors to the two other craft were closed. Most of the earth had been cleaned away, and the dent in the crumpled side gaped forlornly. I could see that once it had been as smooth and shiningly perfect as those that stood there now. But Celene was heading for it with a singular strength of purpose that I could not understand.

Again, I felt the power of Israfel's mind, saw his eyes fixed on Celene with angry desperation. The latter slowed but did not stop. He was forcing himself on, struggling against the bond of Israfel's mind with a determination born of certainty.

Go to the ship, Laura.

The command came abruptly, shocked me into fear.

Israfel, I'm not going with you.

Don't disobey me. Go to the ship. At once.

He needed all his strength to fight Celene, and the burden of Farrand must have weighed heavily in his arms. He still hadn't recovered from the ordeal earlier with the helicopter and had no power left to force me. I hesitated, too distressed and in despair to stop to consider any other motive than the one I already knew.

Laura. NOW!

Forcing one foot before the other, I went. Glancing back once, longingly, I saw he was close behind me, carrying Farrand. Beyond him I could see Maureen staring after me with wide-eyed alarm.

Once again, I was plunged into the shadowy world of unreality. This could not be. I didn't want any of this to happen. Farrand lying there so waxen and still could only be a nightmare. This walk I was taking toward that impossible craft must have been some wild movie I was only watching. I could not be taking part.

The ramp was beneath my feet. The silvery figure stood at the side of the doorway, watching me with enigmatic, almost expressionless amber eyes. The interior was small, circular, soft underfoot. A bank of panels flickered and flashed below a window that was only a translucence in the hull.

Brilliant light suffused the whole area, a soft humming sound, a strange, slightly smoky scent. Much as I willed it, I knew this was no dream.

Israfel was kneeling, gently laying his burden down on the soft floor. He took my hand, a fingertip, and guided it into Farrand's hair. *Press here*, he ordered me silently and was gone.

I knelt there, in the bottomless pit of despair that had swallowed me. Farrand's face, so waxen and still, was one I could only know as dead. The front of his tunic was splashed with stains like wine, and there was no movement, no beat of a pulse in wrist or throat when I laid my other hand tentatively against them. And I was in this alien craft at Israfel's command. I turned once and looked toward the door, saw that it was closed. The silver figure stood before it with those unmoving gold eyes fixed firmly on me. I felt like a prisoner.

I wondered what was happening outside to Jesse and Maureen, Ted and all the people confronting those soldiers. And Israfel and Celene were also out there, locked in that mysterious combat of their own. That huge vessel must still be waiting. Did those on board wonder what was going on down here? Or did they know? What would they do if they knew what had happened to Farrand? Would they wreak some terrible vengeance? And why had Israfel ordered me onto this craft when he knew I wouldn't go with him?

Tears welled in my aching eyes, burning, spilling. One fell onto his cheek, and I wiped it away. The skin was cold beneath my hand, and my tears fell faster and would not stop.

The door opened. Israfel and Celene came in, their eyes raging and faces taut with anger. Celene's mouth was twisted with fury; Israfel's drawn into a tight hard line that softened only slightly when he saw my tearstained face and despairing eyes. The door closed behind them.

Israfel, let me go.

The silver figure went to the control panel.

I can't go without you.

He knelt beside me, his fingers moving swiftly into Farrand's hair.

No.

I will bring you back . . . if there is an earth left to bring you to.

I stared at him numbly, lost in a new unreality. Around me the humming sound became more intense. The craft was lifting, its speed increasing. And

Celene stood on the far side of it, resolute anger in every line of his face and certainty of victory in his eyes.

There was nothing I could do but kneel there helplessly beside Farrand's body while this ship carried me away from my husband, my home and my friends, my horses and the life I had been so determined not to leave. I wondered what Jesse was doing. Did he realize what had happened to me? And he was as helpless as me. He had no way of following, no means of getting me back. And Israfel's last words seethed in my brain as another impossible, illusory nightmare. The earth, with its vast continents and mighty oceans. Its colossal mountains and great masses of polar ice – with towns and cities and teeming populations, forests and jungles, deserts and plains – how could it no longer be?

I stared fearfully at Israfel, at his pale strained face and adamant eyes. At Celene – his angry triumph and curling savage mouth. Farrand – so mortally wounded, the last one to deserve such a cruel fate. Despair was endless, crushing even the persistence of hope.

CHAPTER THIRTY-SEVEN

Λ SHEET OF GOLD SUDDENLY blazed in the window, drawing my eyes in spite of my despair. The hull of the rescue ship reflecting the sun. It was strung with rows of opalescent windows, shining like pearls. Then there was the depth of a passing shadow, followed by a brilliant white light. Israfel lifted Farrand and rose to his feet.

Come, Laura.

In a daze of resignation, I followed, walking behind him blindly to the door as the craft's motion ceased. We went down the ramp with Celene close behind us and into a great hanger where rows and rows of silvery craft stretched as far as I could see. Behind us came the other two, carrying the wreckage from the High Meadow. People were waiting near a wide doorway, men and women with beautiful faces and shining hair, dressed mostly in the ivory and gold I already knew. Two came forward and took Farrand, bearing him swiftly away through another doorway. Another came and stood before us.

Dimly, I became aware of strange, thick white hair and dark eyes that pierced mine with an intelligence that knew no end. My perception sharpened, and then I saw the face. It was magnificent, molded by humor and warmth and a vast understanding, cast into gentleness and an all-encompassing caring that put it far beyond those of mortals.

Although the gaze of those fearful eyes was shattering, I stood and stared in wonder at the face, forgetting for a moment even where I was. An arm slipped round my shoulders, and Israfel's mind reached mine.

Laura, this is my teacher and friend. This is Michael.

Automatically, I made a move to offer my hand, then let it fall as I realized my inferiority and insignificance before this marvelous being. But his hand clasped mine in a grip so warm and strong my heart leaped. He smiled, and it was dazzling.

"Laura, Israfel has spoken of you, of your care and his caring." The voice was like music, and he spoke carefully, as if in an unfamiliar language. "We owe you our gratitude and offer you our hospitality. But charges have been laid, and Israfel will tell you of the inquiry we must now hold and the possible consequences."

He released my hand and turned away, encircling Israfel's shoulders with his arm. The smile was gone, the magnificent face now deeply serious with concern and troubled thoughts. Israfel's arm tightened around me, drew me with him as the whole assemblage moved toward the open doorway.

I stumbled beside him, my mind trying to grapple with the strangeness of my surroundings, the ominous words I had just heard. And what of Farrand? None made any direct reference to him, but they were speaking of charges, an inquiry, and consequences. Of Israfel's mind, all I could gather were streaking flashes.

We passed into a pale blue hallway that suddenly seemed to be moving. The walls were flashing past, blurring into a dizzying nimbus of light that made my head swim. We were moving at a frightening speed. I pressed closer to Israfel, but his concentration was on that wonderful face. There were curious eyes on other faces, and Celene, tight-lipped, still stood beside us. But his eyes avoided mine.

A doorway appeared beside us, and Israfel drew me through it, into a room filled with flowers and light. Huge windows framed a deep blue sky, let in the light of my own golden sun. The floor was cushioned beneath my feet, as green as grass. Soft sculpted couches were grouped around low tables, and masses of flowers in a riot of color spilled from large pots and urns and filled the air with a delicate fragrance that was exquisite.

But I had no time to stare. Israfel was speaking to me with swift urgent words.

Laura, Celene is demanding that the earth be destroyed. He says its people are too dangerous to be left to their own devices, that they pose a threat to the universe and our civilization. He says that humanity has not followed the course of the gods but has chosen corruption and deceit, cruelty and vice, and forfeited their legacy of intelligence and choice. Laura, we came to see if the directions humanity has taken would show us new roads. Instead, we learned of poverty and hunger, greed and exploitation. We came back with a device that we would use to destroy this planet if closer study deemed it advisable. Celene says it has and would have completed the mission at the sacrifice of ourselves. I say not. Celene says I am blinded and can see no farther than you, the woman I have come to love. And this I can't deny. It's possible that he is right. So now there is to be an inquiry. Laura, the earth is on trial, and you and I are its only defenders.

The silence was unnerving. Intensive proceedings were taking place right here in my presence, and I was totally oblivious to what was being said. I could only stand and watch the semicircle of stern faces at the long curving table, see their intent and comprehending eyes go from Celene to Israfel and back again, and feel my heart beating in painful trepidation at the sight of Israfel's unhappy face, the curl of triumph on Celene's lips.

The chamber was vast with a misty ceiling that had no visible substance. The floor was also green and soft, but I stood on it in the utmost diffidence, aware of my hopeless inadequacy in the face of what I was confronting. I was too young, too immature, to be in this position. Those intelligent faces with their allseeing, all-knowing eyes must surely be regarding me, in my homely sweater and slacks, with my unruly hair and unimposing stature, as a creature of utmost insignificance. And I was a member of the race on trial, considered too dangerous to survive, part of the people who had shot Farrand.

Israfel turned to me, his eyes grieving, and spoke to me with a lack of emotion that belied what I could read behind his words.

Laura, tell them about the loyalty of the people who helped protect us, who came long distances, who turned back the army and the police. Tell them about the progress of your sciences, your architecture, music, arts, and literature. Tell them—

A voice spoke from the table. "That will not be necessary, Israfel. You have already told us of this."

I looked toward the speaker and saw a pale, tired face that bore the weight of a heavy decision, a pained concern. He addressed me. His deep blue eyes were intent on my face from beneath a halo of soft white hair. "Laura, let me ask you a few questions."

I glanced appealingly, fearfully, at Israfel. But he had turned away, and his mind was closed to me. He couldn't help me. I was on my own.

The voice was deep, patient, but expecting an answer to every query.

"Israfel has asked you to go with him, to leave that dangerous planet and live with him in love and beauty. You have refused. Will you tell us why?"

I drew a deep breath, hoped my voice wouldn't tremble. "Because . . . because I'm married to another."

"And you regard yourself as being loyal to that man?"

"Yes."

The eyes seemed to look right into mine, to the most secret of my innermost thoughts. "Do you regard your planet as dangerous?"

I stared at him, numb. How was I to answer that? The patient face waited for my answer.

I stumbled over words that wouldn't do, tried to find the right ones. "In . . . in many ways it is . . . but there are laws . . . laws designed to protect the . . . the innocent, to convict the guilty."

"Is it corrupt?"

"I can't condemn millions because of a few," I said faintly. "There is corruption . . . yes. But it is . . . um . . . counteracted by those who are not."

"Is humanity worthy of the fellowship of the universe?"

"I . . . I don't know."

The eyes were piercing. "If you don't know, then it is apparent that the tenets of the fellowship have not been followed. Or have they been lost?"

Again I said, "I don't know."

"Celene insists humanity is not worthy. Israfel says they may yet become so. Do you think humanity has a future of greater promise than that which has been recently attained?"

"I think they are . . . trying."

"Celene has studied your history, tells us it is appalling. Farrand has been severely wounded, presumably with the intent to kill."

"That was the action of one," I said, no longer able to keep my voice steady. "They were stopped by all those who . . . who protected us."

"Us?"

"Israfel . . . Celene . . . and Farrand."

"What was the purpose of attempting to kill Farrand?"

"I . . . I'm not sure. To . . . to capture him, the craft . . . to stop them getting way."

"In so drastic a fashion?"

"We left them with no other options."

There was a short silence. Penetrating eyes studied me from the entire semicircle. Israfel stood still, his head raised and mind closed. Celene's expression did not change.

"So, there were other attempts?"

"To find their craft, yes. It would have been invaluable to any government or army."

Every word I spoke seemed a condemnation. I wasn't being allowed any defense, and I even wondered if I'd be able to find any if I were.

"And to what use would it have been put had it been found?" The question was almost sharp.

"I'm sorry," I whispered. "I'm in no position to know."

"You do not know your government's intentions?"

"No."

"You are not informed?"

"Not of everything, no. There is security, you see."

This was going from bad to worse. I knew it. I gazed at Israfel despairingly, but still, he didn't look at me.

"Security for what purpose?"

"Uh . . . Celene must have told you."

"Of nation armed against nation, yes. And because of misunderstandings that have become traditional or because of differences in philosophies. To us this is incredible."

"I-I'm sorry, but there are many who are trying to bring peace."

There was another silence, heavy with implication. I sank even deeper into my pit of despair.

"We do try," I said between dry stiff lips. "We are trying."

But the eyes had left mine, were turning to the others'. Israfel's head was bending slightly in thought. Only the face of Celene remained unchanged.

A woman came into the room, slender and beautiful with brilliant auburn hair and wide green eyes. She beckoned me to go with her.

Israfel, I implored him. *What must I do? What's going on?*

He turned and gave me the hint of an encouraging smile. *Go with her, Laura. I'll come for you directly.*

I could see that they were all waiting for me to leave. I had no alternative but to force my unwilling feet into motion once more and follow her back to the room with the couches and the flowers and the windows looking out onto the sky.

There I turned to her and asked her if she knew what was happening. She smiled and looked at me enquiringly, obviously not understanding me.

"Farrand?" I asked. "How is Farrand? Do you know?"

The name drew a response, and she smiled again in acknowledgment.

I persisted. "Do you know how he is?"

She framed the word with unaccustomed lips. "Farrand?"

"Yes. Yes." I nodded eagerly.

In answer, she beckoned me again to follow her, and led the way out into that endless corridor. Again the walls streamed past, and the misty ceiling flowed overhead. Another doorway, an alarming descent with the walls flashing upward. I closed my eyes to prevent the dizziness the sensation induced, and she touched my arm, giving me an encouraging smile.

We stood at the entrance to a small, softly lit room. I could hear faint music and smell delicate flowers, but before us was machinery in great banks with glowing lights in rippling bands and a myriad of buttons. She led me forward, and then I saw Farrand's dark hair on a pillow, the waxen pallor of his face. I froze where I stood.

Farrand, shot down when he was guilty of nothing. Farrand, so gentle and kind, industrious and sincere . . . no wonder the earth was on trial. But . . . all those millions: the innocents who lived deep in the jungles or the deserts or the plains; the farmers and children, the men and women who sacrificed their lives . . . surely Farrand would not condone it.

He lay in a thing that looked vaguely like an iron lung. But there was no sound other than the distant music, no movement of any kind. The woman smiled and urged me closer. And when we stood beside him and I looked down at him in my numbing despair, the blue-tinted lids moved, and the dark eyes gazed up at me.

My heart seemed to stop beating, and my head spun far more dizzily than it had in the rushing hallway. I stared at him with my voice locked in my throat and blood roaring in my ears.

The smallest of smiles touched his mouth, and his lips moved. "Laura? Have you decided to come with us?"

Blindly, my eyes filling with tears of relief, I shook my head.

"No? Then why are you here?"

I struggled to speak. "Israfel brought me."

He stared at me, his eyes almost black in the pallor of his face.

"Farrand," I whispered. "I thought you were dead. Are you all right? Are you badly hurt?"

"I'm recovering," he said quietly.

"I . . . I'm so sorry . . . so sorry someone shot at you. I think . . . Israfel killed him."

"Yes."

"They came up from the creek, got through. Those men we didn't trust . . . they let them in."

He frowned. "What happened then?"

"The people . . . they stopped them."

"The people?"

"Yes."

He considered this, then his eyes sought mine. "Laura, why did Israfel bring you?"

"He . . . he says . . . " Helpless tears began to stream down my face, and I choked on the rest of the words. "That he'll take me back . . . if there's an earth left."

"Celene?"

My answer was a harsh sob.

His arm came up, pushed the machine and the soft coverlet that lay over him away. He was dressed in shimmering white, pure cloth unstained, but his movements were slow, difficult. He held his hand out to me. "Laura, help me up."

I dashed my sleeve across my eyes and stared at him in horror. "Farrand! You mustn't move! No! Stay where you are."

He swung his feet to the floor and held his hand out to me again. In the open neck of the robe that covered him, I could see a wound at the base of his throat. It was almost healed, little more than a scar, and below it I could see another. His hand caught mine. "I'm fine, Laura."

With my hand steadying him, he rose slowly to his feet and stood, gathering himself. His face was white and eyes very dark.

"Farrand, I don't think—"

He silenced me with a move of his hand, then leaned on my shoulder. "Come along. It isn't far."

Across the floor to the doorway, his pale bare feet wavering, I supported him as best I could. But my heart filled with fear for him at the pallor of his face.

The walls were rushing downward, flashing with light. Several times he swayed, and I clung to him desperately. "Farrand!"

"No." He shook his head, giving me a faint smile.

The endless corridor lay before us; the walls went streaming by. His lips were tight, head held high – as Israfel's usually was.

But not any longer, I saw, as we stood in the open doorway. I called to him frantically.

But already he was springing to Farrand's side, and those at the table came hurrying, consternation in their eyes. Celene too came forward, astonishment registering briefly on his face, then a frown of misgiving.

A chair was brought for Farrand, and then his eyes, still dark, spoke fervently to those who stood before him. Israfel came to stand by me and relayed what was being said.

Farrand is prepared to dismiss the attack made on him, to forgive those he says were only obeying orders. He says that all should not suffer because of a few and that a sense of justice does prevail, and as there are those who do strive to better the condition of their fellow humans, then we should grant this planet a reprieve.

Celene is arguing that humans are too dangerous a creature, that they have now progressed their technology so far as to venture forth into the universe, and that this poses a threat to its peace and magnificent culture. He says we cannot afford to take the chance of allowing all we have built and achieved to be subjected to this menace. Farrand is reminding him that we too have known wars, that what we have won did not come lightly. And because it happened very long ago doesn't make it any less part of our past than humanity's so recent violent history.

Laura, Michael knows this. He was a warrior long before I was, and where my role had been a protective one, his, centuries ago, had not been. But from it, he learned compassion, and Farrand is appealing now to that compassion. Laura, it is not you and me who might save your planet but Micheal and Farrand.

With the passing of total despair and the return of hope's everready spring, unreality descended on me once again. This extraordinary room with that impossible ceiling, those incredible faces . . . and Farrand, who I had believed dead, a light now in his eyes, was there and speaking silently to those who would presume to condemn my husband and home, my friends and their families, all the living things of my beautiful planet to obliteration. This could only be a nightmare, I remember thinking. It couldn't possibly be real. And yet, when I turned my head, Israfel stood at my shoulder, tall and ethereal, the optimism he had come to know on earth illuminating his face and shining in his eyes.

Again I thought painfully of Jesse, what he was doing at this moment, whether he was thinking I had abandoned him to go away with Israfel, the being he disliked and who I had spent so much of my time with, had defended so resolutely. The familiar rooms of my home formed clear pictures in my mind: the kitchen in the morning sun, its tiles and copper gleaming; a fire burning on the hearth in our warm cedar living room; my blue clay dinner service spread on the old oak dining table; and the horses. I saw Shadrach's exquisite head, felt the silky warmth of Andante's neck, the surge of her body beneath me. And Jesse – his hazel eyes and soft brown hair, the music he conjured from his heart and head and hands. A tear of longing welled in a corner of my eye, slipped, rolled slowly down my cheek. Israfel saw it, knew its source, and I saw the light leave his face, his eyes go gray.

Pain mingled with longing, blinding my eyes to the rooms of my home, my horses, Jesse . . . I reached out, found Israfel's long cool fingers, pressed them with sadness and regret. But I dared not look at him again, keeping my gaze fixed on Farrand's face, the dark eyes that glittered through the veil of my tears.

When Michael turned to the one who had questioned me, and all the other eyes turned in suit, my stomach lurched with the memory of why I was here, what was happening in this incredible place. The two helped Farrand from his chair and carried him away. Celene left the room, moving slowly, with obvious reluctance. And Israfel took my arm and guided me in silence back to the room with the flowers.

The door closed behind us, and he stood and looked down at me, his face drawn and troubled.

What's happening? I asked him anxiously. *Have they decided?*

No, not yet. They are considering what to do.

He turned away, went to the window, and looked out. I waited, breathless with anxiety, very aware of reality now.

Israfel came back. I felt his hands fall lightly on my shoulders, and he gazed at me with the troubled frown still resting on his brow.

Laura, you don't know how torn I was, back in there, during that inquiry. As soon as we arrived, I resigned, and it left me feeling as though I had abdicated my whole life. There was only one thing left, and that was you. And if Celene had his way, won the jurisdiction, then earth would be destroyed and there would be nothing left for you to go back to. It was a very tempting thought – very "human," wouldn't you say? But it was also a very short one. Laura, I do want you to come, but only if you want to. Always remember that. To force you would ruin it. I saw that very clearly. And now I shall be content to wait.

Say nothing, he went on as he saw my face, my effort to speak. *You have said enough. And I'm certain Farrand did too. He also pointed out that Celene was just as guilty in his wish for destruction as well the humans who have killed on earth, and that they would all be equally culpable if they agreed to his demand. Celene has more zeal than I had realized, and Farrand more compassion. Now, while they are reaching the verdict, I am becoming certain of, shall we go and see him?*

I reached up to him, wound my arms tightly around him, and kissed him with an aching gentleness.

Do you think, I whispered, *that Celene learned to be zealous when he saw our history? And that Farrand discovered compassion on earth?*

Yes.

And what did you learn?

He held me away from him, smiled into my eyes. *More things than I had ever imagined. Life, love, and how to dream.*

Farrand was lying pale and still beneath his strange machine, but there was a soft smile on his lips and a look of triumph in his eyes. I kissed his cheek with lips and fresh tears, with an endless gratitude and the pain of parting. And still he smiled.

Israfel placed a starshaped pendant around my throat, his eyes dark but mouth resolved. Michael pressed my hand and smiled at me with his eyes. I did not see Celene again.

At last I stumbled out onto the ramp and entered a different reality. I stopped and stood before a multitude of milling people. Cameras flashed, voices roared, and I heard my name called, and not always by voices I recognized.

I turned to Israfel standing behind me. The dazzle of sunlight filled my eyes with tears, and when I tried to brush them away, they still came.

I looked into those beloved silver eyes, and knew they were also tears of loss – of regret, of the pain of parting.

This pain, I realized, had come because I was now becoming aware of the incredible total love, a miraculous wonder that had come to me from an amazing being of another world. He had filled my heart, my soul, and my mind with unbelievable treasure. And was I only now, on the verge of parting, realizing it?

Laura, you can still come with me. The words spoken in silence echoed in my head and heart.

Images flashed. Deenie, suspended in midair. Israfel racing from the house, catching her. Saving my beautiful filly. Singing with his beautiful voice, playing Jesse's guitar in the shadow of a fireplace in the valley. Then his silent words – *Laura. The song was for you.*

Lifting me from a mass of ice and snow and broken branches. Carrying me across the fields to the house, repairing my broken leg. Then caring for me with a gentle and kind efficiency. Showers – no problem. Changing my clothes – a simple matter. Bringing the meals Celene had prepared to me on trays with a smile, as the dishes were sort of varied. Always edible, though.

He had given me regular reports on the horses, asked questions regarding their care, and passed the answers on to Farrand. They had obviously been getting the best of care. Our silent discourse in the evenings, mind to mind, telling me of the day's happenings, and asking any questions that might have arisen.

Israfel. Now I stood on the edge of his departure and saw more clearly all that I was letting go. Israfel, with his amazing love for me, the treasure of his heart. The pain in mine grew and grew. The tears in my eyes were not only caused by the sun.

Jesse – till death do us part.

Jesse . . . out there in the crowd of people, watching us, wondering why I was still standing there at the door of an alien spacecraft with an alien being I had always had some kind of affinity with – even though he had never really heard us talking together.

There was a gold ring on my finger that belonged to him. A small pendant on my neck that I wondered if he would ever notice. I doubted he ever would.

For better, for worse . . .

Jesse playing and singing, "When Laura Smiles."

I gently touched the pendant and tried to smile into those extraordinary silver eyes.

My love . . . one day . . . but now I must go.

I will be waiting for you. He bent his head and lightly brushed my lips with his.

My tears still flowed as I turned and began to stumble on down the ramp. Then he was beside me, steadying me with his hand on my arm. He let me go when my feet reached the crushed and trampled grass. *Goodbye,* I said. I felt him smile.

Then I was caught by Maureen, breaking from the crowd that was pressing toward me, microphones and cameras waving.

"Laura," she sobbed. "You are here! But what about Farrand? Oh, God! It was awful! Seeing him lying, bleeding on the grass. Just when rescue had finally come. It was heartbreaking!"

"He's all right," I tried to tell her through my own aching throat. "He is alive. He will be all right."

Jesse was right behind her. His eyes were narrow and angry, his lips drawn tight and hard.

I turned back to see Israfel at the top of the ramp. He raised his hand to us, then stepped through the door into the small craft that had brought us down to the High Meadow field.

The ramp slid up and away, the door closed, a gold ring began to spin around the dome, and the small ship slid through the doorway of that enormous waiting ship.

A hush fell over the waiting multitude of people. All eyes were fixed on the incredible sight before them. There was no sound as it began to rise effortlessly skyward. And as it rose, so did the pain in my heart, my chest, my throat.

Goodbye, my love, I said silently. An answer came. *Not goodbye, my dearest.*

I clung to Maureen's hand. She seemed to understand.

We watched as the huge ship rose skywards, catching a golden glow from our brilliant sun, passing through puffs of cloud that were soon left behind.

And so was our precious earth.

Voices began to rise again, cameras and microphones pushing close to my face, and the roar of questions began to deafen me.

A mass of people was holding back the uniforms, helmets, and guns above the creek. What appeared to be a covered body lay on the ground in front of them. The one who had shot Farrand, I learned later. We also heard that there was not a single wound on the body. If there had been an autopsy, we were never given the results.

To the streams of questions, I would only say, "I have nothing to say." I must have said the same words a thousand times.

Many took offense at my stubborn refusal. What right did I have to be so uncooperative? Who did I think I was, anyway? If I did give an answer when I thought it was warranted, I told them I was on my property, and they were trespassing on it and on my privacy.

Dealing with Jesse with another matter.

CHAPTER THIRTY-EIGHT

"WHY DID YOU GO?" JESSE asked me.

During the hours since my return, I had developed a total dread of questions. They had poured at me, been hurled at me with bruising force, battered me, and hurt me with a total lack of consideration for my tearstained eyes and distraught face. It was mainly through Gus Peterson and Norman Forrest's efforts that we were able to reach our truck at all, climb in, and drive away from the High Meadow. Then there were people jamming the roads, pouring along them in both directions. The logging trucks had been forced to move to allow an ambulance through, and that had opened the way for another influx. The rest of the blockades had been lifted now that our visitors were gone, along with that huge ship from the sky, and the house was vulnerable again.

Ted, Gus Peterson, Colin Webb, and a few others tried to keep the reporters and photographers, the television crews, and the police, the curious and the pushy away as much as they could. Maureen, distraught, had gone home. We had taken the telephone receiver off the hook. And Jesse had become angrier and angrier.

I glared at him from red-rimmed eyes. "You make that sound like an accusation," I said. "And besides, I'm sick of questions."

"Okay. So, take it as an accusation. Why did you go?"

The kitchen surrounded me with its colors and plants, its warm hewn wood, and its familiar fixtures, but it was also stifling. We hadn't left any windows open, and the day had become scorching with the sudden arrival of summer we were often subjected to.

"Because I had to," I said irritably.

"You couldn't drag yourself away from him. Is that it?"

"From who?" I stared at him, my face hot.

"Don't act so dumb. You know damn well who I mean."

Remorse for my attitude swept over me. "Jesse," I said unhappily. "Why are we behaving like this?"

"Because there's something here that needs clearing up." He stood facing me, his arms folded in an uncharacteristic pose. And he was watching me with suspicious eyes, with no sympathy, and again my worn nerves jangled.

"Now what are you insinuating?"

"I'm not insinuating. I'm asking."

I filled a glass with cold water, let its chill soothe the burning in my throat, ease the ache that had persisted and seemed to become permanent. And over the rim of the glass, I recognized a nervousness in the flicker of his eyes, an apprehension in the tightness of his lips. Had he been even more worried than I had realized? Would he have missed me that badly? Fresh tears welled in my eyes, tears of regret and concern.

"Darling," I said. "I went because of Farrand."

"But he was dead. Don't you realize the danger you were putting yourself in by going after that happened?"

"Farrand isn't dead." I said. "And if I hadn't gone, we'd never have known."

"Not dead? He sure looked it."

"I know. I'm sure he was, clinically. They revived him on the ship."

"How?"

"I don't know."

"I was expecting all hell to break loose."

"Jesse," I said, a tremor in my voice. "Weren't you concerned about Farrand?"

"Of course, I was. But I was more concerned about you. And what in hell did you expect me to think when I saw you going with them, shut inside that thing?"

"I wondered about it."

"Thanks a bunch."

"Love," I said, my voice trembling with the emotional exhaustion that was draining me. "Can't we just drop it? I came back. It's all over. I'm worn out, just want to forget about it all. It's been a terrible day."

"We're not done with it yet," he said bitterly.

At least he seemed to be dropping his questions, and I was glad of that. For what would he have said if I'd told him why I'd had to go? That this whole planet had been on trial? That it could have been destroyed, and the means to do so had been in the craft he had buried on the High Meadow, hidden there all along? Now I knew what that fierce contention had been between Israfel and Celene. And if Jesse knew that, he would probably say he'd been right in the first place, that we never should have taken them in and protected them the way we had.

Would he have been right? I supposed he would, and yet admitting it would have diminished me, everything our friends had done, and Israfel in a way I couldn't bear to face.

And Jesse was right in that our trials were not yet over. The peace and forgetfulness I longed for began to seem as distant as the stars as police, National Defense officers, reporters, and newscasters beat endlessly on our door. My near-hysteria sent many away, and Jesse's grim refusal to talk and his insolence to any officialdom deterred many more. But others still kept coming and coming, relentless and determined. Initial puzzlement at our refusal to talk all soon turned to anger. Our behavior was tantamount to treason in many eyes. What right did we have to remain silent? To hoard this story? Most people would have been falling over themselves to tell. Why weren't we?

Many were glad at our silence, we knew. There was remarkably little reporting on television newscasts and in the larger newspapers. The crew from Seattle had obtained the only film of it. Much of it had obviously been cut. The rest of the shots were unsteady or surprisingly indistinct. Amateur movies seemed to disappear while being processed. Photographs taken were either over or underexposed. Those developed at home and then published were promptly dismissed as hoaxes. Interviews with the people who had been there were far more authoritative. But again, distortions and erraticism threw doubt, and no two stories were the same. They generally appeared in the tabloid sort of publication or in those devoted to UFO phenomena – strictly sensationalism, of course. And once the discreet government personnel were satisfied that we had no technical information they could use, they left us alone and pleaded ignorance of the whole affair when questioned. They relied on more authoritative journals than the Martian News, they said at a press conference, and after that there was noticeable silence from those quarters.

But not at our home. Tabloid journalists constantly sought interviews with us. But still we held our silence, and I did so with an increasing sense of guilt. Death squads roamed without compunction in the streets of cities in South America and with the backing and support of their governments. A man was caught in Cleveland after he had raped over sixty little girls in eight years, the youngest aged only four. The fire set by an arsonist killed thirty-eight old people in a rest home, and it was later discovered that he had stood by and watched from the beginning to end.

And in my head, I held the information of why our celestial visitors had come here, and I was keeping it there because I didn't want to hurt Jesse or further jeopardize our cherished marriage.

I tried to justify my silence. Humanity must not be forced to learn out of fear. People must not improve their ways only because of a threat to their existence. That would be hollow and meaningless. And yet . . . and yet, in the case of such a total end, shouldn't the warning at least be given?

No matter how many times I tried to find a way of telling only what was necessary, I knew it would have to be at a press conference. And then I would have to answer all questions. For who would believe me otherwise? The words "sensationalism" and "hoax" had been used far more frequently than "we have been visited by aliens from another world."

If I delivered the warning, I would also be proving they were dangerous. They could have destroyed this planet. I was the one who had insisted they be taken into our home, who had implicated Jesse in their protection and concealment. Jesse had then buried their craft with its hideously dangerous cargo on our property, had hidden it from the authorities. It was I who misled the police and army personnel, letting them go on searching in vain. Wasn't a lie as much a lie by omission? Everything would come out, and my motives would be doubted because of my feelings for Israfel. And Jesse would know.

He had questioned my reason for going with Israfel – him, not them. His suspicions had been founded, and I doubted he had dismissed them yet.

How would I answer a barrage of questions without letting something slip? Even a refusal to speak of Israfel would be a form of confession. Tears would come with frightening ease at the very thought of him. Under heavy questioning, they would pour. Jesse would know why.

I had kept my vows and come back to the man who was my husband. But did that make my loyalty and fidelity any more secure? They still weren't in my mind. Why should they be in his?

Our marriage was already suffering. A further blow would kill it. I resolved to wait until time had done its healing, until I could speak of Israfel with no more emotion than a cherished memory and our marriage was again strong.

So I erected a wall of silence to live behind and waited and tried to rebuild our former lives. But time did not heal, the memories did not fade, the emptiness in my mind was a dark void, and Israfel was its only light.

To Jesse, the name was anathema.

"I don't want to talk about him," he said when I once tried to clear the air. His voice was as cold and hard as stone. "Ever again. And you'd better forget him. Completely."

How I wished I could. But the emptiness I lived in was a never-ceasing reminder of him, the house as desolate and silent as my unshared mind, my loneliness without him a torment of sorrow and guilt.

For the first time in my life, the impending show seasons brought me not even a trace of anticipation, even though I had a beautiful foal I named Andromeda to show and Gallant, at maturity, was going to be strong competition. I told myself that it was because there'd be people with questions to contend with, that I was tired from all the pressures I'd been under, that I'd feel better once we were there. But knowing that Israfel wouldn't be there to see the filly I'd wanted him to have made the whole business seem dull.

More and more of the wildflowers bloomed that I wished he could have seen. Moon daisies starred the pasture, then lay across it like drifts of snow. "Weeds!" Jesse insisted and scythed them down in the thousands.

Columbines grew in clumps and tossed their scarlet and yellow flowers on tall thick stems, and delicate wild roses bloomed along the roads and at the forest's edge. Orange honeysuckle hung on vines from the trees and shrubs, their long, luscious trumpets attracting bees and hummingbirds while the spires of mauve and purple lupines cast a haze of blue around the house.

Mountain lilies unfurled their exotic petals in every glade, and even amid the thick alfalfa in the hay field on the High Meadow, the scent of clover was heady and intoxicating, and I breathed it in deeply as I rode Andante over the lush early summer grass while my heart ached with memories. And I gathered the first wild strawberries, served them to Jesse with thick whipped cream, and wished we were not alone on the patio, in the beautiful softness of those rare warm evenings.

Andromeda won her class at her first show. Gallant was named "reserve champion stallion," and Jesse and Astra won the western class and the horse race. But I stood at the sidelines and watched him, saw the determination on his face, and wondered what the point of it all was. Weren't there more important things than good withers and straight hindlegs, another ribbon to hang on the wall? All those people there in the stands, cheering on their own horses and assessing the points of a yearling colt – while people were starving in Africa and India and South America, being taken hostage in a jail riot, and mourning the deaths of two hundred relatives and friends who'd been killed when a bomb planted on a plane had exploded.

"I don't want to show any more," I told Jesse on the long dark drive homeward. "I've had enough."

His head jerked around, and he stared at me in astonishment. "Not show? You sick or something?"

Yes, I thought. *I am sick – sick of false values, of petty importance like winning a ribbon, proving your horse is better than the other guy's, when we should be more concerned about the lack of integrity in high places, about hunger and disease, ignorance and superstition, corruption, about abuse in all its aspects. I'm sick of what my life is becoming.*

But I said nothing. There would only be an argument about the futility of idealism, and if we were to be in the horse breeding business, then the shows were where we did our best advertising, necessarily putting our stock on the line.

"Hey?" Jesse was persisting.

"Maybe," I said tiredly.

It was no answer, and we both knew it. But he said no more because Israfel's shadow suddenly lay between us. My changed behavior had started the day they'd left, after Jesse's accusations. We both realized that my there-is-nothing-wrong face was false. And the marriage I was trying to hold together kept fraying at the seams before the knife of his suspicion, a knife he refused to sheathe. There was no discussing Israfel. The subject was taboo. And so, the threads kept breaking, and the fabric of our marriage became more fragile. My efforts to repair the damage was repeatedly nullified by a tear somewhere else, another zip or split, while we presented a solid structure to the world around us and to each other, pretending that nothing was wrong.

So, Jesse took Astra and Gallant, went alone to the shows, and I stayed at home in the empty house, the phone off the hook, and refused to see anyone.

Summer moved into July, and we had our hay cut and baled, and we brought it in ourselves in the cool of the evening. Evenings were beautiful out on the fields with the sky flaming or hazy blue, the slopes decorated with cyclamen puffs as the sun went down. And the shadow of the mountain lay across the lower slopes while a few rays crept from behind its shoulder, spilling technicolor gold across the patterned stubble.

How Israfel would have loved this! The thought came again and again, hovering like the red-tailed hawk that hung high above us, watching for moles and scuttling field mice. And a doe and her fawn sometimes passed, unafraid, as they were accustomed to seeing us there, and the fragile legs would step and the leaflike ears sway with extraordinary natural elegance. How Israfel would have loved this.

Jesse began to work on another score and was away from home more and more. Most of the visiting mares were gone. Ours were out on the pasture with their foals, and the yearlings we had for sale were displayed in a field near our entrance. Fewer people came – our story was no longer new. And I began to answer the phone again, visit with my friends, and sleep a little.

But there were times when I would wake in the night, my heart thudding loudly. Was that a sound? Had someone come? Was there a horse in trouble in the barn? And I would lie and listen, immediately aware of the emptiness in my mind, the loneliness that nothing would dispel, the loss that nothing could replace.

These were long, dark, lonely nights. I lay staring at the place where I knew the window was, waiting for the first faint beams of dawn – so early, so unpromising. For I moved through the days like an automaton with little direction and few incentives, my mind haunted by that perfect face and silver eyes, the memories of happiness.

Israfel, Israfel. The name was in the rhythms of my brain, the pulse of my blood, and the stream of my life force. There was no escaping it, the memories it brought, the pain it renewed in my heart.

I went to Vernon and looked up the name in the library, almost fearfully, and I gazed in mute astonishment when I finally saw it printed on a page before me, scarcely believing my eyes. "And the angel Israfel, whose heartstrings are a lute, and who has the sweetest voice of all God's creatures." I found these lines before a poem by Edgar Allan Poe. He attributed the quote to the Koran, an ancient religious text.

Numb, I stumbled out into the brilliant sunshine. But I scarcely felt its heat, hardly saw the people who passed by me in their carefree summer clothes, was deaf to the traffic out there on the street.

He had said he'd been here before. Could it possibly be the same person? Once again, I heard that magnificent voice singing in the shadows beyond Maureen's breath, that incredibly beautiful song. "The angel Israfel." Angels – messengers of the gods.

I drove home in a daze and immersed myself in the stillness of the forest, the cooler air of our mountain altitude. And the song echoed in the sound of the birds, the distinct music of the creek. I could hear his voice, its melody, his rare laughter, see the look in his eyes on that day when I had left him here behind the house, and I had told him he had to go alone.

Sleepless nights again beset me. Jesse came home, and I greeted him with mixed emotions, said nothing of my find. After all, the name was still taboo.

Jesse quietly put the gold in the bank, took Astra off to another show, and was engrossed in his music and withdrawn and generally uncommunicative. I tried to question him about his new score and the one he had recently completed for the movie *The Great Plains*. But he brushed my questions aside as though I had only asked out of duty or politeness, and I added another burden to my conscience, an even deeper despair as another seam tore apart in the fabric of our marriage.

A spell of thundery weather brought rain. It settled the dust, freshened the fields, cooled the overheated air. But it also brought a team of UFO researchers from Virginia, and I was for once sorely tempted to tell them the whole story. But Jesse was there, his face closed and disapproving, a frown darkening his hazel eyes, eager to get back to his work, his irritation at the interruption obvious. They were sensitive and understanding, left names and numbers they could be reached at, and went away looking very disappointed. I suffered a pang of regret as their station wagon drove away, but then I thought of all I might have been forced to tell, the details that Jesse did not know. My tattered marriage came first.

Then Jesse went away again and phoned me one night to say he was going to New York, to the premiere of *The Great Plains*.

"Oh!" I cried. "Can I come?"

"I've only got one ticket," he said. My heart cringed as the knife cut again. "And I'm only going to be there for the one night. Besides, you know how hellishly hot New York is in August. Surely you don't want to be here for that."

So, he went by himself and was noncommittal about the film when he came home a short while later.

"It's okay," he said.

"And the music?" I really wanted to know.

"Okay."

I tried to hide my disappointment. "The reviews?"

"Not bad."

"Any idea when it'll be here?"

He shrugged. "Who knows?"

Then he went away again, back to LA, and I was left with my memories and guilt.

But *The Great Plains* came to a Vernon movie theater. I phoned Maureen and asked her if she'd go with me.

"We both want to see it," she told me. "We'll pick you up and all go together."

The anticipation of going lifted me out of my despondency. This was the score that had given Jesse so much trouble that I hadn't heard a single note of, and I could hardly wait for us to get there, the movie to begin.

The Great Plains was undoubtedly a beautiful movie. Its run had been most successful. The opening scenes were spectacular, and I sat in the flickering darkness, enthralled as the fields of undulating wheat glowed copper and gold beneath vast skies of pale azure. Then I was listening to the music as it came, soaring, flowing, rippling – and the screen before my eyes might as well have been blank as the images ceased to form in my mind. The skin on my back crawled and there was a strange pain in my breast, as though my heart were dying. I'm sure I ceased to breathe.

Jesse's hand was unmistakable, his singular stamp, but the music was not his own. I heard Maureen's sharp intake of breath as the melody began to form and the theme began to reveal its shape. She shifted in her seat, a sudden involuntary moment of shock and alarm. I sat frozen, incredulous, wounded to the foundation of my loyalty.

I had heard that glorious music before, but not at Jesse's hands. He had stolen it, used it, taken it without Israfel's permission. And Israfel knew.

My feet and fingers were like ice, and I shivered in the summer warmth. Never had I dreamed that Jesse, my wonderful talented Jesse, could do such an ignominious thing. No wonder he'd been so evasive about the score and hadn't wanted me to go to the premiere. I could no longer think. I pressed my hands to my ears in an attempt to shut out that beautiful, incriminating, heartbreaking sound.

Ted leaned around Maureen and looked at me with disturbed eyes. "Laura," he whispered. "Do you want to stay?"

I shook my head, unable to speak.

"Let's go," he said.

We hurried out, murmuring apologies to those who had to move for us. He took my arm in the foyer and squeezed it comfortingly. Maureen was pale, biting her lip and glancing at me with shared understanding and disappointment. I found I couldn't look at either of them.

Ted drove us home along the familiar winding highway that now seemed to lead nowhere. The hills were gold in the last of the sun, the sky a soft blue haze. But I saw nothing of the beauty – only the face and eyes of Israfel.

Maureen suddenly exploded. "Never," she declared, "would I have suspected Jesse of doing such a thing. Never! How could he have stolen Rafe's music? How could he!"

I swallowed hard. "His name is Israfel, Maureen."

"Israfel?"

"Yes. Rafe was the name we gave him for the sake of simplicity among our friends."

" 'None sing so wildly well as the angel Israfel,' " Ted quoted.

"What?"

"A poem by Edgar Allan Poe. Based on a line in the Koran."

"I found that," I said.

"Good heavens!" Maureen said and nothing more.

We drove on without speaking, immersed in disturbing thought. *How could he?* I asked myself again and again. *How could Jesse have done such a thing?*

"Why not?" he said when I put the question to him. My face flamed with anger, my eyes scalding with tears. "It was perfect – just what I needed."

The highway sped toward us. We left the airport behind. I had gone to pick him up, boiling with pent-up fury and disappointment. I had made him drive home, no longer trusting myself.

"You stole it!" I shouted at him. "You . . . you thief!"

"Aw, c'mon, Laura! What's gotten into you?"

"I saw *The Great Plains*!" I yelled. "I heard the music – not your music. Israfel's!"

"So?"

"And your name was on the credits."

"Well, of course. I wrote the score, put it together—"

"His music."

"Okay, so I got the theme from him. But why should he care? He's gone, forever."

"Do you think he didn't know?" I demanded, the tears now spilling over to run unchecked down my face. "Hey?"

"Know? How could he?"

"He knew far more than you ever realized – than either of us realized."

"But what difference does it make? Laura, he's gone. That's it. Anyway, it's done now. The movie's a big box office hit. Mancini is cutting a record of the score. This could the biggest thing I've done for a long time."

"But it isn't yours!"

"Sure, it is. All I took was the theme. There wasn't any copyright on it, nothing like that."

"That isn't the point," I stormed. "You stole it, took it without his permission."

His jaw hardened. "Do you think he'd care? He's gone. Gone. You hear me? And why the hell are you getting so uptight about it?"

"I care!" I cried, sobs rising in my throat, anger shaking me. "I care about it."

"There's no need to get hysterical," he said sharply.

I subsided, hurt and furious and bitterly disappointed. My long-held loyalty slipped from another of its moorings, letting me swing like a ship on the flow of the tide, secured by the anchor of my marriage and little else.

We didn't speak of it again. Jesse never mentioned anything connected with Israfel, no matter how remote. Maureen and Ted avoided him, the Jesse they had once so fervently admired. Gone were the lovely evenings together with music on the patio or beside a fire. Jesse must have noticed the change in their attitude toward him, but he either ignored it or deliberately said nothing, and I was too embarrassed to do anything about it.

More and more, when he was at home, I found myself saddling Andante or Gallant and riding out into the leaf-strewn woods in the golden sun of waning summer, the berries red and white, thistledown drifting on the air. This was my favorite season, but the cloudy shadow of regret lay over it like a pall. The love Jesse and I had shared was tarnished, spoiled, without its shine, even its sharing gone. All my attempts at resurrection had been met by a corpse that refused to live while bound in winding sheets of disappointment beside a tomb of betrayal. And the red leaves of maple, the bronze of bracken, and gold of birch spoke constantly to me, telling me that Israfel had gone and could not share the beauty with me.

For better or for worse, till death do us part. I clung to the words as I rode on the glowing forest trails. Our wedding had been beautiful at his home in Oregon, my father's only brother giving me away. Jesse's music had played on the organ in the church and had moved me to tears. His mother's flowers had spilled color everywhere, and friends and relatives had come to wish us well. Our honeymoon in Hawaii had been a dream of sea and sun and laughter, Jesse's humor reflecting happiness in his eyes that had made my love grow stronger every day.

Could that die? No. Never, I told myself. We had been happy, rarely differing, exchanging very few sharp words. An idyllic marriage, I had always thought, on a foundation I had considered unshakable.

So, a few stones fell out of it during the course of years. Inevitable. People changed, grew older, were shaped by their experiences into different molds. Nothing remained constant in life. One had to flow with the stream, bend with the wind, be tolerant and compassionate, forgiving and generous.

I tried to forgive him for the theft of Israfel's music but found it more than hard to do. If he had asked me to, perhaps then it would have been easier, but he never did. And I knew the loneliness of differing opinions, the isolation of conflicting codes of ethics, and the never-ending pain of loss.

October was beautiful, cold. The birches were burnished, spreading carpets of gold on the grass and the High Meadow Road. Mountains were blue, hazy, higher, further, ethereal. The fragrance of wood smoke hung in the air as I kept the fires stoked. The forest was silent in the still, waiting air. Jesse was away in Los Angeles. The music from *The Great Plains* was being played on the radio, haunting me with that magnificent voice, the touching mind, the song intended for me. And Jesse's mark on it provoked me into anger and bitter tears.

Now it was November. The day was cold and the ground frozen as hard as iron. Frank McKinnon's card in my pocket had become a goad, a taunting of its own, a reminder of guilt. There was one question I must ask Jesse next time he came home.

Fire on the hearth, coffee in a mug, Jesse tired and strained, sprawling in his favorite chair. We sat in this beautiful room with mellow cedar, rich deep rugs, curtains drawn against the night, warm firelight dancing golden on polished floors and heavy log walls.

"Jesse." I phrased the question carefully, trying to be casual to conceal the tension holding me in its vice. "What would you have done if their ship had never come? About the theme of *The Great Plains*?"

He did not look at me, his half-closed eyes watching the fire. "I'd already used it."

"Already? Before what?"

"Before the ship came."

"What . . . what would you have done if he had heard it?"

I saw him stiffen. His eyes opened wider, but still, he didn't look at me. His voice was too casual. "I tried to make damn sure he never would."

My blood seemed to freeze in my veins, chilling me to ice. My voice was locked in my rigid throat. I saw like a stone, the implication of his words hammering me, driving nails of painful knowledge.

The fire crackled in the silence. I could see he was waiting for me to break into anger. He was preparing his defense by resuming his attitude of suspicion.

"Was it you . . . " I forced the words to form. " . . . who advised the authorities they were here?"

"Sure. Might as well tell you now they're gone, but I wanted that music, and the whole business was getting to be too much. ET looking down his bloody nose at me, you acting like a damn idiot."

He glanced sidelong at me, and his eyes widened with disbelief. "Laura, I did what I thought was best. Tried not to implicate us directly—"

"Why didn't you tell me?" My voice was shaking, trembling with rage and pain.

"Because you had it in your head to protect them, keep them here."

"I promised," I whispered hoarsely.

"But I never did."

"This," I said, my lips quivering, "is my house."

"Our house, you always said," he interjected, his voice hardening.

"It was, but no longer. Will you please leave?"

"Laura! What in hell's gotten into you? The whole thing's finished with, and I wish to God I'd done what I'd wanted to do and called the authorities in the first place. Then none of this would have happened."

"None of what?"

"You acting like this."

"I'm not acting. I'm deadly serious. Israfel knew! He knew what you had done, and he didn't tell me because . . . Oh, never mind! Just get out. Go away. And I don't want to see you again, ever."

Painful words, incredible words, like a surgeon's knife cutting into the flesh of my existence, ripping open all I had so long cherished and nurtured and held so dear. With no anesthetic, the scalpel of destruction was rending my life apart, and it was my hand guiding it.

"Laura!" He rose to his feet, staring at me in wounded astonishment. "What're you saying?"

"You heard me." My voice climbed an octave, cracked. "Get out."

"You're getting hysterical again. For chrissakes, Laura! Will you try to listen to reason?"

"What reason? I've heard your reasons, and they're lousy. They stink. Just get out. Now!"

He turned away. "I'm not going to listen to you carrying on like this. I'm going to bed, and I hope you'll be more rational in the morning."

After he had gone, I washed my face, drank some water, put on my old coat, and then went out to the barn. Although the wounds of my words still hurt painfully, the cancer was gone and had left a calm, deep, and healing comfort. Now I could clearly see all that I had masked from my vision. Now I could see the lies, and they would all be made right. Frank McKinnon would have his story and the world its warning, and Israfel would have the whole love he was waiting for.

Now I knew that my love for Jesse had grown out of sharing; I had fallen in love with Israfel the moment I had seen his face.

There in the barn, I made my plans. Calliope, Andromeda, Shadrach, Andante, and Argente, Alla Bay, Gallant, Bint Amiri, and Arabi Rose; the best of the yearling fillies; and Sally. I must have their halters ready, make sure they're fed for the journey.

The house stood solidly amid its trees, but I felt only a small pang as I looked at it. Home was where the heart was, and mine was no longer there. It was already winging beyond the stars to where it belonged. There was only one place I wanted to be, one person I wanted to be with. My fingers did not tremble as they found the pendant at my throat and twisted the point of the star that moved. It clicked into its position, and the pendant started vibrating slightly, not visibly, but I could feel it as though it was alive against my skin.

I've left these notes with Maureen, with instructions to give them to Frank McKinnon after I've gone. I believe she'll understand.

The house was silent. Jesse had returned to Los Angeles. I listened to the stillness and watched the sky and waited.

THE END

EPILOGUE

I AM LAURA. YOU MAY have read my earlier story about the UFO that crashed on my ranch in Trinity Valley, a part of British Columbia where my grandfather had built his rugged log house. He left the house to me, his only heir. And then, at the early age of seventeen, I became an orphan.

My mother had given me an Arabian mare when I was fourteen. I was horse crazy. After I lost both my parents, my mother's brother and his wife Mary took me in, horse and all. They cared for me as if I was their own.

I met Jesse Tremayne at a horse show where I was riding my mother's prized gift to me.

He had the nerve to catch my rein as I was leaving the ring after the English pleasure riding class. He teased me about never having smiled throughout the entire competition.

This brash young man with a plain face and long hair under a rather fancy hat did not attract me in the slightest. I dragged my rein away from his grasp and left him standing, watching me ride away. I did not learn until much later on that he composed musical scores for the movies.

He sent me a record, a single, his own composition with voice and guitar. I was overwhelmed. Never had I been given something so special. And when the song "When Laura Smiles" rose to the top of the Hit Parade music charts for several months, I was truly impressed. I never imagined someone would do something like that for me! I had to write to thank him. From there we conversed regularly, and six months later, I married him.

When Israfel crashed into my life a few years later and lay unconscious in one of our bedrooms, we quickly realized he was determined to die. I looked at his beautiful face and the unhappy faces of Celene and Farrand – his crew members we'd also rescued from the damaged craft.

So, what happened to me and Israfel after that terrible day on the High Meadow? I waited and watched the skies, feeling the gentle pulsing of the pendant that Israfel had placed around my neck.

I shall let Israfel complete the story in his own words.

⬭

The High Arctic was an area I had never been before. Previous visits to this planet had only been to the southern climates, to deserts of rock and sand where it was hot and dry.

Coming down from the north over the snow and ice – many miles before there were any signs of patches of green on the tundra – this landscape seemed eternal. It eventually developed into forests of trees, the Rocky Mountains, and below that, lush grassy fields and flowing rivers. We were captivated by the beauty of the land.

But, back to the task at hand, it was not the scenery we had come to this planet for. Out in the universe, concern was growing that the inhabitants of earth were breaking away, venturing into what they called "space," and were becoming entitled to go wherever they were able.

The moon had been their first successful venture, and now more ambitious humans were looking for other areas to explore. They wondered what else was out there for the taking. Invasions and wars seemed to be the way these humans achieved their goals and took what they considered to be theirs. Anyone who stood in their way was seemingly expendable: shot and bombed, no matter if they were a man, woman, or child.

Was this true? This is what we came to find out, and we eventually did find our answer.

Continuing southward, we saw lakes, streams, rivers, and a few hamlets with small houses. We decided to follow one of the rivers to a deeper canyon. From there, we rose higher toward a graying sky of thin clouds. This was where it all changed.

A plane we hadn't seen at first was suddenly upon us and firing a blaze of bullets. I took us around a green grassy mountain at top speed, away from where the plane had been. We did not see it again. However, I soon realized that our craft was damaged. We were losing power, and we needed to get down to the ground and hide as best we could.

On the east side of that grassy mountain, I had a view of a long narrow field. Could I make it there? We had to.

So, here we were. I had lost control of my ship, my command, and almost my life. It was Laura, riding a frightened horse, who came to our rescue.

And now to present day, I answered the call of the pulsing pendant at my neck that matched the one I'd given her. I returned to her with a ship large enough to carry horses and hay. I took the long journey back to the High Meadow, and there she was, standing in the grass in the early morning sun, giving me life again. I ran down the ramp and into her arms. I held her as if I would never let her go.

She now lies beside me as I write this – another message we're sending to earth in the "mail" system Farrand has created. It's going to the care of Ted and Maureen, our ever-trusted friends.

We have cushions on the velvet grass before the white pavilion of our home where I play my music and sing the songs she never seems to tire of. When she came to me, she brought the document that finalized her marriage to Jesse. We put it in a drawer and never looked upon it again. The animals we brought have recovered following the initial shock of traveling on a starship. The dogs and stallions love being knee-deep in the lush green grass. The stallions have separate fields where their yearlings play.

My longtime teacher and very special friend Michael came to visit us very soon after we arrived. He smiled and reminded us of that desperate day when we had stood before him and the council as the future of the planet earth had hung in the balance. Laura had stumbled so awkwardly through their questions while Farrand, grievously wounded, had clung to her and defended earth. Pleading that there were still people worthy of saving, people who had protected them in their time of need. And finally, there was Laura, who had determinedly saved my life.

I now thank her for that every day, for the love she gives me and the joy of sharing our existence together. For happiness.

—Israfel

AUTHOR'S NOTE

I WROTE THIS STORY NEARLY 50 years ago. I was in a creative writing course in Okanagan College and there were about 18 young people and one young man wanted to read what I had written. I lent him a copy and I can still see him; he came skidding onto our property in his car, waving the manuscript, shouting, "It was the music, it was the music! The story is just wonderful!

I wrote this when my husband, Roy, and I were living in a cottage and building our new home as depicted in my previous book *Stories of Silverado Ranch*. As time went on and the busier we became, the manuscript ended up in a box under the bed in the spare room. Over the past few years working with my great-niece, Christina, in Manitoba, we have unearthed this piece and brought *Israfel* to the world. I would like to dedicate this book to her, for without her, it would still be tucked away under the bed. I hope you enjoy it!

Bless you all,

Anthea McLean

Milton Keynes UK
Ingram Content Group UK Ltd.
UKHW020218040724
444921UK00010B/125/J